# EVOlutioN

Created by Joe Infurnari . Joseph Keatinge . Christopher Sebela . Joshua Williamson

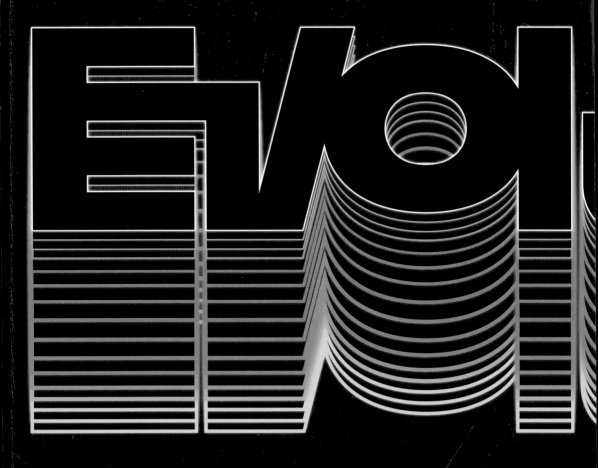

**WRITERS**
## James Asmus
## Joseph Keatinge
## Christopher Sebela

**COLORIST**
## Jordan Boyd

**ARTIST**
## Joe Infurnari

**LETTERER**
## Pat Brosseau

EVOLUTION VOLUME 2. FIRST PRINTING. DECEMBER 2018. PUBLISHED BY IMAGE COMICS, INC. OFFICE OF PUBLICATION: 2701 NW VAUGHN ST., STE. 780, PORTLAND, OR 97210. ORIGINALLY PUBLISHED IN SINGLE MAGAZINE FORM AS EVOLUTION #7-12. EVOLUTION™ (INCLUDING ALL PROMINENT CHARACTERS FEATURED HEREIN), ITS LOGO AND ALL CHARACTER LIKENESSES ARE TRADEMARKS OF SKYBOUND, LLC, UNLESS OTHERWISE NOTED. IMAGE COMICS® AND ITS LOGOS ARE REGISTERED TRADEMARKS AND COPYRIGHTS OF IMAGE COMICS, INC. ALL RIGHTS RESERVED. NO PART OF THIS PUBLICATION MAY BE REPRODUCED OR TRANSMITTED IN ANY FORM OR BY ANY MEANS (EXCEPT FOR SHORT EXCERPTS FOR REVIEW PURPOSES) WITHOUT THE EXPRESS WRITTEN PERMISSION OF IMAGE COMICS, INC. ALL NAMES, CHARACTERS, EVENTS AND LOCALES IN THIS PUBLICATION ARE ENTIRELY FICTIONAL. ANY RESEMBLANCE TO ACTUAL PERSONS (LIVING OR DEAD), EVENTS OR PLACES, WITHOUT SATIRIC INTENT, IS COINCIDENTAL. PRINTED IN THE U.S.A. FOR INFORMATION REGARDING THE CPSIA ON THIS PRINTED MATERIAL CALL: 203-595-3636 ISBN: 978-1-5343-0878-7

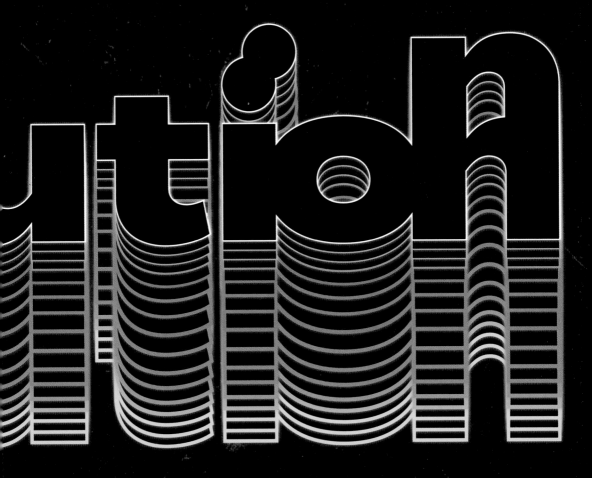

**ASSOCIATE EDITOR**
**Arielle Basich**

**COVER ART**
**Joe Infurnari**
**Jordan Boyd**

**LOGO DESIGN**
**Andres Juarez**

**EDITOR**
**Jon Moisan**

**PRODUCTION DESIGN**
**Carina Taylor**

SKYBOUND LLC. ROBERT KIRKMAN CHAIRMAN DAVID ALPERT CEO SEAN MACKIEWICZ SVP, EDITOR-IN-CHIEF SHAWN KIRKHAM SVP, BUSINESS DEVELOPMENT BRIAN HUNTINGTON VP ONLINE CONTENT SHAUNA WYNNE PUBLICITY DIRECTOR ANDRES JUAREZ ART DIRECTOR JON MOISAN EDITOR ARIELLE BASICH ASSOCIATE EDITOR CARINA TAYLOR PRODUCTION ARTIST PAUL SHIN BUSINESS DEVELOPMENT COORDINATOR JOHNNY O'DELL SOCIAL MEDIA MANAGER SALLY JACKA SKYBOUND RETAILER RELATIONS DAN PETERSEN SR. DIRECTOR OF OPERATIONS & EVENTS INTERNATIONAL INQUIRIES: AG@SEQUENTIALRIGHTS.COM LICENSING INQUIRIES:CONTACT@SKYBOUND.COM WWW.SKYBOUND.COM

IMAGE COMICS, INC. ROBERT KIRKMAN CHIEF OPERATING OFFICER ERIK LARSEN CHIEF FINANCIAL OFFICER TODD MCFARLANE PRESIDENT MARC SILVESTRI CHIEF EXECUTIVE OFFICER JIM VALENTINO VICE PRESIDENT ERIC STEPHENSON PUBLISHER/CHIEF CREATIVE OFFICER COREY HART DIRECTOR OF SALES JEFF BOISON DIRECTOR OF PUBLISHING PLANNING & BOOK TRADE SALES CHRIS ROSS DIRECTOR OF DIGITAL SALES JEFF STANG DIRECTOR OF SPECIALTY SALES KAT SALAZAR DIRECTOR OF PR & MARKETING DREW GILL ART DIRECTOR HEATHER DOORNINK PRODUCTION DIRECTOR NICOLE LAPALME CONTROLLER WWW.IMAGECOMICS.COM

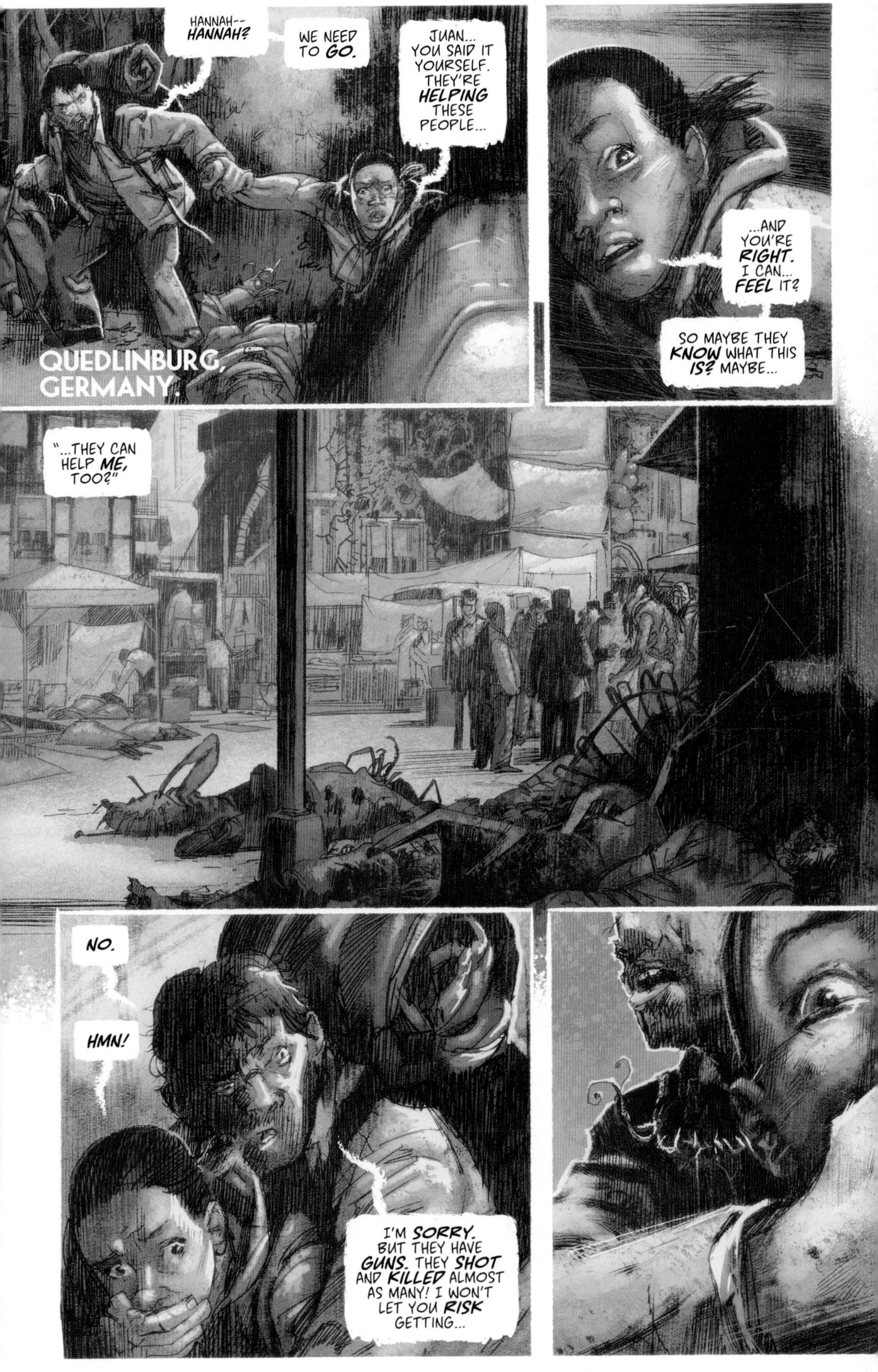
HANNAH--
HANNAH?
WE NEED TO GO.
JUAN... YOU SAID IT YOURSELF. THEY'RE HELPING THESE PEOPLE...
QUEDLINBURG, GERMANY.
...AND YOU'RE RIGHT. I CAN... FEEL IT?
SO MAYBE THEY KNOW WHAT THIS IS? MAYBE...
"...THEY CAN HELP ME, TOO?"
NO.
HMN!
I'M SORRY. BUT THEY HAVE GUNS. THEY SHOT AND KILLED ALMOST AS MANY! I WON'T LET YOU RISK GETTING...

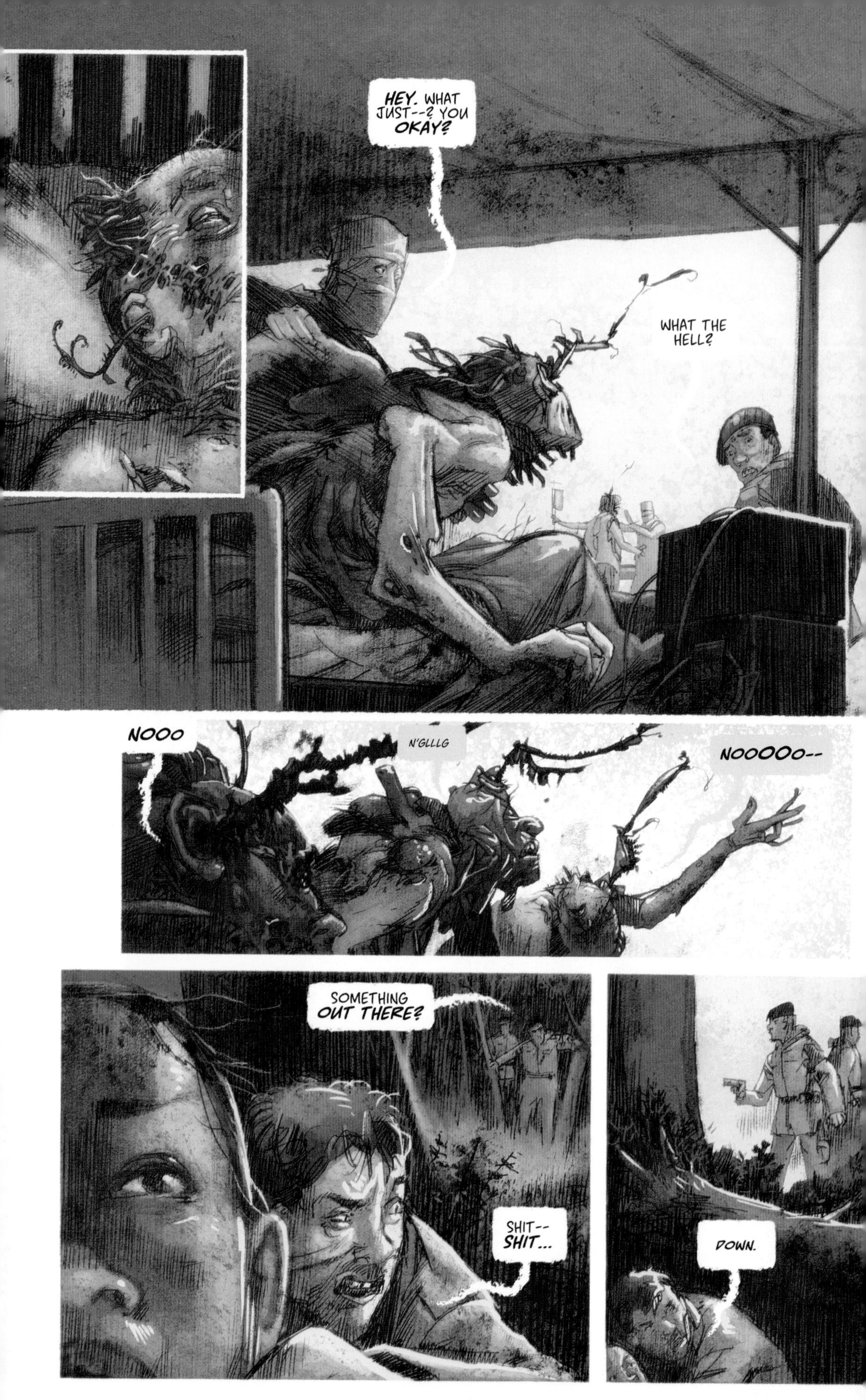
HEY. WHAT JUST--? YOU OKAY?
WHAT THE HELL?
NOOO
N'GLLLG
NOOOOO--
SOMETHING OUT THERE?
SHIT-- SHIT...
DOWN.

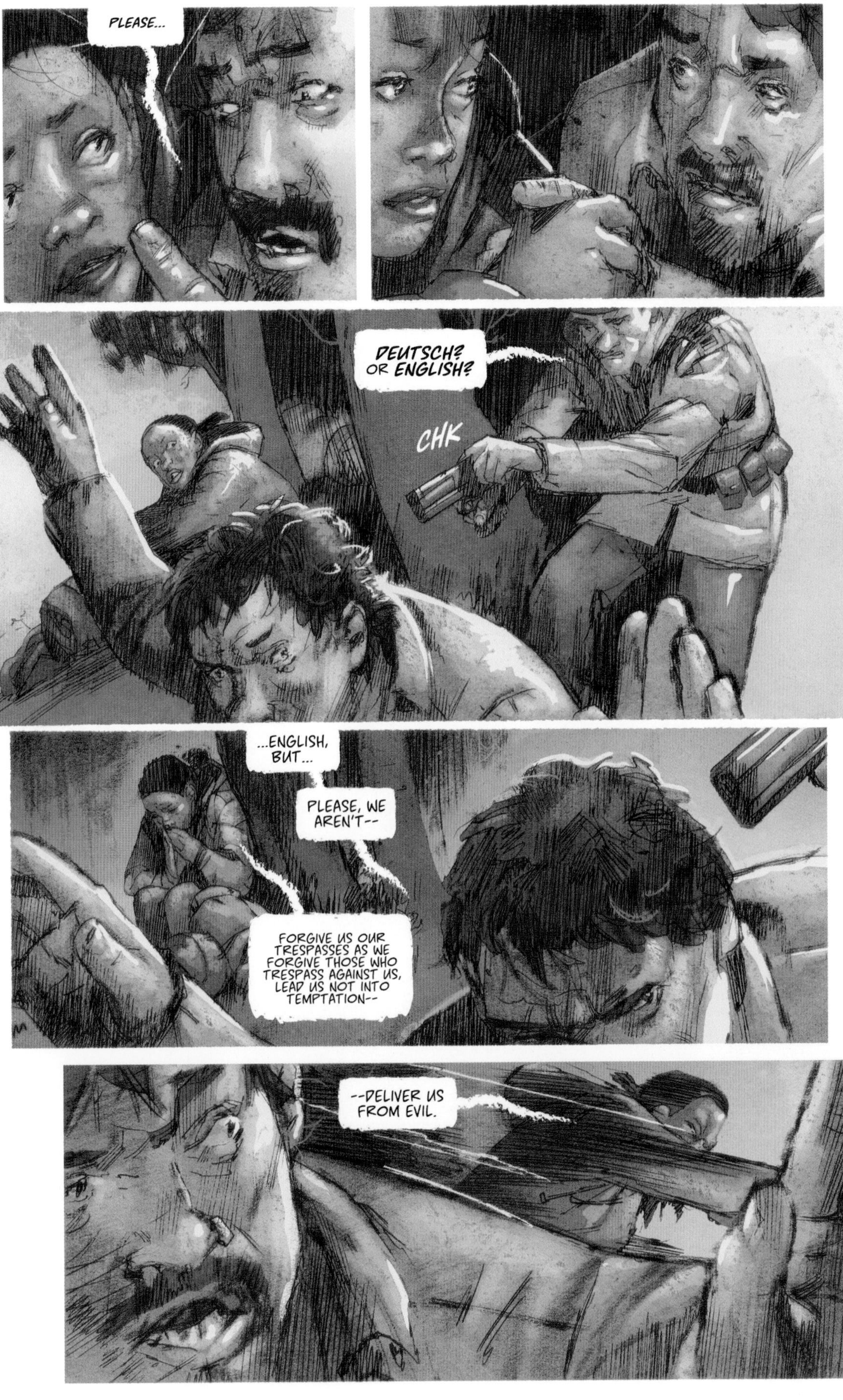
PLEASE...
DEUTSCH? OR ENGLISH?
CHK
...ENGLISH, BUT...
PLEASE, WE AREN'T--
FORGIVE US OUR TRESPASSES AS WE FORGIVE THOSE WHO TRESPASS AGAINST US, LEAD US NOT INTO TEMPTATION--
--DELIVER US FROM EVIL.

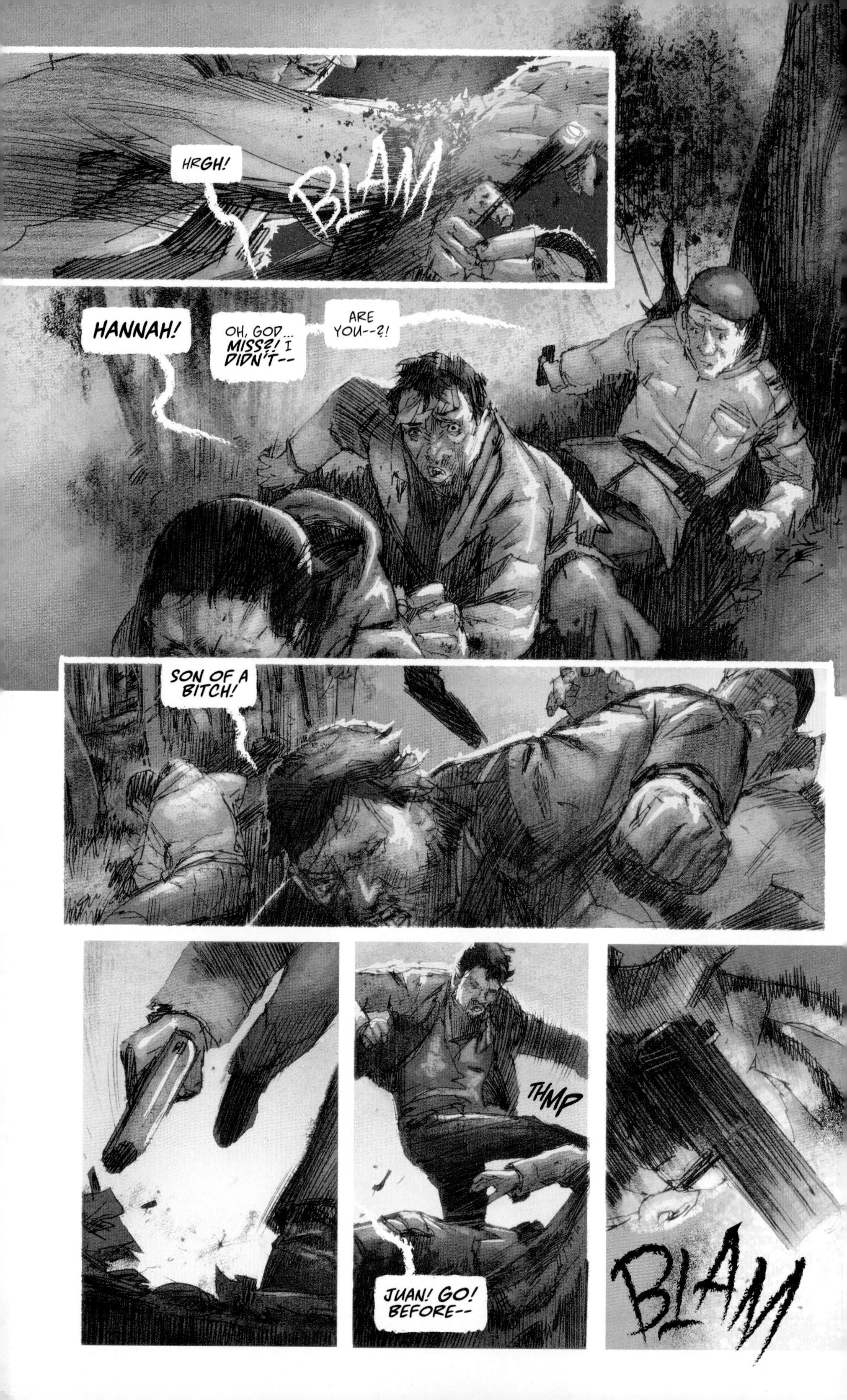
HRGH!
BLAM
HANNAH!
OH, GOD... MISS?! I DIDN'T--
ARE YOU--?!
SON OF A BITCH!
THMP
JUAN! GO! BEFORE--
BLAM

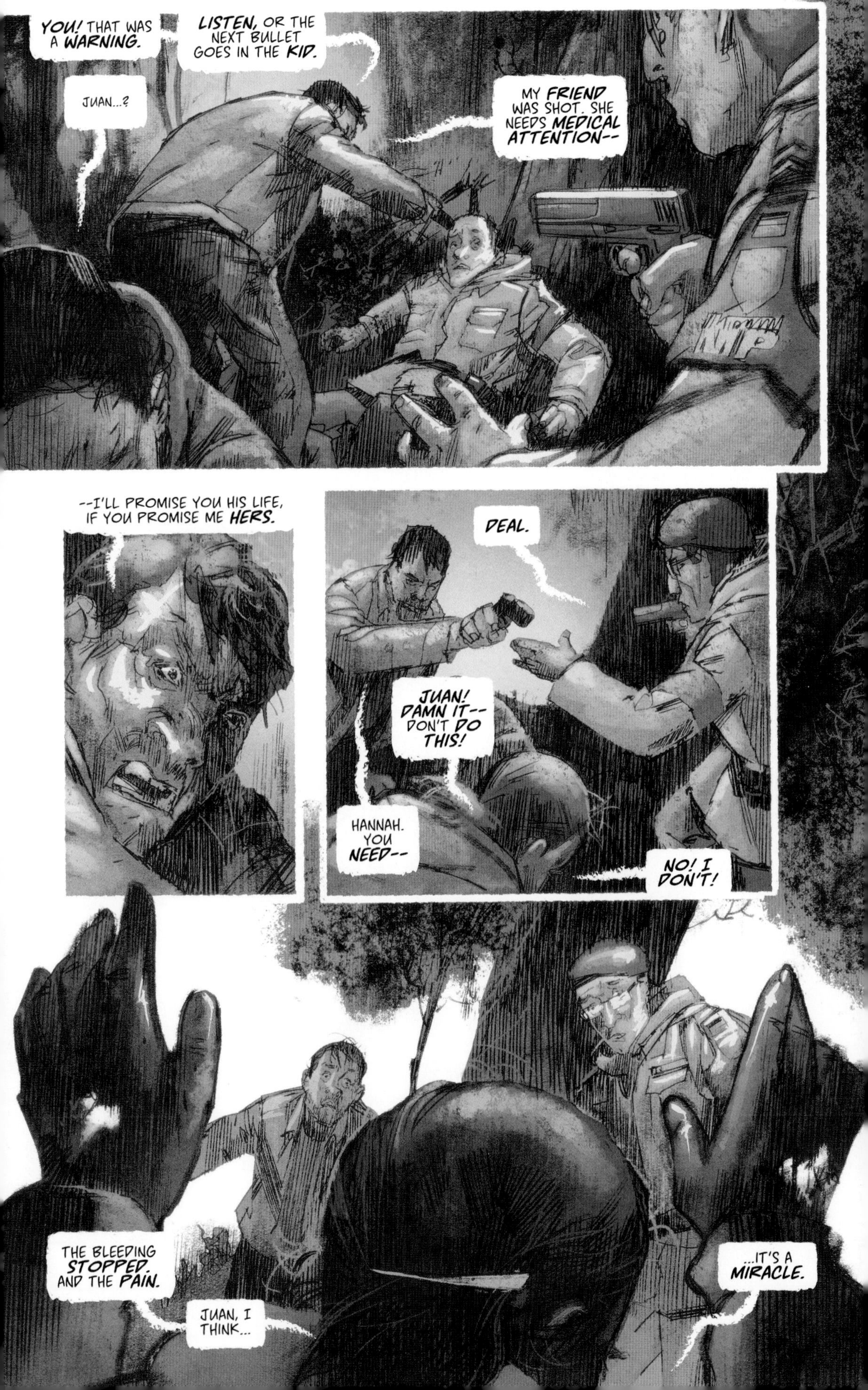
YOU! THAT WAS A WARNING.
LISTEN, OR THE NEXT BULLET GOES IN THE KID.
JUAN...?
MY FRIEND WAS SHOT. SHE NEEDS MEDICAL ATTENTION--
--I'LL PROMISE YOU HIS LIFE, IF YOU PROMISE ME HERS.
DEAL.
JUAN! DAMN IT-- DON'T DO THIS!
HANNAH. YOU NEED--
NO! I DON'T!
THE BLEEDING STOPPED. AND THE PAIN.
JUAN, I THINK...
...IT'S A MIRACLE.

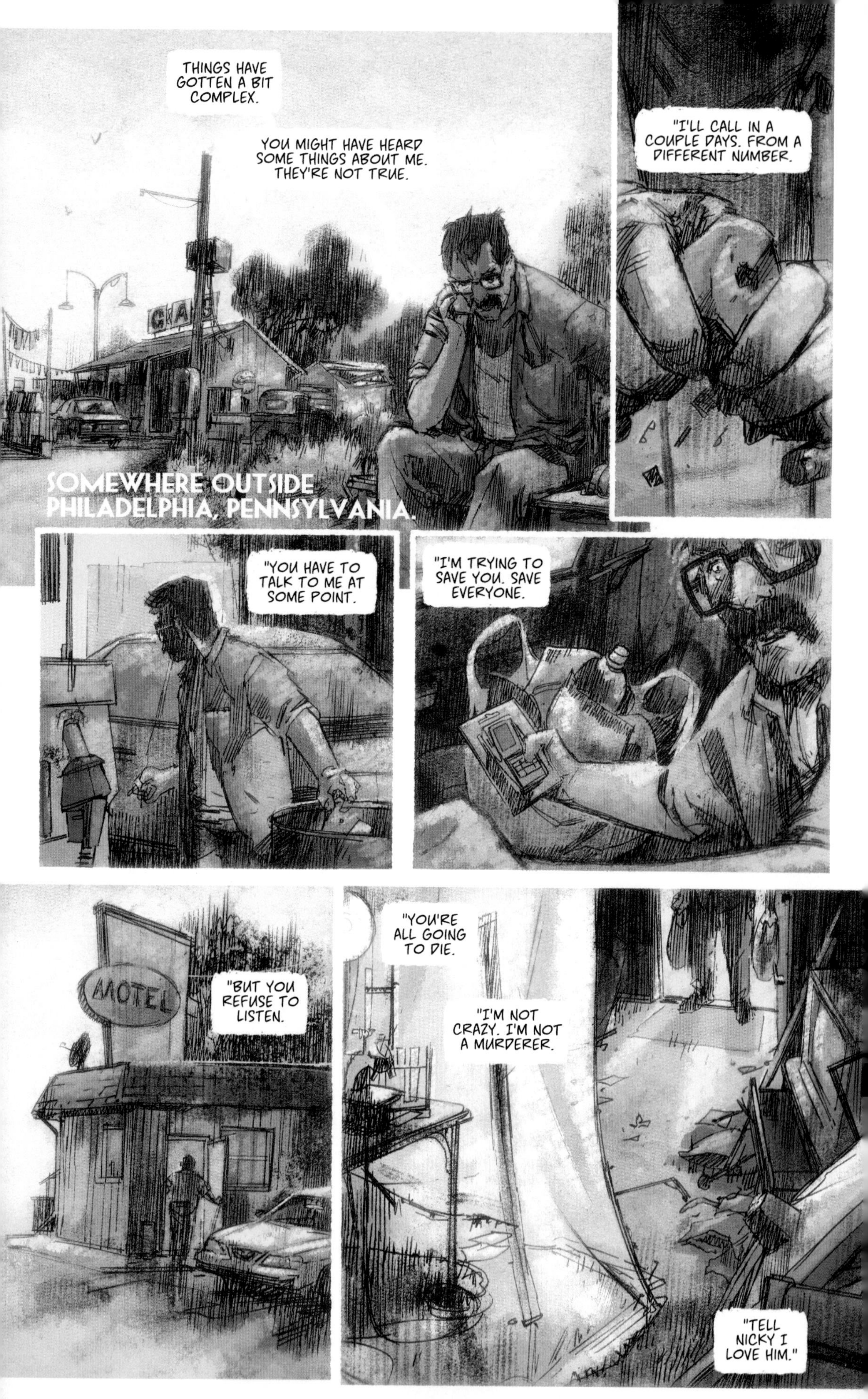
THINGS HAVE GOTTEN A BIT COMPLEX.
YOU MIGHT HAVE HEARD SOME THINGS ABOUT ME. THEY'RE NOT TRUE.
SOMEWHERE OUTSIDE PHILADELPHIA, PENNSYLVANIA.
"I'LL CALL IN A COUPLE DAYS. FROM A DIFFERENT NUMBER.
"YOU HAVE TO TALK TO ME AT SOME POINT.
"I'M TRYING TO SAVE YOU. SAVE EVERYONE.
MOTEL
"BUT YOU REFUSE TO LISTEN.
"YOU'RE ALL GOING TO DIE.
"I'M NOT CRAZY. I'M NOT A MURDERER.
"TELL NICKY I LOVE HIM."

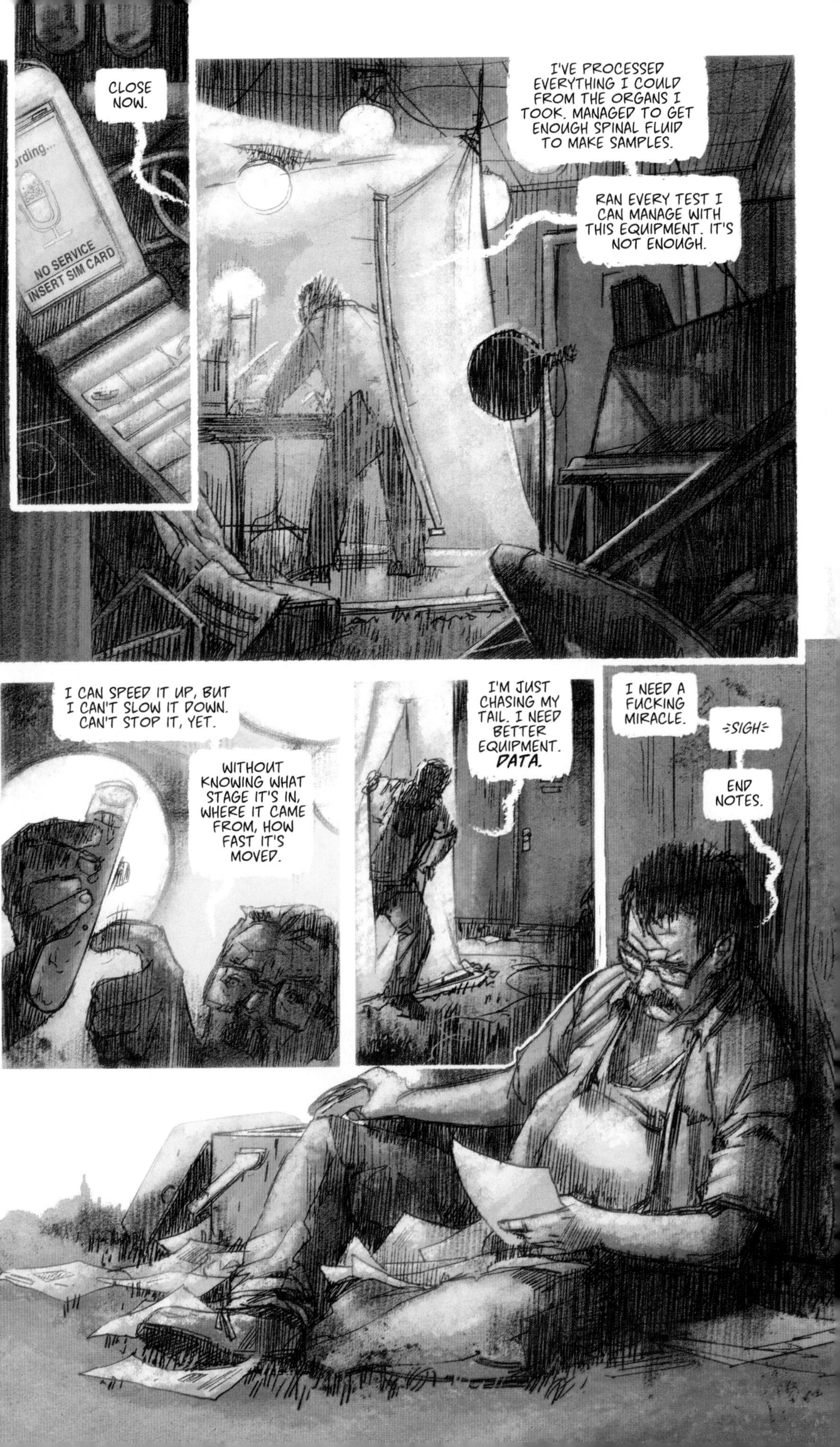
CLOSE NOW.
...ording...
NO SERVICE
INSERT SIM CARD
I'VE PROCESSED EVERYTHING I COULD FROM THE ORGANS I TOOK. MANAGED TO GET ENOUGH SPINAL FLUID TO MAKE SAMPLES.
RAN EVERY TEST I CAN MANAGE WITH THIS EQUIPMENT. IT'S NOT ENOUGH.
I CAN SPEED IT UP, BUT I CAN'T SLOW IT DOWN. CAN'T STOP IT, YET.
WITHOUT KNOWING WHAT STAGE IT'S IN, WHERE IT CAME FROM, HOW FAST IT'S MOVED.
I'M JUST CHASING MY TAIL. I NEED BETTER EQUIPMENT. DATA.
I NEED A FUCKING MIRACLE.
=SIGH=
END NOTES.

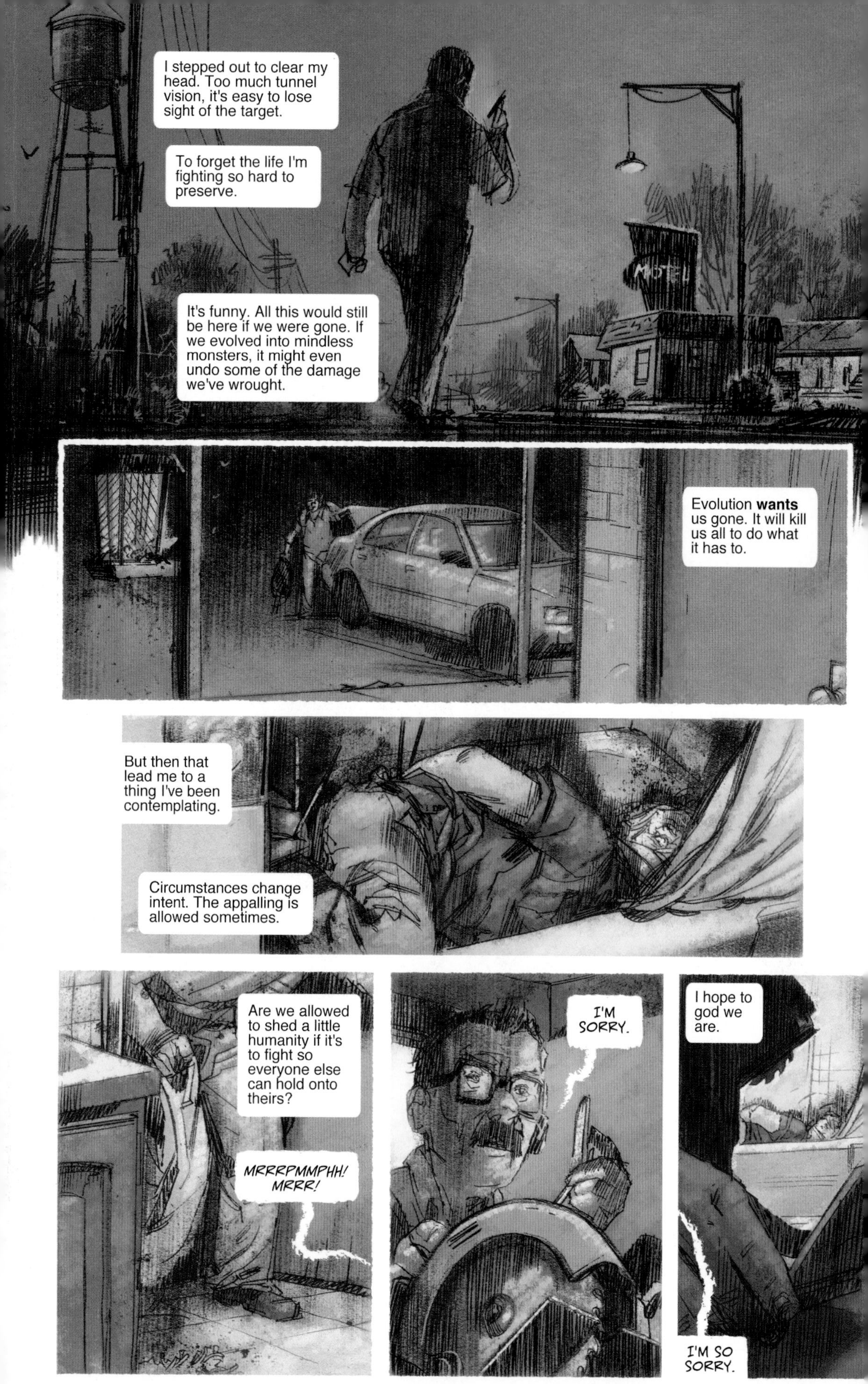

I stepped out to clear my head. Too much tunnel vision, it's easy to lose sight of the target.
To forget the life I'm fighting so hard to preserve.
It's funny. All this would still be here if we were gone. If we evolved into mindless monsters, it might even undo some of the damage we've wrought.
MOTEL
Evolution **wants** us gone. It will kill us all to do what it has to.
But then that lead me to a thing I've been contemplating.
Circumstances change intent. The appalling is allowed sometimes.
Are we allowed to shed a little humanity if it's to fight so everyone else can hold onto theirs?
MRRRPMMPHH! MRRR!
I'M SORRY.
I hope to god we are.
I'M SO SORRY.

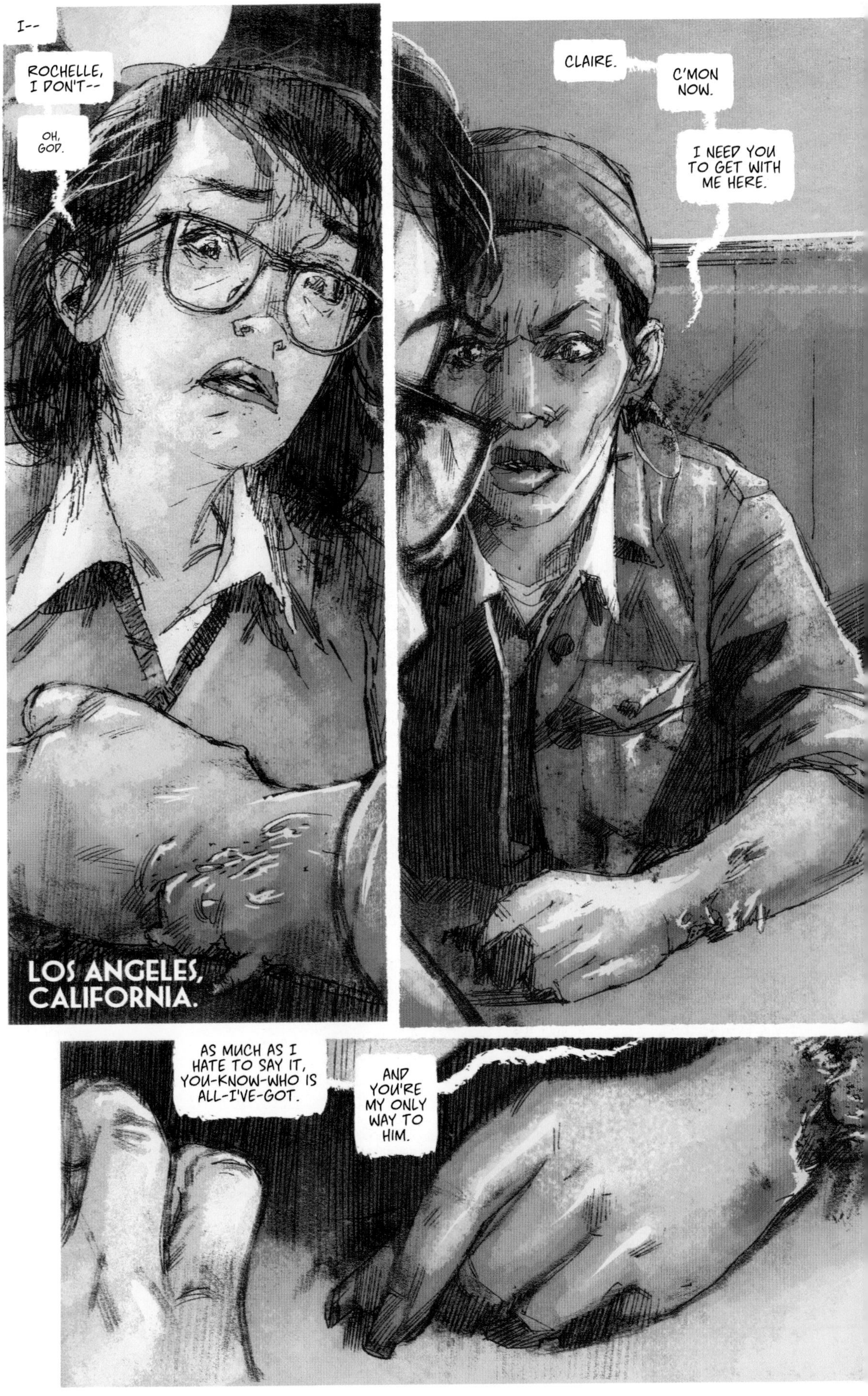
I--
ROCHELLE, I DON'T--
OH, GOD.
LOS ANGELES, CALIFORNIA.
CLAIRE.
C'MON NOW.
I NEED YOU TO GET WITH ME HERE.
AS MUCH AS I HATE TO SAY IT, YOU-KNOW-WHO IS ALL-I'VE-GOT.
AND YOU'RE MY ONLY WAY TO HIM.

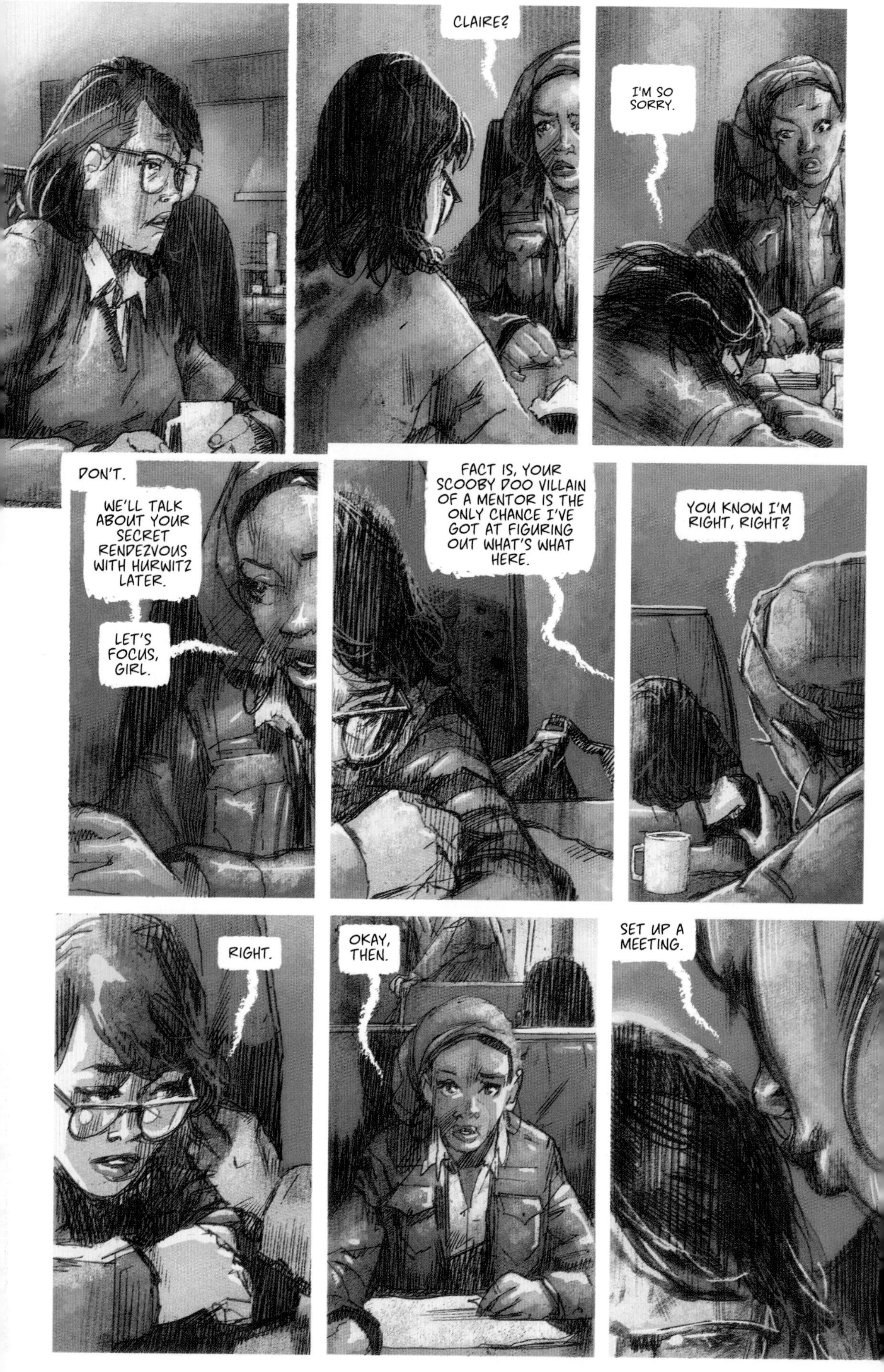
CLAIRE?
I'M SO SORRY.
DON'T.
WE'LL TALK ABOUT YOUR SECRET RENDEZVOUS WITH HURWITZ LATER.
LET'S FOCUS, GIRL.
FACT IS, YOUR SCOOBY DOO VILLAIN OF A MENTOR IS THE ONLY CHANCE I'VE GOT AT FIGURING OUT WHAT'S WHAT HERE.
YOU KNOW I'M RIGHT, RIGHT?
RIGHT.
OKAY, THEN.
SET UP A MEETING.

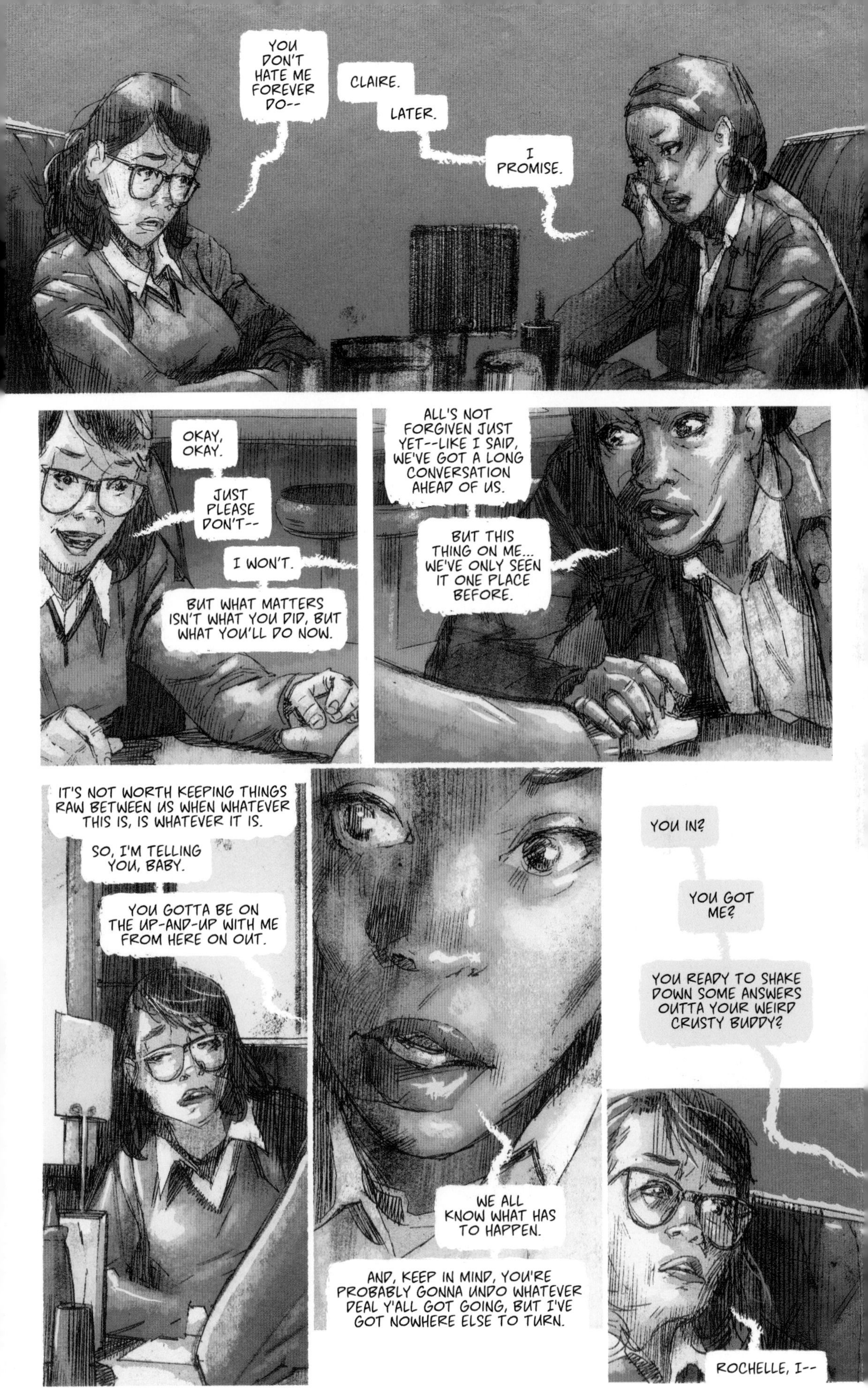
YOU DON'T HATE ME FOREVER DO--
CLAIRE.
LATER.
I PROMISE.
OKAY, OKAY.
JUST PLEASE DON'T--
I WON'T.
BUT WHAT MATTERS ISN'T WHAT YOU DID, BUT WHAT YOU'LL DO NOW.
ALL'S NOT FORGIVEN JUST YET--LIKE I SAID, WE'VE GOT A LONG CONVERSATION AHEAD OF US.
BUT THIS THING ON ME... WE'VE ONLY SEEN IT ONE PLACE BEFORE.
IT'S NOT WORTH KEEPING THINGS RAW BETWEEN US WHEN WHATEVER THIS IS, IS WHATEVER IT IS.
SO, I'M TELLING YOU, BABY.
YOU GOTTA BE ON THE UP-AND-UP WITH ME FROM HERE ON OUT.
WE ALL KNOW WHAT HAS TO HAPPEN.
AND, KEEP IN MIND, YOU'RE PROBABLY GONNA UNDO WHATEVER DEAL Y'ALL GOT GOING, BUT I'VE GOT NOWHERE ELSE TO TURN.
YOU IN?
YOU GOT ME?
YOU READY TO SHAKE DOWN SOME ANSWERS OUTTA YOUR WEIRD CRUSTY BUDDY?
ROCHELLE, I--

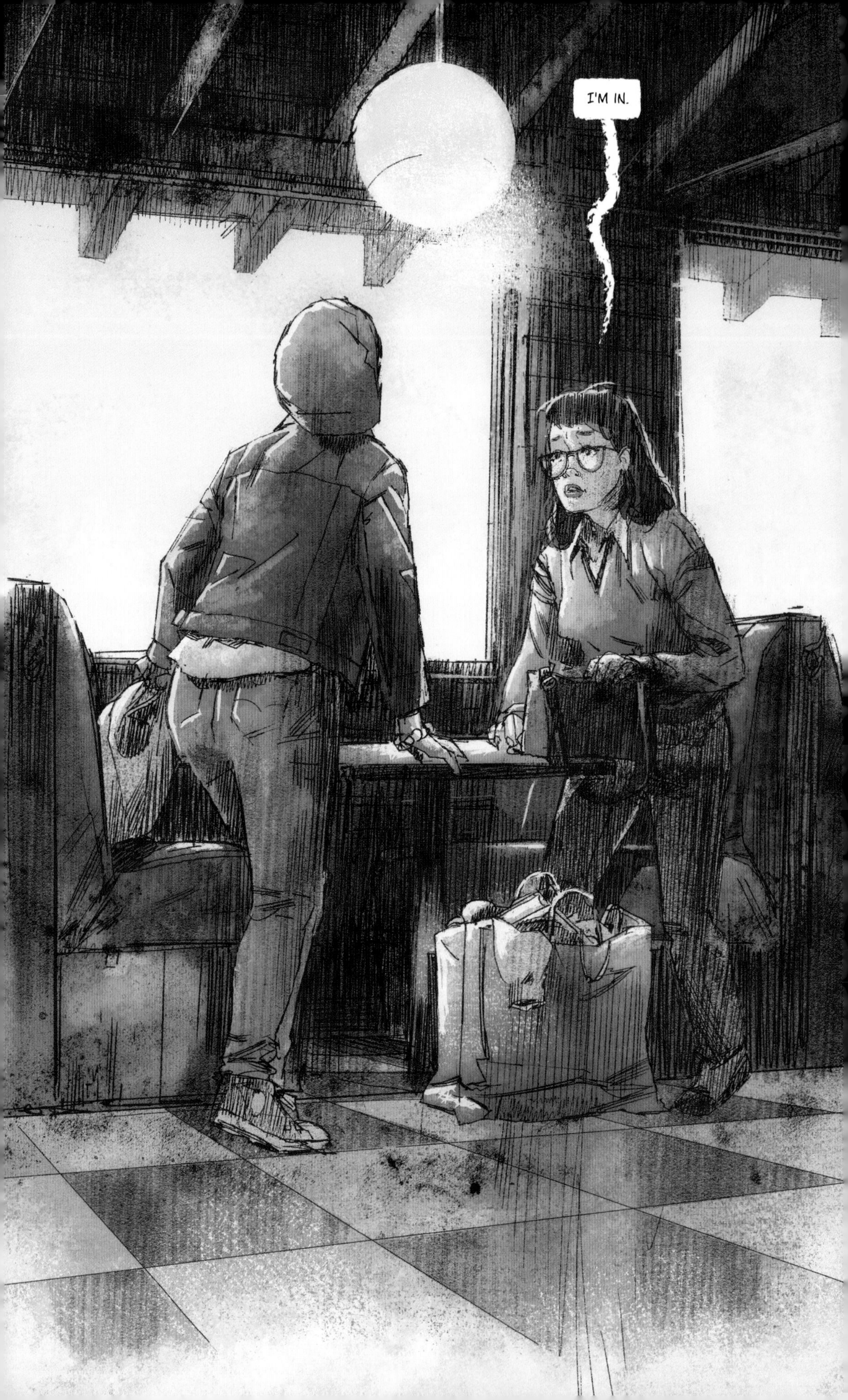
I'M IN.

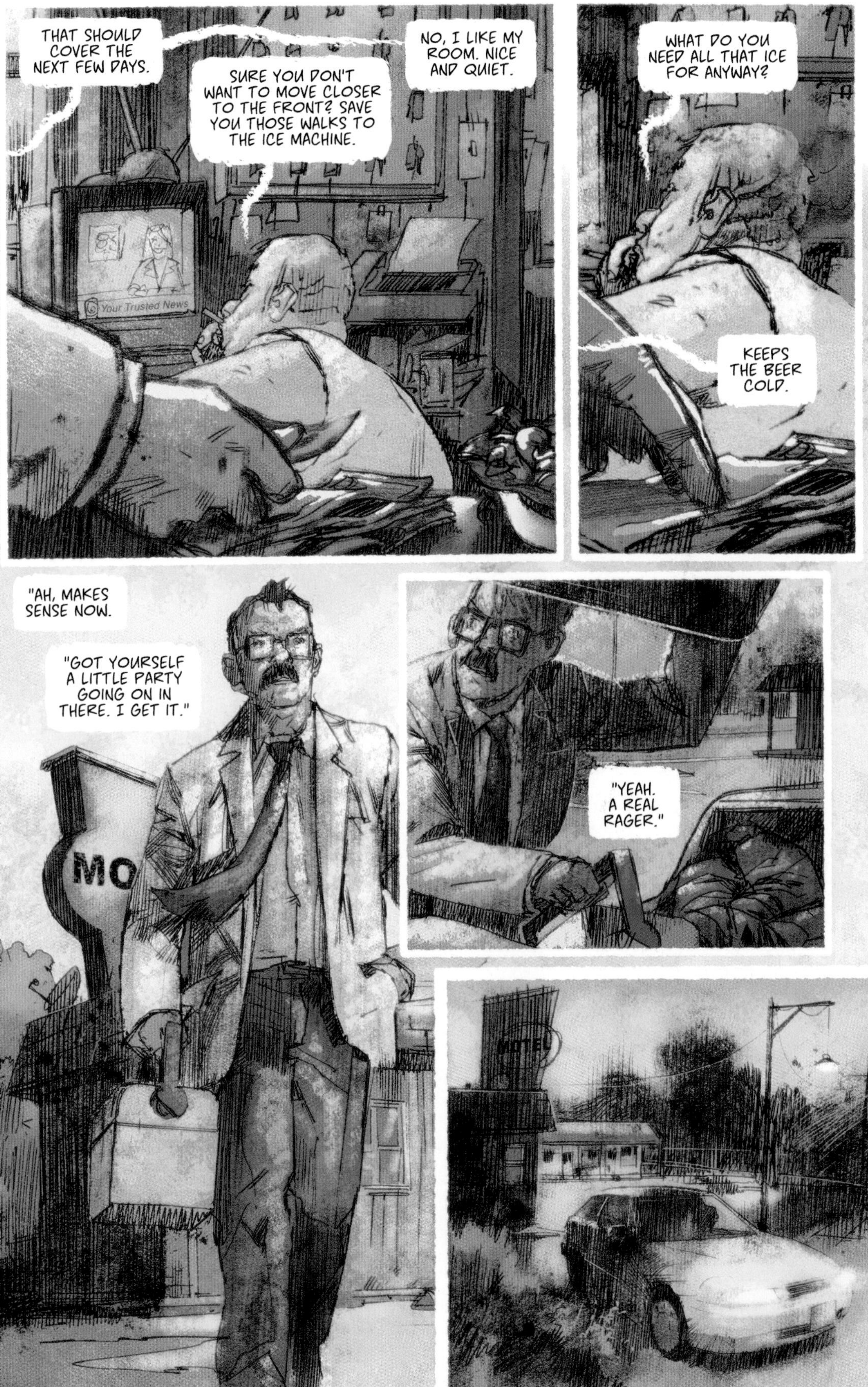

THAT SHOULD COVER THE NEXT FEW DAYS.
SURE YOU DON'T WANT TO MOVE CLOSER TO THE FRONT? SAVE YOU THOSE WALKS TO THE ICE MACHINE.
NO, I LIKE MY ROOM. NICE AND QUIET.
Your Trusted News
WHAT DO YOU NEED ALL THAT ICE FOR ANYWAY?
KEEPS THE BEER COLD.
"AH, MAKES SENSE NOW.
"GOT YOURSELF A LITTLE PARTY GOING ON IN THERE. I GET IT."
MO
"YEAH. A REAL RAGER."
MOTEL

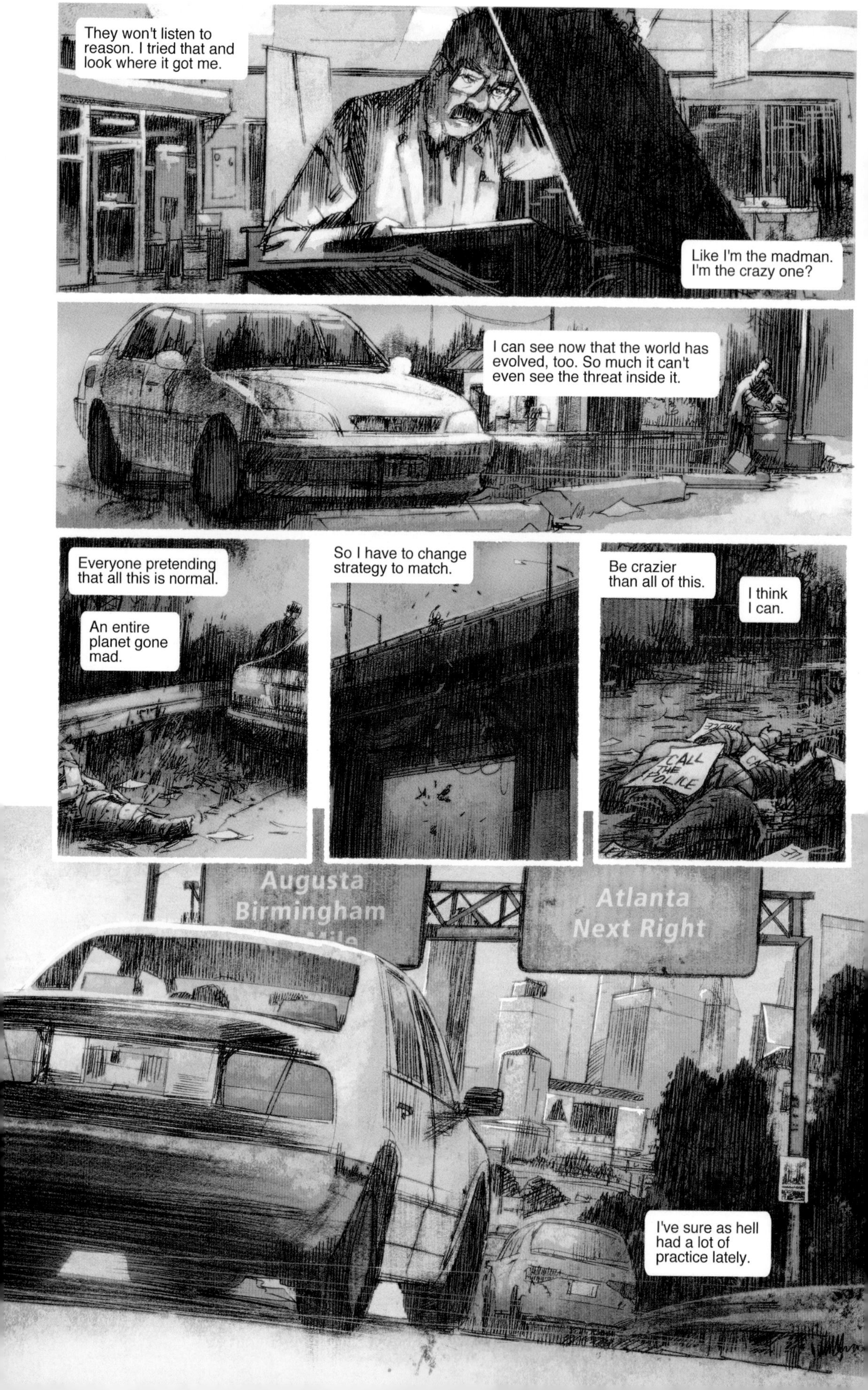
They won't listen to reason. I tried that and look where it got me.
Like I'm the madman. I'm the crazy one?
I can see now that the world has evolved, too. So much it can't even see the threat inside it.
Everyone pretending that all this is normal.
An entire planet gone mad.
So I have to change strategy to match.
Be crazier than all of this.
I think I can.
CALL THE POLICE
Augusta
Birmingham
Atlanta
Next Right
I've sure as hell had a lot of practice lately.

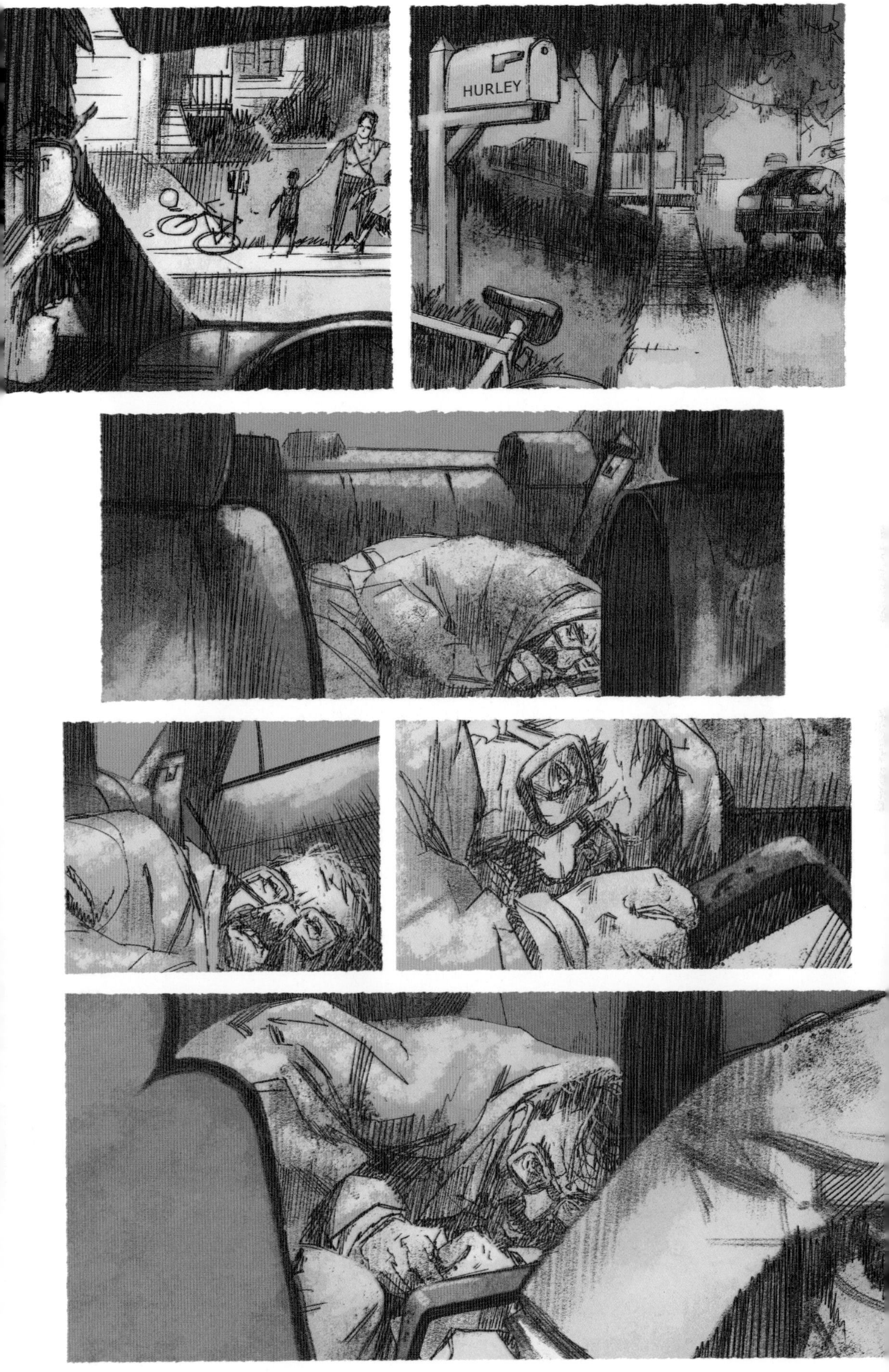
HURLEY

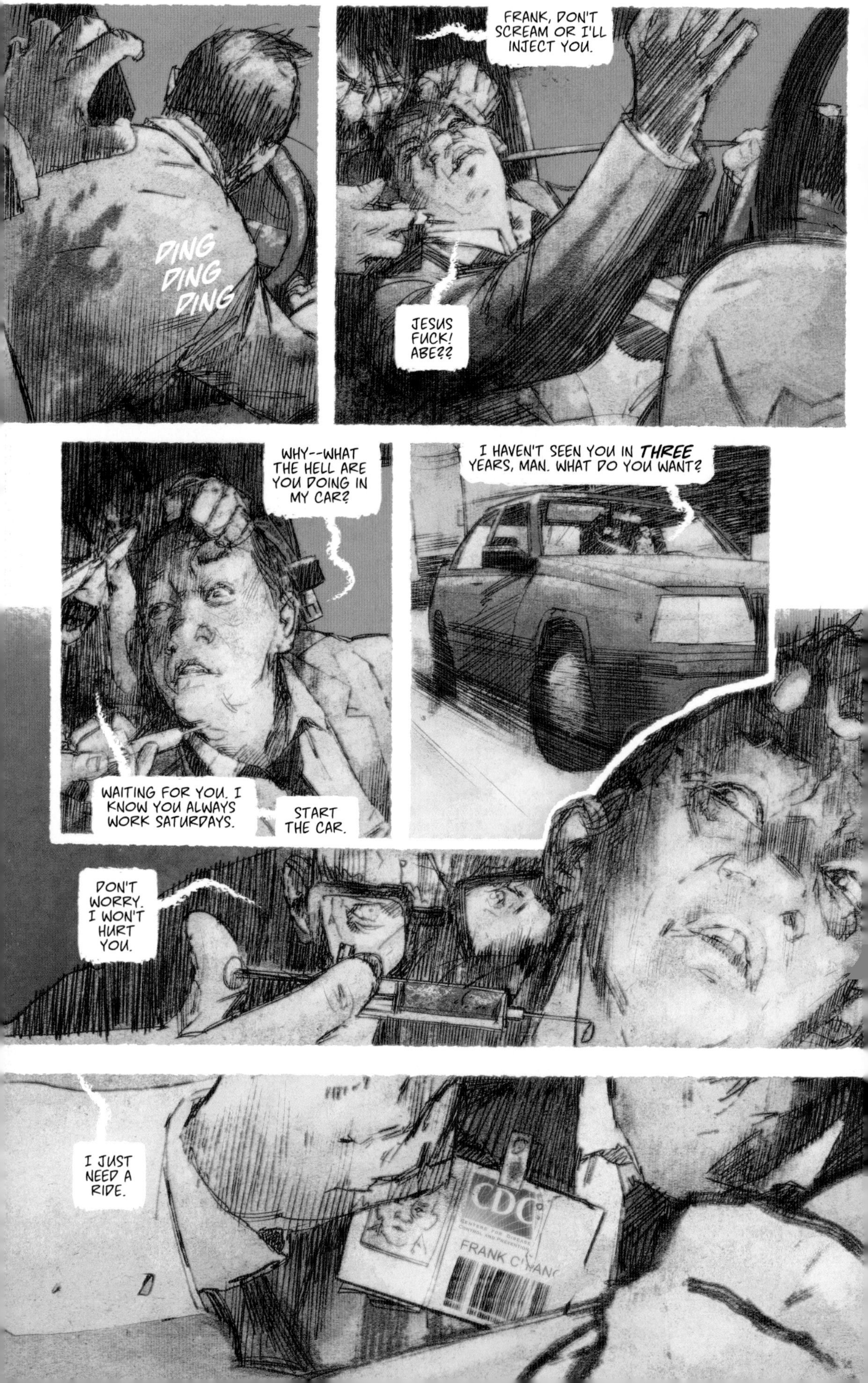
DING
DING
DING
FRANK, DON'T SCREAM OR I'LL INJECT YOU.
JESUS FUCK! ABE??
WHY--WHAT THE HELL ARE YOU DOING IN MY CAR?
WAITING FOR YOU. I KNOW YOU ALWAYS WORK SATURDAYS.
START THE CAR.
I HAVEN'T SEEN YOU IN THREE YEARS, MAN. WHAT DO YOU WANT?
DON'T WORRY. I WON'T HURT YOU.
I JUST NEED A RIDE.
CDC
FRANK C'HANG

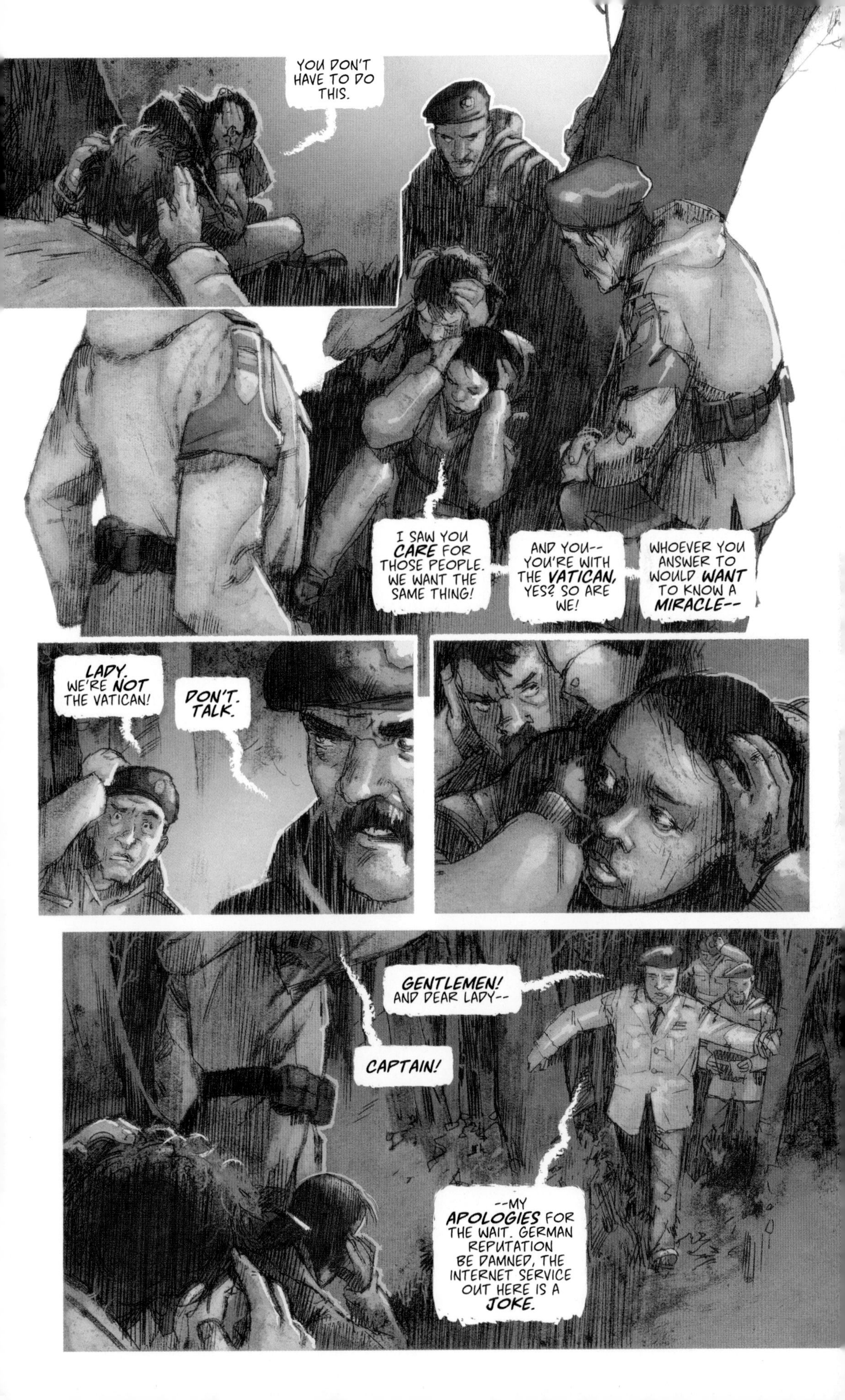

YOU DON'T HAVE TO DO THIS.
I SAW YOU CARE FOR THOSE PEOPLE. WE WANT THE SAME THING!
AND YOU-- YOU'RE WITH THE VATICAN, YES? SO ARE WE!
WHOEVER YOU ANSWER TO WOULD WANT TO KNOW A MIRACLE--
LADY. WE'RE NOT THE VATICAN!
DON'T. TALK.
GENTLEMEN! AND DEAR LADY--
CAPTAIN!
--MY APOLOGIES FOR THE WAIT. GERMAN REPUTATION BE DAMNED, THE INTERNET SERVICE OUT HERE IS A JOKE.

WE RAN YOUR PASSPORTS.

THANK YOU FOR BRINGING THOSE, BY THE WAY.

BUT, EVENTUALLY, WE FOUND YOUR *REAL* NAME, TOO--

--HANNAH PAULSON.

OF COURSE--WE DIDN'T KNOW WHO YOU WERE AT THE TIME OF THE *MIRACLE.* BUT AS YOU MIGHT IMAGINE, EVERY PIECE OF THAT EVENT WAS OF *GREAT INTEREST*--

YOU MEAN...MY *HANDS?*

HANDS--? *NO.*

YOU WERE *THERE,* WEREN'T YOU?

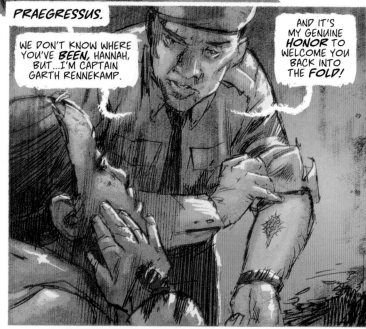

*PRAEGRESSUS.*

WE DON'T KNOW WHERE YOU'VE *BEEN,* HANNAH, BUT...I'M CAPTAIN GARTH RENNEKAMP.

AND IT'S MY GENUINE *HONOR* TO WELCOME YOU BACK INTO THE *FOLD!*

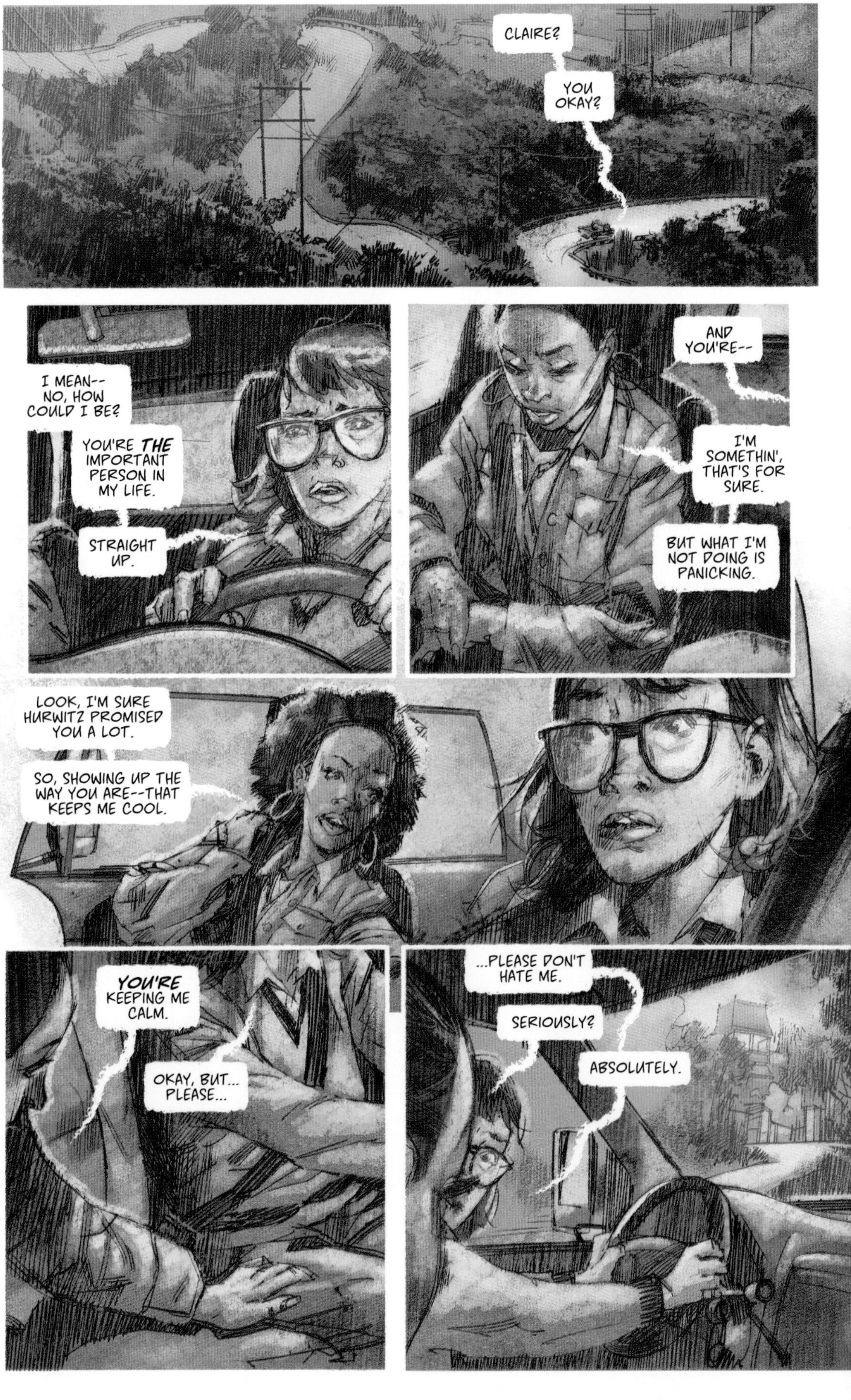
CLAIRE?
YOU OKAY?
I MEAN-- NO, HOW COULD I BE?
YOU'RE **THE** IMPORTANT PERSON IN MY LIFE.
STRAIGHT UP.
AND YOU'RE--
I'M SOMETHIN', THAT'S FOR SURE.
BUT WHAT I'M NOT DOING IS PANICKING.
LOOK, I'M SURE HURWITZ PROMISED YOU A LOT.
SO, SHOWING UP THE WAY YOU ARE--THAT KEEPS ME COOL.
***YOU'RE*** KEEPING ME CALM.
OKAY, BUT... PLEASE...
...PLEASE DON'T HATE ME.
SERIOUSLY?
ABSOLUTELY.

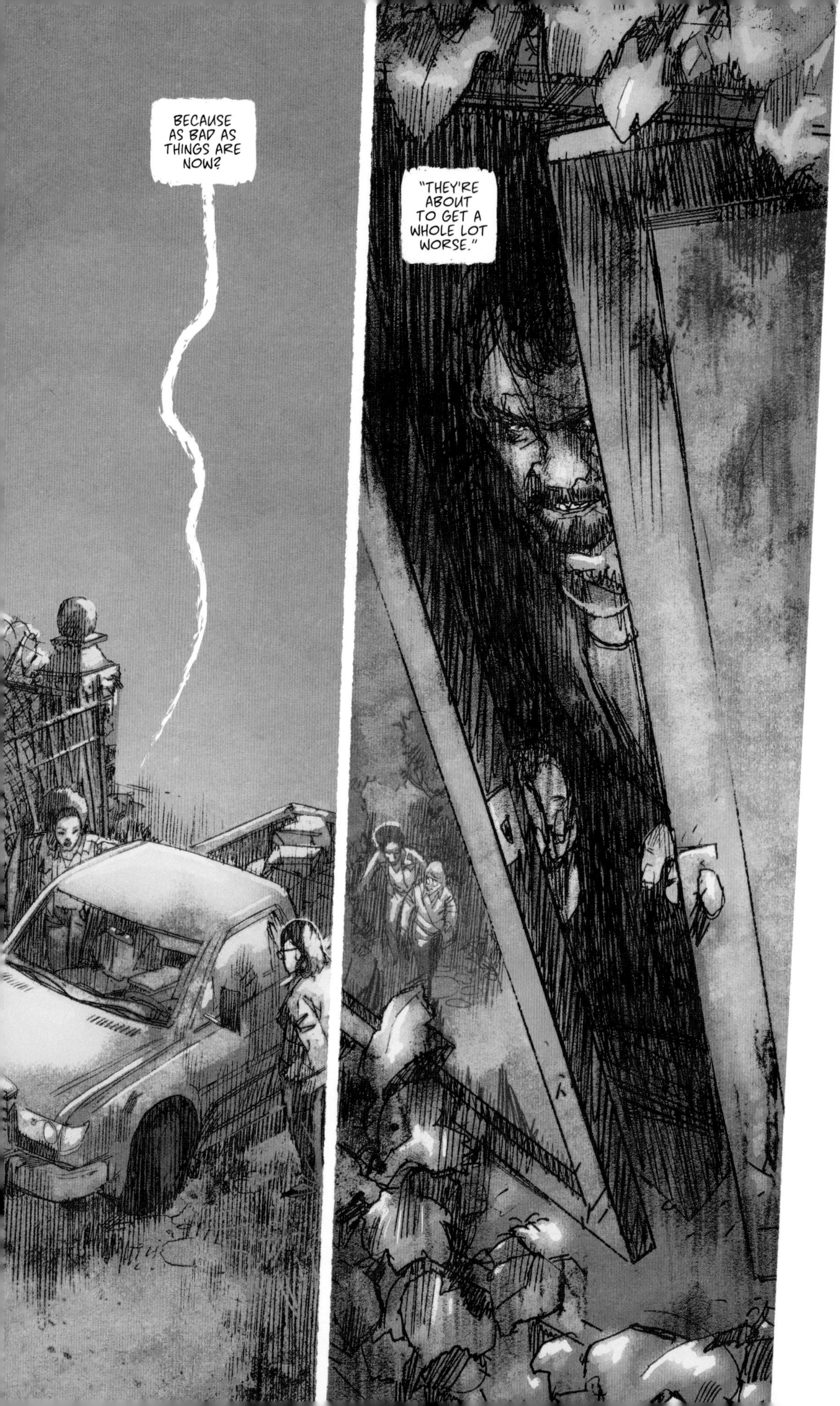
BECAUSE AS BAD AS THINGS ARE NOW?
"THEY'RE ABOUT TO GET A WHOLE LOT WORSE."

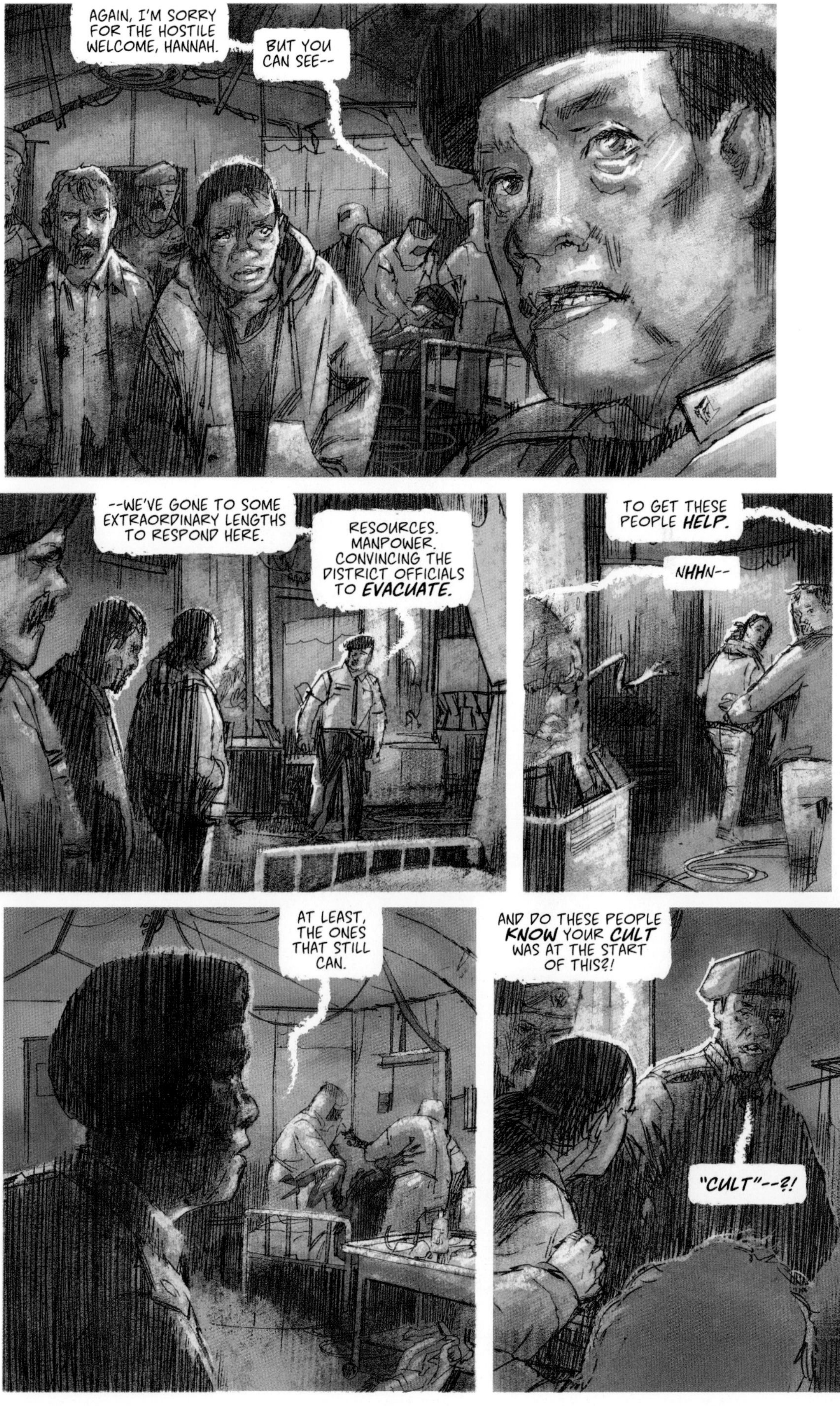
AGAIN, I'M SORRY FOR THE HOSTILE WELCOME, HANNAH.
BUT YOU CAN SEE--
--WE'VE GONE TO SOME EXTRAORDINARY LENGTHS TO RESPOND HERE.
RESOURCES. MANPOWER. CONVINCING THE DISTRICT OFFICIALS TO EVACUATE.
TO GET THESE PEOPLE HELP.
NHHN--
AT LEAST, THE ONES THAT STILL CAN.
AND DO THESE PEOPLE KNOW YOUR CULT WAS AT THE START OF THIS?!
"CULT"--?!

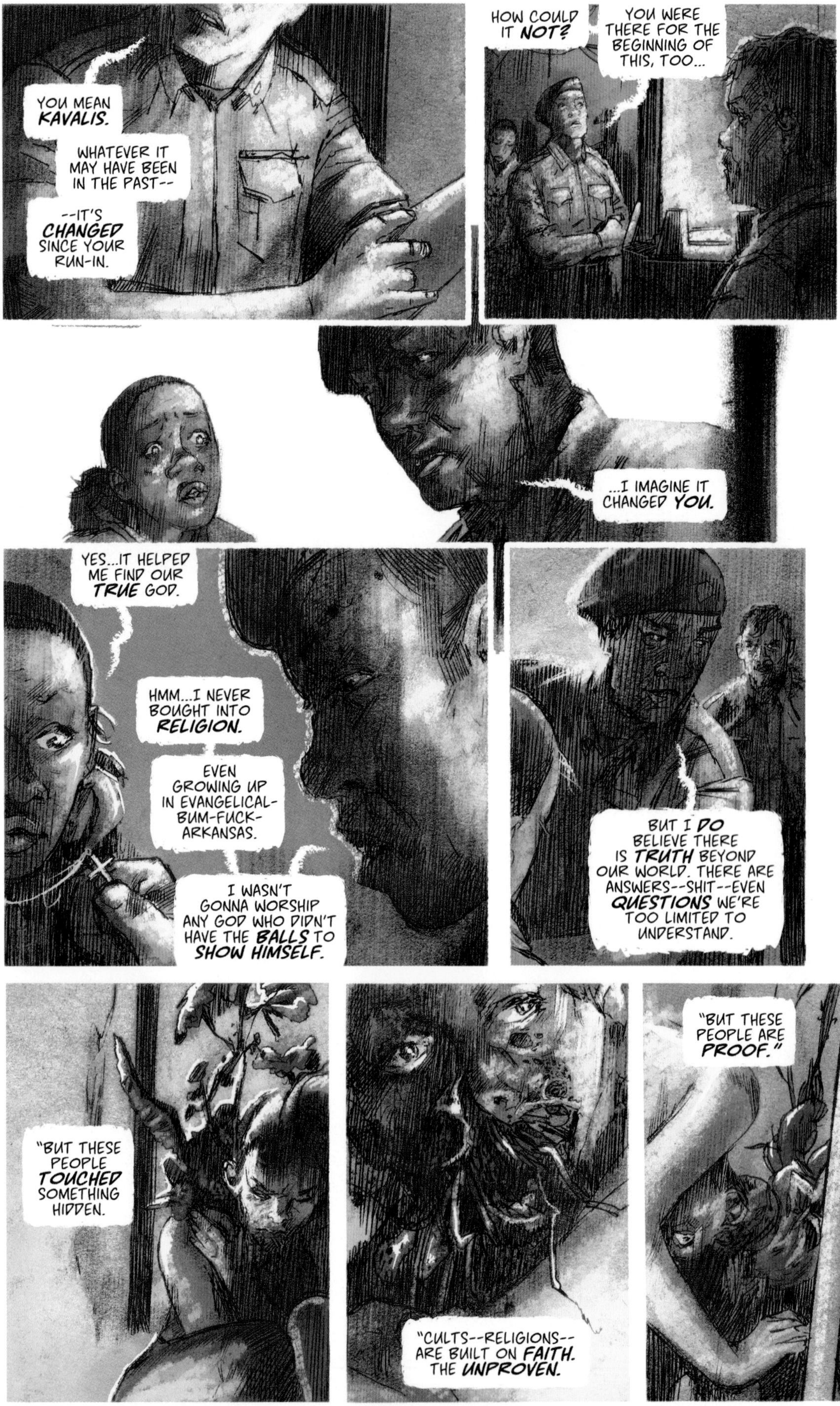
YOU MEAN KAVALIS.
WHATEVER IT MAY HAVE BEEN IN THE PAST--
--IT'S CHANGED SINCE YOUR RUN-IN.
HOW COULD IT NOT?
YOU WERE THERE FOR THE BEGINNING OF THIS, TOO...
...I IMAGINE IT CHANGED YOU.
YES...IT HELPED ME FIND OUR TRUE GOD.
HMM...I NEVER BOUGHT INTO RELIGION.
EVEN GROWING UP IN EVANGELICAL-BUM-FUCK-ARKANSAS.
I WASN'T GONNA WORSHIP ANY GOD WHO DIDN'T HAVE THE BALLS TO SHOW HIMSELF.
BUT I DO BELIEVE THERE IS TRUTH BEYOND OUR WORLD. THERE ARE ANSWERS--SHIT--EVEN QUESTIONS WE'RE TOO LIMITED TO UNDERSTAND.
"BUT THESE PEOPLE TOUCHED SOMETHING HIDDEN.
"CULTS--RELIGIONS--ARE BUILT ON FAITH. THE UNPROVEN.
"BUT THESE PEOPLE ARE PROOF."

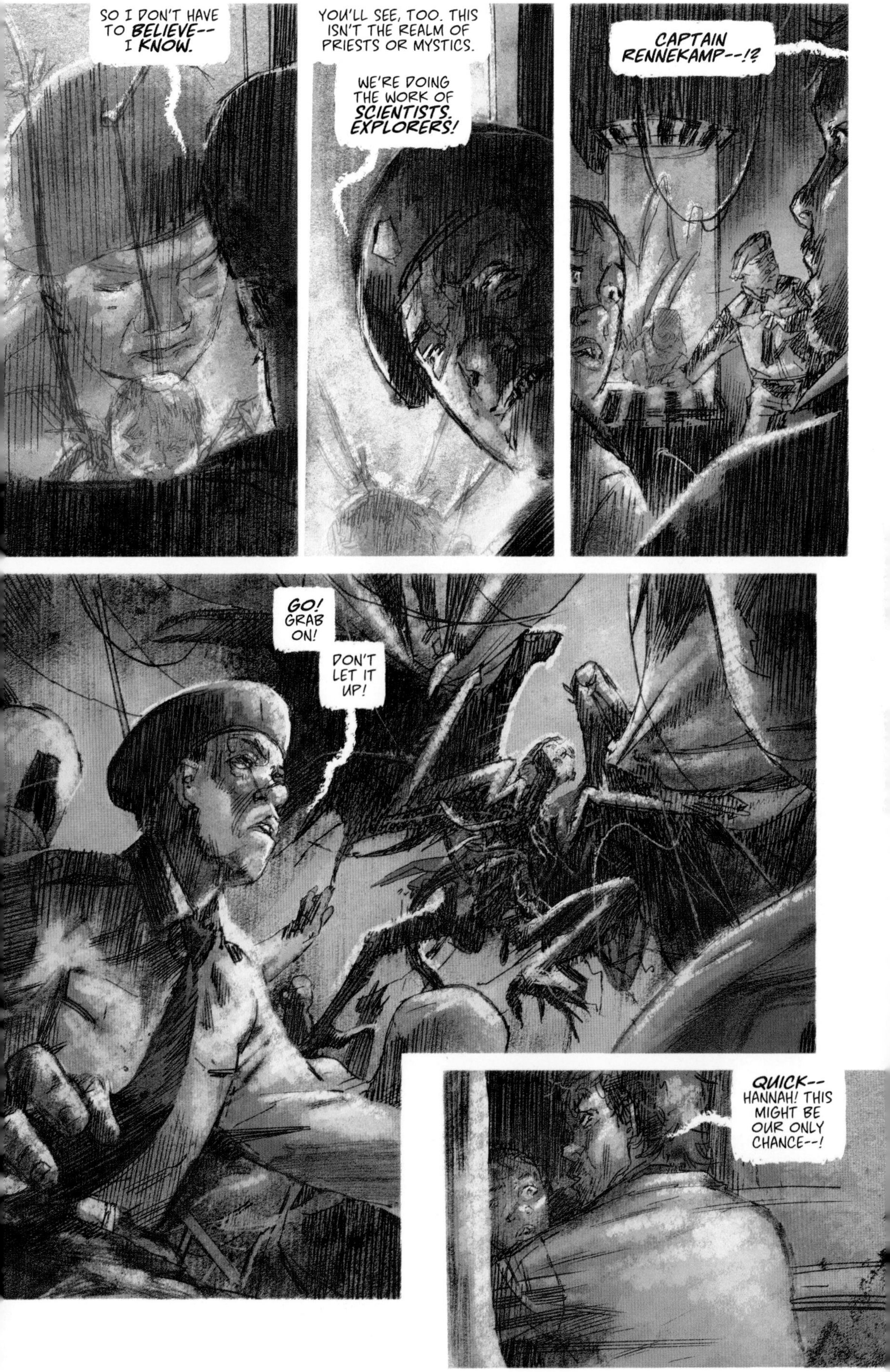
SO I DON'T HAVE TO BELIEVE-- I KNOW.
YOU'LL SEE, TOO. THIS ISN'T THE REALM OF PRIESTS OR MYSTICS.
WE'RE DOING THE WORK OF SCIENTISTS. EXPLORERS!
CAPTAIN RENNEKAMP--!?
GO! GRAB ON!
DON'T LET IT UP!
QUICK-- HANNAH! THIS MIGHT BE OUR ONLY CHANCE--!

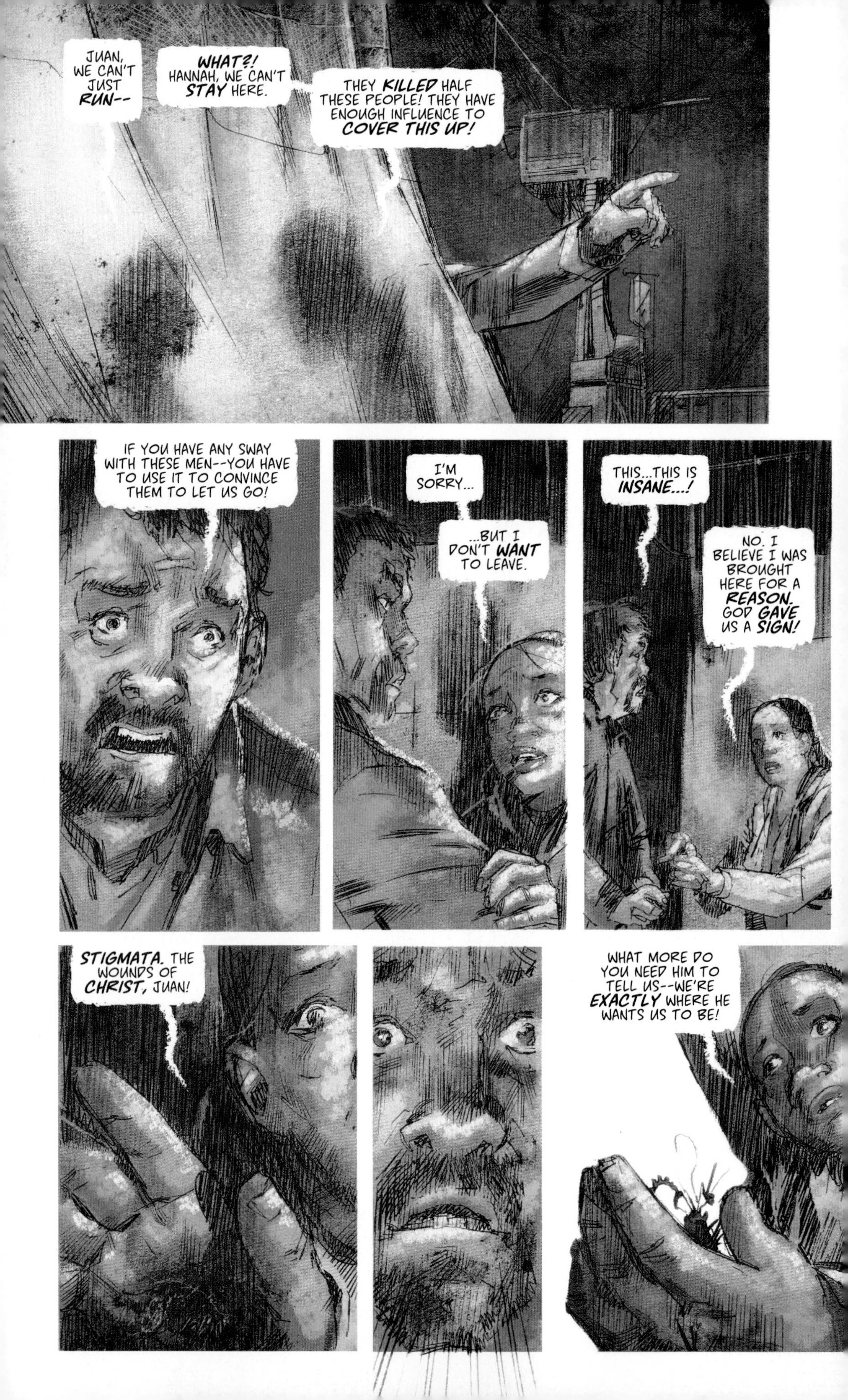

JUAN, WE CAN'T JUST RUN--
WHAT?! HANNAH, WE CAN'T STAY HERE.
THEY KILLED HALF THESE PEOPLE! THEY HAVE ENOUGH INFLUENCE TO COVER THIS UP!
IF YOU HAVE ANY SWAY WITH THESE MEN--YOU HAVE TO USE IT TO CONVINCE THEM TO LET US GO!
I'M SORRY...
...BUT I DON'T WANT TO LEAVE.
THIS...THIS IS INSANE...!
NO. I BELIEVE I WAS BROUGHT HERE FOR A REASON. GOD GAVE US A SIGN!
STIGMATA. THE WOUNDS OF CHRIST, JUAN!
WHAT MORE DO YOU NEED HIM TO TELL US--WE'RE EXACTLY WHERE HE WANTS US TO BE!

YOU KNOW WHAT YOU ARE, DON'T YOU?
YOU-- YOU'RE WORSE THAN ANY MADMAN!
YOU'RE HUMAN WITHOUT HUMANITY!
ALIVE WITHOUT A SOUL!
YOU'RE NOTHING, I TELL YOU!
NOTHING AT ALL!
TO THE PITS WITH YOU!
DAMN YOU--DAMN YOU TO HELL!
UNDERSTAND ONE THING, CHILD.
I AM GREATER THAN HUMANITY.
MY ACTIONS ARE GREATER THAN YOU COULD EVER COMPREHEND.
YOU SEE, YOUNG FOOL, I AM NO MAN.
I AM A GOD.
DING
DONG

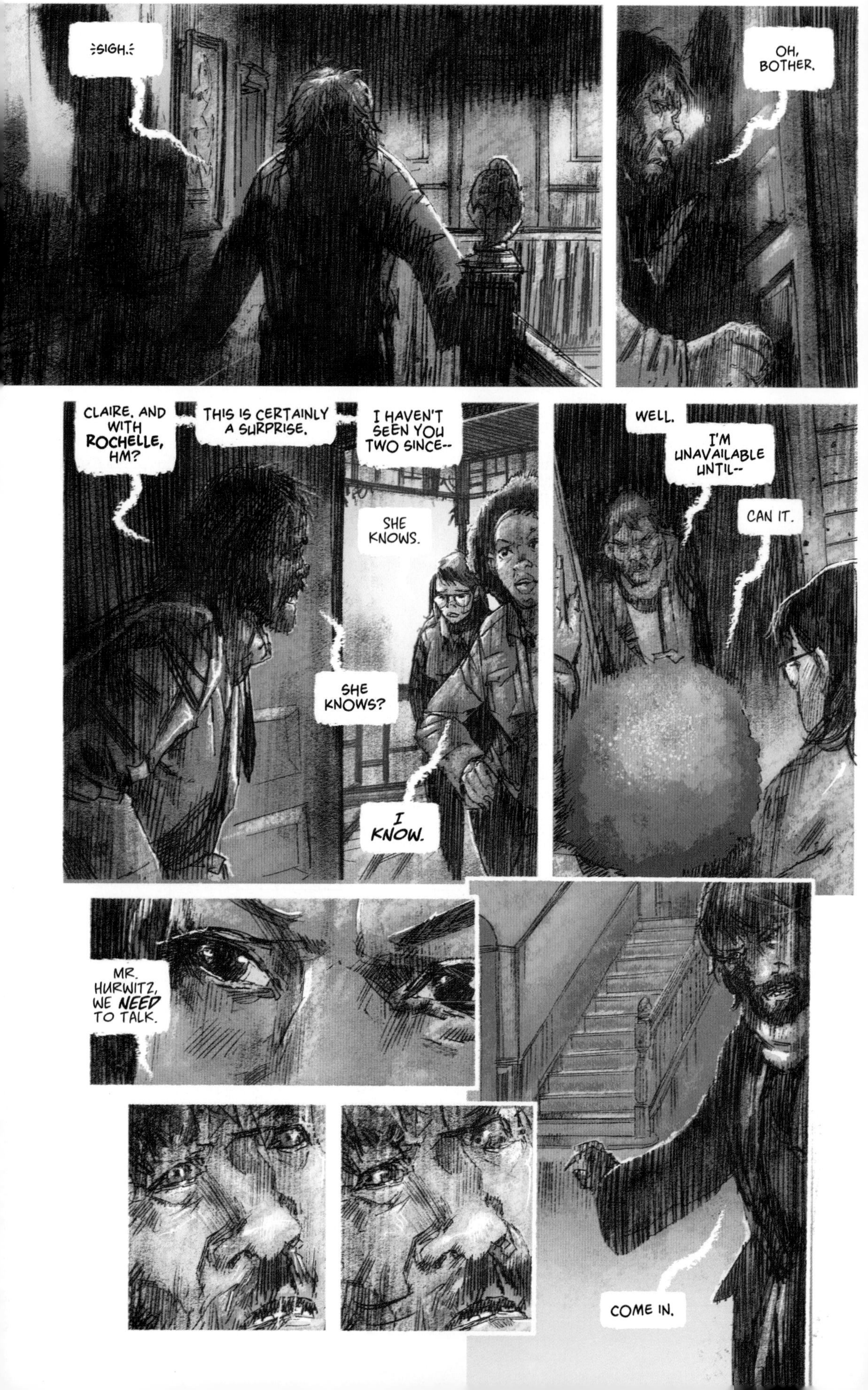

⁝SIGH.⁝
OH, BOTHER.
CLAIRE. AND WITH ROCHELLE, HM?
THIS IS CERTAINLY A SURPRISE.
I HAVEN'T SEEN YOU TWO SINCE--
SHE KNOWS.
SHE KNOWS?
I KNOW.
WELL.
I'M UNAVAILABLE UNTIL--
CAN IT.
MR. HURWITZ, WE NEED TO TALK.
COME IN.

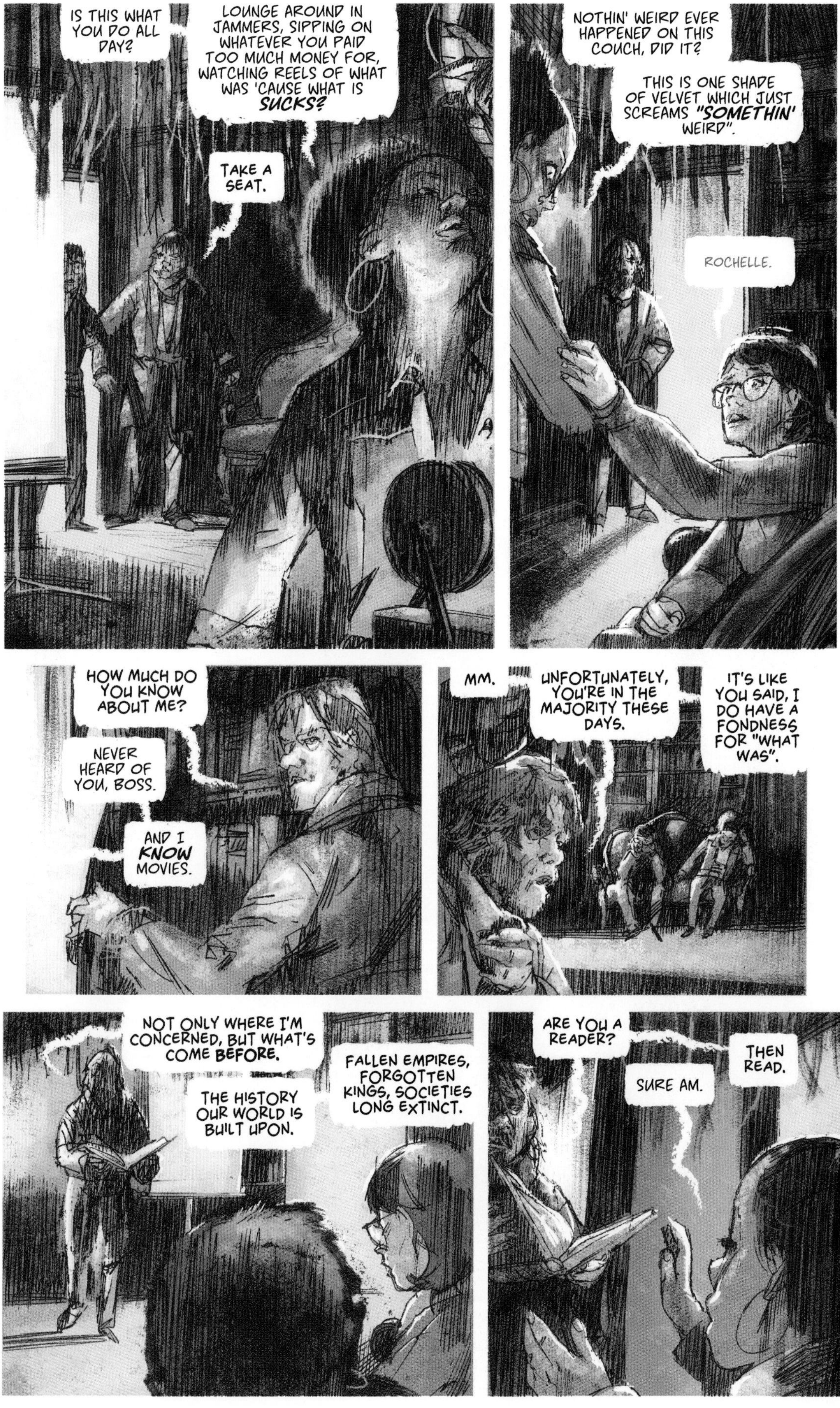
IS THIS WHAT YOU DO ALL DAY?
LOUNGE AROUND IN JAMMERS, SIPPING ON WHATEVER YOU PAID TOO MUCH MONEY FOR, WATCHING REELS OF WHAT WAS 'CAUSE WHAT IS SUCKS?
TAKE A SEAT.
NOTHIN' WEIRD EVER HAPPENED ON THIS COUCH, DID IT?
THIS IS ONE SHADE OF VELVET WHICH JUST SCREAMS "SOMETHIN' WEIRD".
ROCHELLE.
HOW MUCH DO YOU KNOW ABOUT ME?
NEVER HEARD OF YOU, BOSS.
AND I KNOW MOVIES.
MM.
UNFORTUNATELY, YOU'RE IN THE MAJORITY THESE DAYS.
IT'S LIKE YOU SAID, I DO HAVE A FONDNESS FOR "WHAT WAS".
NOT ONLY WHERE I'M CONCERNED, BUT WHAT'S COME BEFORE.
THE HISTORY OUR WORLD IS BUILT UPON.
FALLEN EMPIRES, FORGOTTEN KINGS, SOCIETIES LONG EXTINCT.
ARE YOU A READER?
SURE AM.
THEN READ.

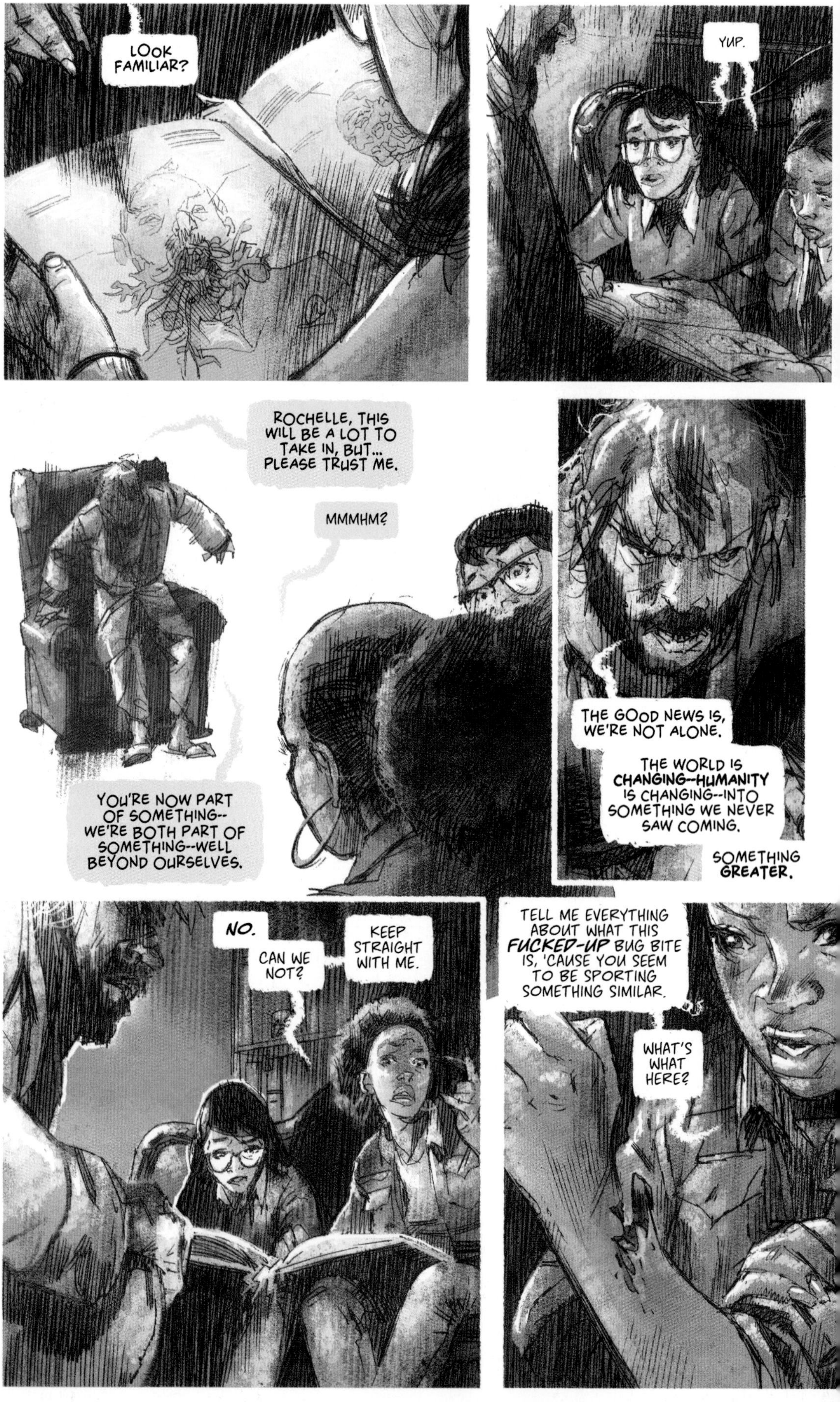
LOOK FAMILIAR?
YUP.
ROCHELLE, THIS WILL BE A LOT TO TAKE IN, BUT... PLEASE TRUST ME.
MMMHM?
YOU'RE NOW PART OF SOMETHING-- WE'RE BOTH PART OF SOMETHING--WELL BEYOND OURSELVES.
THE GOOD NEWS IS, WE'RE NOT ALONE.
THE WORLD IS CHANGING--HUMANITY IS CHANGING--INTO SOMETHING WE NEVER SAW COMING.
SOMETHING GREATER.
KEEP STRAIGHT WITH ME.
NO.
CAN WE NOT?
TELL ME EVERYTHING ABOUT WHAT THIS FUCKED-UP BUG BITE IS, 'CAUSE YOU SEEM TO BE SPORTING SOMETHING SIMILAR.
WHAT'S WHAT HERE?

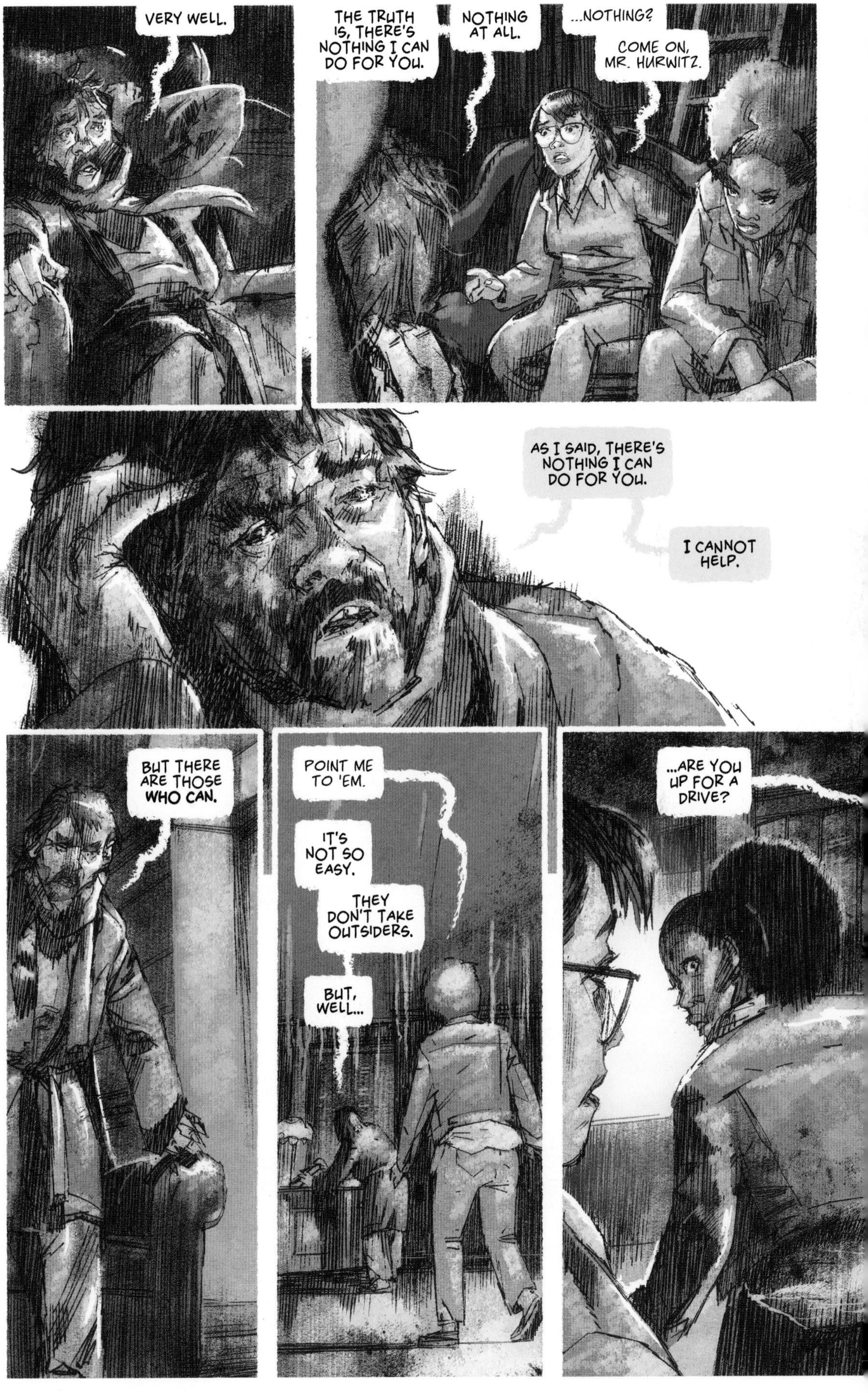
VERY WELL.
THE TRUTH IS, THERE'S NOTHING I CAN DO FOR YOU.
NOTHING AT ALL.
...NOTHING?
COME ON, MR. HURWITZ.
AS I SAID, THERE'S NOTHING I CAN DO FOR YOU.
I CANNOT HELP.
BUT THERE ARE THOSE **WHO CAN.**
POINT ME TO 'EM.
IT'S NOT SO EASY.
THEY DON'T TAKE OUTSIDERS.
BUT, WELL...
...ARE YOU UP FOR A DRIVE?

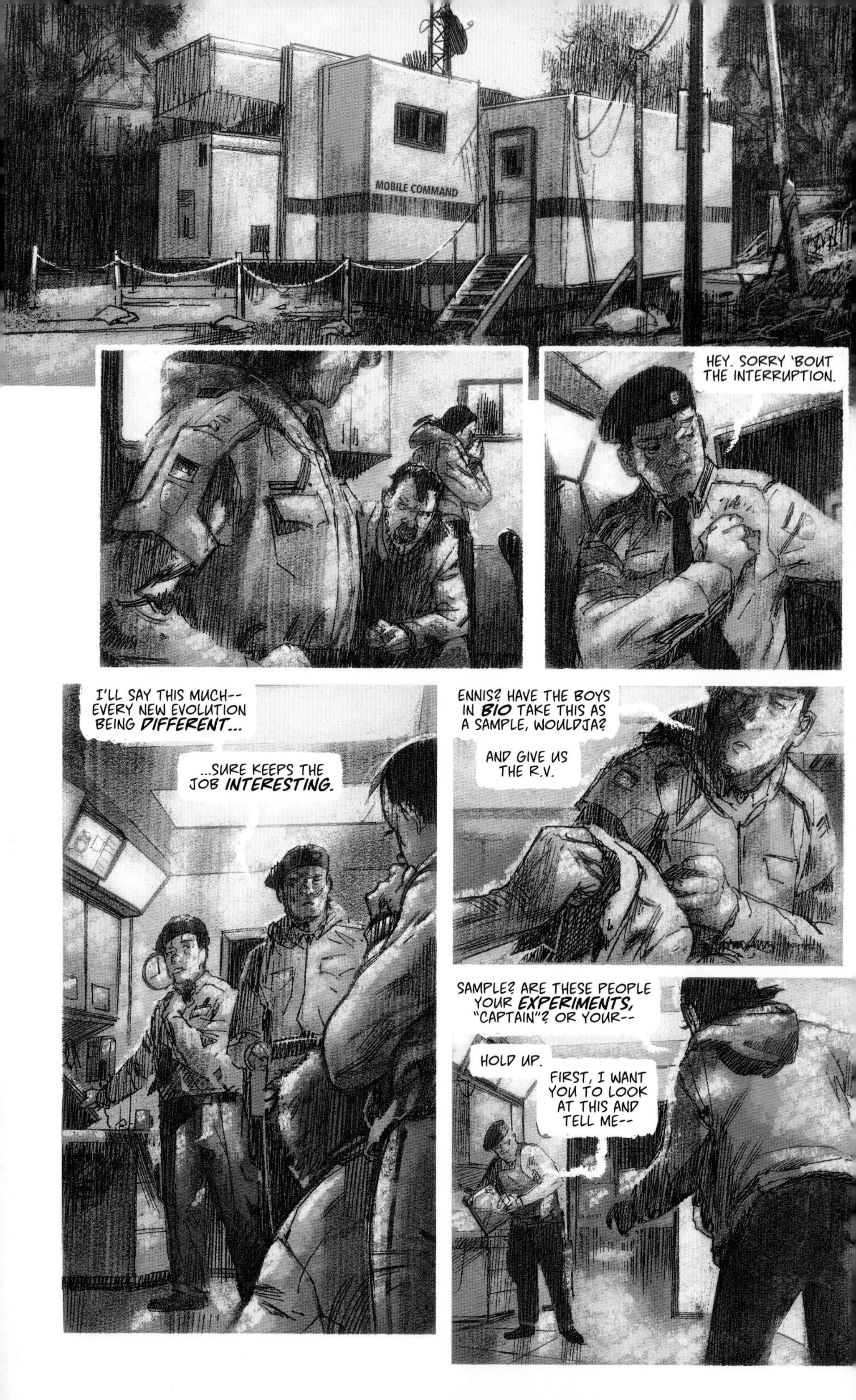
MOBILE COMMAND
HEY. SORRY 'BOUT THE INTERRUPTION.
I'LL SAY THIS MUCH--EVERY NEW EVOLUTION BEING DIFFERENT...
...SURE KEEPS THE JOB INTERESTING.
ENNIS? HAVE THE BOYS IN BIO TAKE THIS AS A SAMPLE, WOULDJA?
AND GIVE US THE R.V.
SAMPLE? ARE THESE PEOPLE YOUR EXPERIMENTS, "CAPTAIN"? OR YOUR--
HOLD UP.
FIRST, I WANT YOU TO LOOK AT THIS AND TELL ME--

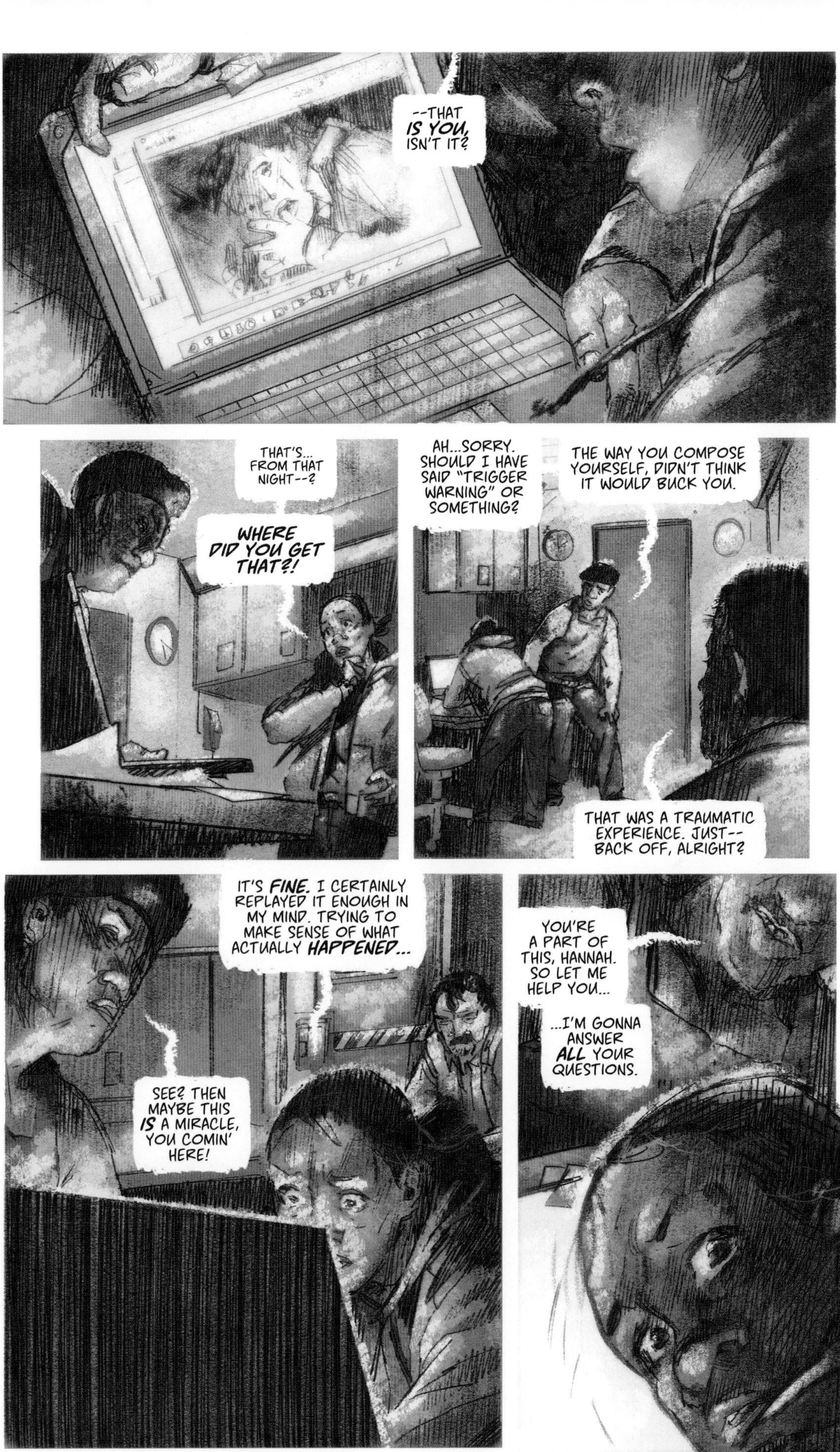
--THAT IS YOU, ISN'T IT?
THAT'S... FROM THAT NIGHT--?
WHERE DID YOU GET THAT?!
AH...SORRY. SHOULD I HAVE SAID "TRIGGER WARNING" OR SOMETHING?
THE WAY YOU COMPOSE YOURSELF, DIDN'T THINK IT WOULD BUCK YOU.
THAT WAS A TRAUMATIC EXPERIENCE. JUST-- BACK OFF, ALRIGHT?
IT'S FINE. I CERTAINLY REPLAYED IT ENOUGH IN MY MIND. TRYING TO MAKE SENSE OF WHAT ACTUALLY HAPPENED...
SEE? THEN MAYBE THIS IS A MIRACLE, YOU COMIN' HERE!
YOU'RE A PART OF THIS, HANNAH. SO LET ME HELP YOU...
...I'M GONNA ANSWER ALL YOUR QUESTIONS.

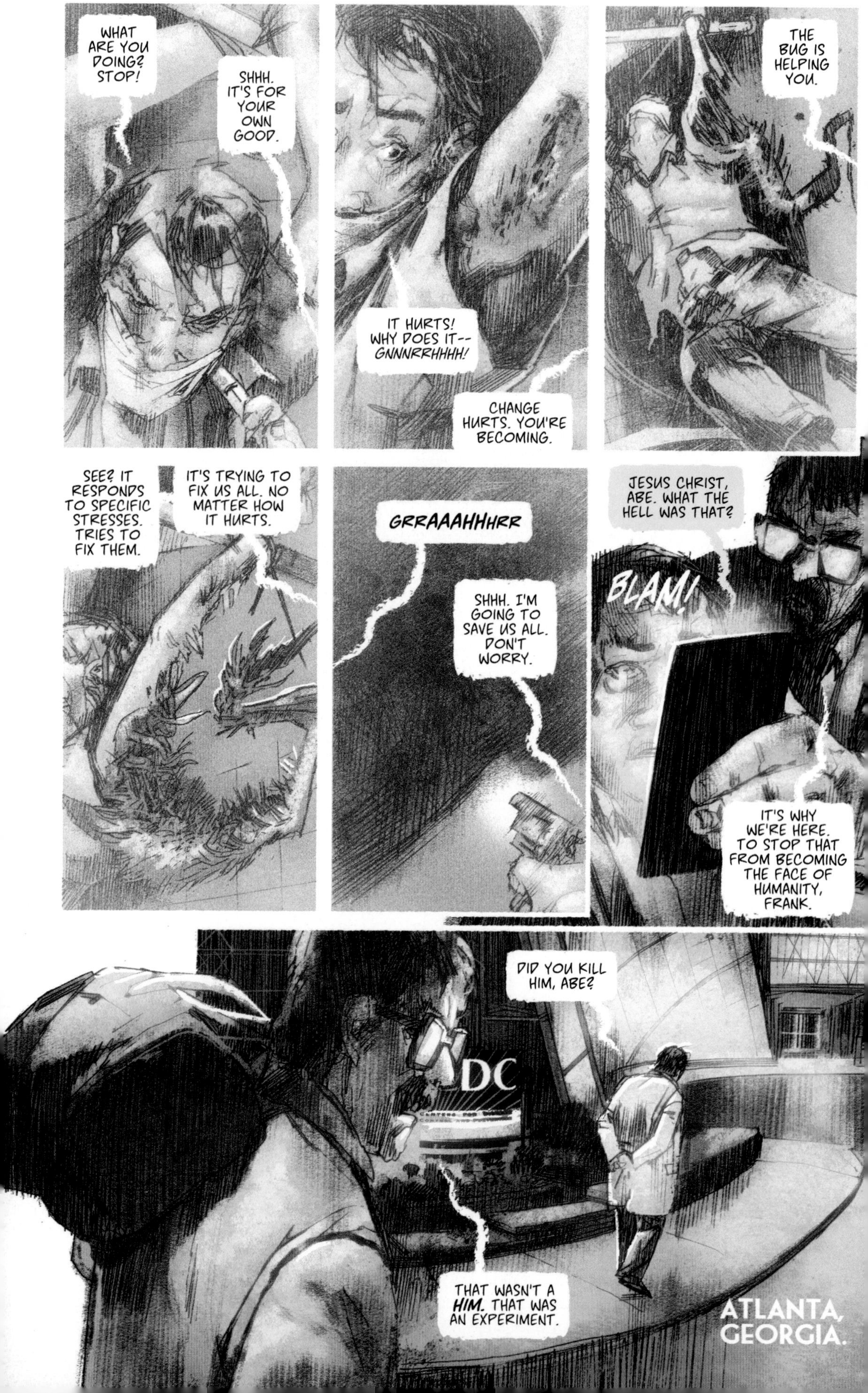
WHAT ARE YOU DOING? STOP!
SHHH. IT'S FOR YOUR OWN GOOD.
IT HURTS! WHY DOES IT-- GNNNRHHHH!
CHANGE HURTS. YOU'RE BECOMING.
THE BUG IS HELPING YOU.
SEE? IT RESPONDS TO SPECIFIC STRESSES. TRIES TO FIX THEM.
IT'S TRYING TO FIX US ALL. NO MATTER HOW IT HURTS.
GRRAAAHHHRR
SHHH. I'M GOING TO SAVE US ALL. DON'T WORRY.
BLAM!
JESUS CHRIST, ABE. WHAT THE HELL WAS THAT?
IT'S WHY WE'RE HERE. TO STOP THAT FROM BECOMING THE FACE OF HUMANITY, FRANK.
DID YOU KILL HIM, ABE?
DC
THAT WASN'T A **HIM.** THAT WAS AN EXPERIMENT.
ATLANTA, GEORGIA.

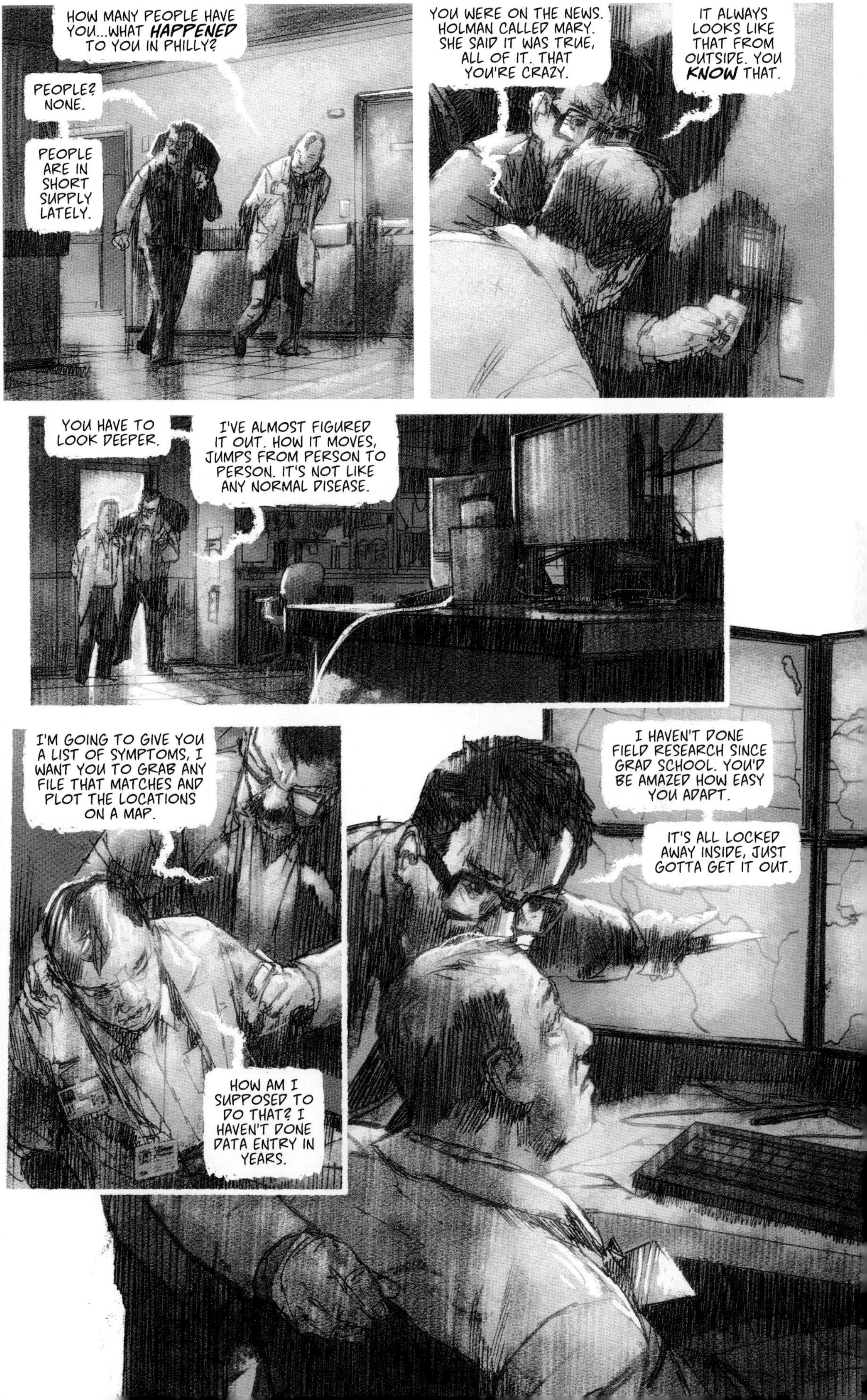
HOW MANY PEOPLE HAVE YOU...WHAT HAPPENED TO YOU IN PHILLY?
PEOPLE? NONE.
PEOPLE ARE IN SHORT SUPPLY LATELY.
YOU WERE ON THE NEWS. HOLMAN CALLED MARY. SHE SAID IT WAS TRUE, ALL OF IT. THAT YOU'RE CRAZY.
IT ALWAYS LOOKS LIKE THAT FROM OUTSIDE. YOU KNOW THAT.
YOU HAVE TO LOOK DEEPER.
I'VE ALMOST FIGURED IT OUT. HOW IT MOVES, JUMPS FROM PERSON TO PERSON. IT'S NOT LIKE ANY NORMAL DISEASE.
I'M GOING TO GIVE YOU A LIST OF SYMPTOMS, I WANT YOU TO GRAB ANY FILE THAT MATCHES AND PLOT THE LOCATIONS ON A MAP.
HOW AM I SUPPOSED TO DO THAT? I HAVEN'T DONE DATA ENTRY IN YEARS.
I HAVEN'T DONE FIELD RESEARCH SINCE GRAD SCHOOL. YOU'D BE AMAZED HOW EASY YOU ADAPT.
IT'S ALL LOCKED AWAY INSIDE, JUST GOTTA GET IT OUT.

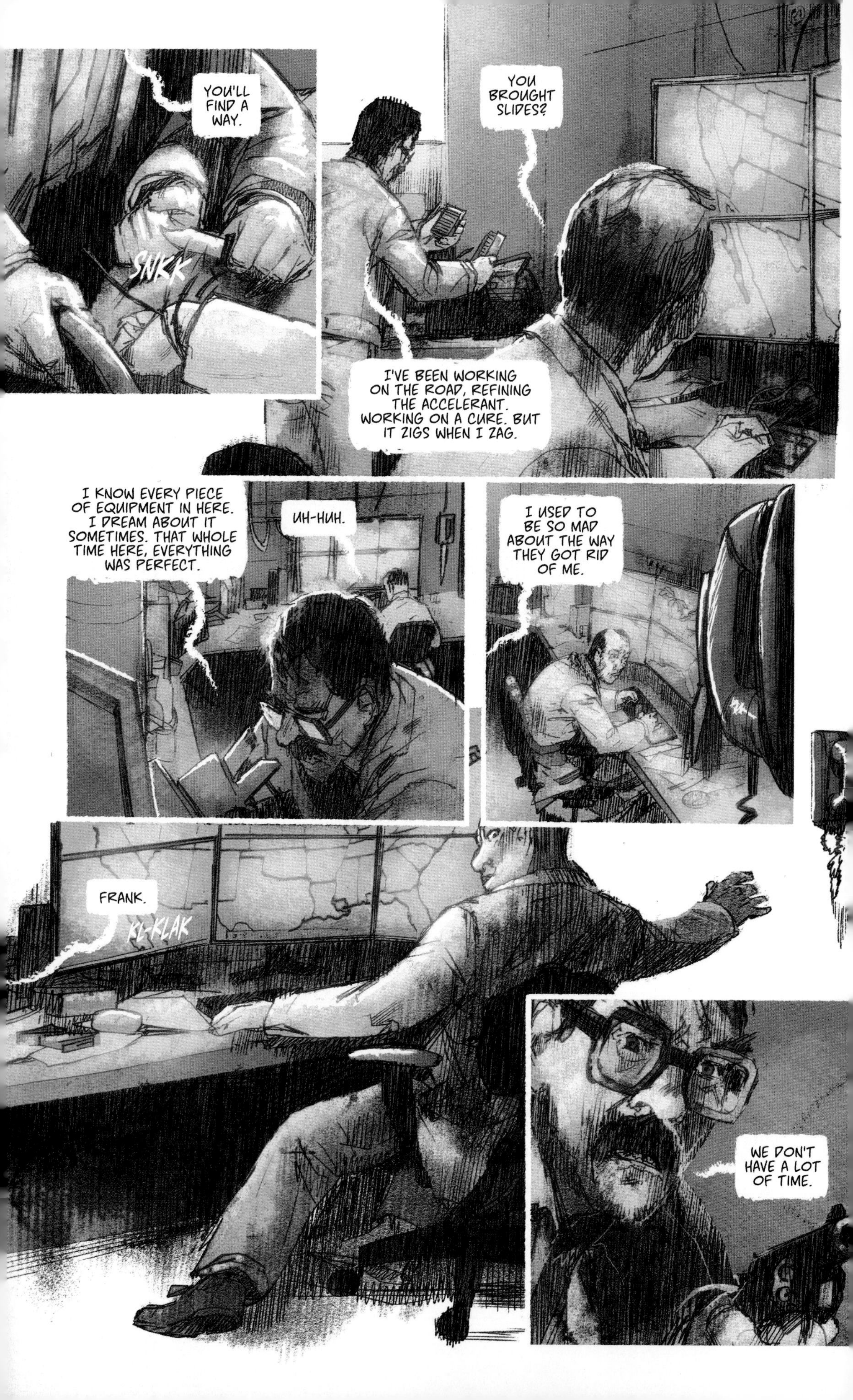

YOU'LL FIND A WAY.
SNKK
YOU BROUGHT SLIDES?
I'VE BEEN WORKING ON THE ROAD, REFINING THE ACCELERANT. WORKING ON A CURE. BUT IT ZIGS WHEN I ZAG.
I KNOW EVERY PIECE OF EQUIPMENT IN HERE. I DREAM ABOUT IT SOMETIMES. THAT WHOLE TIME HERE, EVERYTHING WAS PERFECT.
UH-HUH.
I USED TO BE SO MAD ABOUT THE WAY THEY GOT RID OF ME.
FRANK.
KL-KLAK
WE DON'T HAVE A LOT OF TIME.

THE BUG ISN'T EVEN **HIDING** ANYMORE. IS IT TOO LATE? HAS IT INFECTED ENOUGH PEOPLE THAT WE CAN'T STOP IT?

IT DOESN'T BEHAVE LIKE ANY ORGANISM OR VIRUS. IT'S SOMETHING ELSE. IT HASN'T **SPREAD.** EVERYONE HAS IT.

IT'S BEEN HIDDEN INSIDE US AND NOW IT'S WAKING UP. SOMETHING IS TRIGGERING IT. TURNING IT ON.

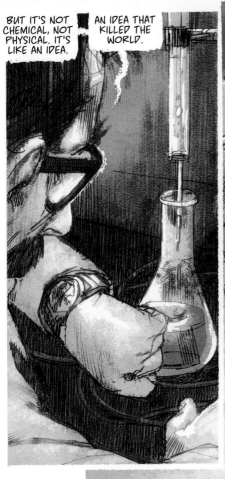

BUT IT'S NOT CHEMICAL, NOT PHYSICAL. IT'S LIKE AN IDEA.

AN IDEA THAT KILLED THE WORLD.

ABE? WHO... WHO YOU TALKING TO?

THE **FUTURE,** FRANK.

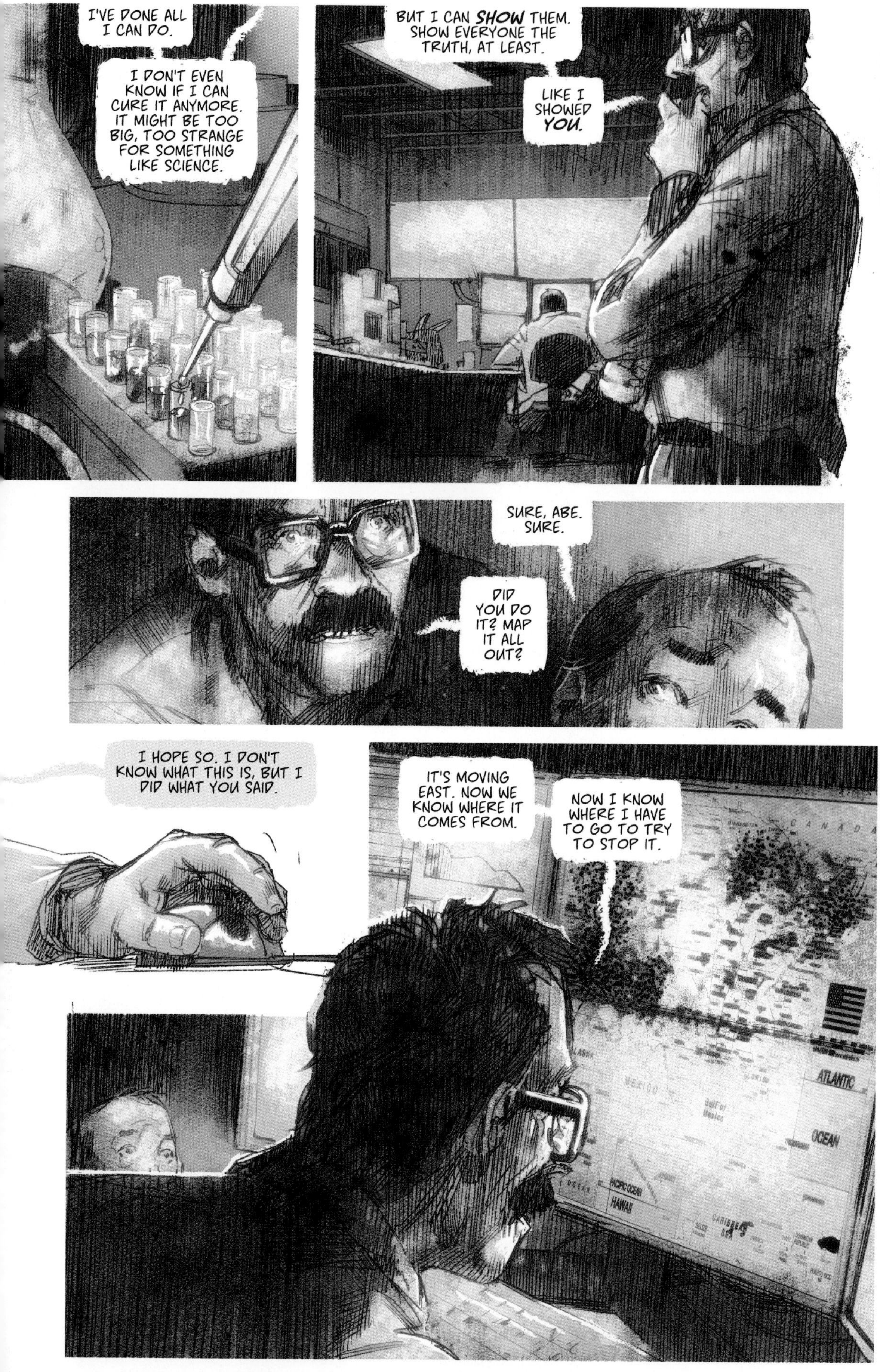
I'VE DONE ALL I CAN DO.
I DON'T EVEN KNOW IF I CAN CURE IT ANYMORE. IT MIGHT BE TOO BIG, TOO STRANGE FOR SOMETHING LIKE SCIENCE.
BUT I CAN SHOW THEM. SHOW EVERYONE THE TRUTH, AT LEAST.
LIKE I SHOWED YOU.
SURE, ABE. SURE.
DID YOU DO IT? MAP IT ALL OUT?
I HOPE SO. I DON'T KNOW WHAT THIS IS, BUT I DID WHAT YOU SAID.
IT'S MOVING EAST. NOW WE KNOW WHERE IT COMES FROM.
NOW I KNOW WHERE I HAVE TO GO TO TRY TO STOP IT.
CANADA
MEXICO
ATLANTIC
OCEAN
PACIFIC OCEAN
HAWAII
CARIBBEAN SEA

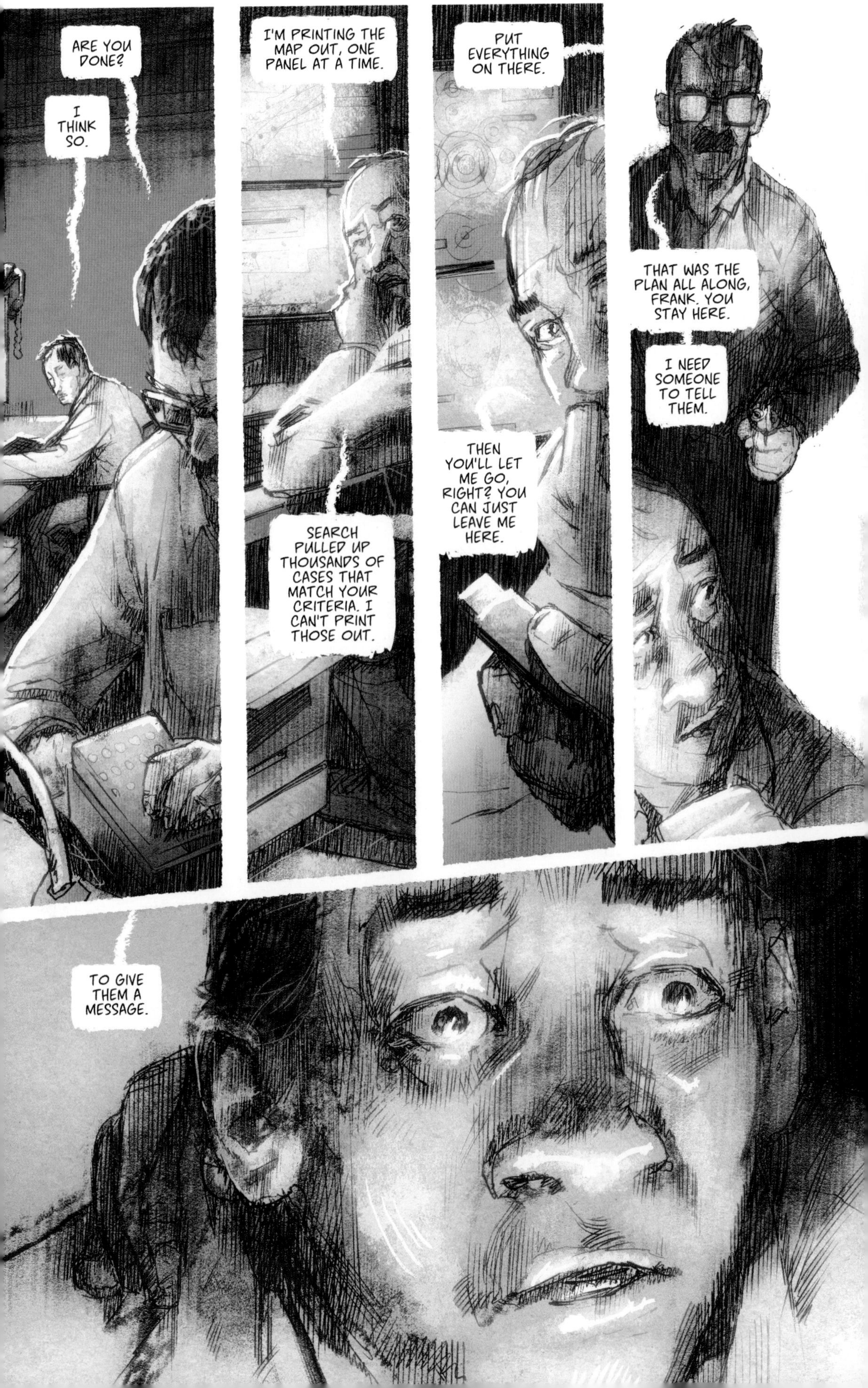
ARE YOU DONE?
I THINK SO.
I'M PRINTING THE MAP OUT, ONE PANEL AT A TIME.
SEARCH PULLED UP THOUSANDS OF CASES THAT MATCH YOUR CRITERIA. I CAN'T PRINT THOSE OUT.
PUT EVERYTHING ON THERE.
THEN YOU'LL LET ME GO, RIGHT? YOU CAN JUST LEAVE ME HERE.
THAT WAS THE PLAN ALL ALONG, FRANK. YOU STAY HERE.
I NEED SOMEONE TO TELL THEM.
TO GIVE THEM A MESSAGE.

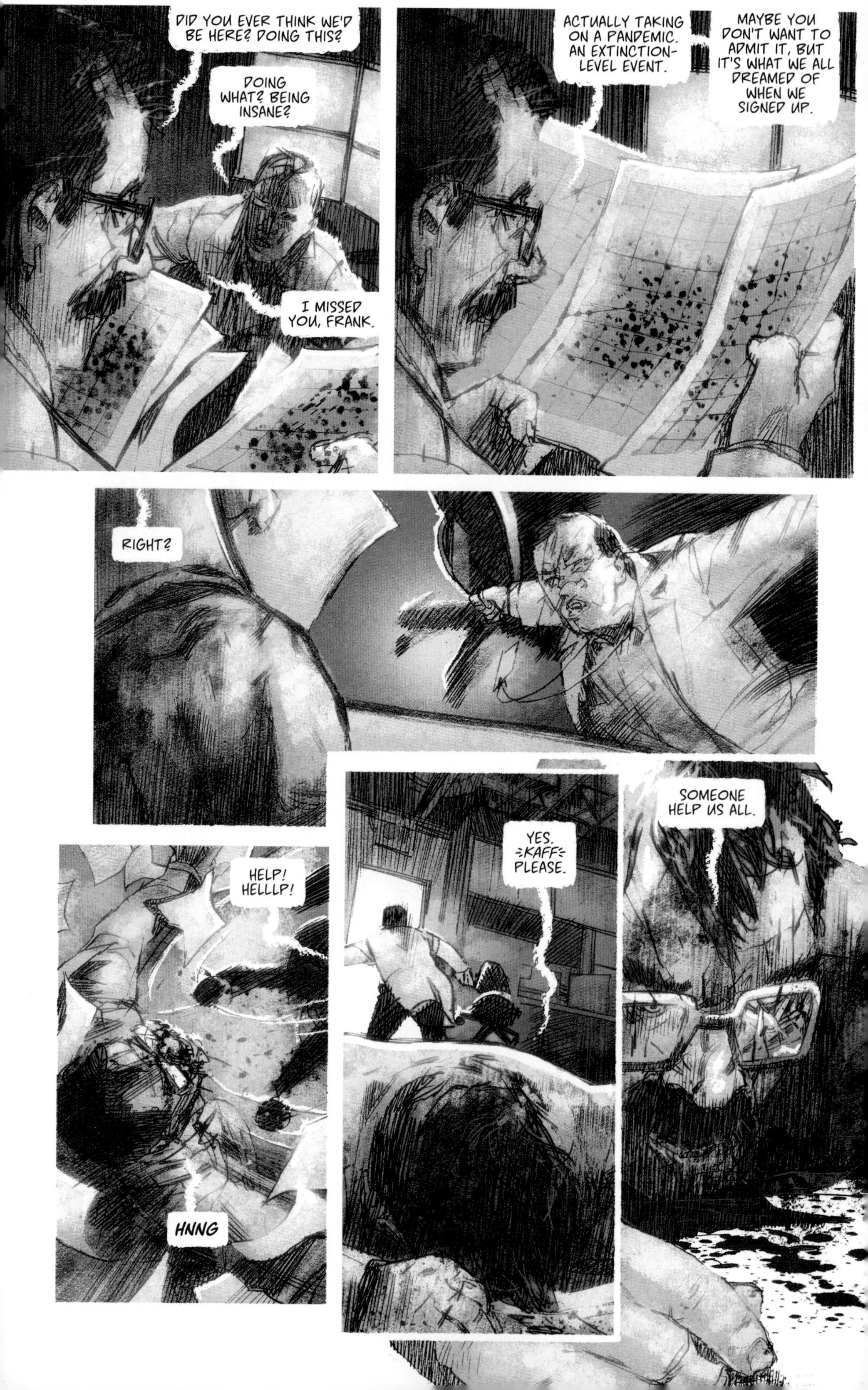
DID YOU EVER THINK WE'D BE HERE? DOING THIS?
DOING WHAT? BEING INSANE?
I MISSED YOU, FRANK.
ACTUALLY TAKING ON A PANDEMIC. AN EXTINCTION-LEVEL EVENT.
MAYBE YOU DON'T WANT TO ADMIT IT, BUT IT'S WHAT WE ALL DREAMED OF WHEN WE SIGNED UP.
RIGHT?
HELP! HELLLP!
HNNG
YES. KAFF PLEASE.
SOMEONE HELP US ALL.

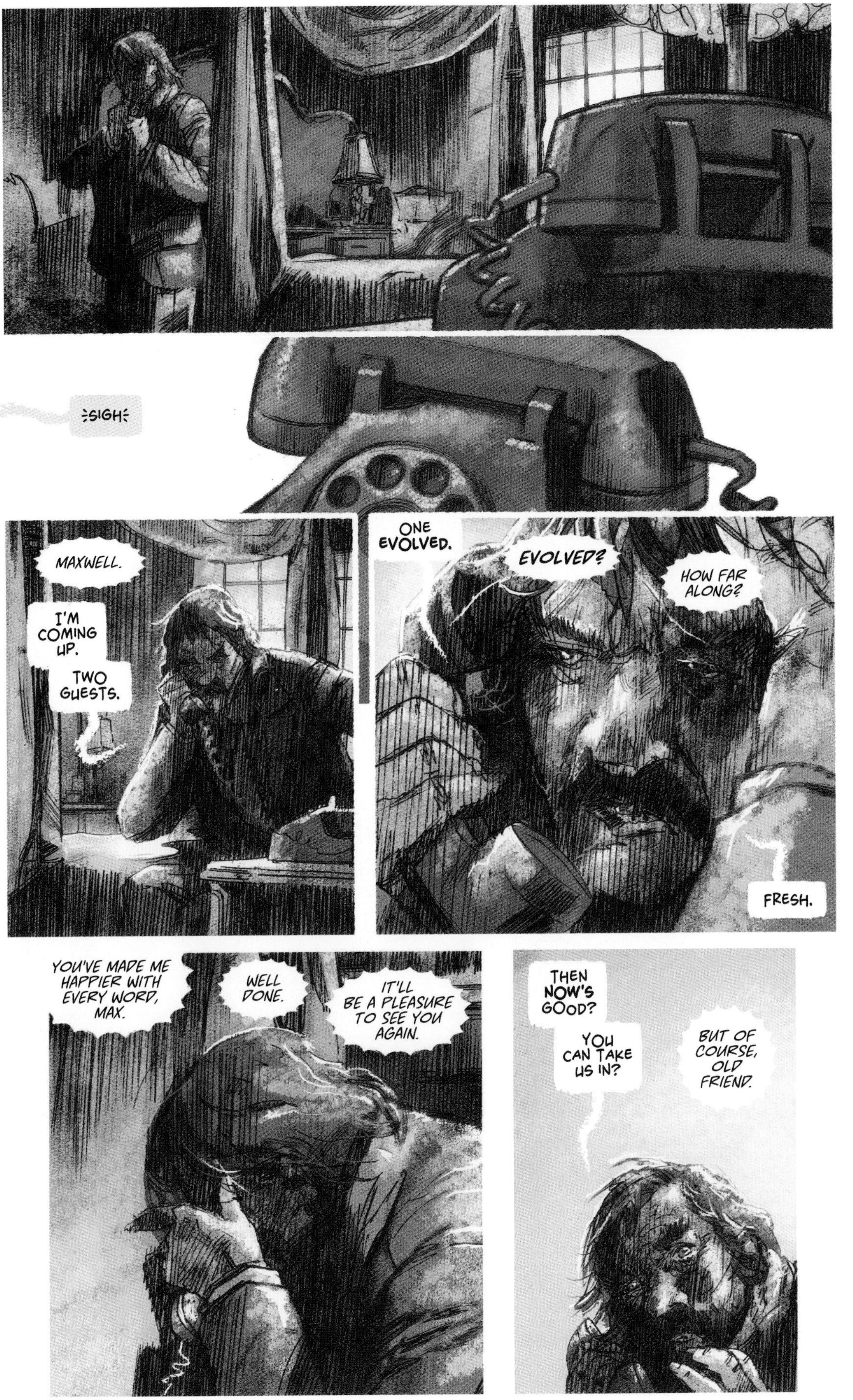
SIGH
MAXWELL.
I'M COMING UP.
TWO GUESTS.
ONE EVOLVED.
EVOLVED?
HOW FAR ALONG?
FRESH.
YOU'VE MADE ME HAPPIER WITH EVERY WORD, MAX.
WELL DONE.
IT'LL BE A PLEASURE TO SEE YOU AGAIN.
THEN NOW'S GOOD?
YOU CAN TAKE US IN?
BUT OF COURSE, OLD FRIEND.

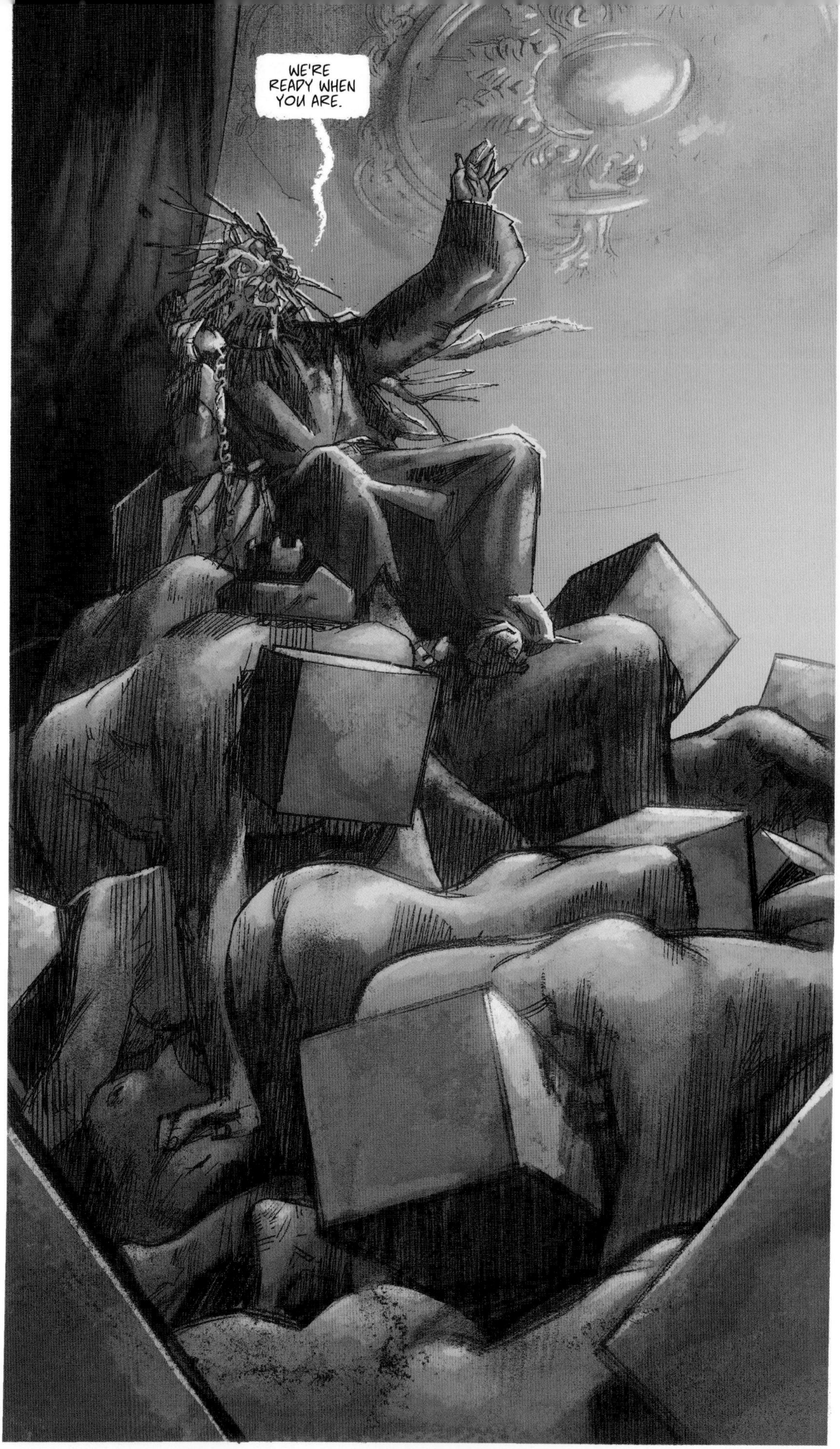
WE'RE READY WHEN YOU ARE.

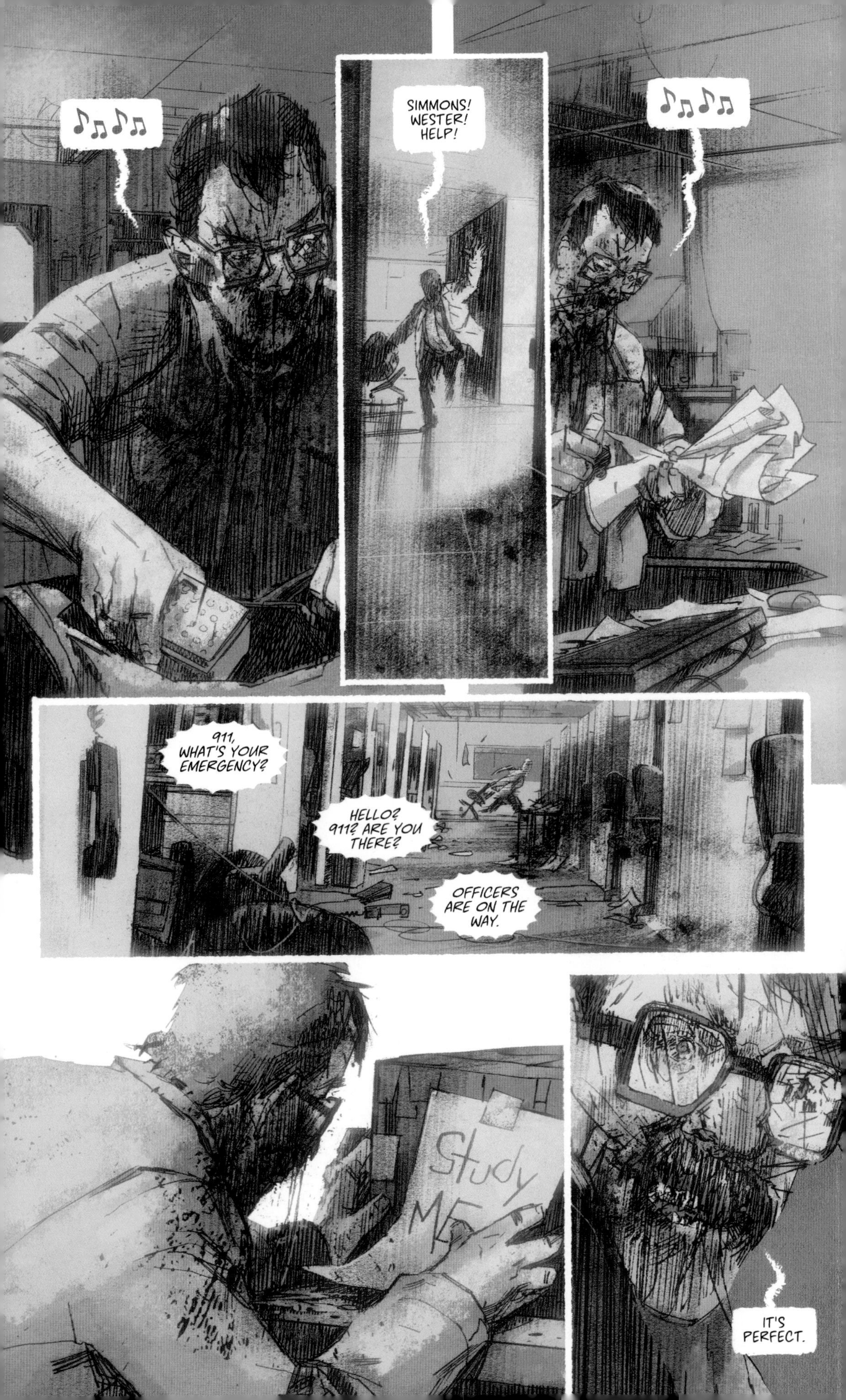
♪♫♪♫
SIMMONS! WESTER! HELP!
♪♫♪♫
911, WHAT'S YOUR EMERGENCY?
HELLO? 911? ARE YOU THERE?
OFFICERS ARE ON THE WAY.
Study ME
IT'S PERFECT.

THINK OF IT AS A TWO-STAGE SOLUTION, FRANK.

PART BIOLOGY, PART IDEOLOGY.

THE BIOLOGY PART, I'VE GOT THAT HANDLED.

I UNDERSTAND IT AS WELL AS ANYONE COULD.

BUT THE IDEOLOGY PART...

...IT'S SO MUCH HARDER.

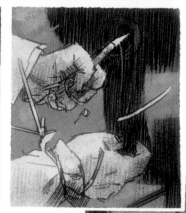

HFF HFF HFF

BWONNG BWONNG BWONNG

THANKS, FRANK. YOU SAVED ME THE TROUBLE.

NOW LET'S TALK.

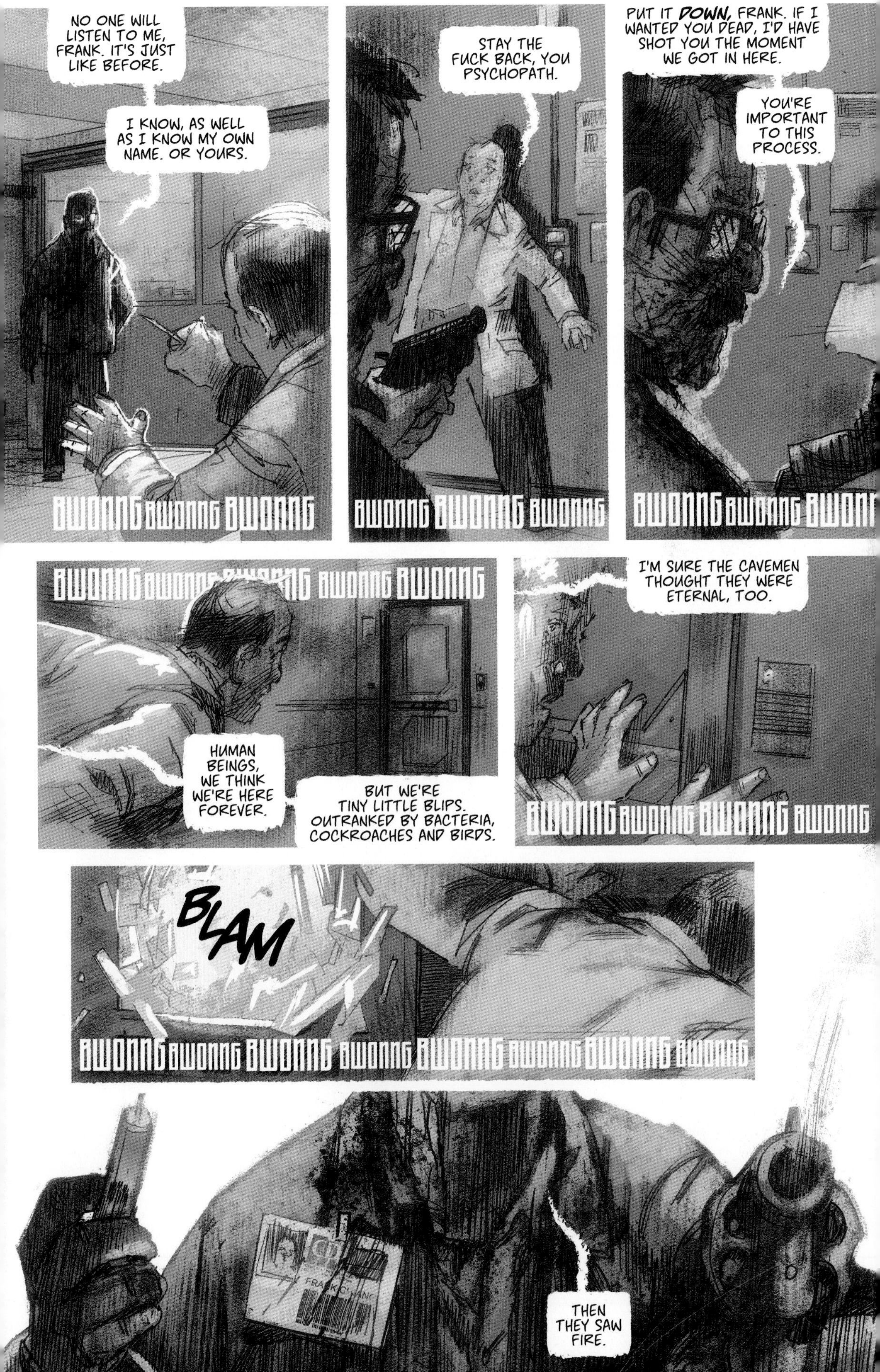
NO ONE WILL LISTEN TO ME, FRANK. IT'S JUST LIKE BEFORE.
I KNOW, AS WELL AS I KNOW MY OWN NAME. OR YOURS.
BWONNG BWONNG BWONNG
STAY THE FUCK BACK, YOU PSYCHOPATH.
BWONNG BWONNG BWONNG
PUT IT DOWN, FRANK. IF I WANTED YOU DEAD, I'D HAVE SHOT YOU THE MOMENT WE GOT IN HERE.
YOU'RE IMPORTANT TO THIS PROCESS.
BWONNG BWONNG
BWONNG BWONNG BWONNG BWONNG
HUMAN BEINGS, WE THINK WE'RE HERE FOREVER.
BUT WE'RE TINY LITTLE BLIPS. OUTRANKED BY BACTERIA, COCKROACHES AND BIRDS.
I'M SURE THE CAVEMEN THOUGHT THEY WERE ETERNAL, TOO.
BWONNG BWONNG BWONNG BWONNG
BLAM
BWONNG BWONNG BWONNG BWONNG BWONNG BWONNG BWONNG BWONNG
THEN THEY SAW FIRE.

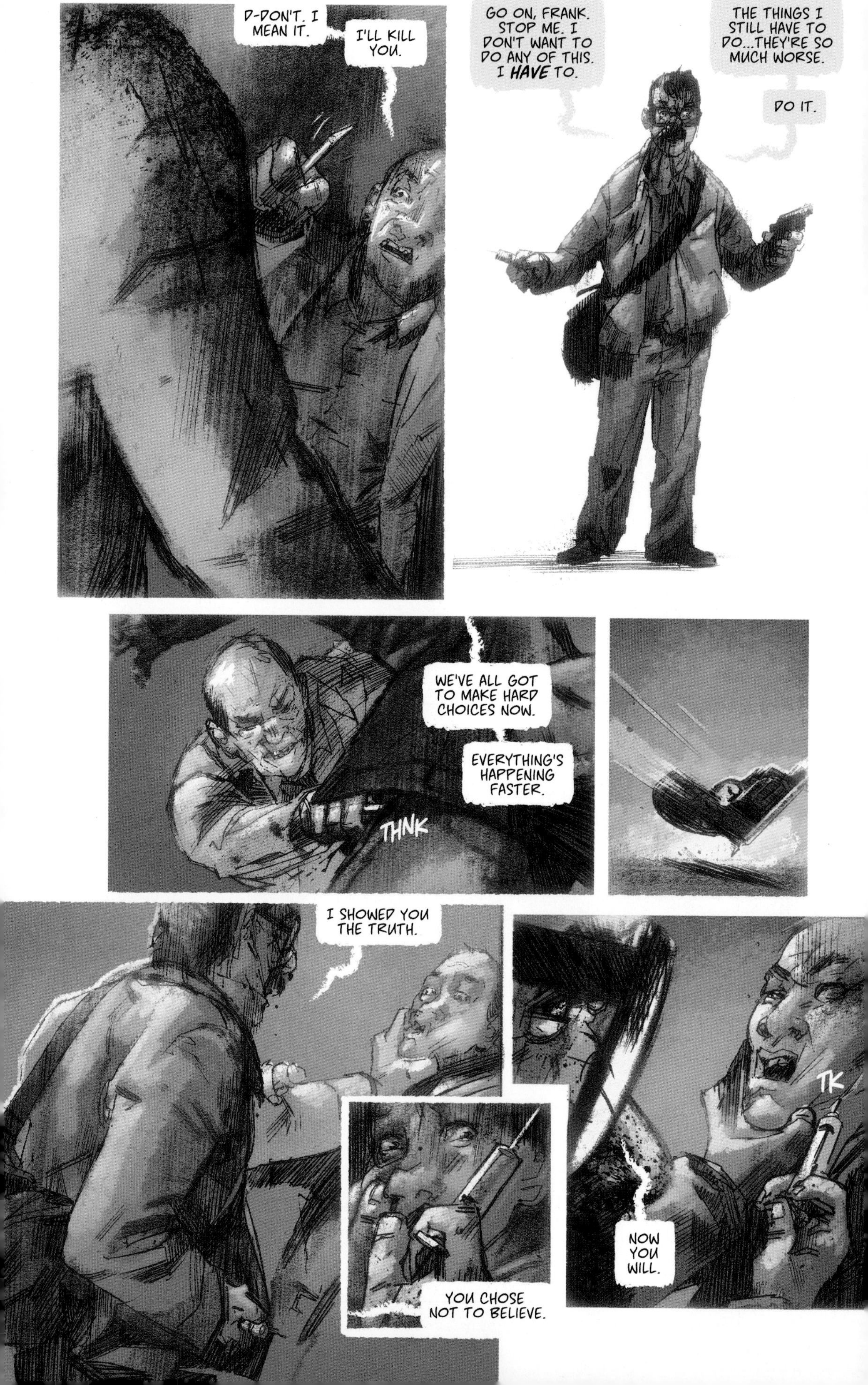
D-DON'T. I MEAN IT.
I'LL KILL YOU.
GO ON, FRANK. STOP ME. I DON'T WANT TO DO ANY OF THIS. I HAVE TO.
THE THINGS I STILL HAVE TO DO...THEY'RE SO MUCH WORSE.
DO IT.
WE'VE ALL GOT TO MAKE HARD CHOICES NOW.
EVERYTHING'S HAPPENING FASTER.
THNK
I SHOWED YOU THE TRUTH.
YOU CHOSE NOT TO BELIEVE.
TK
NOW YOU WILL.

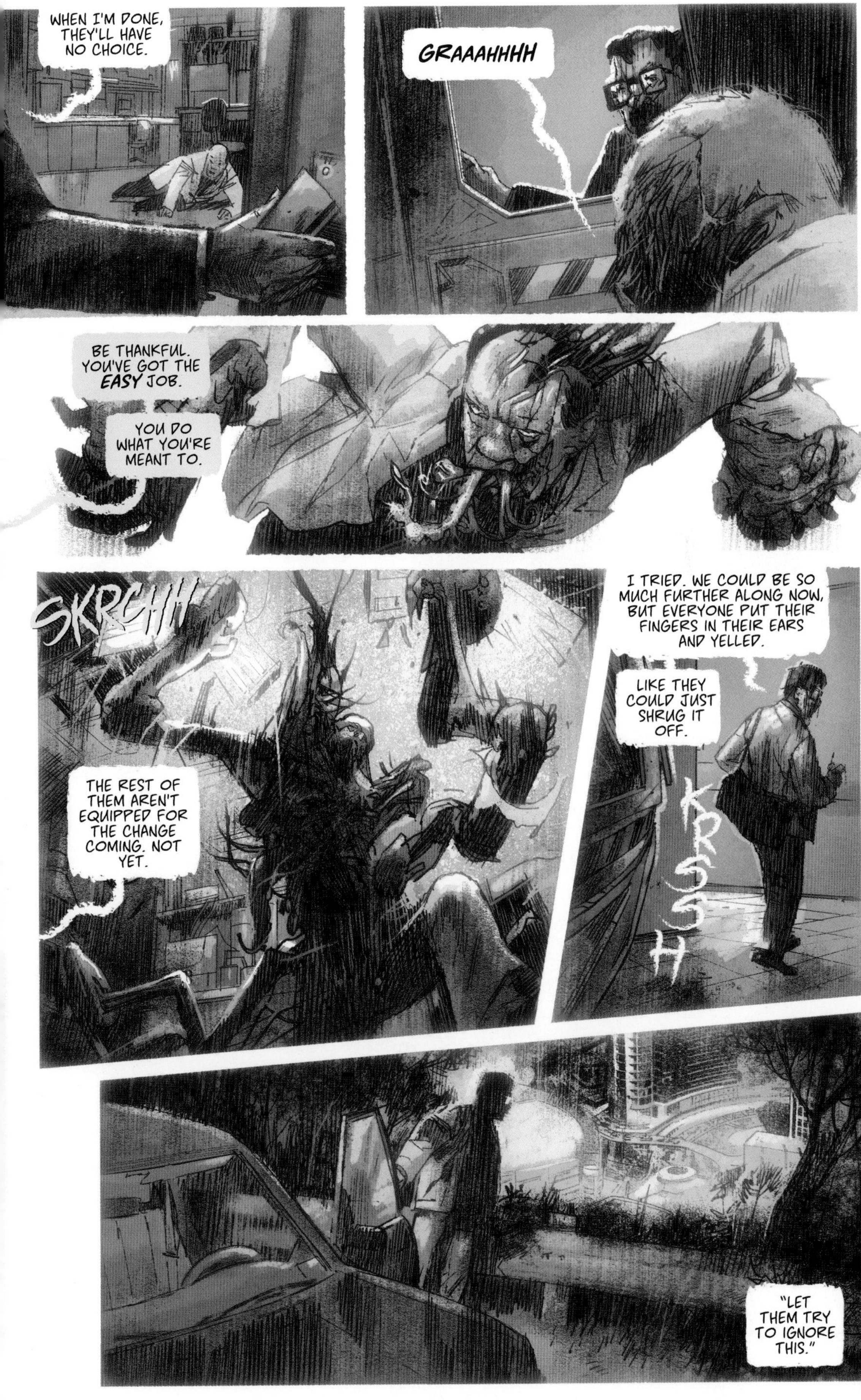
WHEN I'M DONE, THEY'LL HAVE NO CHOICE.
GRAAAHHHH
BE THANKFUL. YOU'VE GOT THE EASY JOB.
YOU DO WHAT YOU'RE MEANT TO.
SKRCHH
THE REST OF THEM AREN'T EQUIPPED FOR THE CHANGE COMING. NOT YET.
I TRIED. WE COULD BE SO MUCH FURTHER ALONG NOW, BUT EVERYONE PUT THEIR FINGERS IN THEIR EARS AND YELLED.
LIKE THEY COULD JUST SHRUG IT OFF.
KRSSH
"LET THEM TRY TO IGNORE THIS."

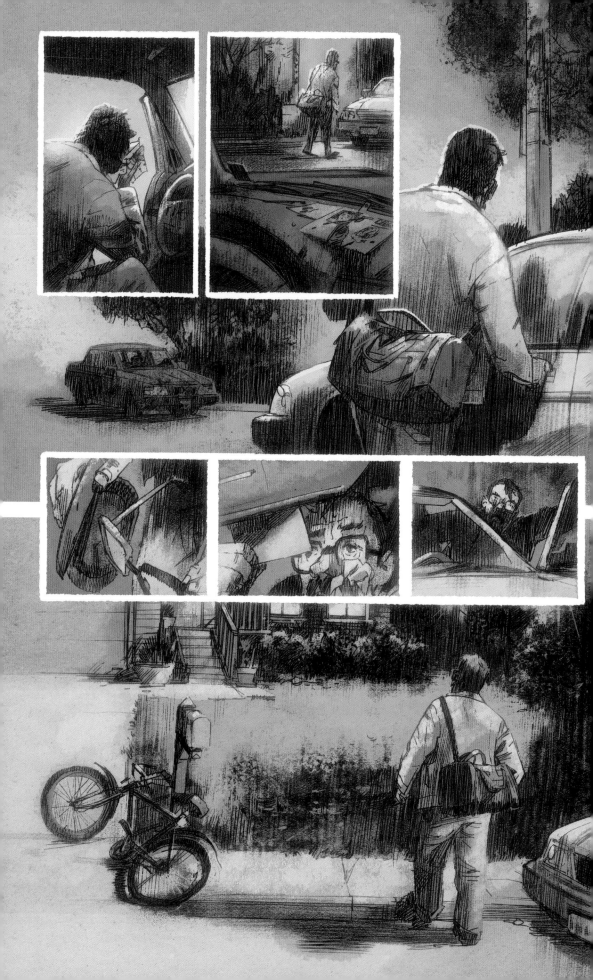

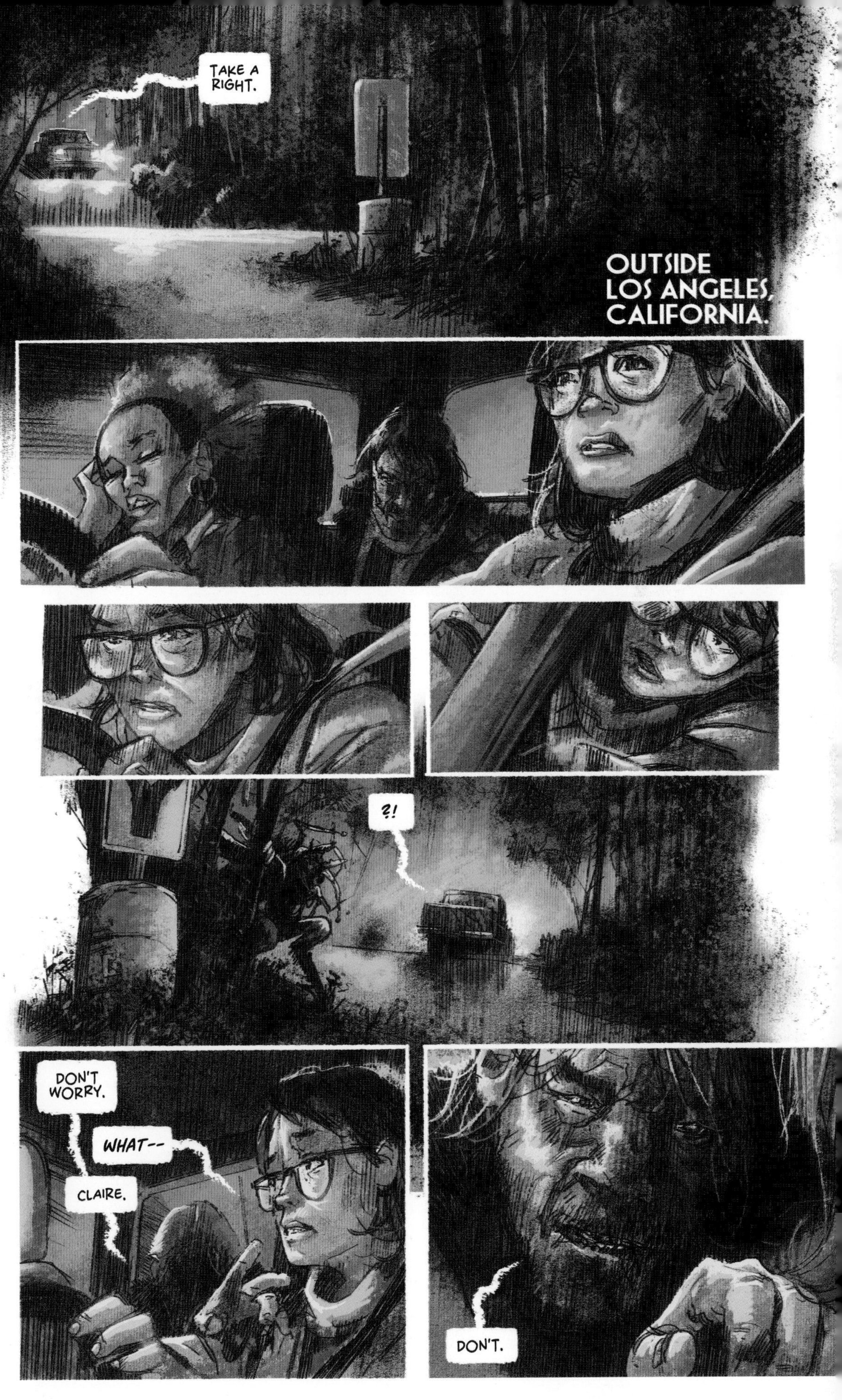
TAKE A RIGHT.
OUTSIDE LOS ANGELES, CALIFORNIA.
?!
DON'T WORRY.
WHAT--
CLAIRE.
DON'T.

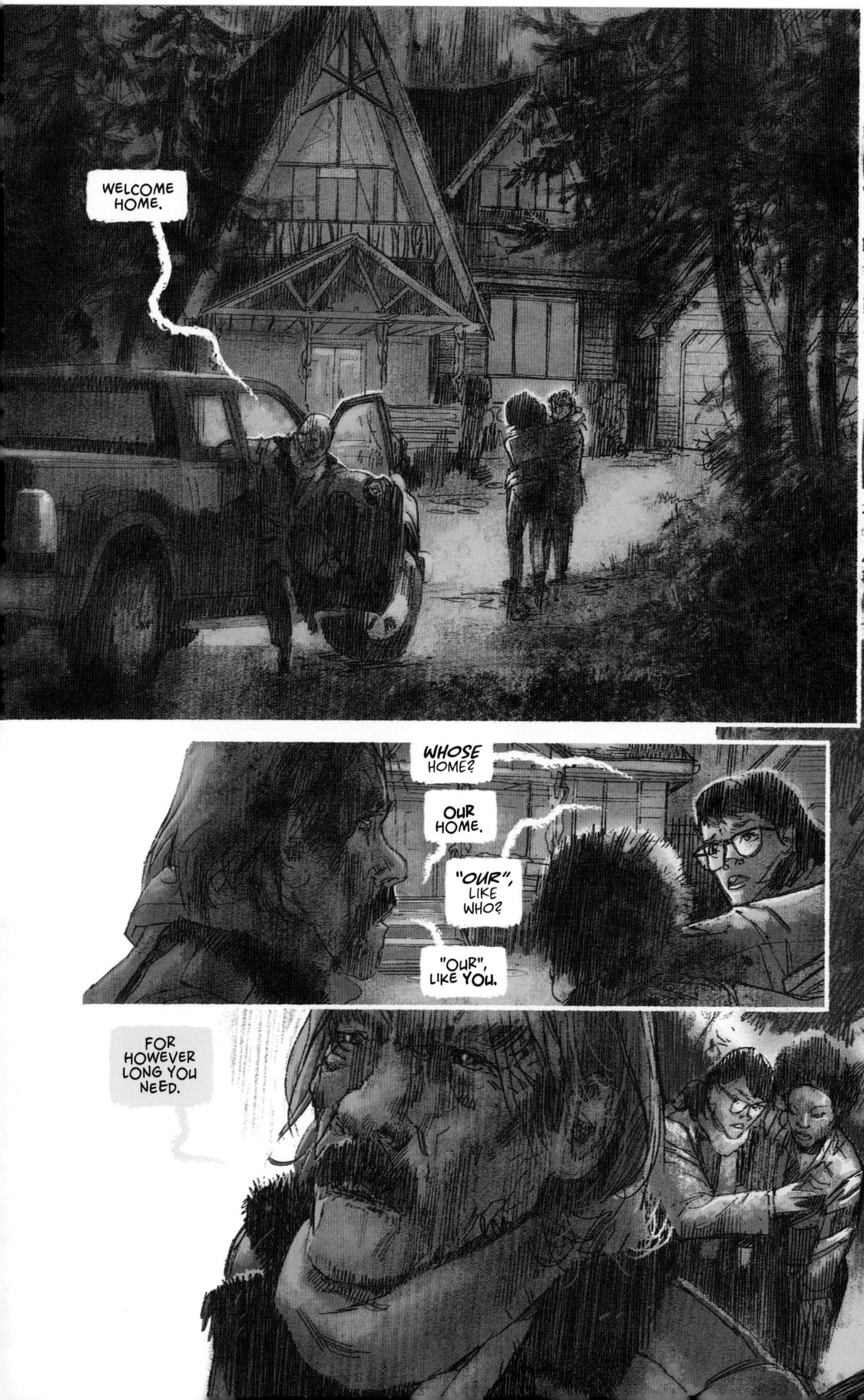
WELCOME HOME.
WHOSE HOME?
OUR HOME.
"OUR", LIKE WHO?
"OUR", LIKE YOU.
FOR HOWEVER LONG YOU NEED.

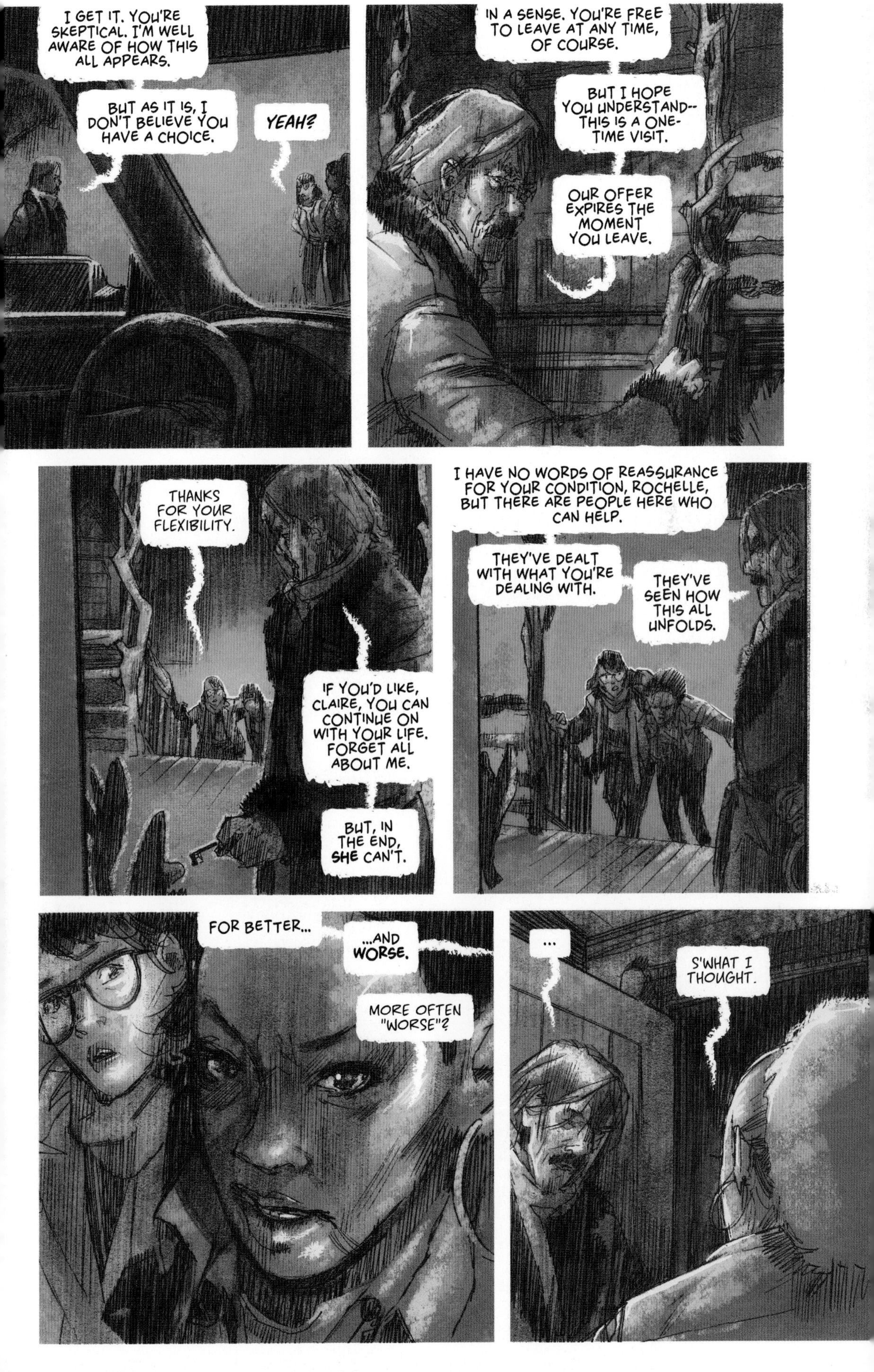
I GET IT. YOU'RE SKEPTICAL. I'M WELL AWARE OF HOW THIS ALL APPEARS.
BUT AS IT IS, I DON'T BELIEVE YOU HAVE A CHOICE.
YEAH?
IN A SENSE. YOU'RE FREE TO LEAVE AT ANY TIME, OF COURSE.
BUT I HOPE YOU UNDERSTAND-- THIS IS A ONE-TIME VISIT.
OUR OFFER EXPIRES THE MOMENT YOU LEAVE.
THANKS FOR YOUR FLEXIBILITY.
IF YOU'D LIKE, CLAIRE, YOU CAN CONTINUE ON WITH YOUR LIFE. FORGET ALL ABOUT ME.
BUT, IN THE END, SHE CAN'T.
I HAVE NO WORDS OF REASSURANCE FOR YOUR CONDITION, ROCHELLE, BUT THERE ARE PEOPLE HERE WHO CAN HELP.
THEY'VE DEALT WITH WHAT YOU'RE DEALING WITH.
THEY'VE SEEN HOW THIS ALL UNFOLDS.
FOR BETTER...
...AND WORSE.
MORE OFTEN "WORSE"?
...
S'WHAT I THOUGHT.

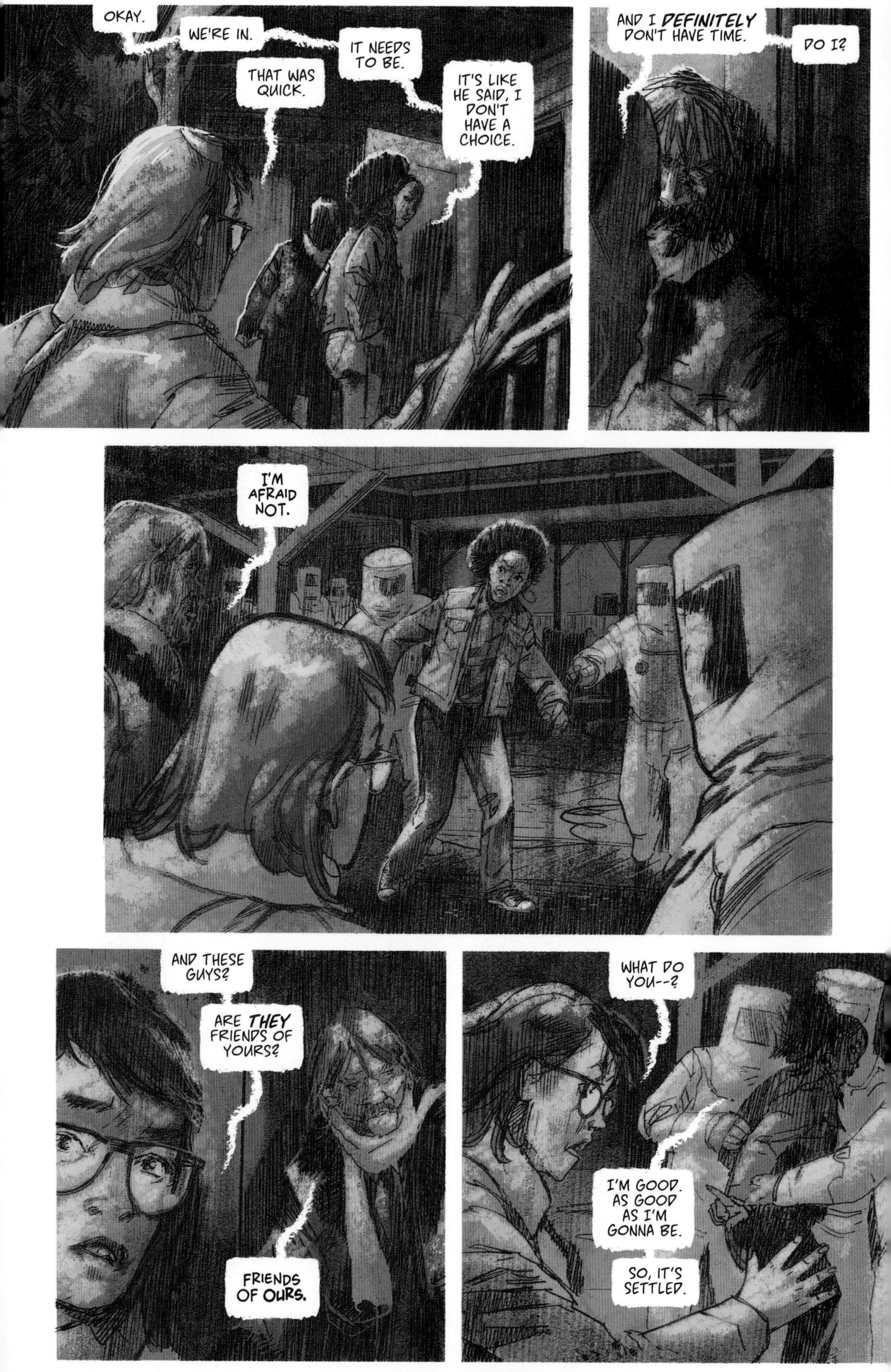
OKAY.
WE'RE IN.
THAT WAS QUICK.
IT NEEDS TO BE.
IT'S LIKE HE SAID, I DON'T HAVE A CHOICE.
AND I *DEFINITELY* DON'T HAVE TIME.
DO I?
I'M AFRAID NOT.
AND THESE GUYS?
ARE *THEY* FRIENDS OF YOURS?
FRIENDS OF **OURS.**
WHAT DO YOU--?
I'M GOOD. AS GOOD AS I'M GONNA BE.
SO, IT'S SETTLED.

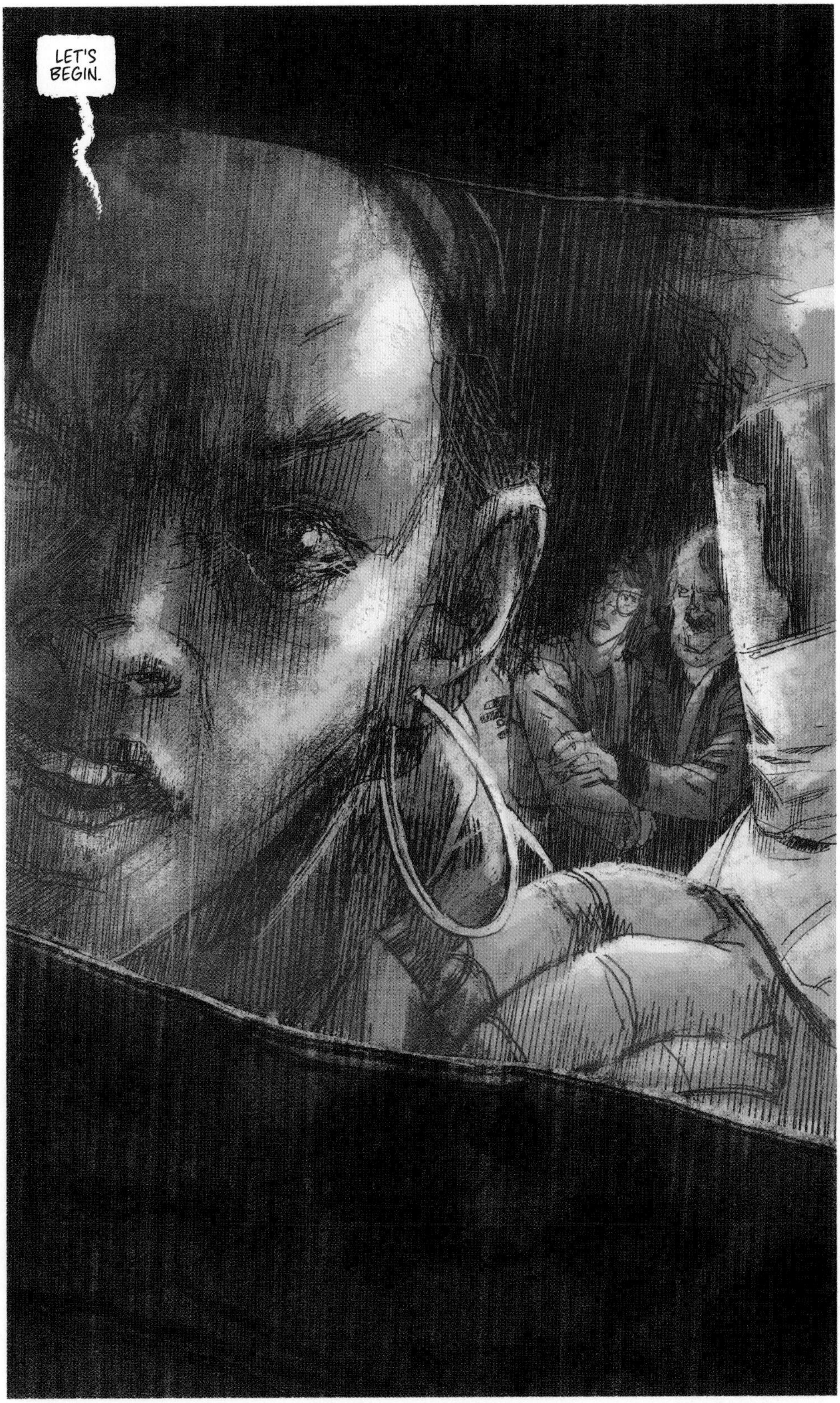
LET'S BEGIN.

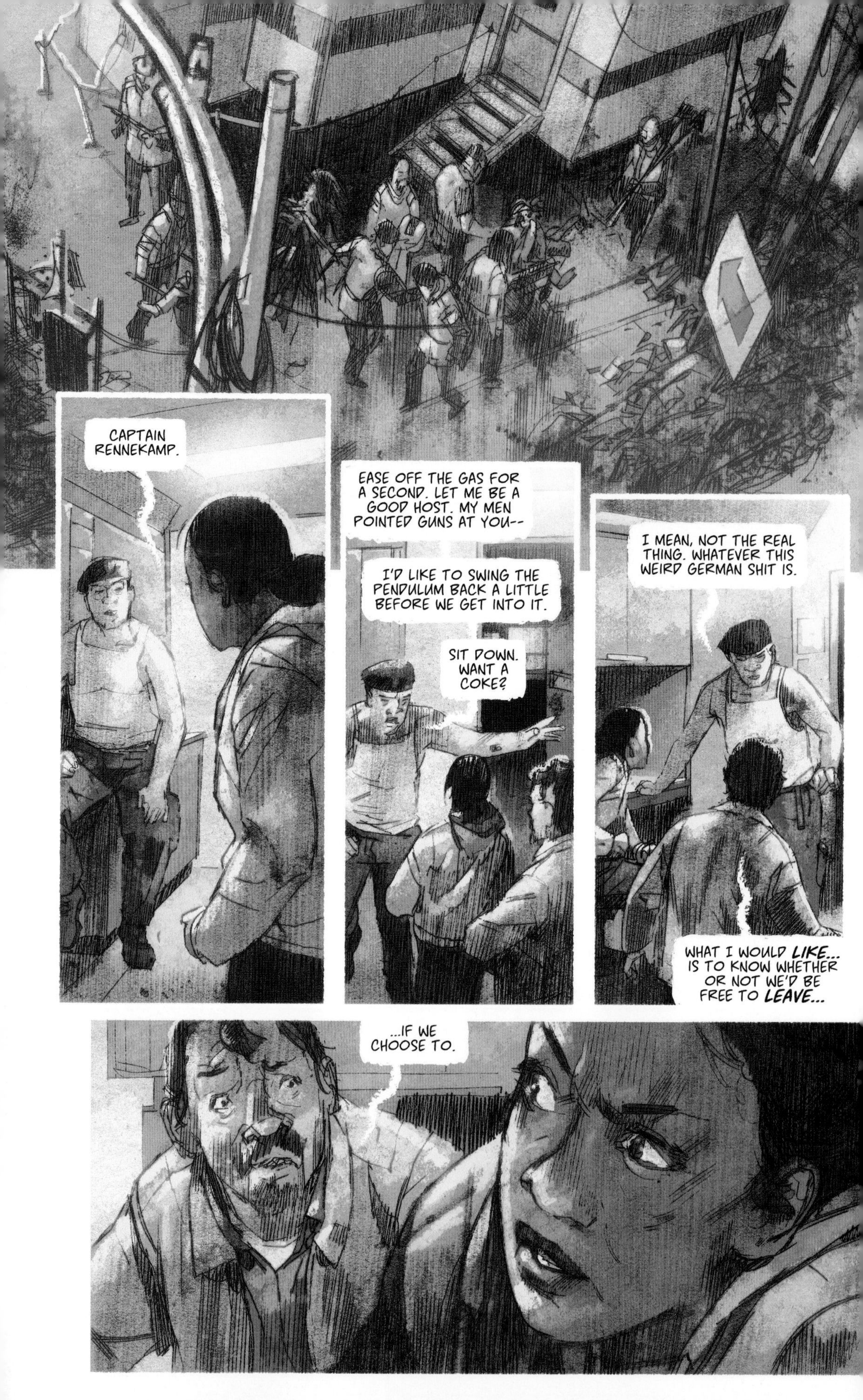
CAPTAIN RENNEKAMP.
EASE OFF THE GAS FOR A SECOND. LET ME BE A GOOD HOST. MY MEN POINTED GUNS AT YOU--
I'D LIKE TO SWING THE PENDULUM BACK A LITTLE BEFORE WE GET INTO IT.
SIT DOWN. WANT A COKE?
I MEAN, NOT THE REAL THING. WHATEVER THIS WEIRD GERMAN SHIT IS.
WHAT I WOULD LIKE... IS TO KNOW WHETHER OR NOT WE'D BE FREE TO LEAVE...
...IF WE CHOOSE TO.

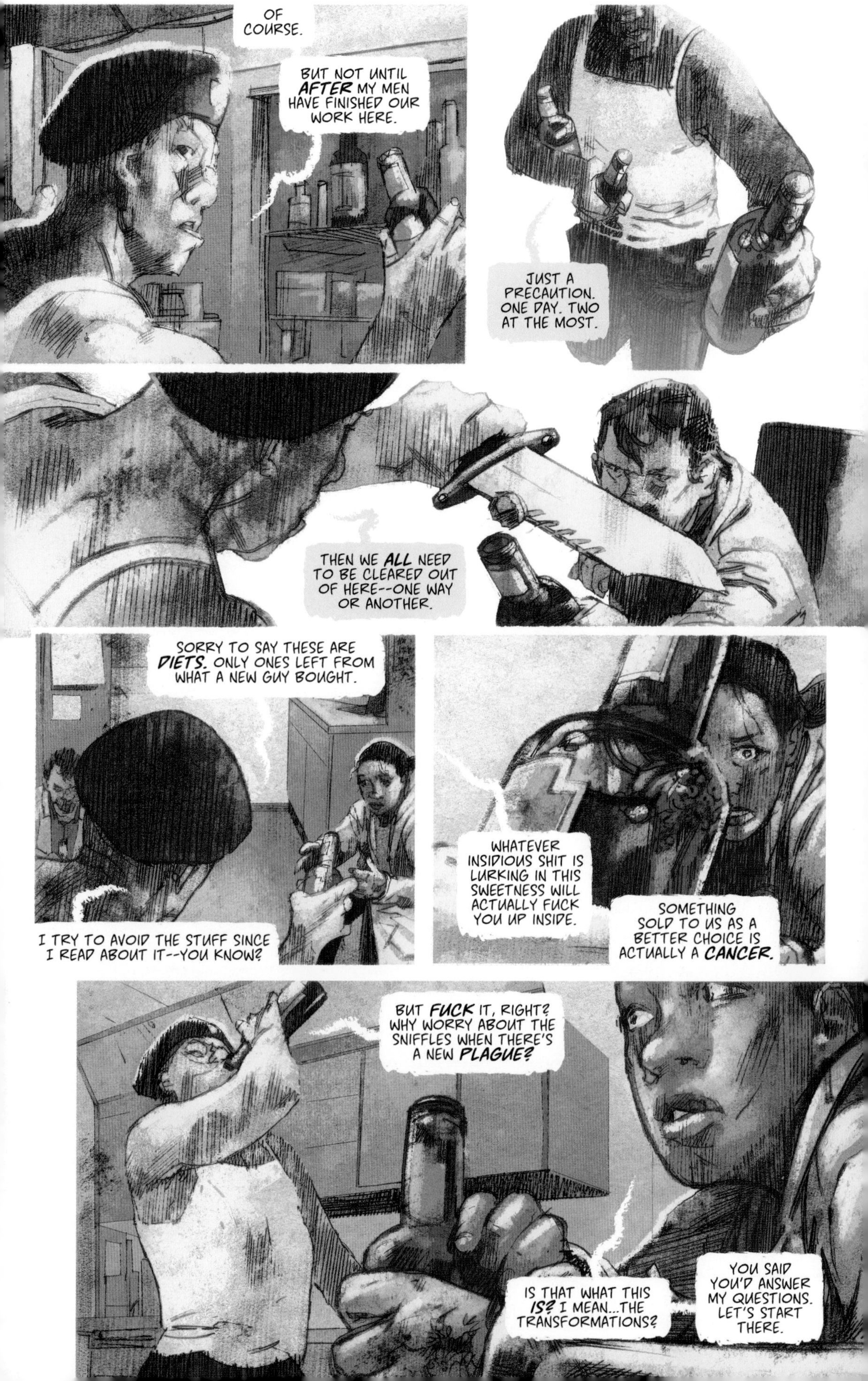
OF COURSE.
BUT NOT UNTIL AFTER MY MEN HAVE FINISHED OUR WORK HERE.
JUST A PRECAUTION. ONE DAY. TWO AT THE MOST.
THEN WE ALL NEED TO BE CLEARED OUT OF HERE--ONE WAY OR ANOTHER.
SORRY TO SAY THESE ARE DIETS. ONLY ONES LEFT FROM WHAT A NEW GUY BOUGHT.
I TRY TO AVOID THE STUFF SINCE I READ ABOUT IT--YOU KNOW?
WHATEVER INSIDIOUS SHIT IS LURKING IN THIS SWEETNESS WILL ACTUALLY FUCK YOU UP INSIDE.
SOMETHING SOLD TO US AS A BETTER CHOICE IS ACTUALLY A CANCER.
BUT FUCK IT, RIGHT? WHY WORRY ABOUT THE SNIFFLES WHEN THERE'S A NEW PLAGUE?
IS THAT WHAT THIS IS? I MEAN...THE TRANSFORMATIONS?
YOU SAID YOU'D ANSWER MY QUESTIONS. LET'S START THERE.

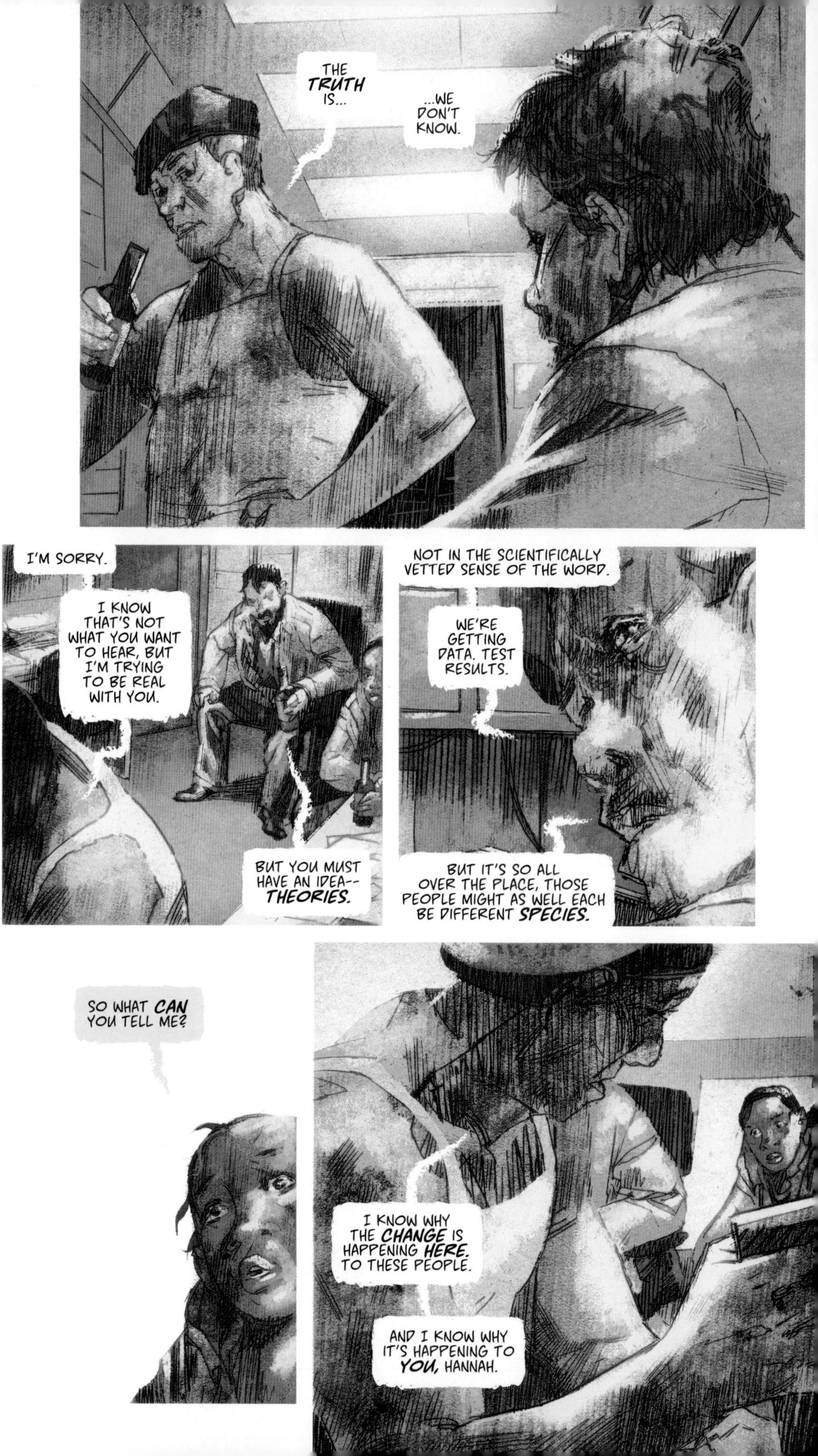
THE TRUTH IS...
...WE DON'T KNOW.
I'M SORRY.
I KNOW THAT'S NOT WHAT YOU WANT TO HEAR, BUT I'M TRYING TO BE REAL WITH YOU.
BUT YOU MUST HAVE AN IDEA-- THEORIES.
NOT IN THE SCIENTIFICALLY VETTED SENSE OF THE WORD.
WE'RE GETTING DATA. TEST RESULTS.
BUT IT'S SO ALL OVER THE PLACE, THOSE PEOPLE MIGHT AS WELL EACH BE DIFFERENT SPECIES.
SO WHAT CAN YOU TELL ME?
I KNOW WHY THE CHANGE IS HAPPENING HERE. TO THESE PEOPLE.
AND I KNOW WHY IT'S HAPPENING TO YOU, HANNAH.

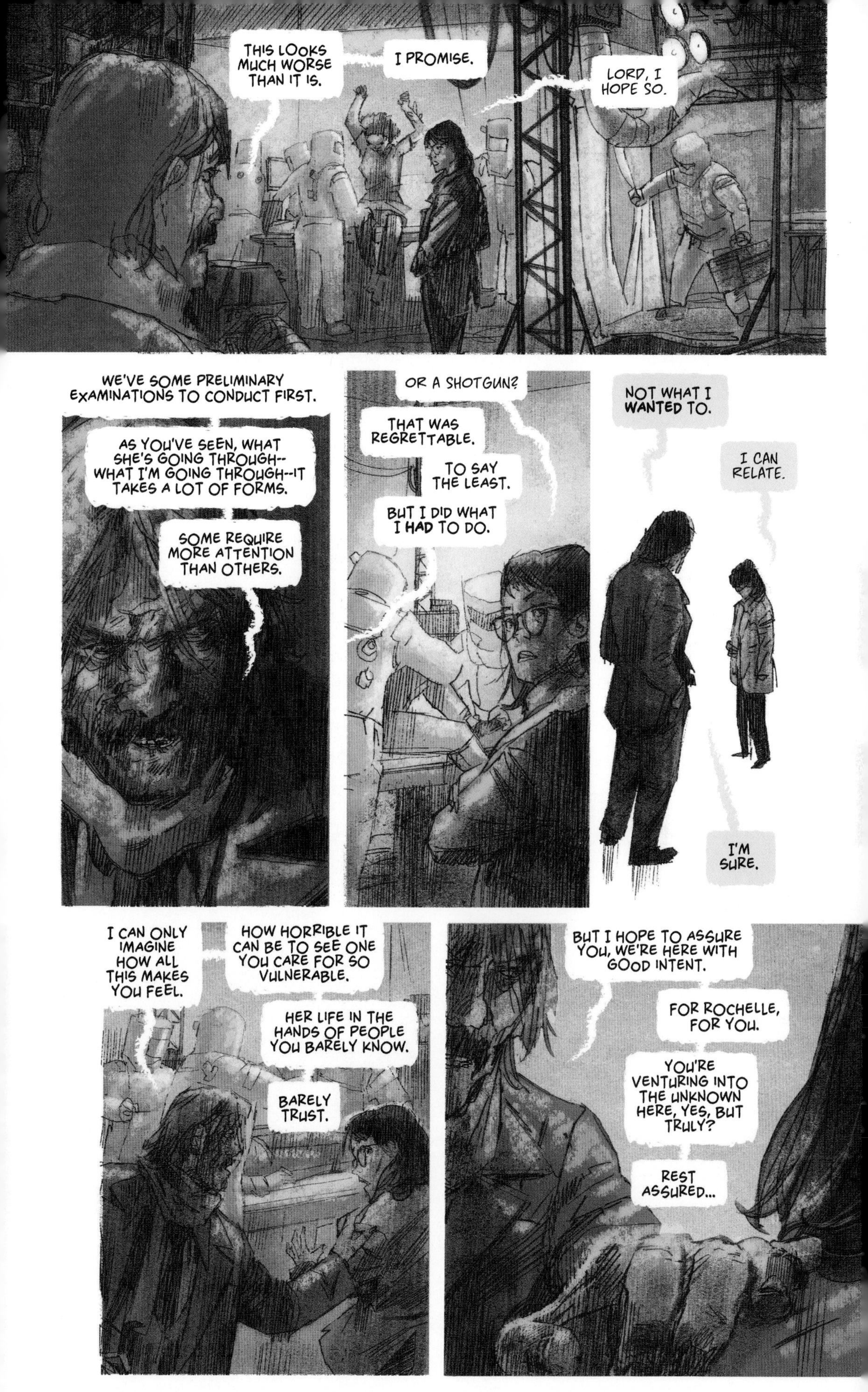
THIS LOOKS MUCH WORSE THAN IT IS.
I PROMISE.
LORD, I HOPE SO.
WE'VE SOME PRELIMINARY EXAMINATIONS TO CONDUCT FIRST.
AS YOU'VE SEEN, WHAT SHE'S GOING THROUGH-- WHAT I'M GOING THROUGH--IT TAKES A LOT OF FORMS.
SOME REQUIRE MORE ATTENTION THAN OTHERS.
OR A SHOTGUN?
THAT WAS REGRETTABLE.
TO SAY THE LEAST.
BUT I DID WHAT I HAD TO DO.
NOT WHAT I WANTED TO.
I CAN RELATE.
I'M SURE.
I CAN ONLY IMAGINE HOW ALL THIS MAKES YOU FEEL.
HOW HORRIBLE IT CAN BE TO SEE ONE YOU CARE FOR SO VULNERABLE.
HER LIFE IN THE HANDS OF PEOPLE YOU BARELY KNOW.
BARELY TRUST.
BUT I HOPE TO ASSURE YOU, WE'RE HERE WITH GOOD INTENT.
FOR ROCHELLE, FOR YOU.
YOU'RE VENTURING INTO THE UNKNOWN HERE, YES, BUT TRULY?
REST ASSURED...

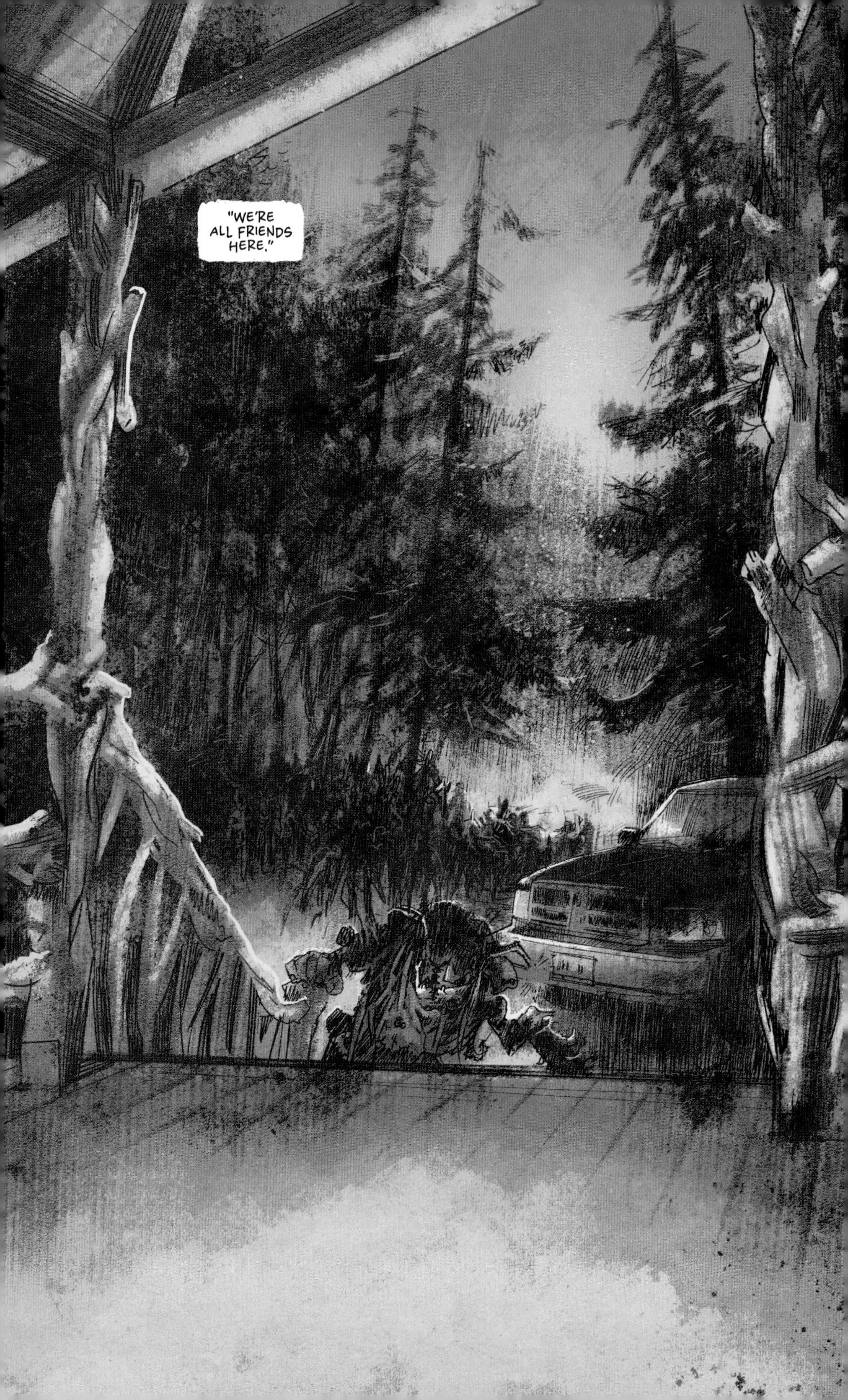
"WE'RE ALL FRIENDS HERE."

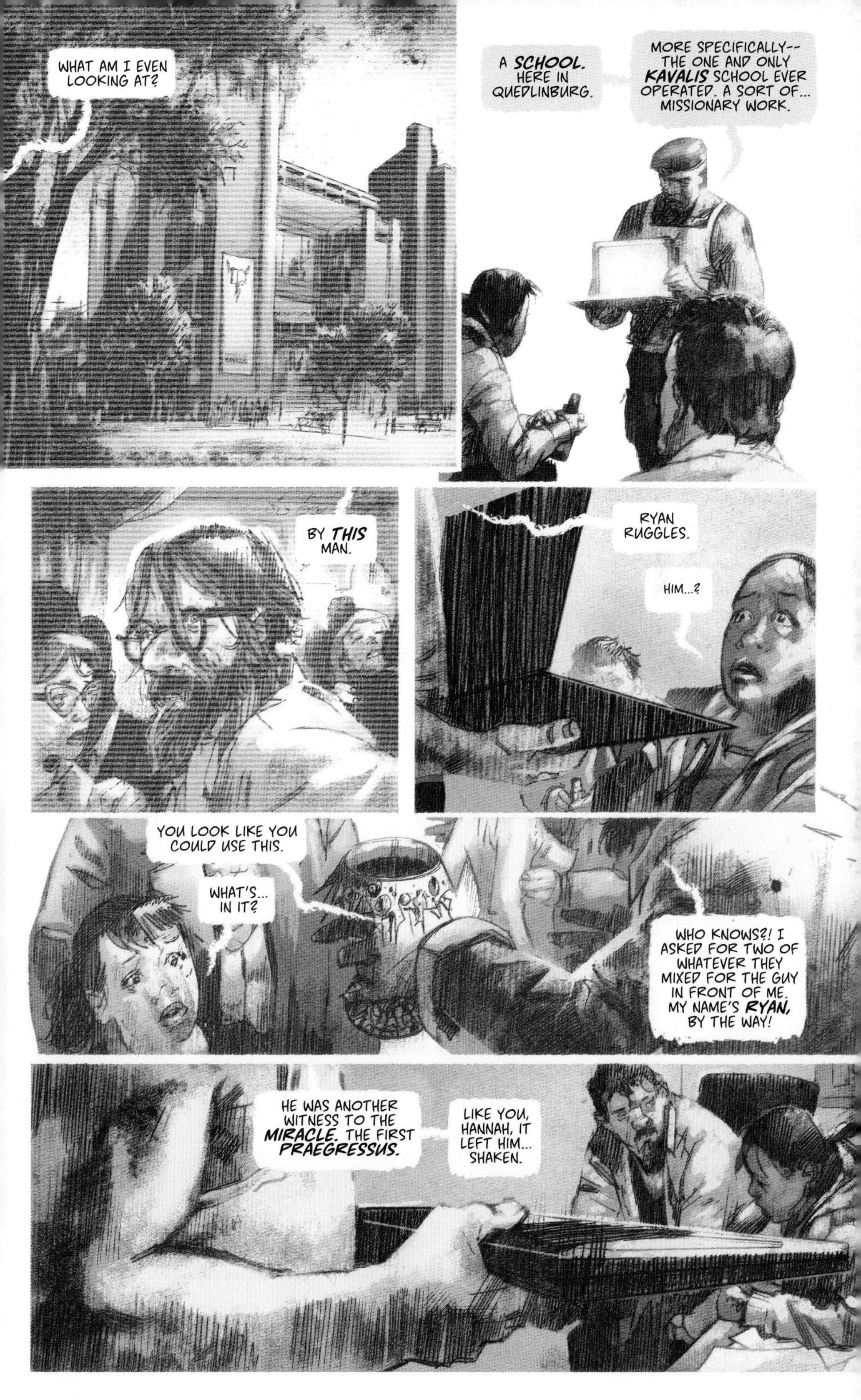
WHAT AM I EVEN LOOKING AT?
A SCHOOL. HERE IN QUEDLINBURG.
MORE SPECIFICALLY-- THE ONE AND ONLY KAVALIS SCHOOL EVER OPERATED. A SORT OF... MISSIONARY WORK.
BY THIS MAN.
RYAN RUGGLES.
HIM...?
YOU LOOK LIKE YOU COULD USE THIS.
WHAT'S... IN IT?
WHO KNOWS?! I ASKED FOR TWO OF WHATEVER THEY MIXED FOR THE GUY IN FRONT OF ME. MY NAME'S RYAN, BY THE WAY!
HE WAS ANOTHER WITNESS TO THE MIRACLE. THE FIRST PRAEGRESSUS.
LIKE YOU, HANNAH, IT LEFT HIM... SHAKEN.

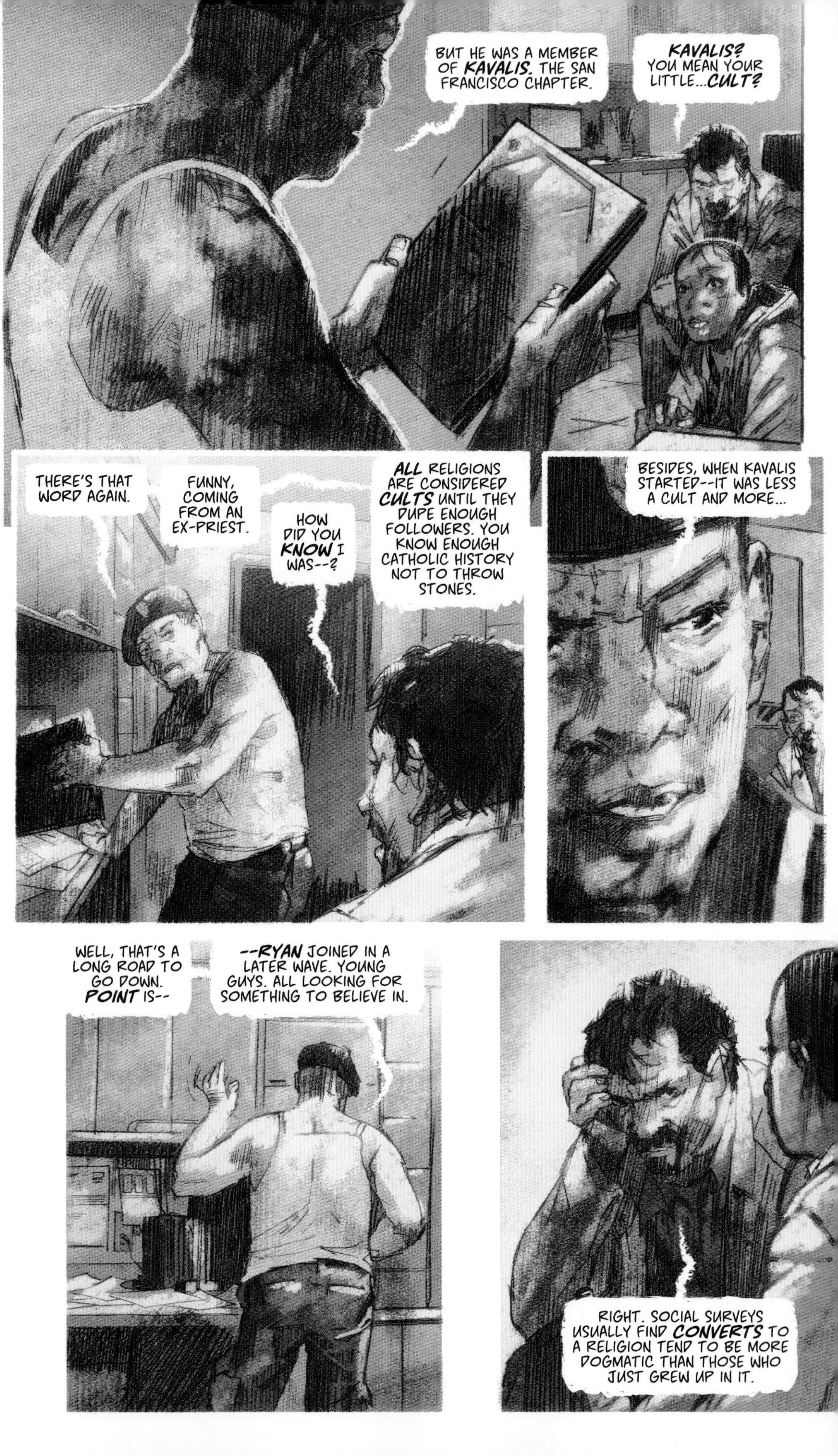
BUT HE WAS A MEMBER OF KAVALIS. THE SAN FRANCISCO CHAPTER.
KAVALIS? YOU MEAN YOUR LITTLE...CULT?
THERE'S THAT WORD AGAIN.
FUNNY, COMING FROM AN EX-PRIEST.
HOW DID YOU KNOW I WAS--?
ALL RELIGIONS ARE CONSIDERED CULTS UNTIL THEY DUPE ENOUGH FOLLOWERS. YOU KNOW ENOUGH CATHOLIC HISTORY NOT TO THROW STONES.
BESIDES, WHEN KAVALIS STARTED--IT WAS LESS A CULT AND MORE...
WELL, THAT'S A LONG ROAD TO GO DOWN. POINT IS--
--RYAN JOINED IN A LATER WAVE. YOUNG GUYS. ALL LOOKING FOR SOMETHING TO BELIEVE IN.
RIGHT. SOCIAL SURVEYS USUALLY FIND CONVERTS TO A RELIGION TEND TO BE MORE DOGMATIC THAN THOSE WHO JUST GREW UP IN IT.

"EXACTLY. AND AS A CONVERT, HE WAS DEVOTED--NO MATTER WHAT.
"AND AS A DEVOUT MAN WITH A GUILTY CONSCIENCE, HE STARTED LOOKING TO **ATONE.**
"FOR GOD KNOWS WHAT REASON--IN MR. RUGGLES' CASE, THAT MEANT OPENING AN ENGLISH LANGUAGE SCHOOL AND COMMUNITY CENTER IN FINANCIALLY STRUGGLING EAST GERMANY.
PSYCH
ADOLESCENCE
EARLY CHILDHOOD EDUCATION
"SOME OF THE MEN RUNNING KAVALIS LIKED THE IDEA THAT A NONPROFIT SCHOOL MIGHT PROP UP THEIR CASE FOR BEING A RELIGION--
"--IN THE EYES OF A SKEPTICAL I.R.S.
"BUT THAT CAME WITH THE REQUIREMENT HE ***TEACH*** THE KAVALIS BELIEFS--SUCH AS THEY WERE.
CHURCH OF KAVALIS
OPEN HOUSE TODAY!
"THE TOWN WAS HAPPY TO HAVE THE INVESTMENT, BUT DIVIDED ON KAVALIS' IDEAS. EVEN DURING COMMUNISM, CHRISTIANITY KEPT ROOTS HERE."
AND MAYBE THE SKEPTICS WERE ***RIGHT.*** IF HE TURNED OUT TO BE ***PATIENT ZERO*** FOR...WHATEVER THE HELL CHANGED THESE PEOPLE.
BUT THE QUESTION I CAN'T GET OUT OF ***MY*** HEAD IS--

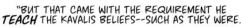

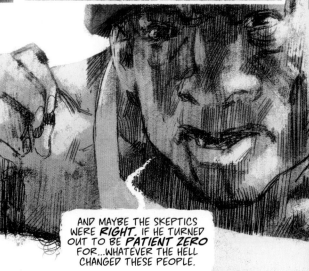

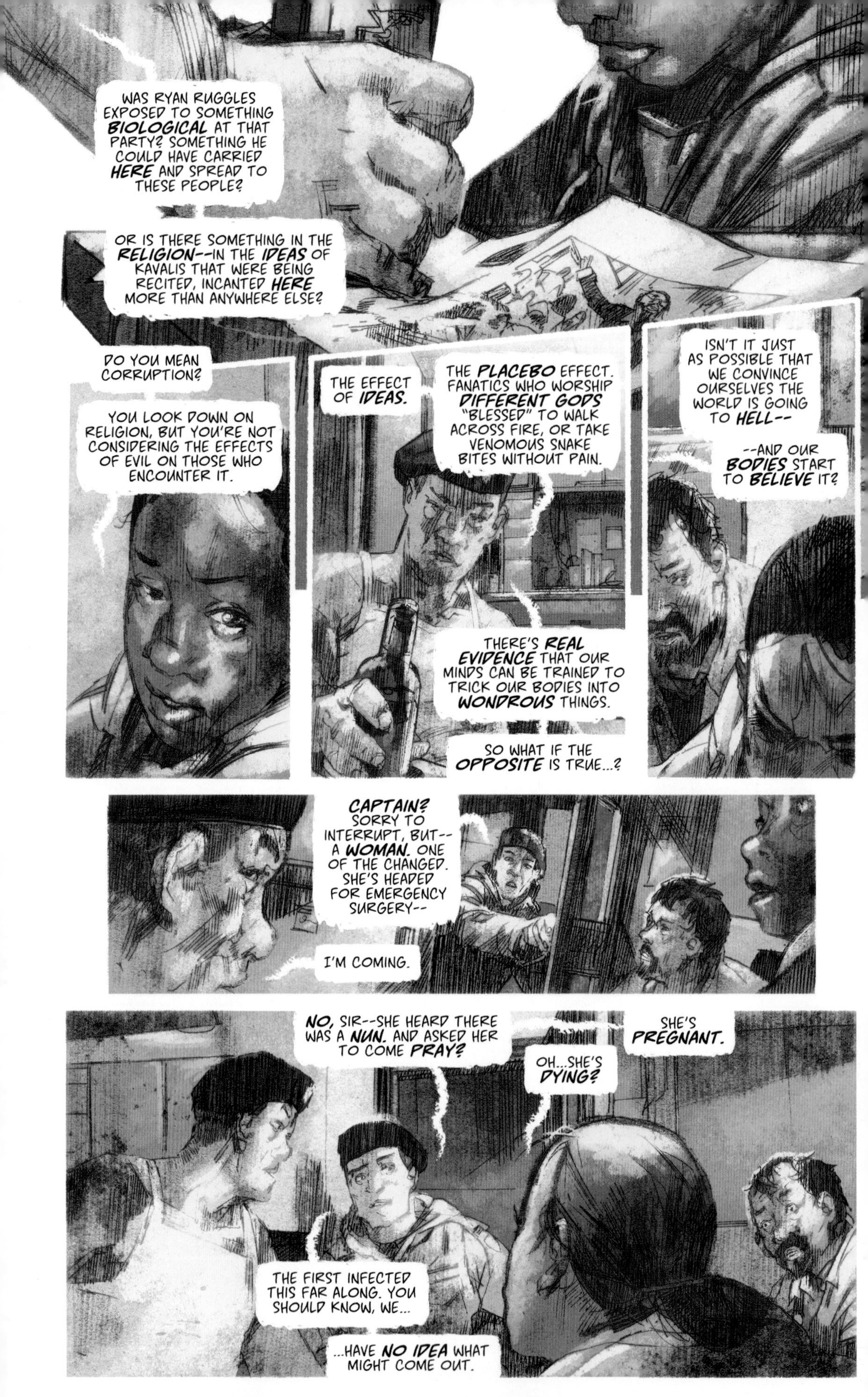
WAS RYAN RUGGLES EXPOSED TO SOMETHING BIOLOGICAL AT THAT PARTY? SOMETHING HE COULD HAVE CARRIED HERE AND SPREAD TO THESE PEOPLE?
OR IS THERE SOMETHING IN THE RELIGION--IN THE IDEAS OF KAVALIS THAT WERE BEING RECITED, INCANTED HERE MORE THAN ANYWHERE ELSE?
DO YOU MEAN CORRUPTION?
YOU LOOK DOWN ON RELIGION, BUT YOU'RE NOT CONSIDERING THE EFFECTS OF EVIL ON THOSE WHO ENCOUNTER IT.
THE EFFECT OF IDEAS.
THE PLACEBO EFFECT. FANATICS WHO WORSHIP DIFFERENT GODS "BLESSED" TO WALK ACROSS FIRE, OR TAKE VENOMOUS SNAKE BITES WITHOUT PAIN.
THERE'S REAL EVIDENCE THAT OUR MINDS CAN BE TRAINED TO TRICK OUR BODIES INTO WONDROUS THINGS.
SO WHAT IF THE OPPOSITE IS TRUE...?
ISN'T IT JUST AS POSSIBLE THAT WE CONVINCE OURSELVES THE WORLD IS GOING TO HELL--
--AND OUR BODIES START TO BELIEVE IT?
CAPTAIN? SORRY TO INTERRUPT, BUT--A WOMAN. ONE OF THE CHANGED. SHE'S HEADED FOR EMERGENCY SURGERY--
I'M COMING.
NO, SIR--SHE HEARD THERE WAS A NUN. AND ASKED HER TO COME PRAY?
OH...SHE'S DYING?
SHE'S PREGNANT.
THE FIRST INFECTED THIS FAR ALONG. YOU SHOULD KNOW, WE...
...HAVE NO IDEA WHAT MIGHT COME OUT.

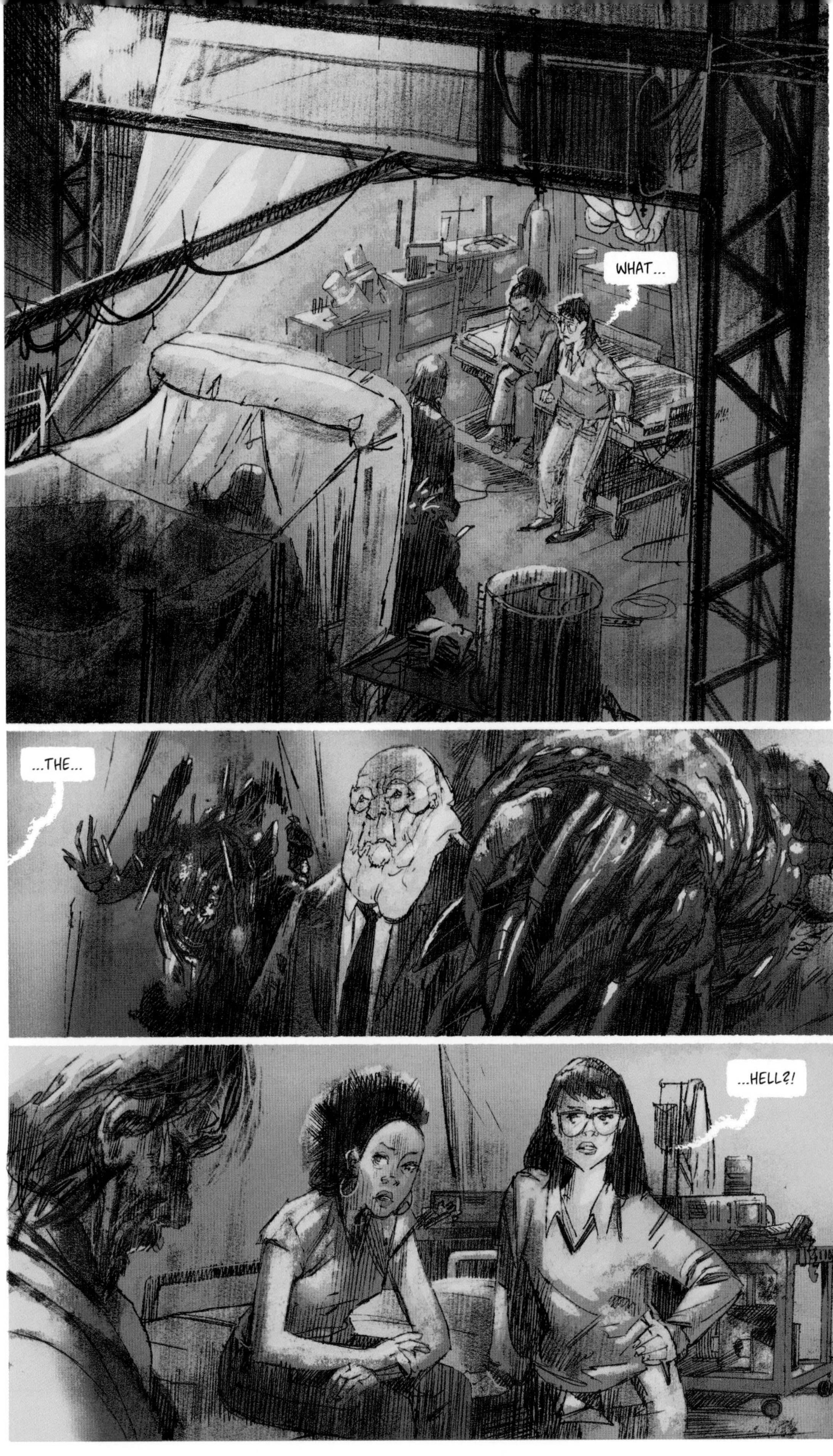
WHAT...
...THE...
...HELL?!

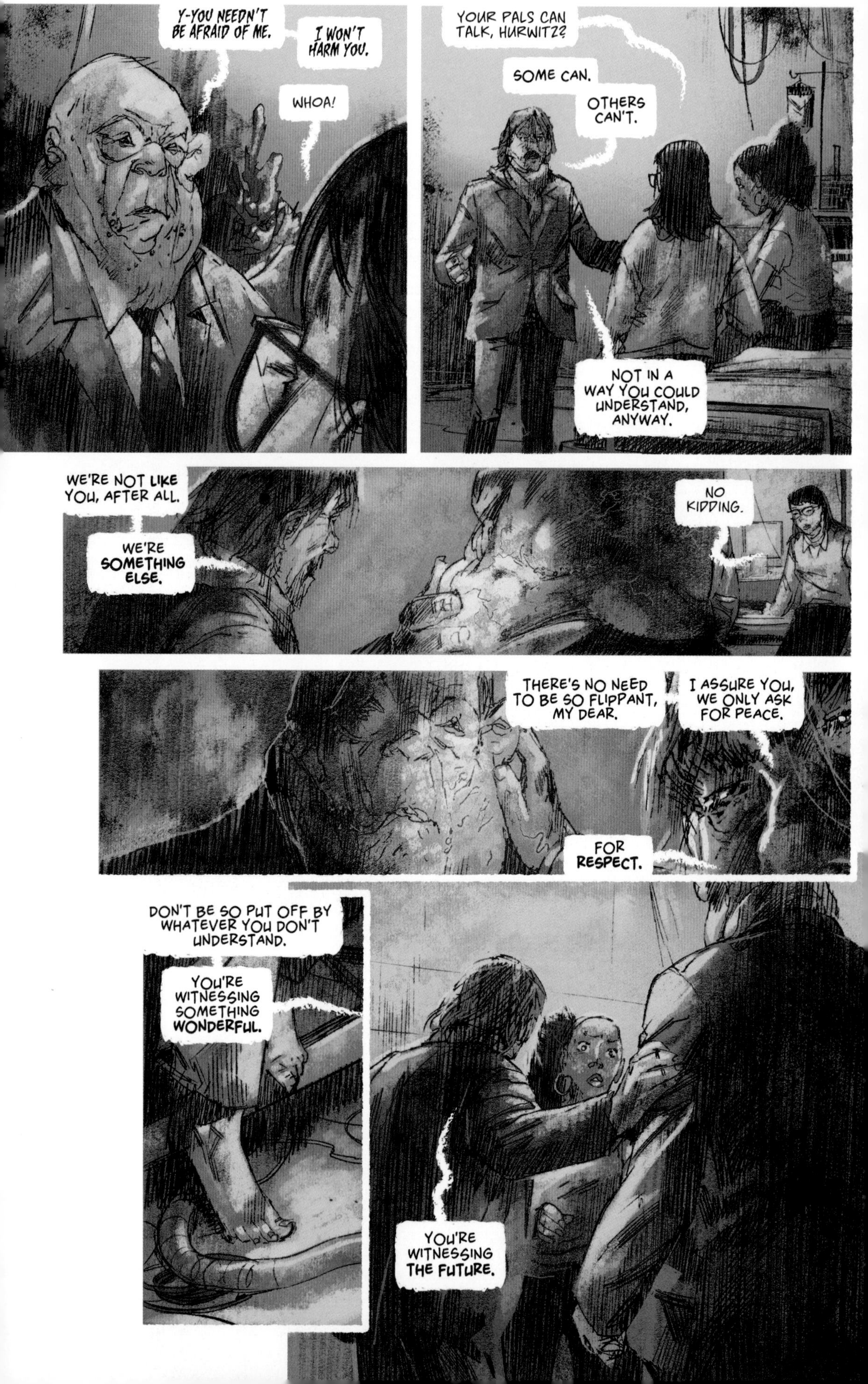
Y-YOU NEEDN'T BE AFRAID OF ME.
I WON'T HARM YOU.
WHOA!
YOUR PALS CAN TALK, HURWITZ?
SOME CAN.
OTHERS CAN'T.
NOT IN A WAY YOU COULD UNDERSTAND, ANYWAY.
WE'RE NOT LIKE YOU, AFTER ALL.
WE'RE SOMETHING ELSE.
NO KIDDING.
THERE'S NO NEED TO BE SO FLIPPANT, MY DEAR.
I ASSURE YOU, WE ONLY ASK FOR PEACE.
FOR RESPECT.
DON'T BE SO PUT OFF BY WHATEVER YOU DON'T UNDERSTAND.
YOU'RE WITNESSING SOMETHING WONDERFUL.
YOU'RE WITNESSING THE FUTURE.

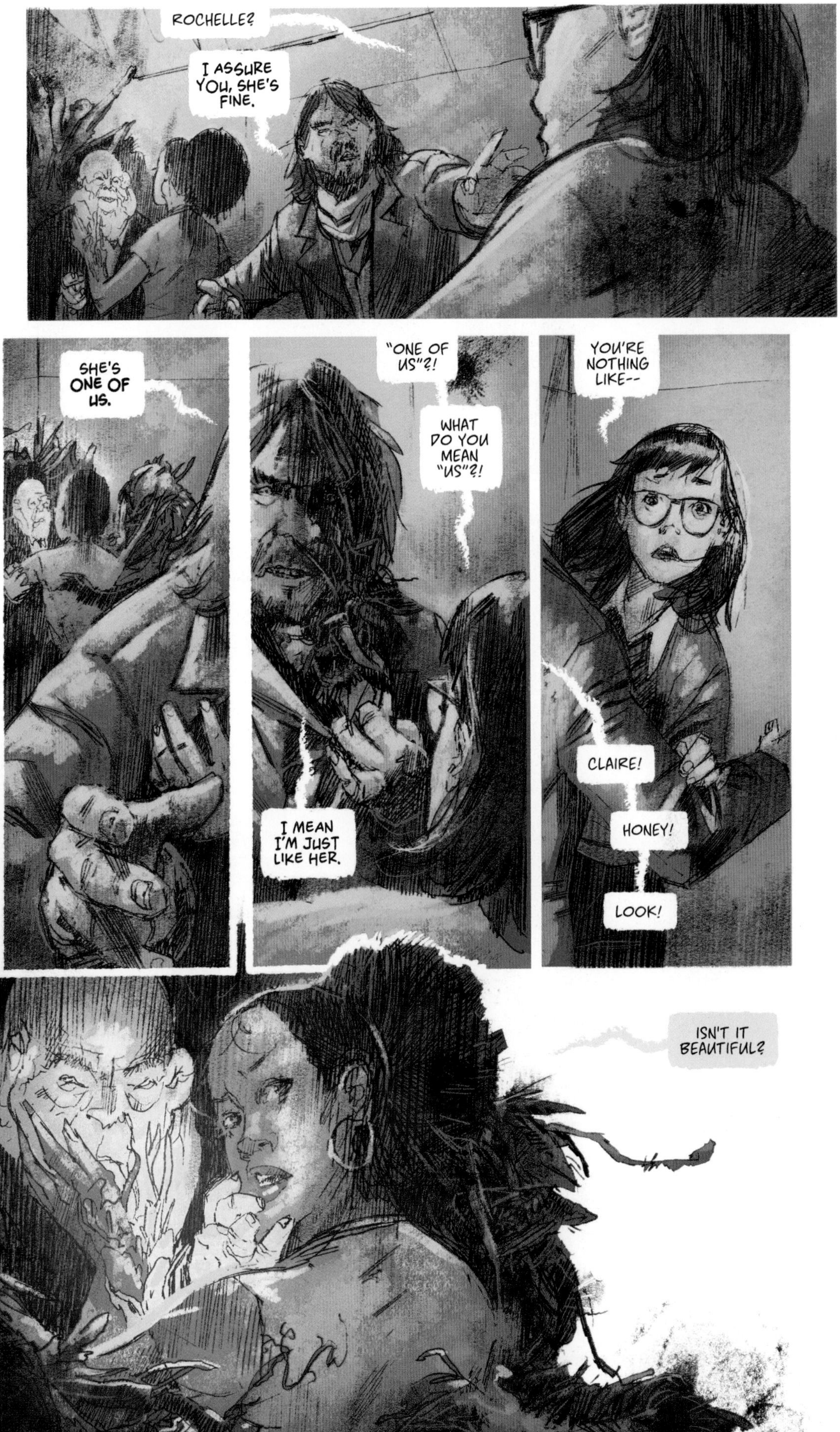
ROCHELLE?
I ASSURE YOU, SHE'S FINE.
SHE'S ONE OF US.
"ONE OF US"?!
WHAT DO YOU MEAN "US"?!
I MEAN I'M JUST LIKE HER.
YOU'RE NOTHING LIKE--
CLAIRE!
HONEY!
LOOK!
ISN'T IT BEAUTIFUL?

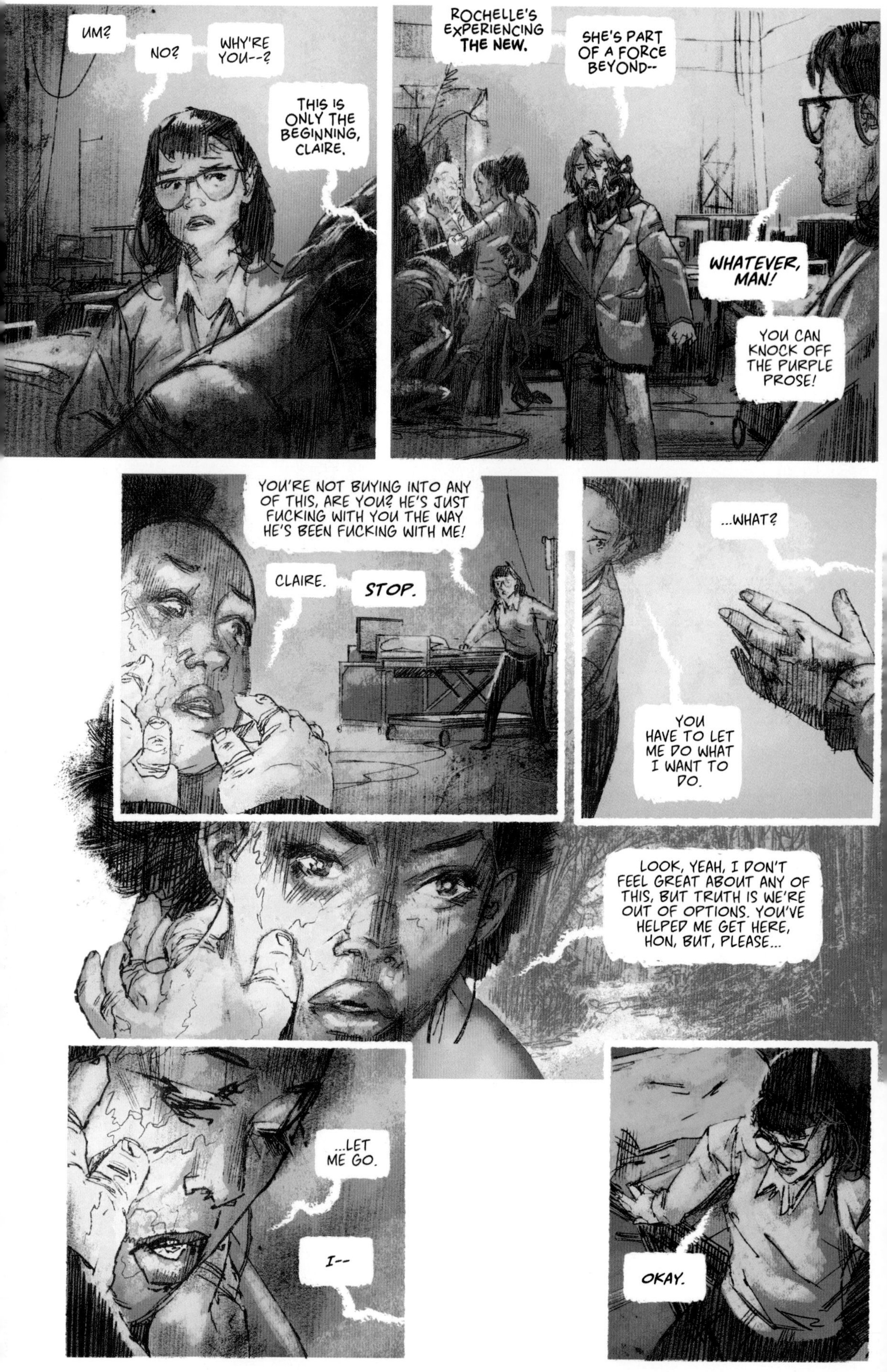
UM?
NO?
WHY'RE YOU--?
THIS IS ONLY THE BEGINNING, CLAIRE.
ROCHELLE'S EXPERIENCING THE NEW.
SHE'S PART OF A FORCE BEYOND--
WHATEVER, MAN!
YOU CAN KNOCK OFF THE PURPLE PROSE!
YOU'RE NOT BUYING INTO ANY OF THIS, ARE YOU? HE'S JUST FUCKING WITH YOU THE WAY HE'S BEEN FUCKING WITH ME!
CLAIRE.
STOP.
...WHAT?
YOU HAVE TO LET ME DO WHAT I WANT TO DO.
LOOK, YEAH, I DON'T FEEL GREAT ABOUT ANY OF THIS, BUT TRUTH IS WE'RE OUT OF OPTIONS. YOU'VE HELPED ME GET HERE, HON, BUT, PLEASE...
...LET ME GO.
I--
OKAY.

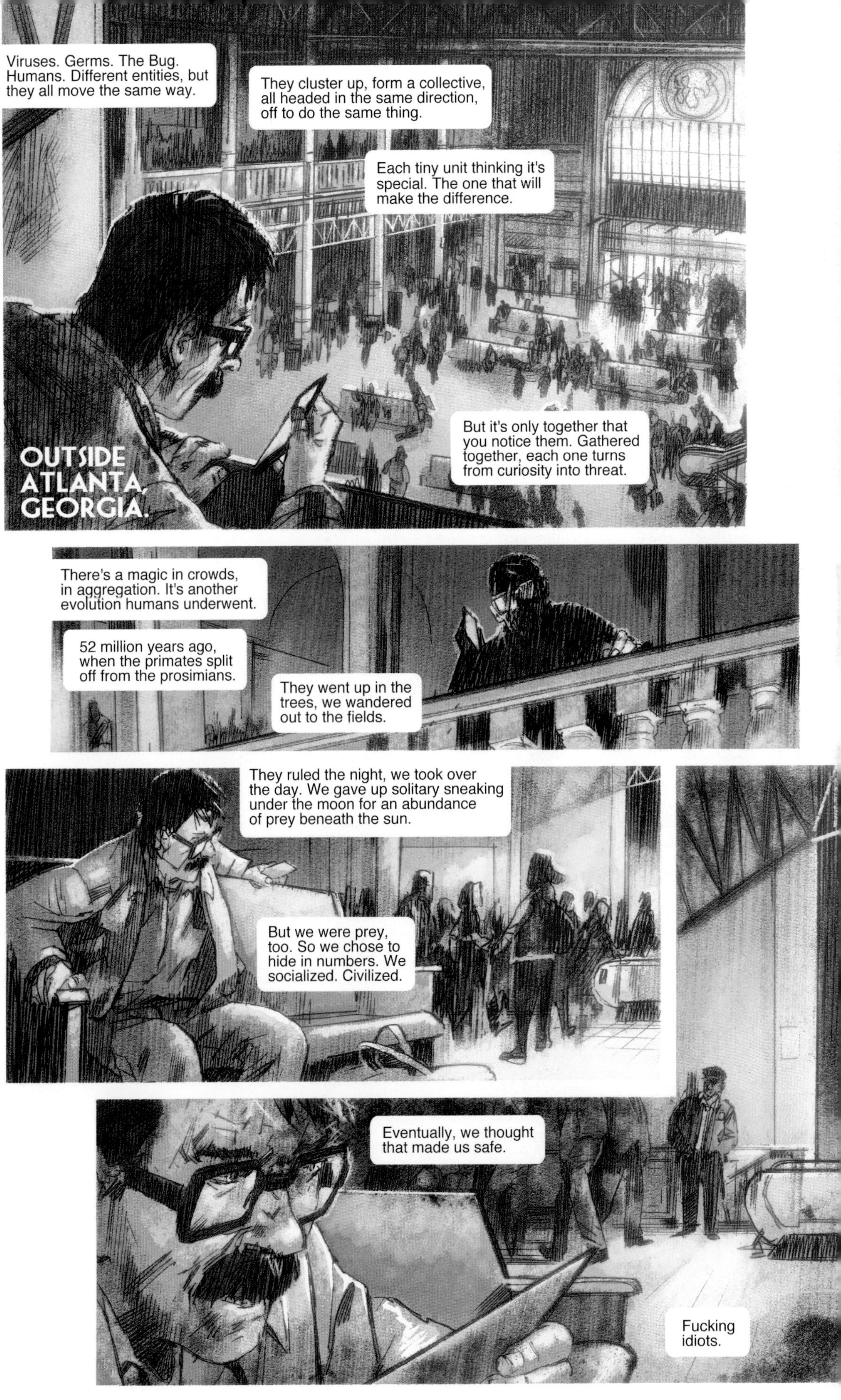
Viruses. Germs. The Bug. Humans. Different entities, but they all move the same way.
They cluster up, form a collective, all headed in the same direction, off to do the same thing.
Each tiny unit thinking it's special. The one that will make the difference.
But it's only together that you notice them. Gathered together, each one turns from curiosity into threat.
OUTSIDE ATLANTA, GEORGIA.
There's a magic in crowds, in aggregation. It's another evolution humans underwent.
52 million years ago, when the primates split off from the prosimians.
They went up in the trees, we wandered out to the fields.
They ruled the night, we took over the day. We gave up solitary sneaking under the moon for an abundance of prey beneath the sun.
But we were prey, too. So we chose to hide in numbers. We socialized. Civilized.
Eventually, we thought that made us safe.
Fucking idiots.

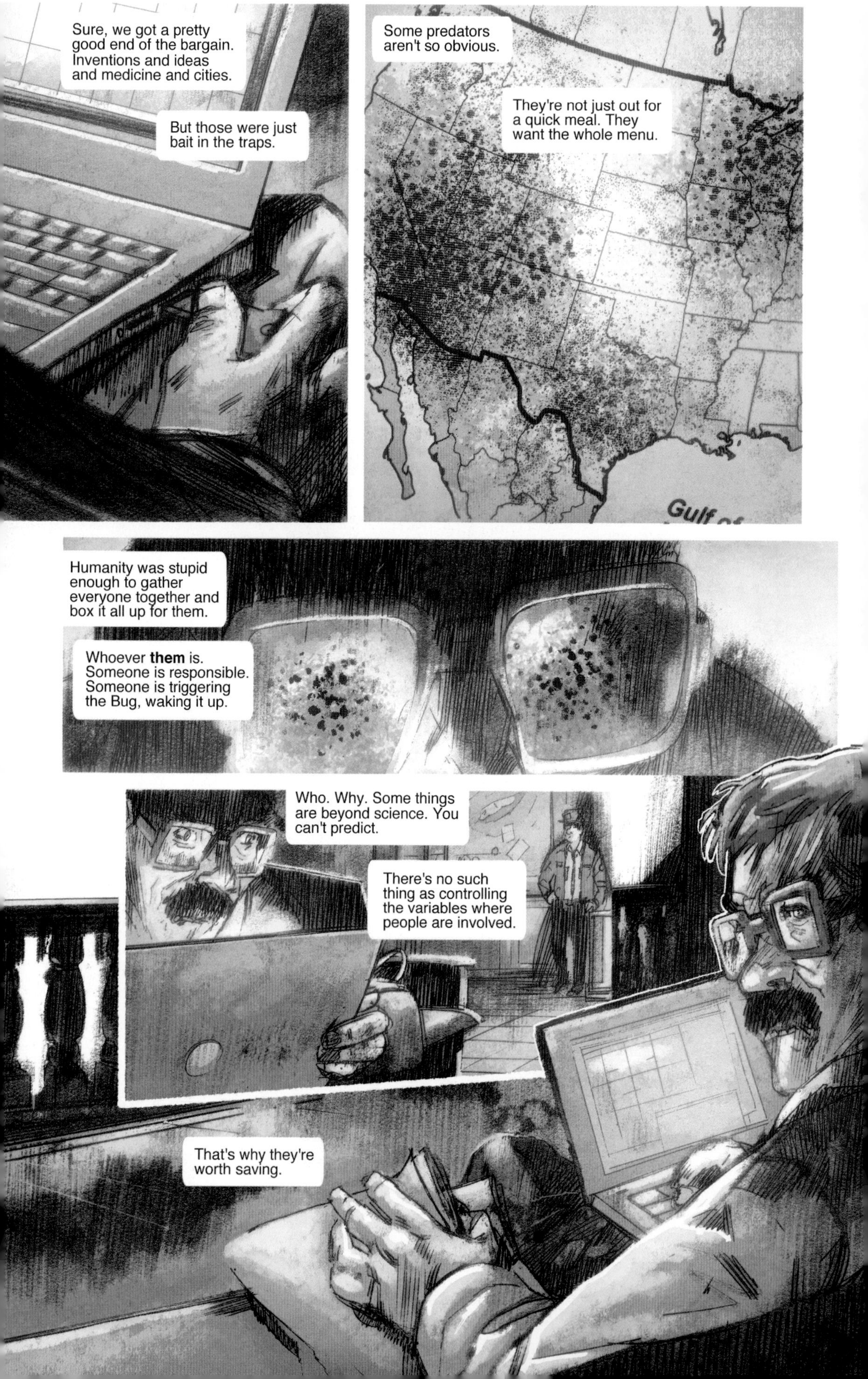
Sure, we got a pretty good end of the bargain. Inventions and ideas and medicine and cities.
But those were just bait in the traps.
Some predators aren't so obvious.
They're not just out for a quick meal. They want the whole menu.
Gulf of
Humanity was stupid enough to gather everyone together and box it all up for them.
Whoever **them** is. Someone is responsible. Someone is triggering the Bug, waking it up.
Who. Why. Some things are beyond science. You can't predict.
There's no such thing as controlling the variables where people are involved.
That's why they're worth saving.

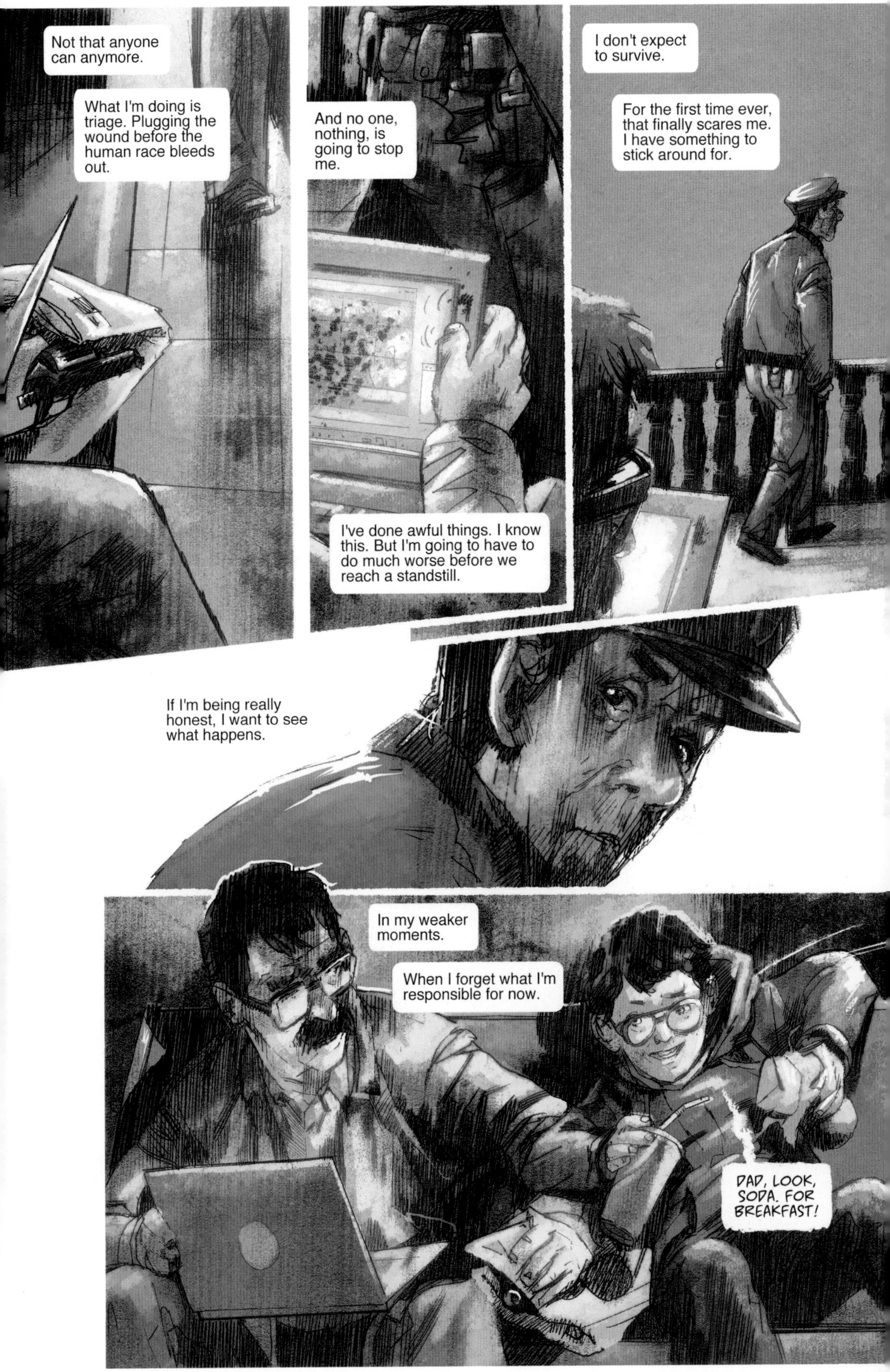
Not that anyone can anymore.
What I'm doing is triage. Plugging the wound before the human race bleeds out.
And no one, nothing, is going to stop me.
I've done awful things. I know this. But I'm going to have to do much worse before we reach a standstill.
I don't expect to survive.
For the first time ever, that finally scares me. I have something to stick around for.
If I'm being really honest, I want to see what happens.
In my weaker moments.
When I forget what I'm responsible for now.
DAD, LOOK, SODA. FOR BREAKFAST!

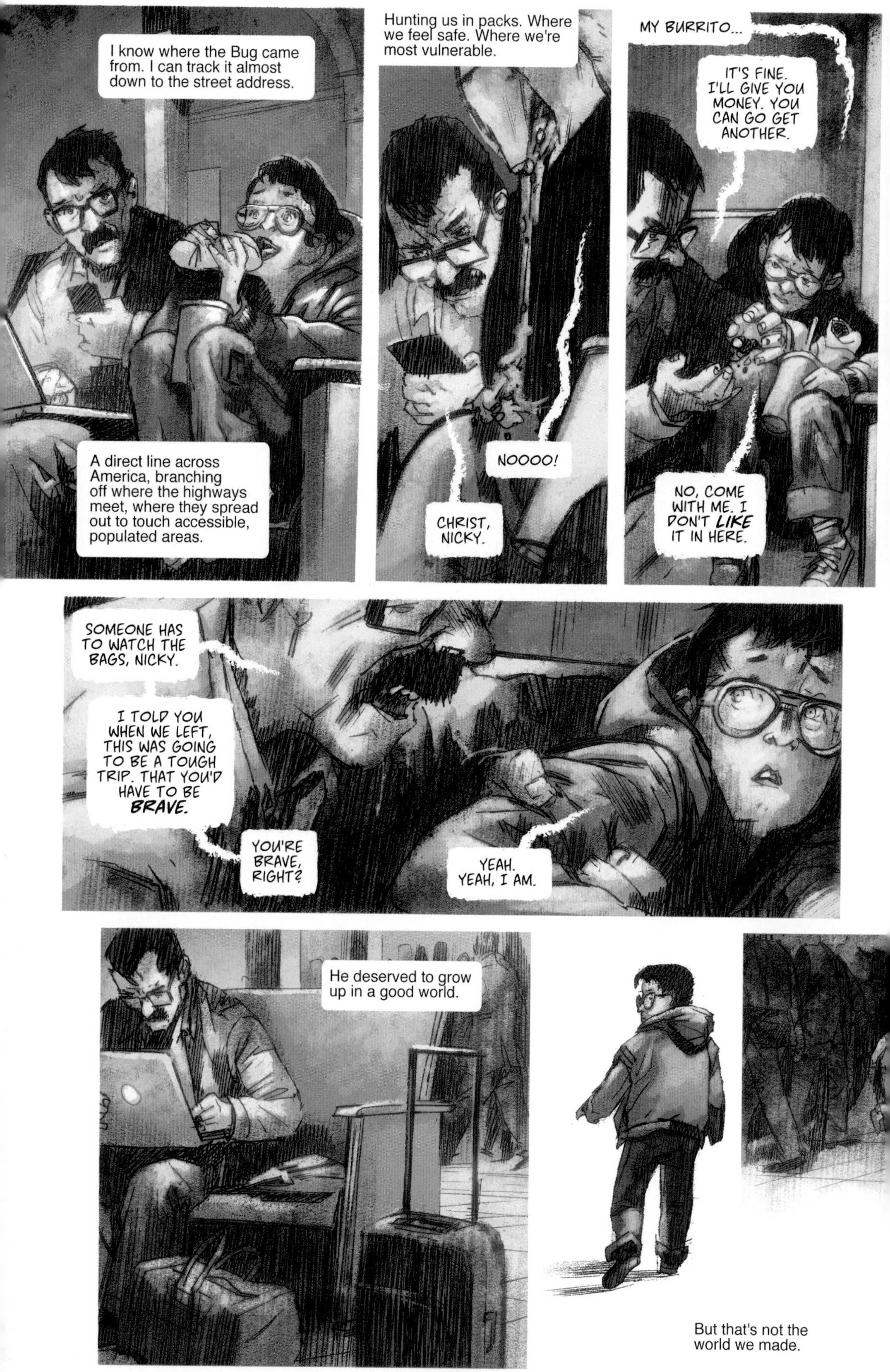
I know where the Bug came from. I can track it almost down to the street address.
A direct line across America, branching off where the highways meet, where they spread out to touch accessible, populated areas.
Hunting us in packs. Where we feel safe. Where we're most vulnerable.
NOOOO!
CHRIST, NICKY.
MY BURRITO...
IT'S FINE. I'LL GIVE YOU MONEY. YOU CAN GO GET ANOTHER.
NO, COME WITH ME. I DON'T LIKE IT IN HERE.
SOMEONE HAS TO WATCH THE BAGS, NICKY.
I TOLD YOU WHEN WE LEFT, THIS WAS GOING TO BE A TOUGH TRIP. THAT YOU'D HAVE TO BE BRAVE.
YOU'RE BRAVE, RIGHT?
YEAH. YEAH, I AM.
He deserved to grow up in a good world.
But that's not the world we made.

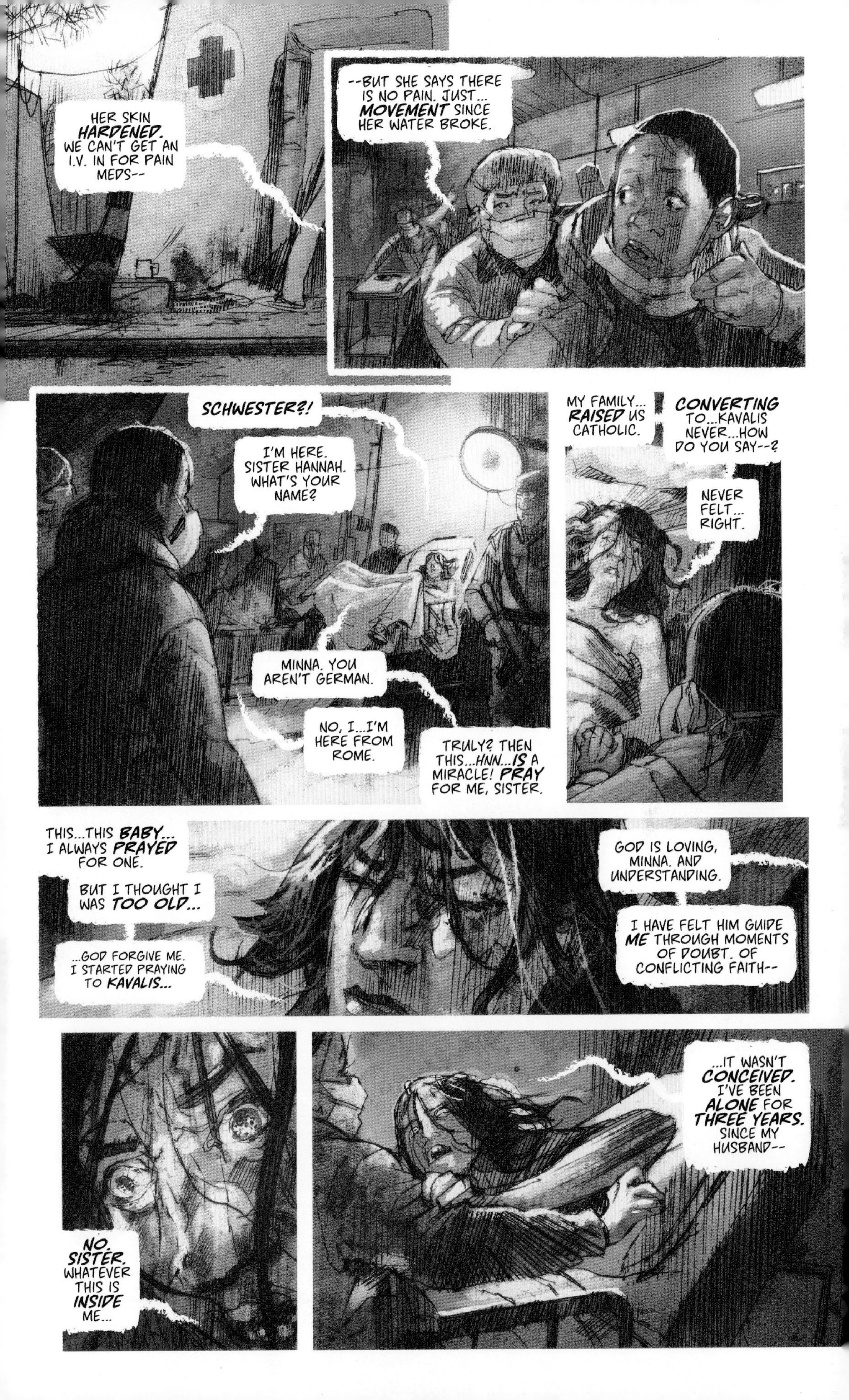
HER SKIN HARDENED. WE CAN'T GET AN I.V. IN FOR PAIN MEDS--
--BUT SHE SAYS THERE IS NO PAIN. JUST... MOVEMENT SINCE HER WATER BROKE.
SCHWESTER?!
I'M HERE. SISTER HANNAH. WHAT'S YOUR NAME?
MINNA. YOU AREN'T GERMAN.
NO, I...I'M HERE FROM ROME.
TRULY? THEN THIS...HNN...IS A MIRACLE! PRAY FOR ME, SISTER.
MY FAMILY... RAISED US CATHOLIC.
CONVERTING TO...KAVALIS NEVER...HOW DO YOU SAY--?
NEVER FELT... RIGHT.
THIS...THIS BABY... I ALWAYS PRAYED FOR ONE.
BUT I THOUGHT I WAS TOO OLD...
...GOD FORGIVE ME. I STARTED PRAYING TO KAVALIS...
GOD IS LOVING, MINNA. AND UNDERSTANDING.
I HAVE FELT HIM GUIDE ME THROUGH MOMENTS OF DOUBT. OF CONFLICTING FAITH--
NO. SISTER. WHATEVER THIS IS INSIDE ME...
...IT WASN'T CONCEIVED. I'VE BEEN ALONE FOR THREE YEARS. SINCE MY HUSBAND--

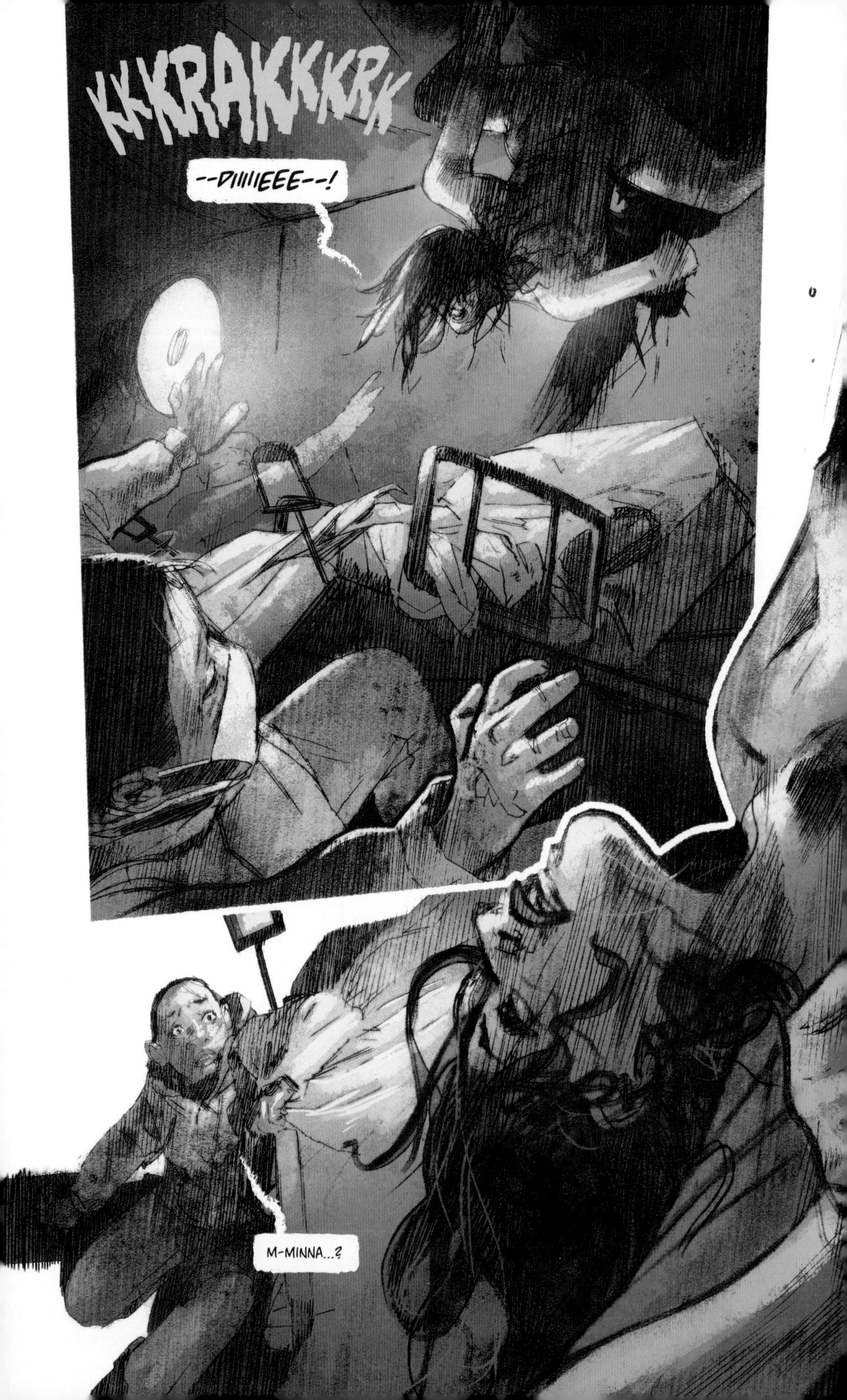
KKKRAKKKRK
--DIIIIIEEE--!
M-MINNA...?

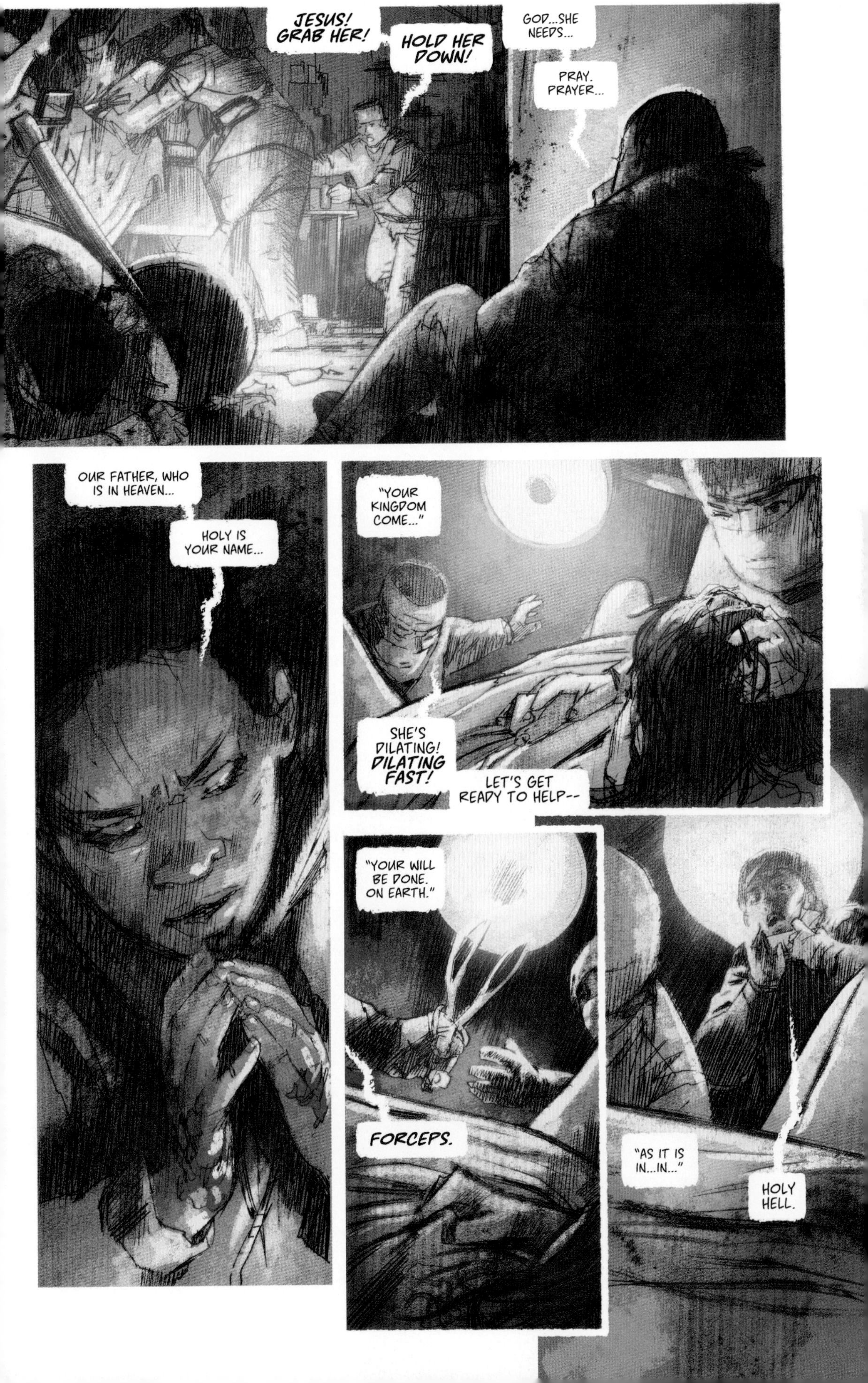
JESUS! GRAB HER!
HOLD HER DOWN!
GOD...SHE NEEDS...
PRAY. PRAYER...
OUR FATHER, WHO IS IN HEAVEN...
HOLY IS YOUR NAME...
"YOUR KINGDOM COME..."
SHE'S DILATING! DILATING FAST!
LET'S GET READY TO HELP--
"YOUR WILL BE DONE. ON EARTH."
FORCEPS.
"AS IT IS IN...IN..."
HOLY HELL.

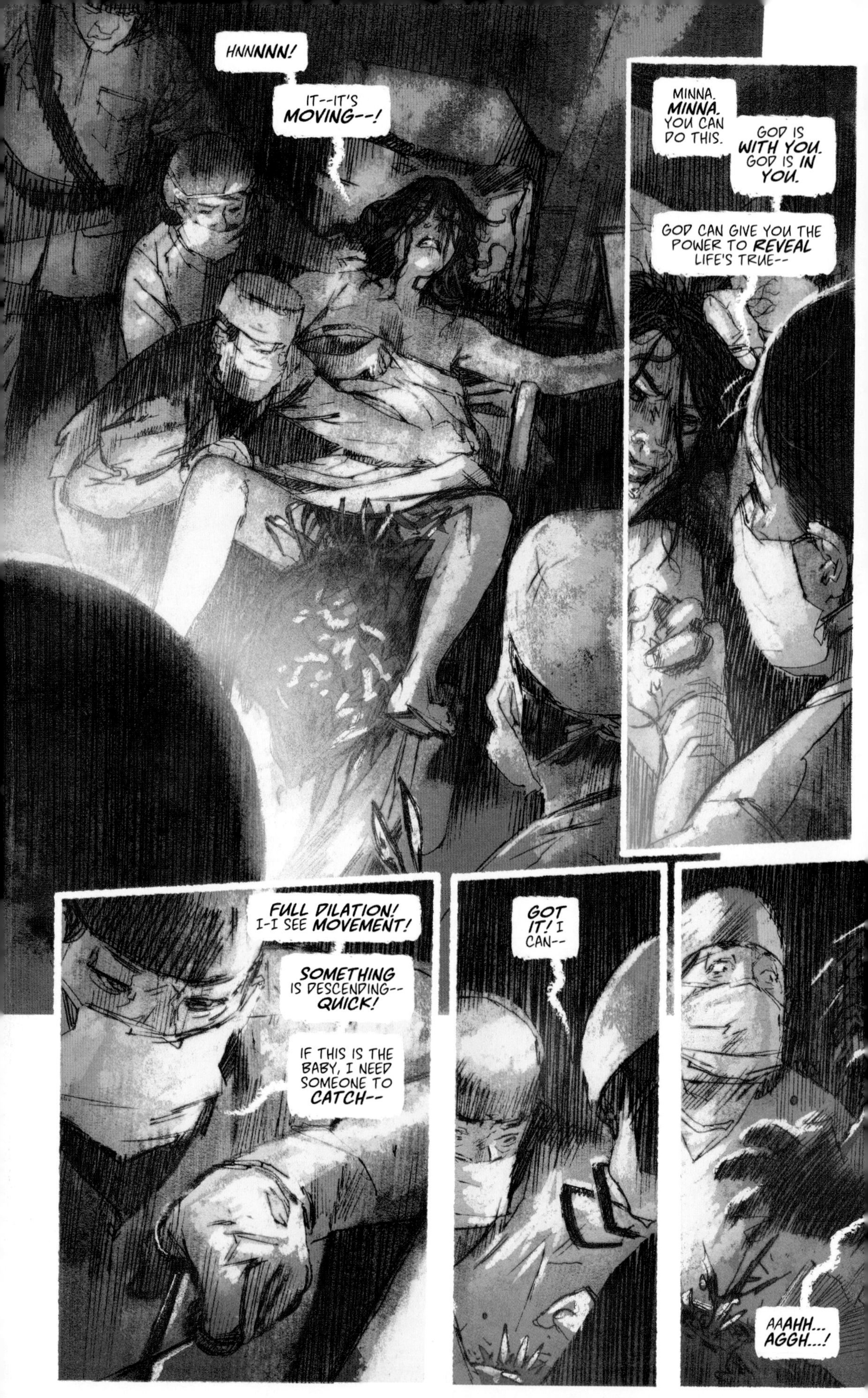
HNNNNN!
IT--IT'S MOVING--!
MINNA. MINNA. YOU CAN DO THIS.
GOD IS WITH YOU. GOD IS IN YOU.
GOD CAN GIVE YOU THE POWER TO REVEAL LIFE'S TRUE--
FULL DILATION! I-I SEE MOVEMENT!
SOMETHING IS DESCENDING-- QUICK!
IF THIS IS THE BABY, I NEED SOMEONE TO CATCH--
GOT IT! I CAN--
AAAHH... AGGH...!

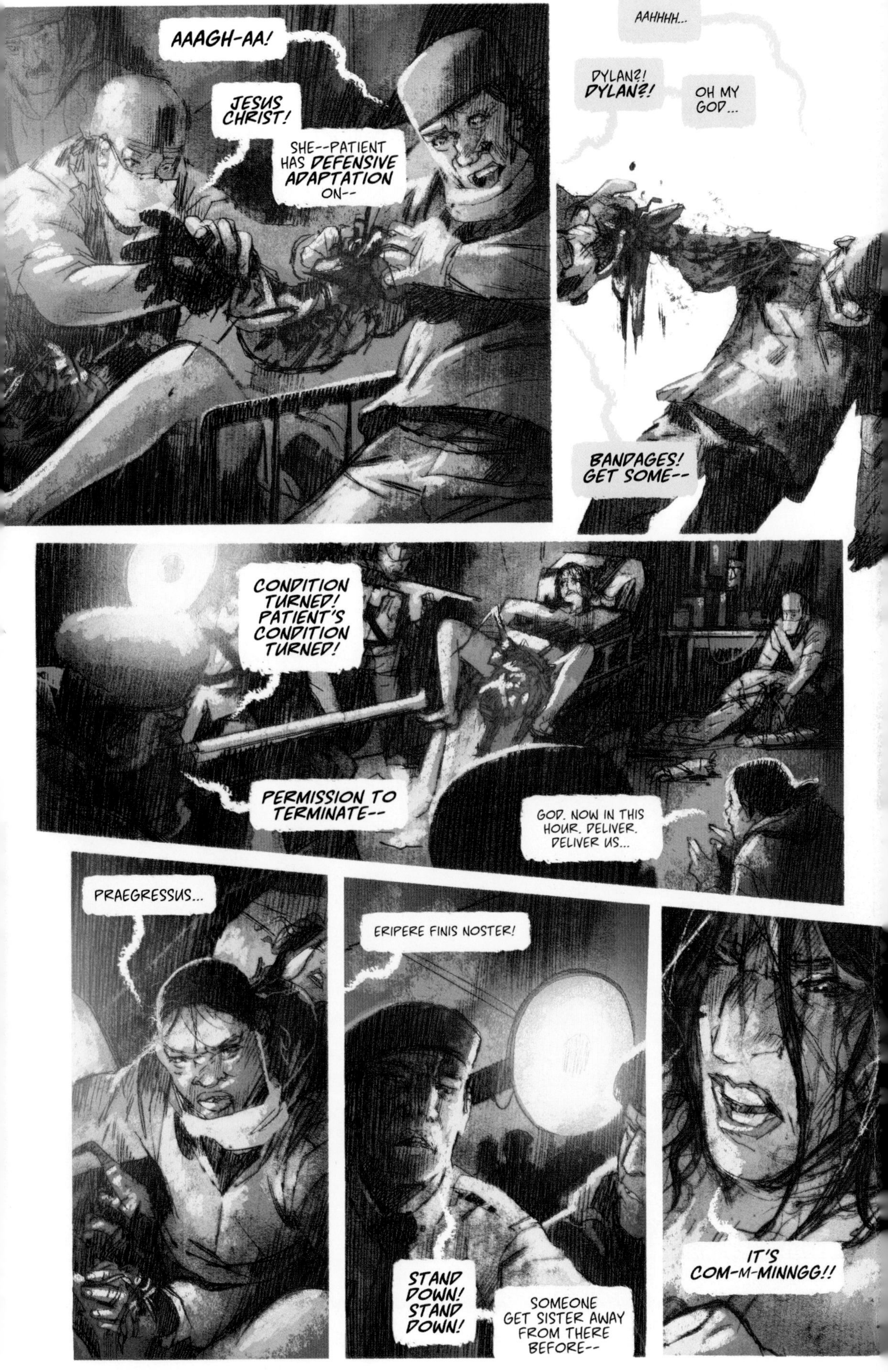
AAAGH-AA!
JESUS CHRIST!
SHE--PATIENT HAS DEFENSIVE ADAPTATION ON--
AAHHHH...
DYLAN?! DYLAN?!
OH MY GOD...
BANDAGES! GET SOME--
CONDITION TURNED! PATIENT'S CONDITION TURNED!
PERMISSION TO TERMINATE--
GOD. NOW IN THIS HOUR. DELIVER. DELIVER US...
PRAEGRESSUS...
ERIPERE FINIS NOSTER!
STAND DOWN! STAND DOWN!
SOMEONE GET SISTER AWAY FROM THERE BEFORE--
IT'S COM-M-MINNGG!!

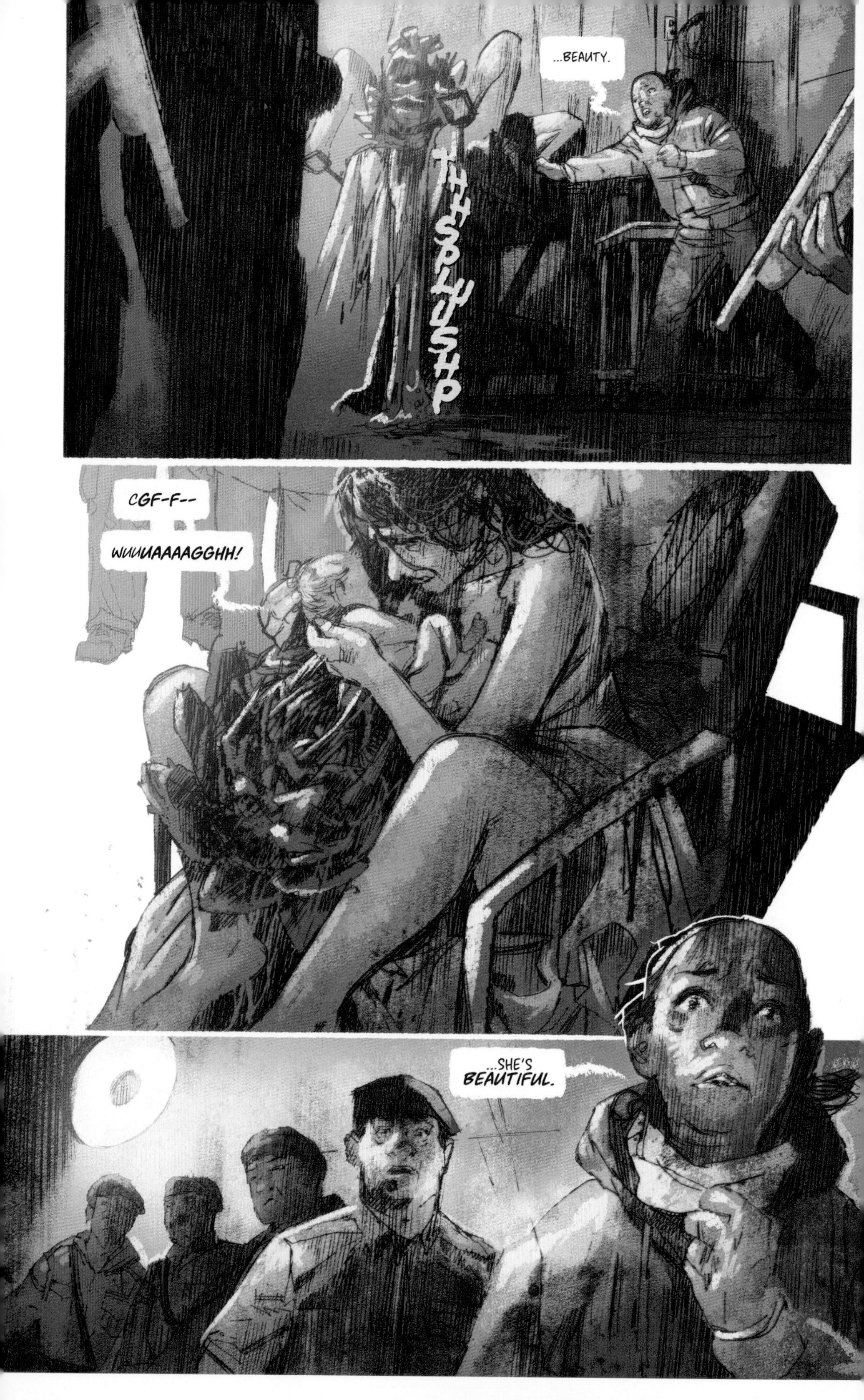
...BEAUTY.
THHSPLUSHP
CGF-F--
WUUUAAAAGGHH!
...SHE'S BEAUTIFUL.

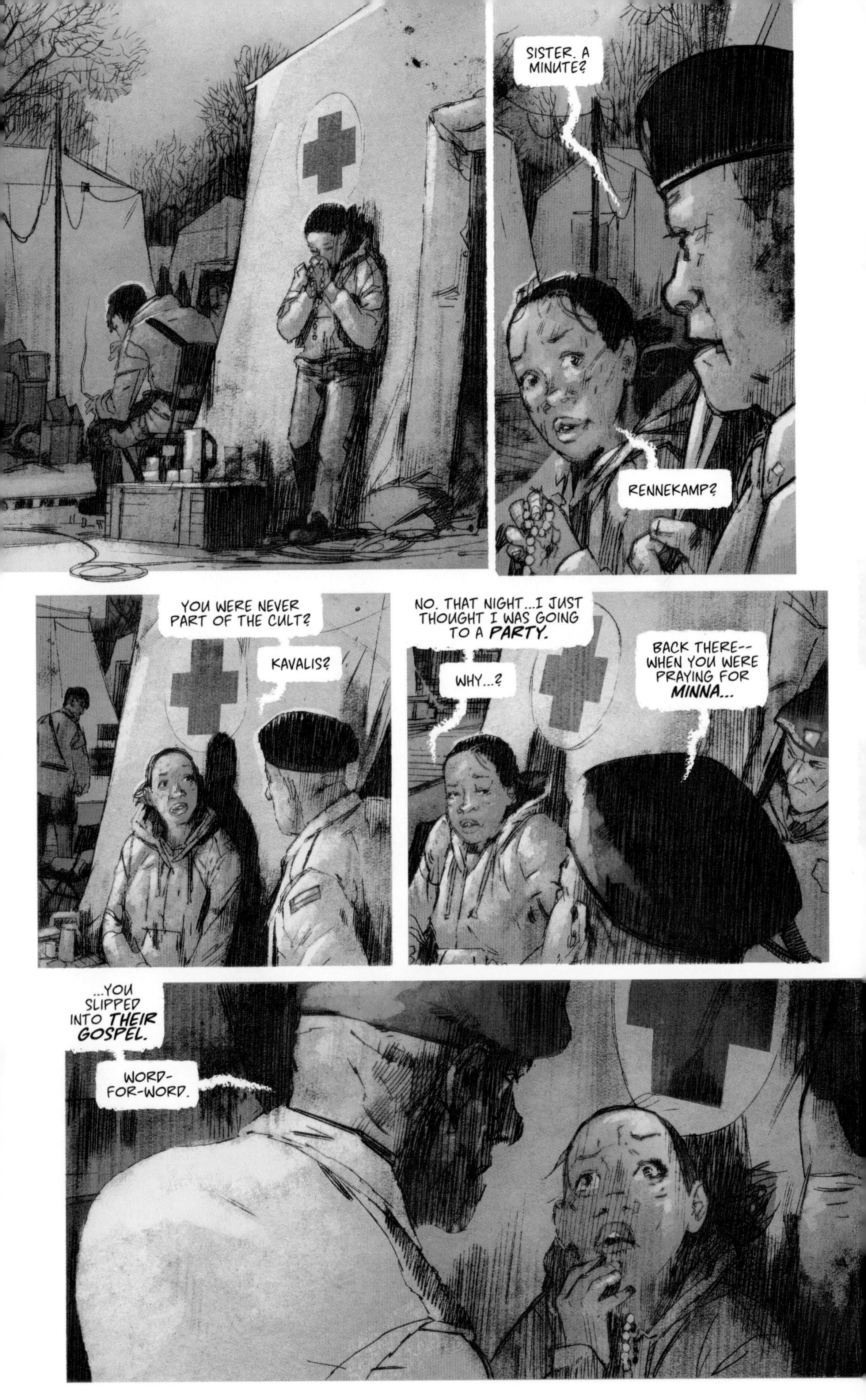
SISTER. A MINUTE?
RENNEKAMP?
YOU WERE NEVER PART OF THE CULT?
KAVALIS?
NO. THAT NIGHT...I JUST THOUGHT I WAS GOING TO A PARTY.
WHY...?
BACK THERE--WHEN YOU WERE PRAYING FOR MINNA...
...YOU SLIPPED INTO THEIR GOSPEL.
WORD-FOR-WORD.

We made a world where everyone is alone.

Full of locked doors and safe rooms, away from the horor.

But we're all locked in with the monsters.

The ones we create.

The ones we are.

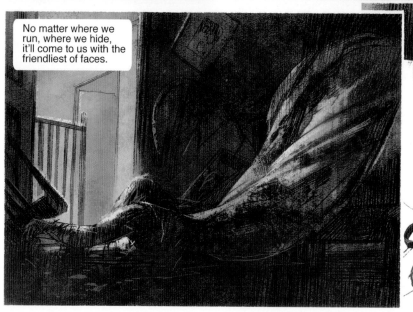

No matter where we run, where we hide, it'll come to us with the friendliest of faces.

A kind of love in its eyes. Because we belong to it now. And we always did.

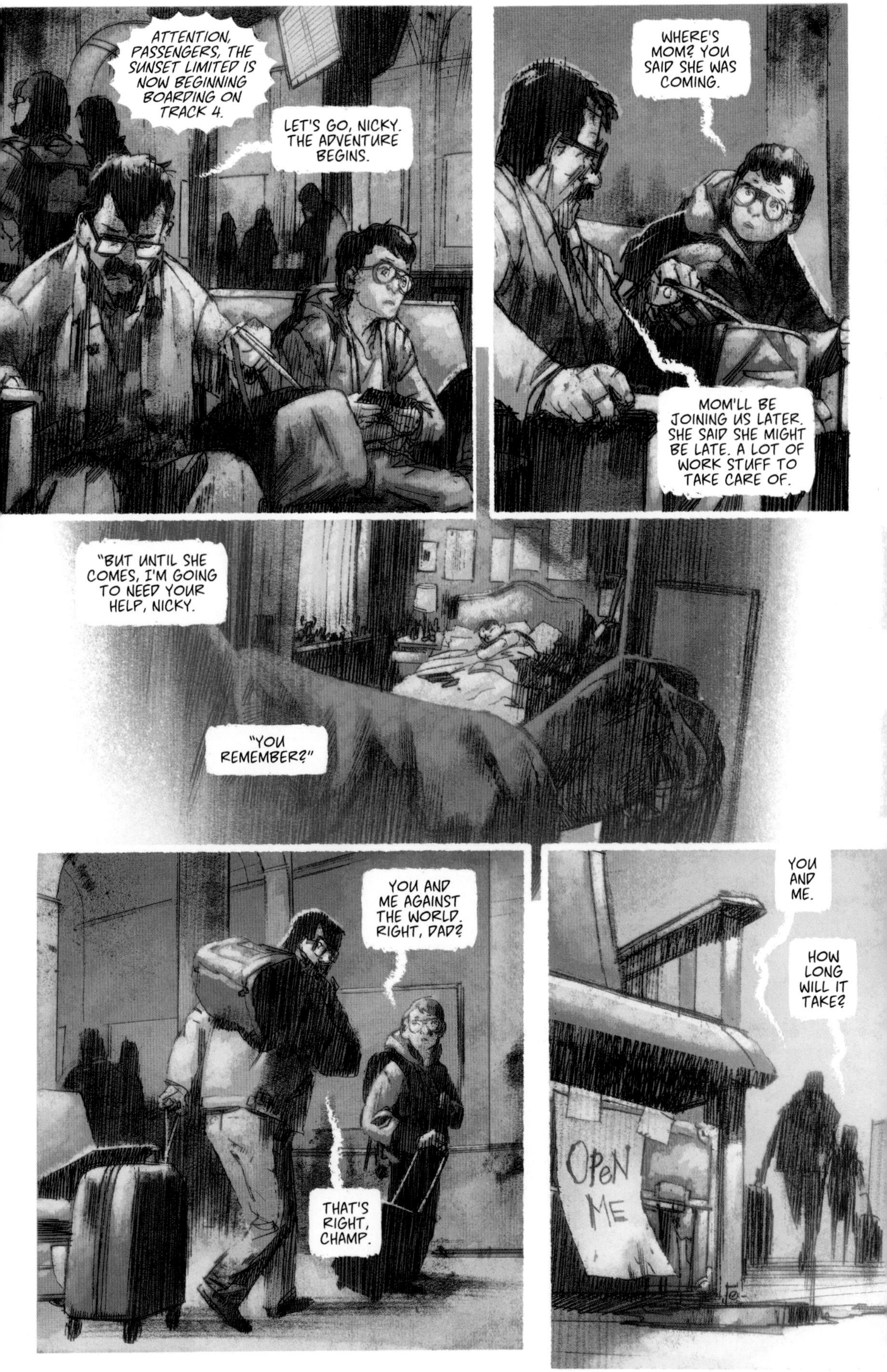
ATTENTION, PASSENGERS, THE SUNSET LIMITED IS NOW BEGINNING BOARDING ON TRACK 4.
LET'S GO, NICKY. THE ADVENTURE BEGINS.
WHERE'S MOM? YOU SAID SHE WAS COMING.
MOM'LL BE JOINING US LATER. SHE SAID SHE MIGHT BE LATE. A LOT OF WORK STUFF TO TAKE CARE OF.
"BUT UNTIL SHE COMES, I'M GOING TO NEED YOUR HELP, NICKY.
"YOU REMEMBER?"
YOU AND ME AGAINST THE WORLD. RIGHT, DAD?
THAT'S RIGHT, CHAMP.
YOU AND ME.
HOW LONG WILL IT TAKE?
OPEN ME

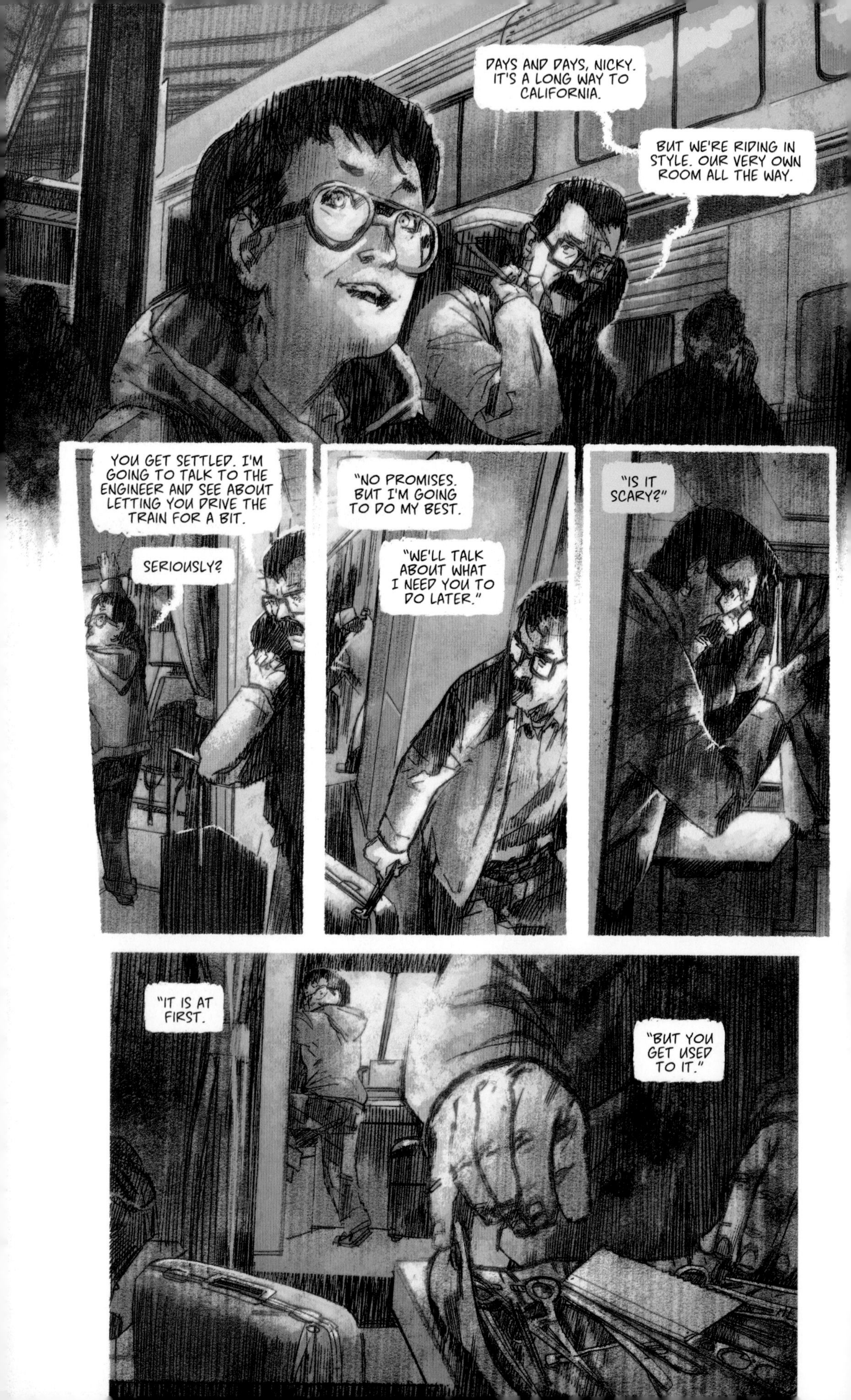
DAYS AND DAYS, NICKY. IT'S A LONG WAY TO CALIFORNIA.
BUT WE'RE RIDING IN STYLE. OUR VERY OWN ROOM ALL THE WAY.
YOU GET SETTLED. I'M GOING TO TALK TO THE ENGINEER AND SEE ABOUT LETTING YOU DRIVE THE TRAIN FOR A BIT.
SERIOUSLY?
"NO PROMISES. BUT I'M GOING TO DO MY BEST.
"WE'LL TALK ABOUT WHAT I NEED YOU TO DO LATER."
"IS IT SCARY?"
"IT IS AT FIRST.
"BUT YOU GET USED TO IT."

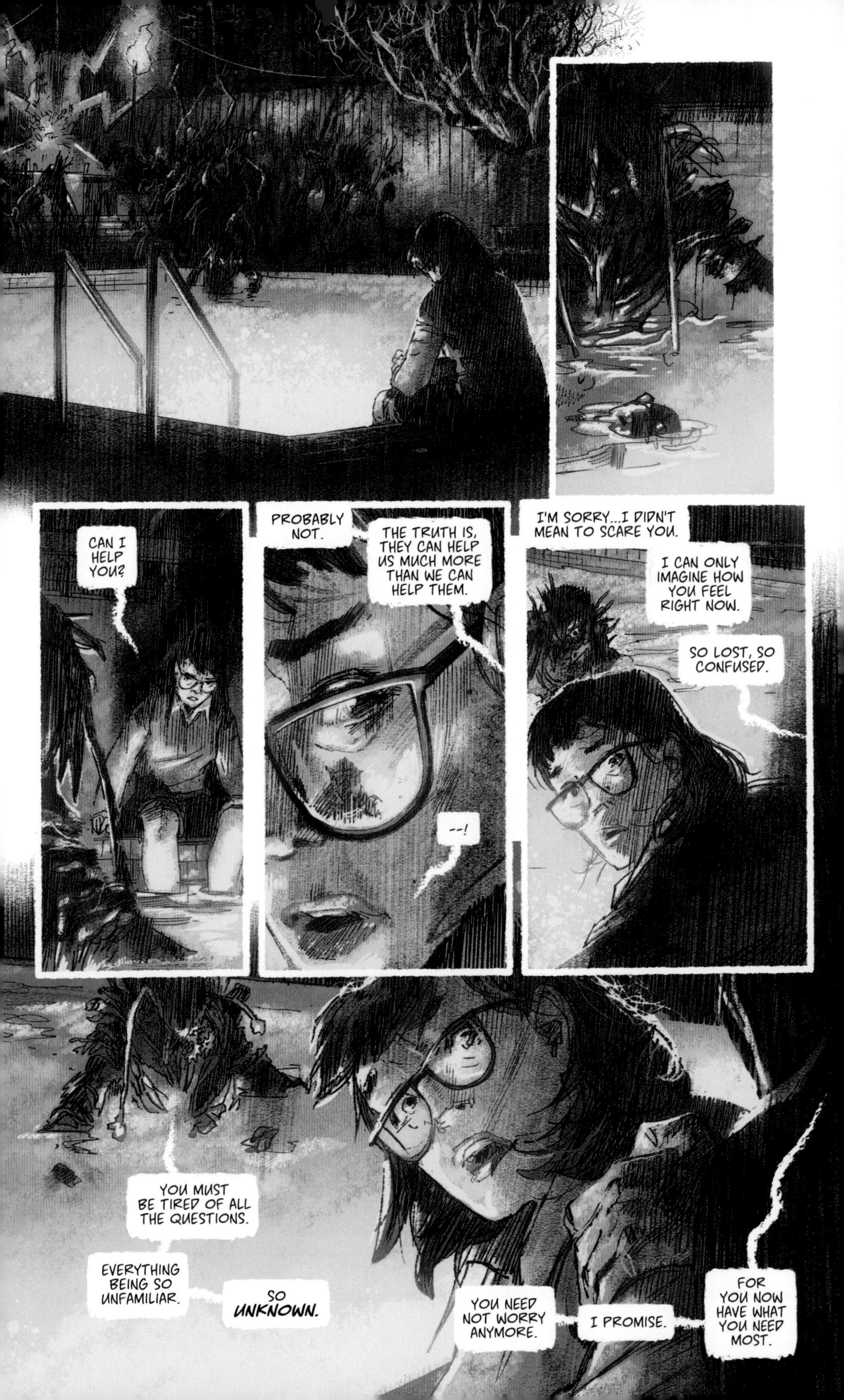

CAN I HELP YOU?
PROBABLY NOT.
THE TRUTH IS, THEY CAN HELP US MUCH MORE THAN WE CAN HELP THEM.
--!
I'M SORRY...I DIDN'T MEAN TO SCARE YOU.
I CAN ONLY IMAGINE HOW YOU FEEL RIGHT NOW.
SO LOST, SO CONFUSED.
YOU MUST BE TIRED OF ALL THE QUESTIONS.
EVERYTHING BEING SO UNFAMILIAR.
SO *UNKNOWN.*
YOU NEED NOT WORRY ANYMORE.
I PROMISE.
FOR YOU NOW HAVE WHAT YOU NEED MOST.

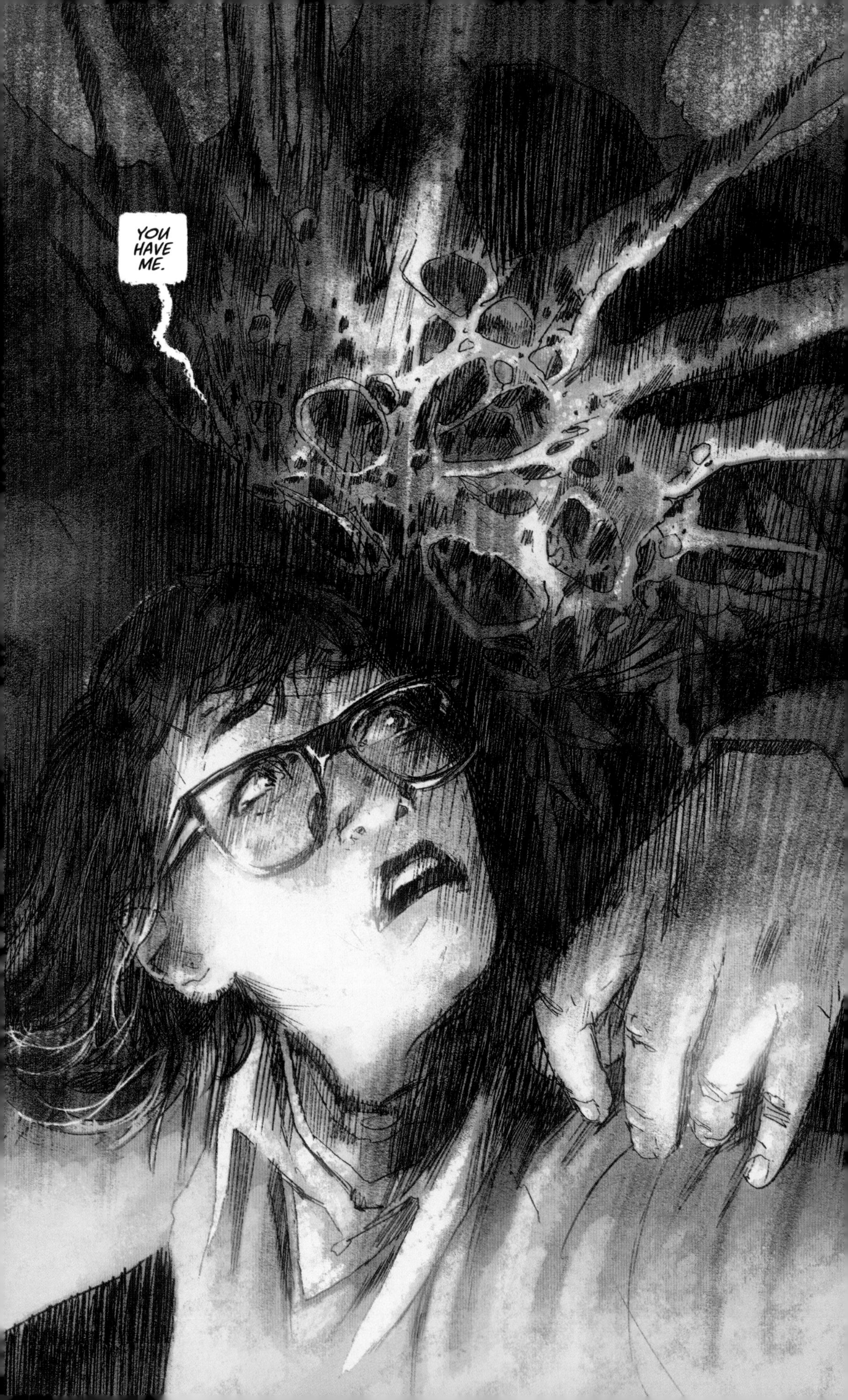
YOU HAVE ME.

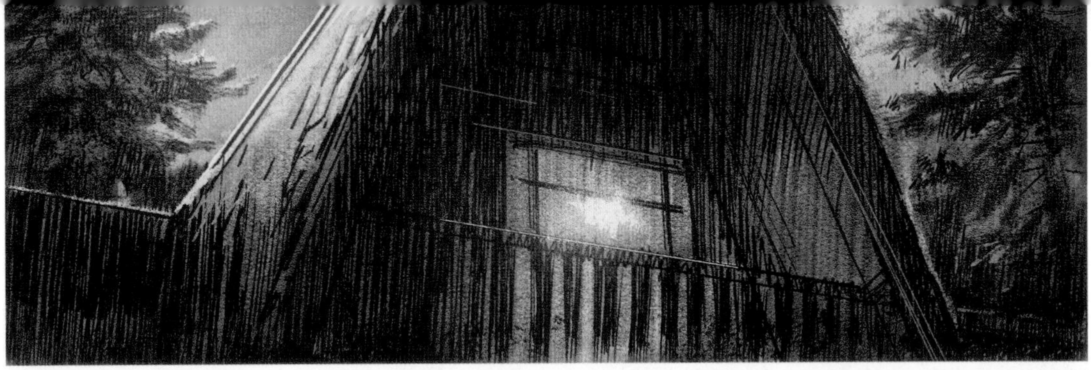

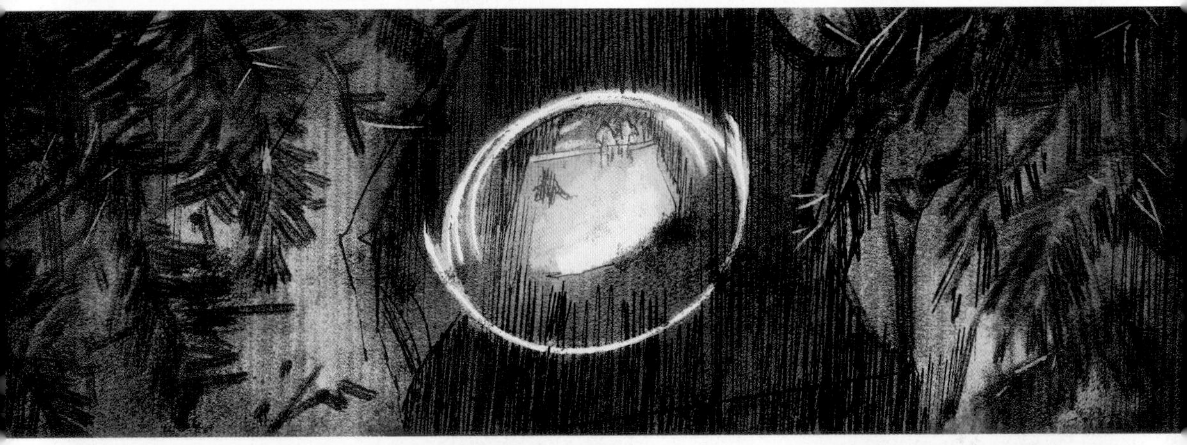

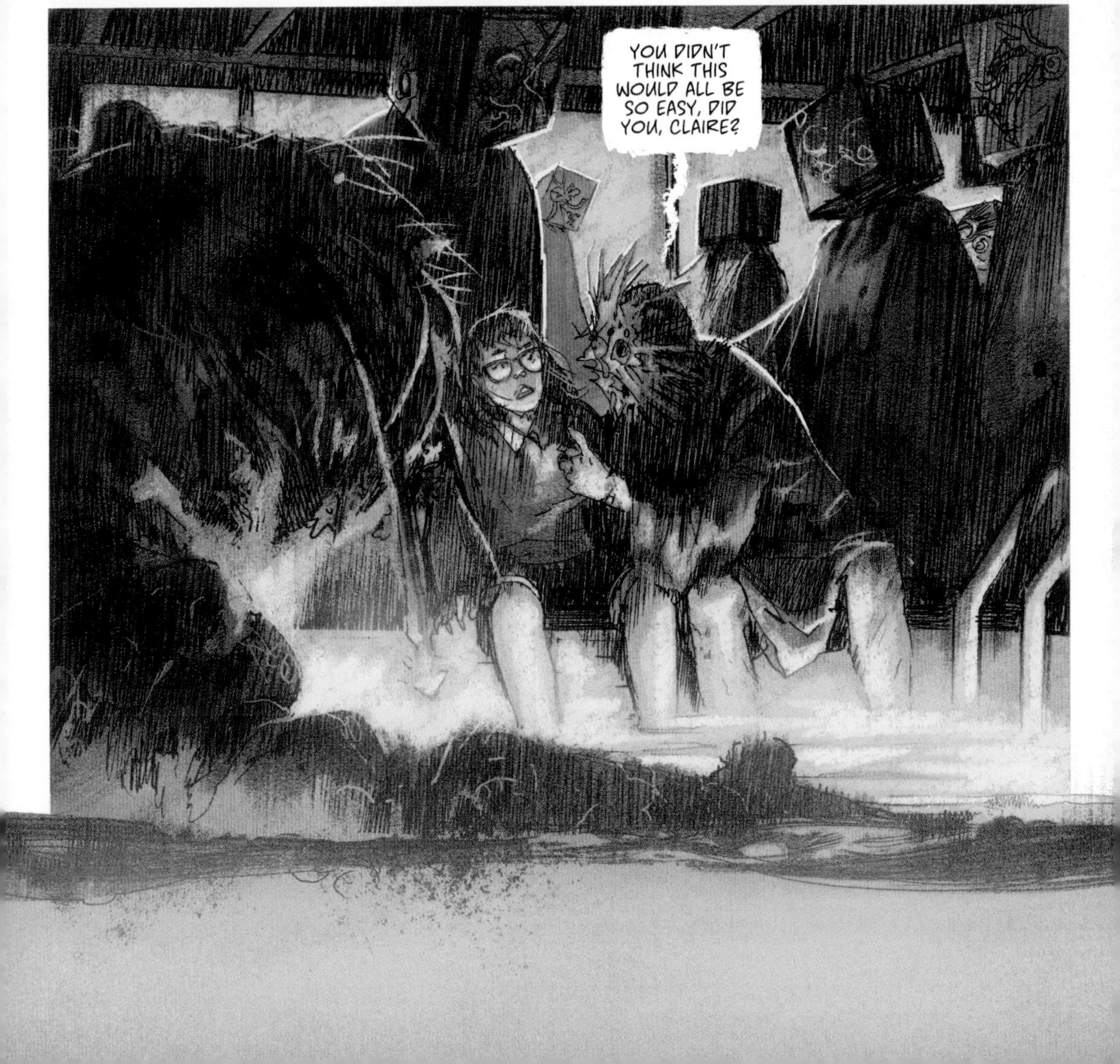
YOU DIDN'T THINK THIS WOULD ALL BE SO EASY, DID YOU, CLAIRE?

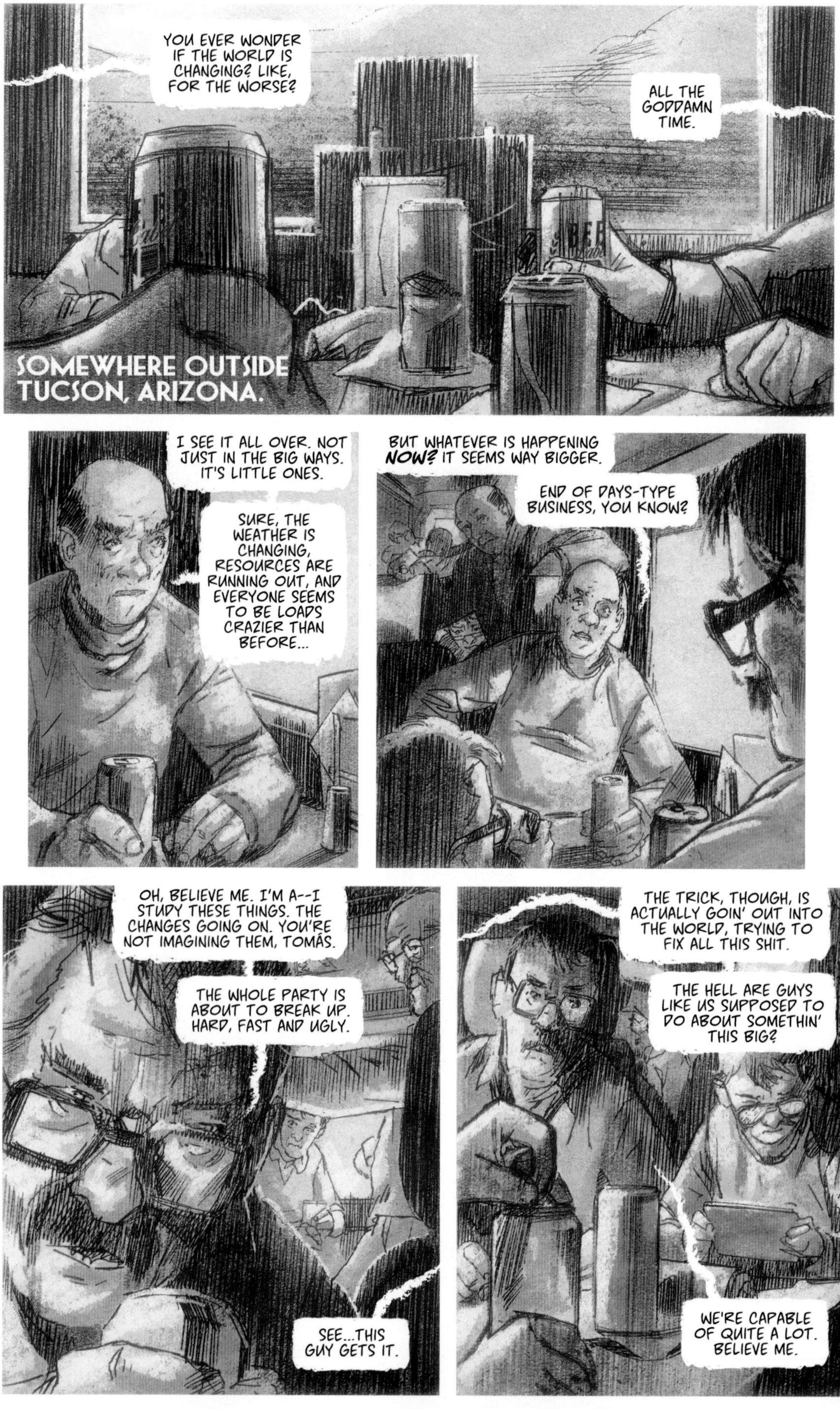
YOU EVER WONDER IF THE WORLD IS CHANGING? LIKE, FOR THE WORSE?
ALL THE GODDAMN TIME.
SOMEWHERE OUTSIDE TUCSON, ARIZONA.
I SEE IT ALL OVER. NOT JUST IN THE BIG WAYS. IT'S LITTLE ONES.
SURE, THE WEATHER IS CHANGING, RESOURCES ARE RUNNING OUT, AND EVERYONE SEEMS TO BE LOADS CRAZIER THAN BEFORE...
BUT WHATEVER IS HAPPENING NOW? IT SEEMS WAY BIGGER.
END OF DAYS-TYPE BUSINESS, YOU KNOW?
OH, BELIEVE ME. I'M A--I STUDY THESE THINGS. THE CHANGES GOING ON. YOU'RE NOT IMAGINING THEM, TOMÁS.
THE WHOLE PARTY IS ABOUT TO BREAK UP. HARD, FAST AND UGLY.
SEE...THIS GUY GETS IT.
THE TRICK, THOUGH, IS ACTUALLY GOIN' OUT INTO THE WORLD, TRYING TO FIX ALL THIS SHIT.
THE HELL ARE GUYS LIKE US SUPPOSED TO DO ABOUT SOMETHIN' THIS BIG?
WE'RE CAPABLE OF QUITE A LOT. BELIEVE ME.

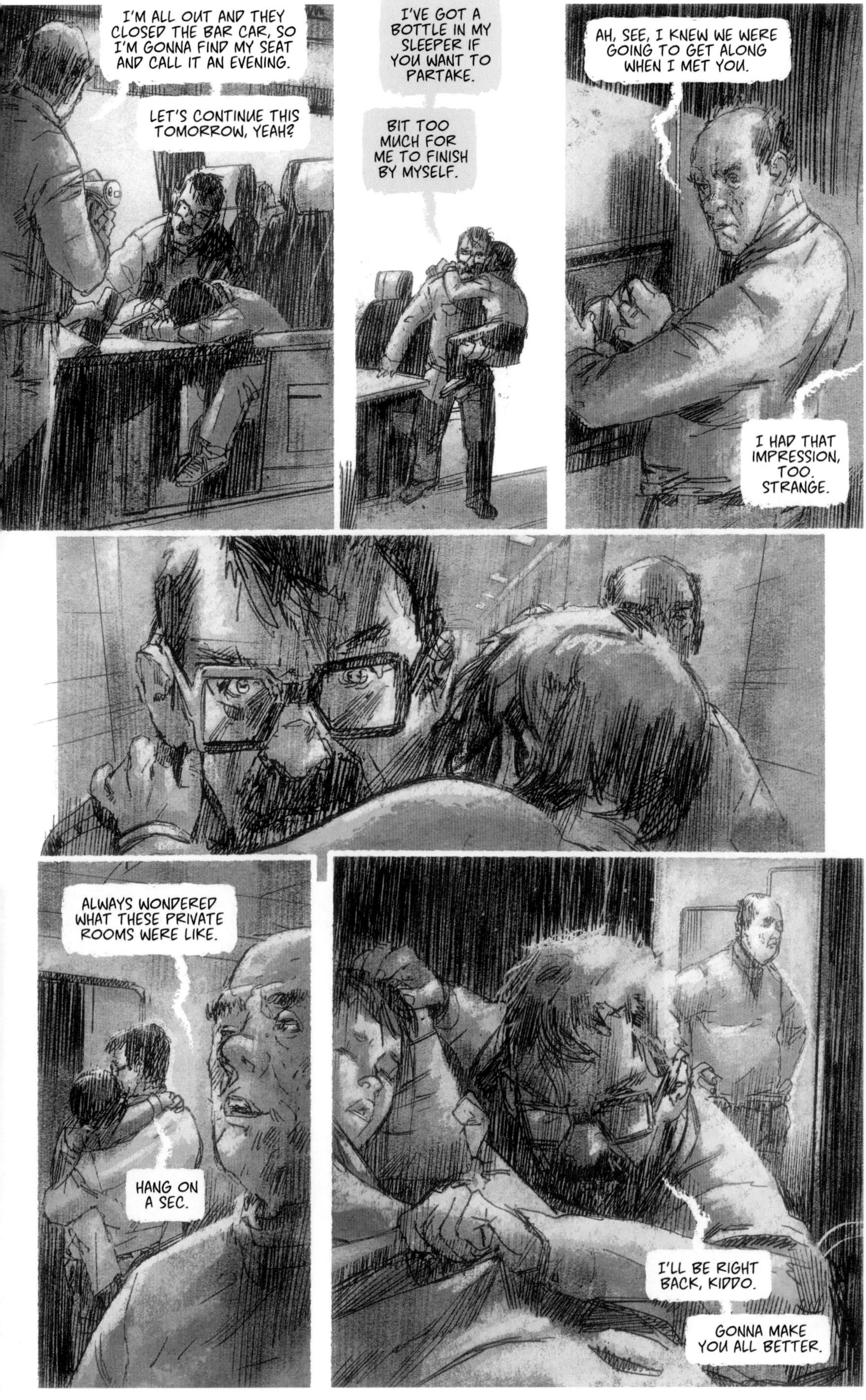
I'M ALL OUT AND THEY CLOSED THE BAR CAR, SO I'M GONNA FIND MY SEAT AND CALL IT AN EVENING.
LET'S CONTINUE THIS TOMORROW, YEAH?
I'VE GOT A BOTTLE IN MY SLEEPER IF YOU WANT TO PARTAKE.
BIT TOO MUCH FOR ME TO FINISH BY MYSELF.
AH, SEE, I KNEW WE WERE GOING TO GET ALONG WHEN I MET YOU.
I HAD THAT IMPRESSION, TOO. STRANGE.
ALWAYS WONDERED WHAT THESE PRIVATE ROOMS WERE LIKE.
HANG ON A SEC.
I'LL BE RIGHT BACK, KIDDO.
GONNA MAKE YOU ALL BETTER.

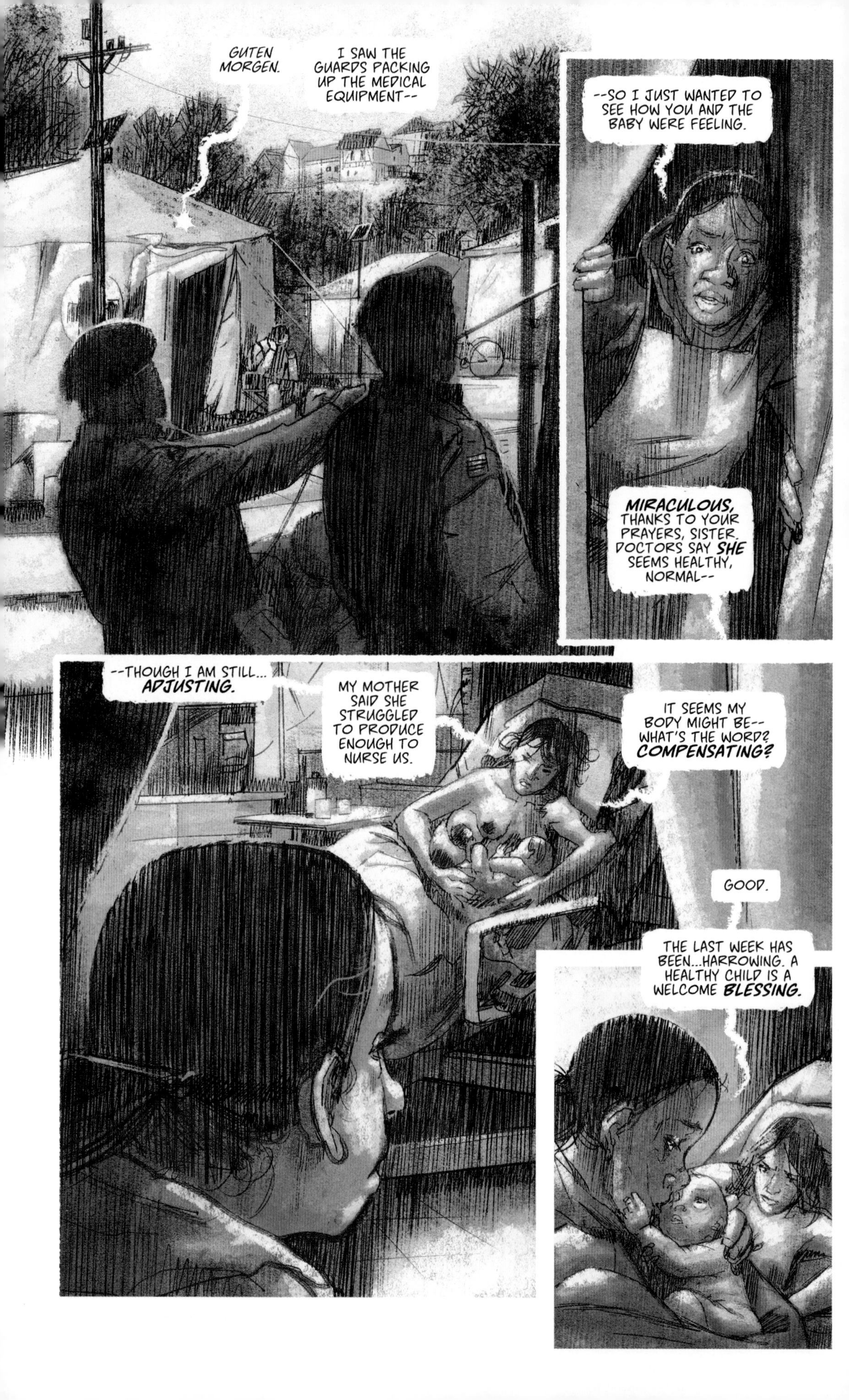
GUTEN MORGEN.
I SAW THE GUARDS PACKING UP THE MEDICAL EQUIPMENT--
--SO I JUST WANTED TO SEE HOW YOU AND THE BABY WERE FEELING.
MIRACULOUS, THANKS TO YOUR PRAYERS, SISTER. DOCTORS SAY SHE SEEMS HEALTHY, NORMAL--
--THOUGH I AM STILL... ADJUSTING.
MY MOTHER SAID SHE STRUGGLED TO PRODUCE ENOUGH TO NURSE US.
IT SEEMS MY BODY MIGHT BE-- WHAT'S THE WORD? COMPENSATING?
GOOD.
THE LAST WEEK HAS BEEN...HARROWING. A HEALTHY CHILD IS A WELCOME BLESSING.

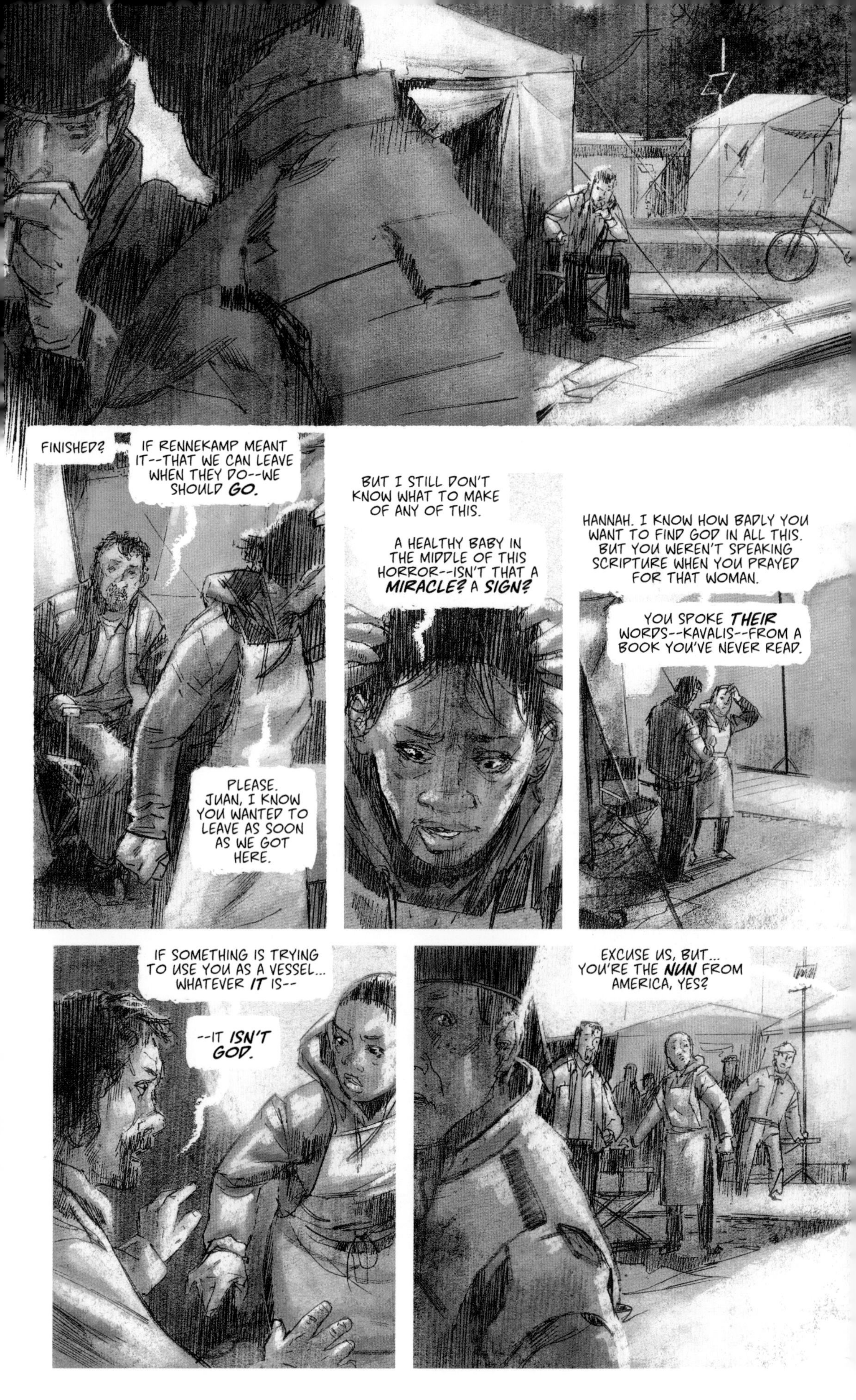
FINISHED?
IF RENNEKAMP MEANT IT--THAT WE CAN LEAVE WHEN THEY DO--WE SHOULD GO.
PLEASE. JUAN, I KNOW YOU WANTED TO LEAVE AS SOON AS WE GOT HERE.
BUT I STILL DON'T KNOW WHAT TO MAKE OF ANY OF THIS.
A HEALTHY BABY IN THE MIDDLE OF THIS HORROR--ISN'T THAT A MIRACLE? A SIGN?
HANNAH. I KNOW HOW BADLY YOU WANT TO FIND GOD IN ALL THIS. BUT YOU WEREN'T SPEAKING SCRIPTURE WHEN YOU PRAYED FOR THAT WOMAN.
YOU SPOKE THEIR WORDS--KAVALIS--FROM A BOOK YOU'VE NEVER READ.
IF SOMETHING IS TRYING TO USE YOU AS A VESSEL... WHATEVER IT IS--
--IT ISN'T GOD.
EXCUSE US, BUT... YOU'RE THE NUN FROM AMERICA, YES?

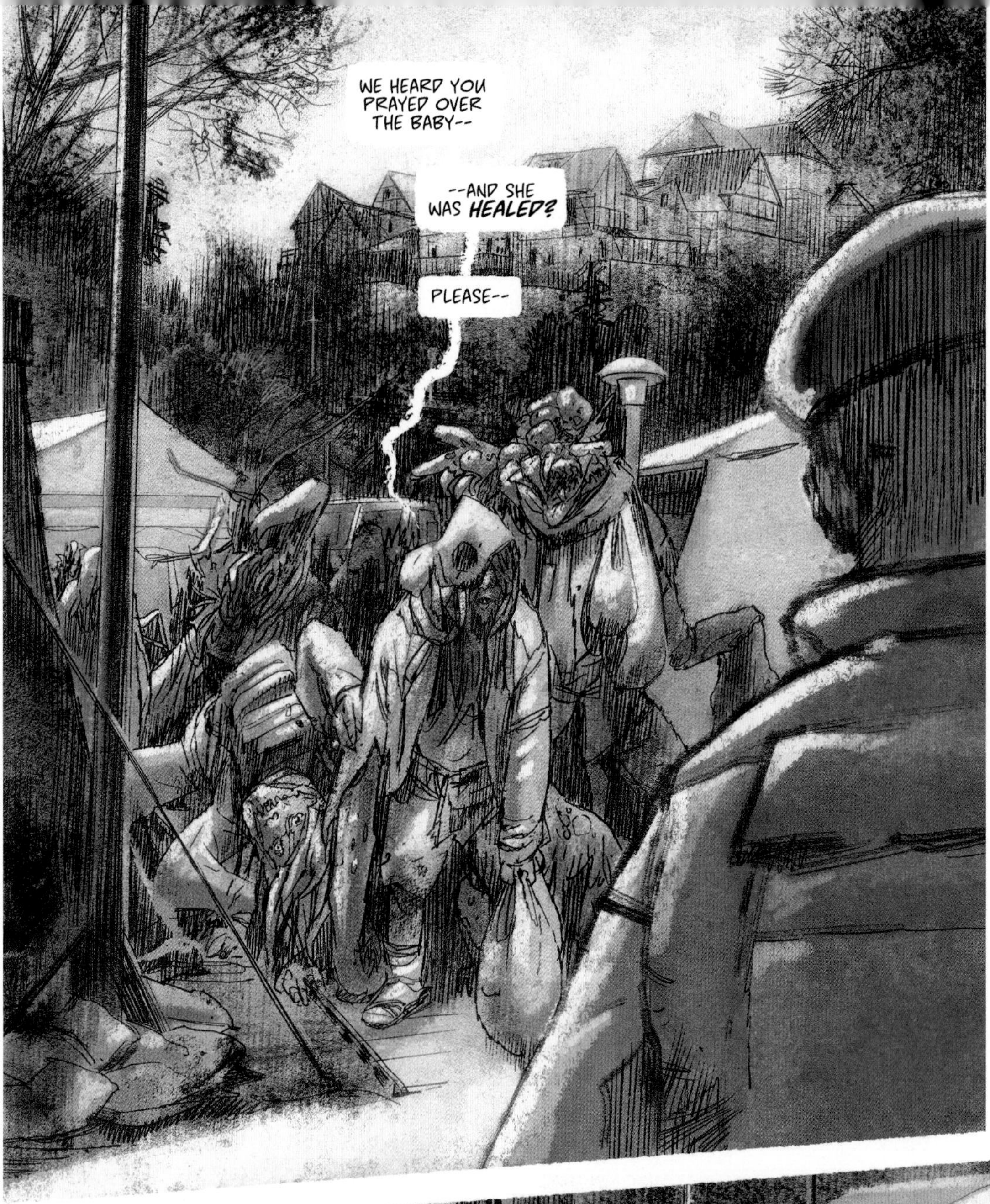
WE HEARD YOU PRAYED OVER THE BABY--
--AND SHE WAS HEALED?
PLEASE--
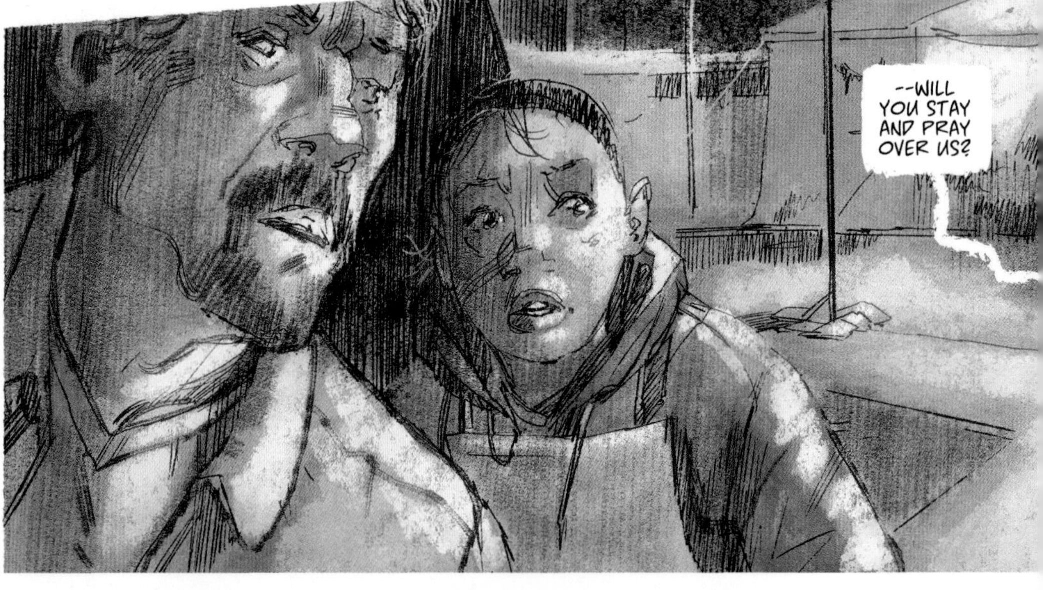
--WILL YOU STAY AND PRAY OVER US?

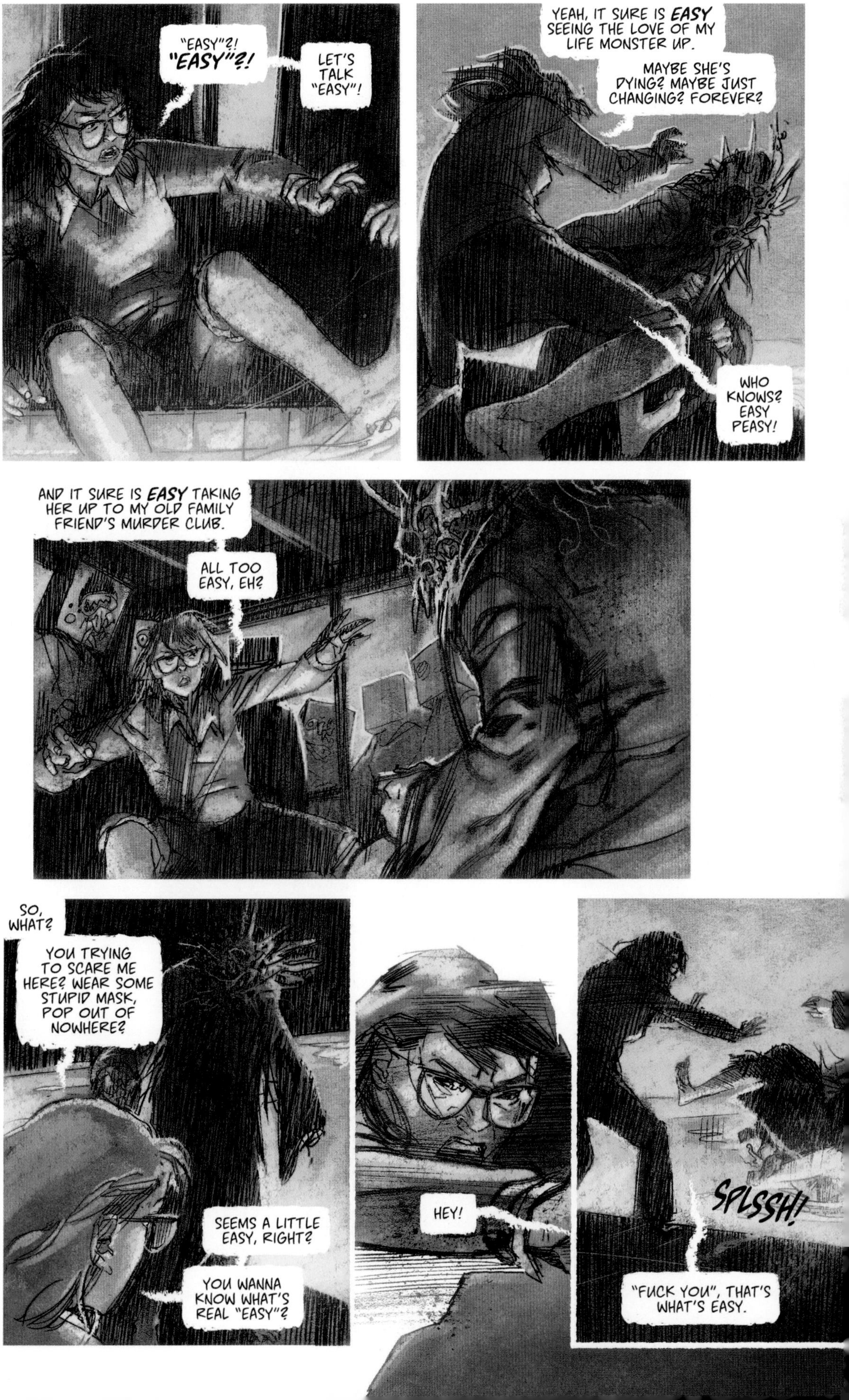
"EASY"?! "EASY"?!
LET'S TALK "EASY"!
YEAH, IT SURE IS EASY SEEING THE LOVE OF MY LIFE MONSTER UP.
MAYBE SHE'S DYING? MAYBE JUST CHANGING? FOREVER?
WHO KNOWS? EASY PEASY!
AND IT SURE IS EASY TAKING HER UP TO MY OLD FAMILY FRIEND'S MURDER CLUB.
ALL TOO EASY, EH?
SO, WHAT?
YOU TRYING TO SCARE ME HERE? WEAR SOME STUPID MASK, POP OUT OF NOWHERE?
SEEMS A LITTLE EASY, RIGHT?
YOU WANNA KNOW WHAT'S REAL "EASY"?
HEY!
SPLSSH!
"FUCK YOU", THAT'S WHAT'S EASY.

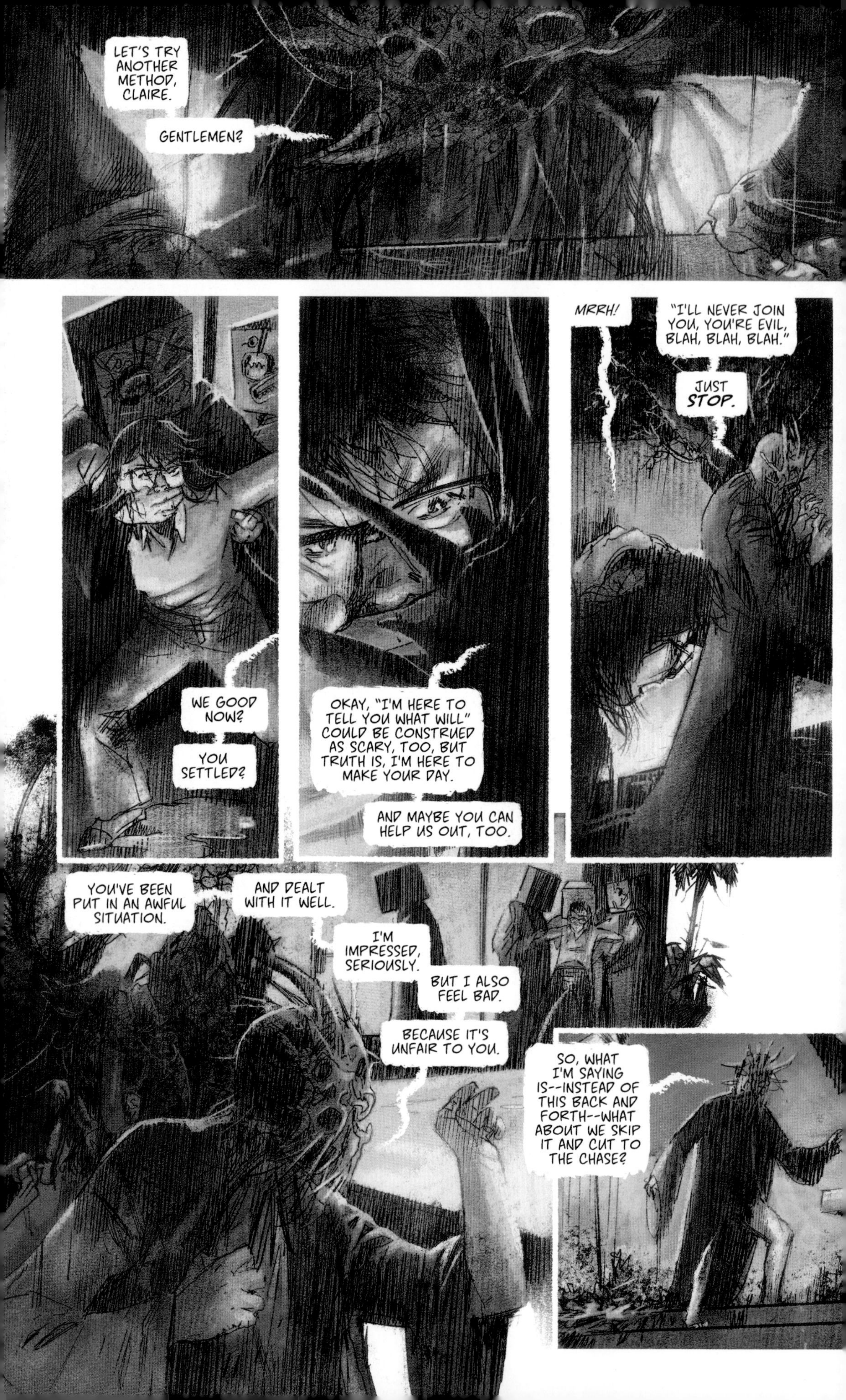
LET'S TRY ANOTHER METHOD, CLAIRE.
GENTLEMEN?
WE GOOD NOW?
YOU SETTLED?
OKAY, "I'M HERE TO TELL YOU WHAT WILL" COULD BE CONSTRUED AS SCARY, TOO, BUT TRUTH IS, I'M HERE TO MAKE YOUR DAY.
AND MAYBE YOU CAN HELP US OUT, TOO.
MRRH!
"I'LL NEVER JOIN YOU, YOU'RE EVIL, BLAH, BLAH, BLAH."
JUST STOP.
YOU'VE BEEN PUT IN AN AWFUL SITUATION.
AND DEALT WITH IT WELL.
I'M IMPRESSED, SERIOUSLY.
BUT I ALSO FEEL BAD.
BECAUSE IT'S UNFAIR TO YOU.
SO, WHAT I'M SAYING IS--INSTEAD OF THIS BACK AND FORTH--WHAT ABOUT WE SKIP IT AND CUT TO THE CHASE?

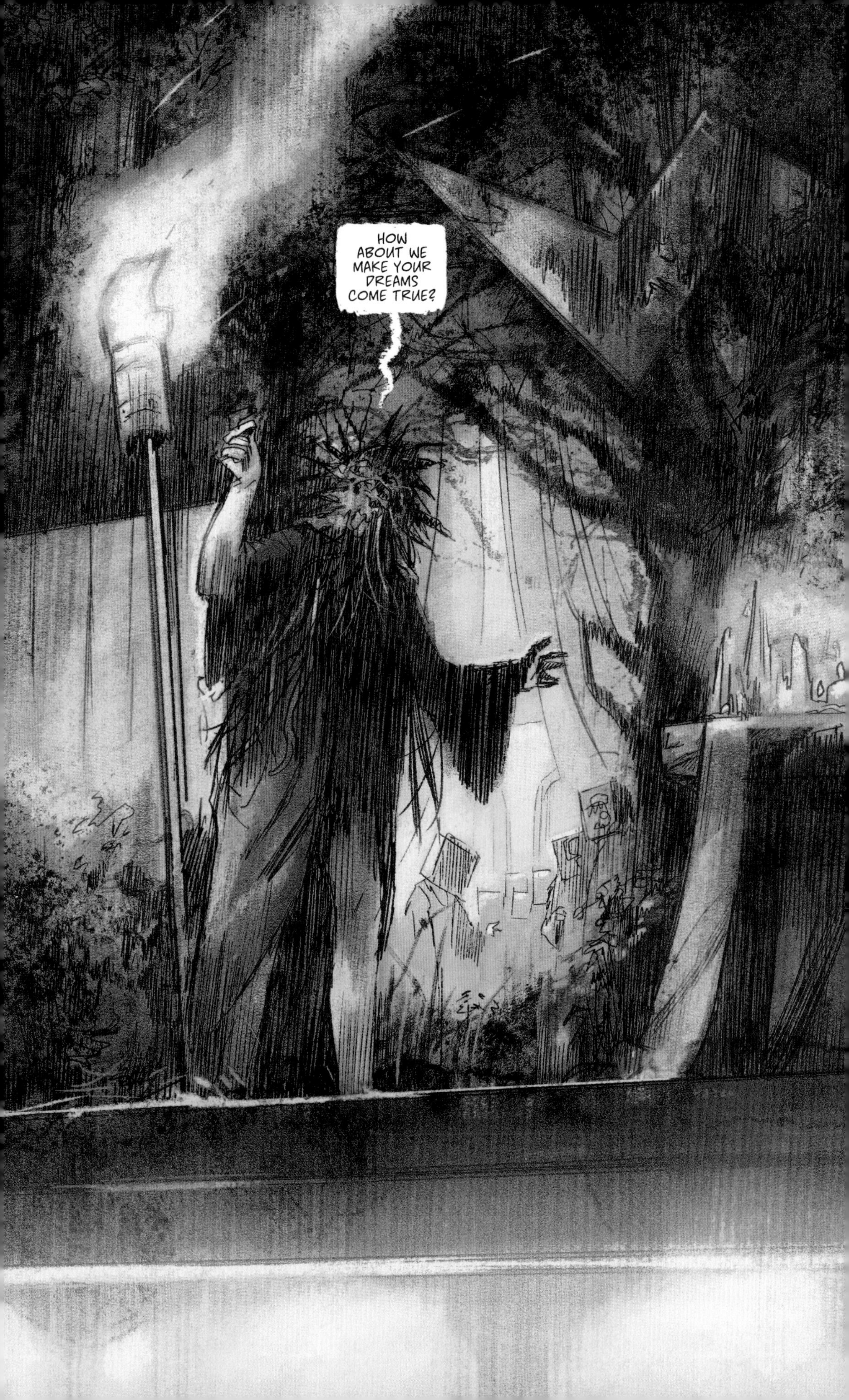
HOW ABOUT WE MAKE YOUR DREAMS COME TRUE?

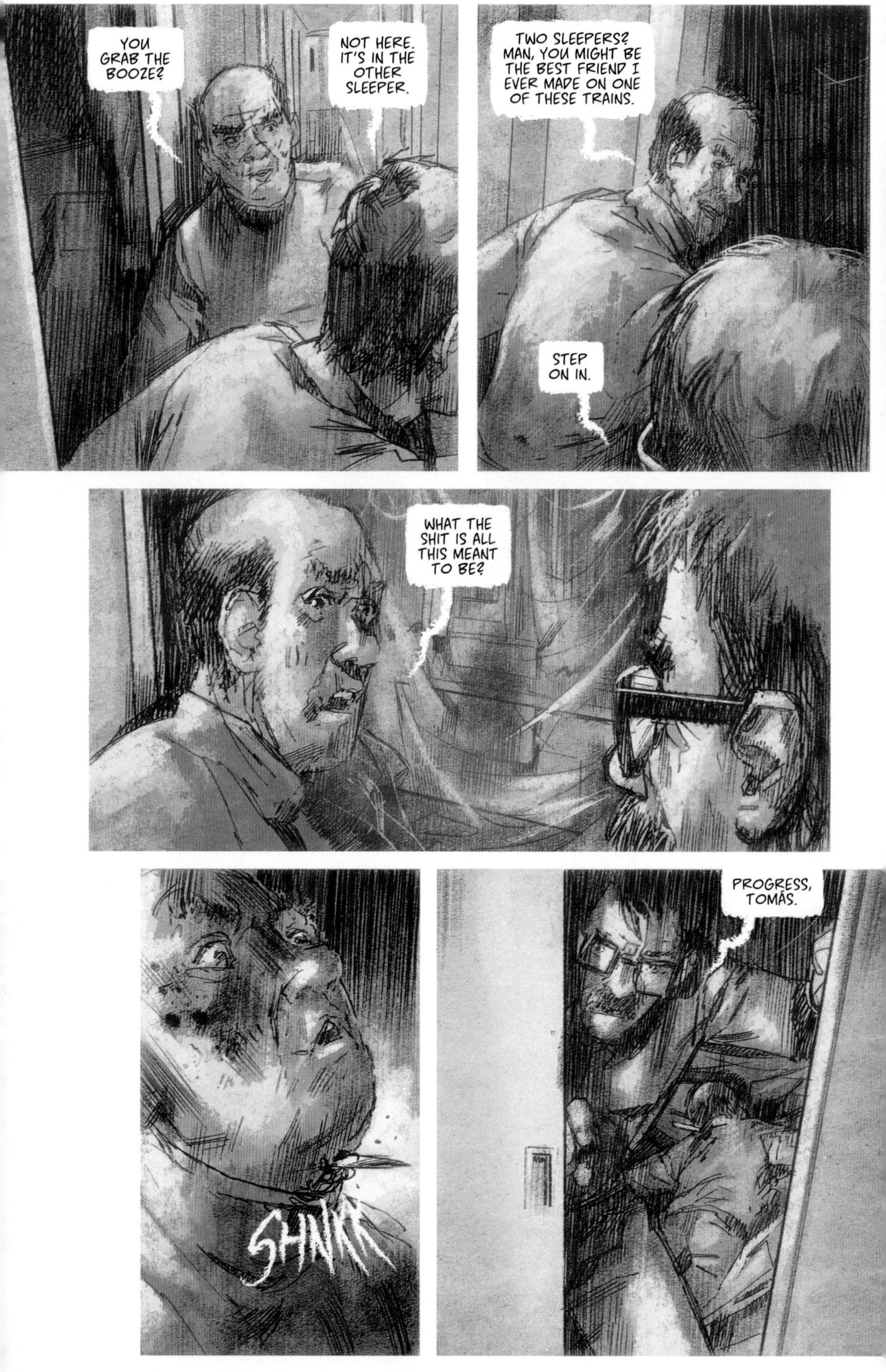
YOU GRAB THE BOOZE?
NOT HERE. IT'S IN THE OTHER SLEEPER.
TWO SLEEPERS? MAN, YOU MIGHT BE THE BEST FRIEND I EVER MADE ON ONE OF THESE TRAINS.
STEP ON IN.
WHAT THE SHIT IS ALL THIS MEANT TO BE?
SHNKK
PROGRESS, TOMÁS.

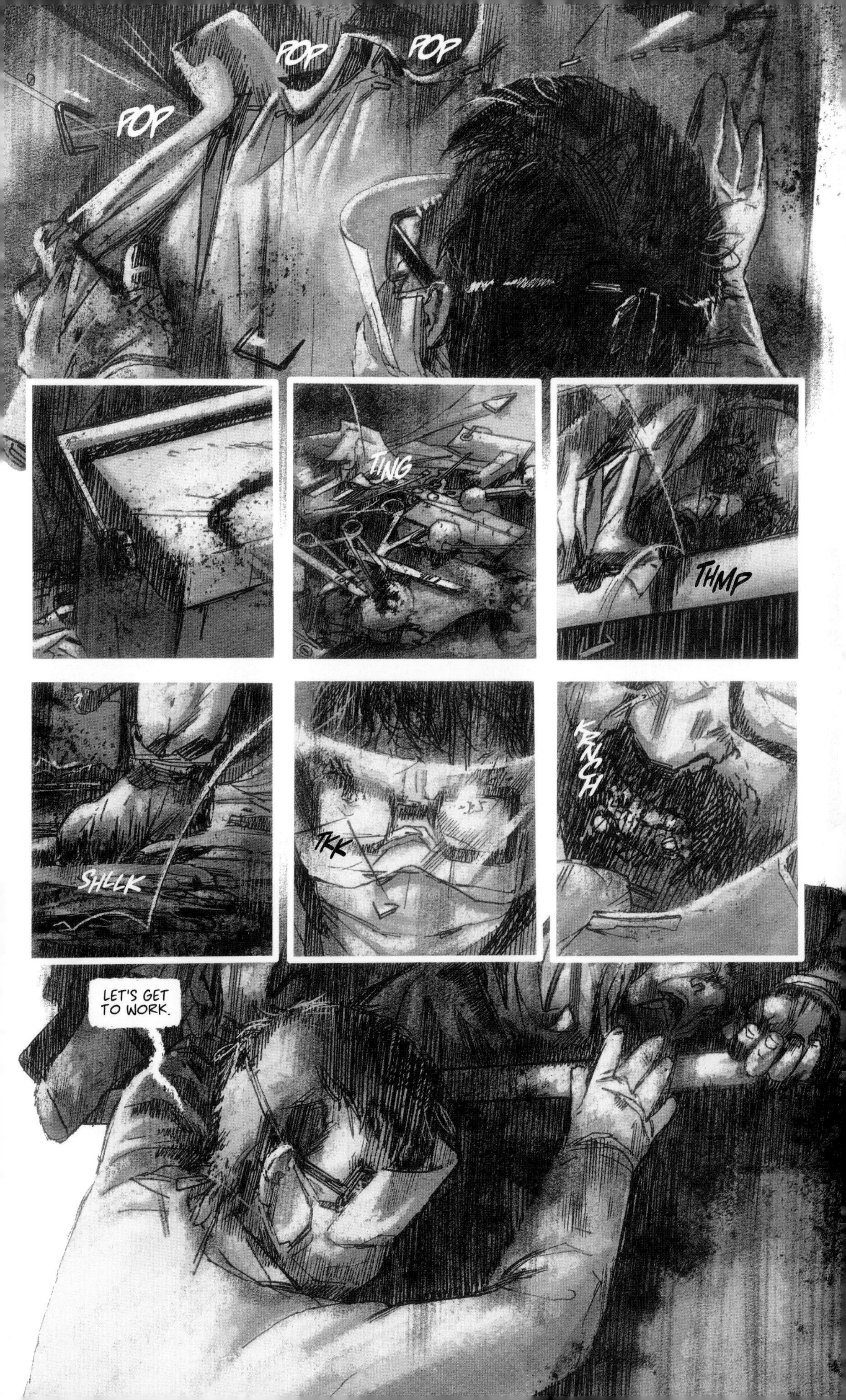
POP
POP
POP
TING
THMP
SHLK
TKK
KRNCH
LET'S GET TO WORK.

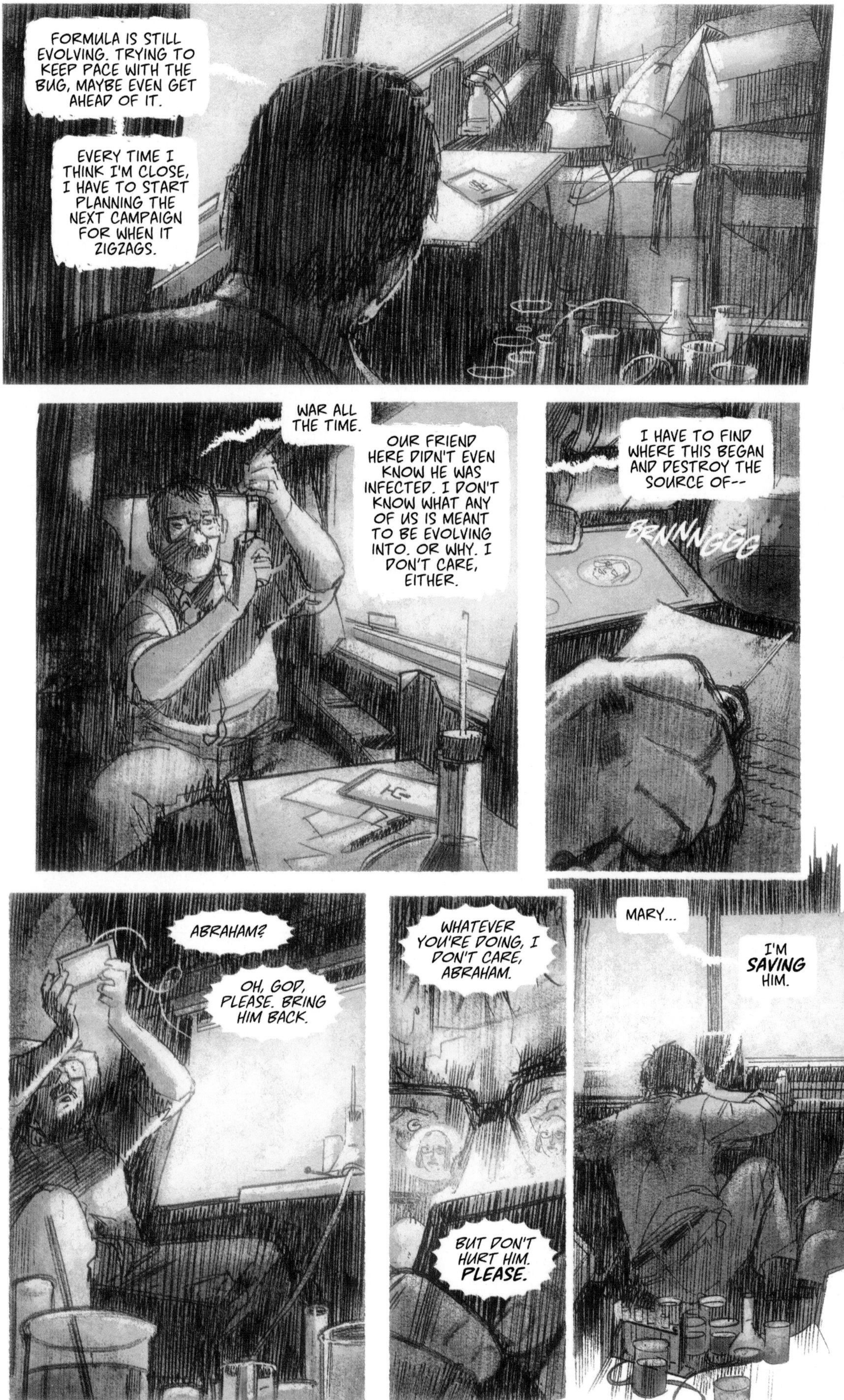
FORMULA IS STILL EVOLVING. TRYING TO KEEP PACE WITH THE BUG, MAYBE EVEN GET AHEAD OF IT.
EVERY TIME I THINK I'M CLOSE, I HAVE TO START PLANNING THE NEXT CAMPAIGN FOR WHEN IT ZIGZAGS.
WAR ALL THE TIME.
OUR FRIEND HERE DIDN'T EVEN KNOW HE WAS INFECTED. I DON'T KNOW WHAT ANY OF US IS MEANT TO BE EVOLVING INTO. OR WHY. I DON'T CARE, EITHER.
I HAVE TO FIND WHERE THIS BEGAN AND DESTROY THE SOURCE OF--
BRNNNGGG
ABRAHAM?
OH, GOD, PLEASE. BRING HIM BACK.
WHATEVER YOU'RE DOING, I DON'T CARE, ABRAHAM.
BUT DON'T HURT HIM. PLEASE.
MARY...
I'M SAVING HIM.

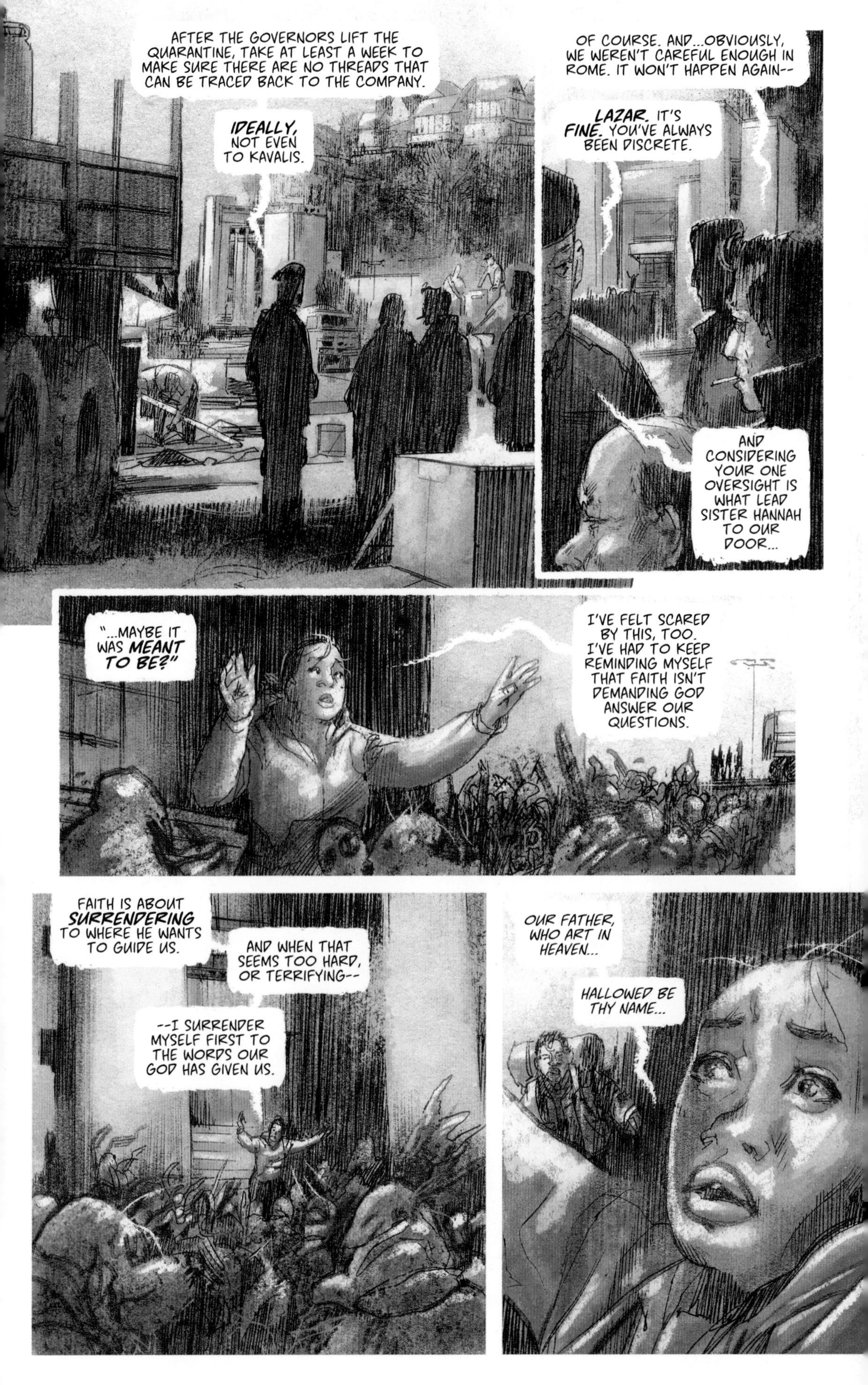
AFTER THE GOVERNORS LIFT THE QUARANTINE, TAKE AT LEAST A WEEK TO MAKE SURE THERE ARE NO THREADS THAT CAN BE TRACED BACK TO THE COMPANY.
IDEALLY, NOT EVEN TO KAVALIS.
OF COURSE. AND...OBVIOUSLY, WE WEREN'T CAREFUL ENOUGH IN ROME. IT WON'T HAPPEN AGAIN--
LAZAR. IT'S FINE. YOU'VE ALWAYS BEEN DISCRETE.
AND CONSIDERING YOUR ONE OVERSIGHT IS WHAT LEAD SISTER HANNAH TO OUR DOOR...
"...MAYBE IT WAS MEANT TO BE?"
I'VE FELT SCARED BY THIS, TOO. I'VE HAD TO KEEP REMINDING MYSELF THAT FAITH ISN'T DEMANDING GOD ANSWER OUR QUESTIONS.
FAITH IS ABOUT SURRENDERING TO WHERE HE WANTS TO GUIDE US.
AND WHEN THAT SEEMS TOO HARD, OR TERRIFYING--
--I SURRENDER MYSELF FIRST TO THE WORDS OUR GOD HAS GIVEN US.
OUR FATHER, WHO ART IN HEAVEN...
HALLOWED BE THY NAME...

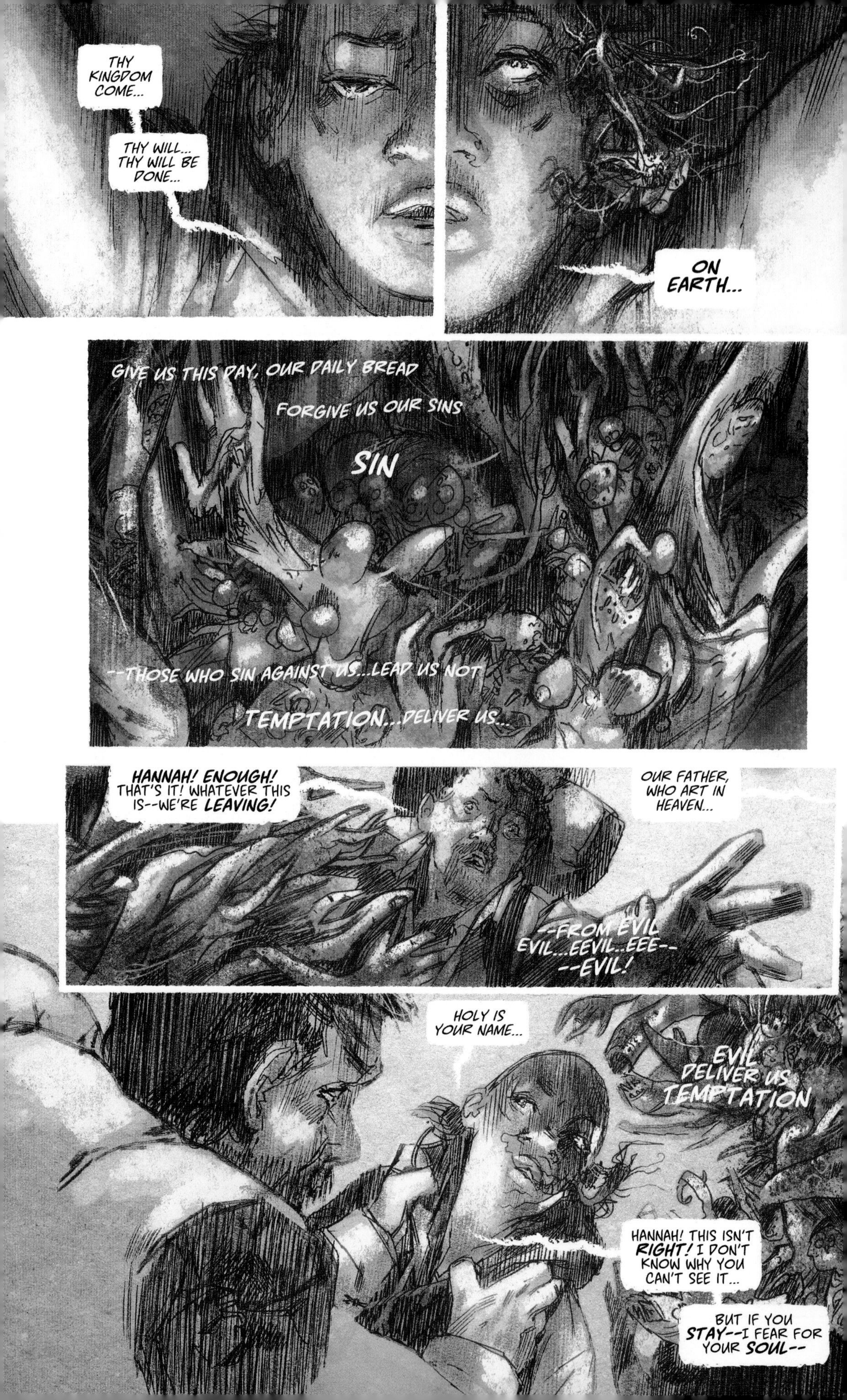
THY KINGDOM COME...
THY WILL... THY WILL BE DONE...
ON EARTH...
GIVE US THIS DAY, OUR DAILY BREAD
FORGIVE US OUR SINS
SIN
--THOSE WHO SIN AGAINST US...LEAD US NOT
TEMPTATION...DELIVER US...
HANNAH! ENOUGH! THAT'S IT! WHATEVER THIS IS--WE'RE LEAVING!
OUR FATHER, WHO ART IN HEAVEN...
--FROM EVIL
EVIL...EEVIL..EEE--
--EVIL!
HOLY IS YOUR NAME...
EVIL
DELIVER US
TEMPTATION
HANNAH! THIS ISN'T RIGHT! I DON'T KNOW WHY YOU CAN'T SEE IT...
BUT IF YOU STAY--I FEAR FOR YOUR SOUL--

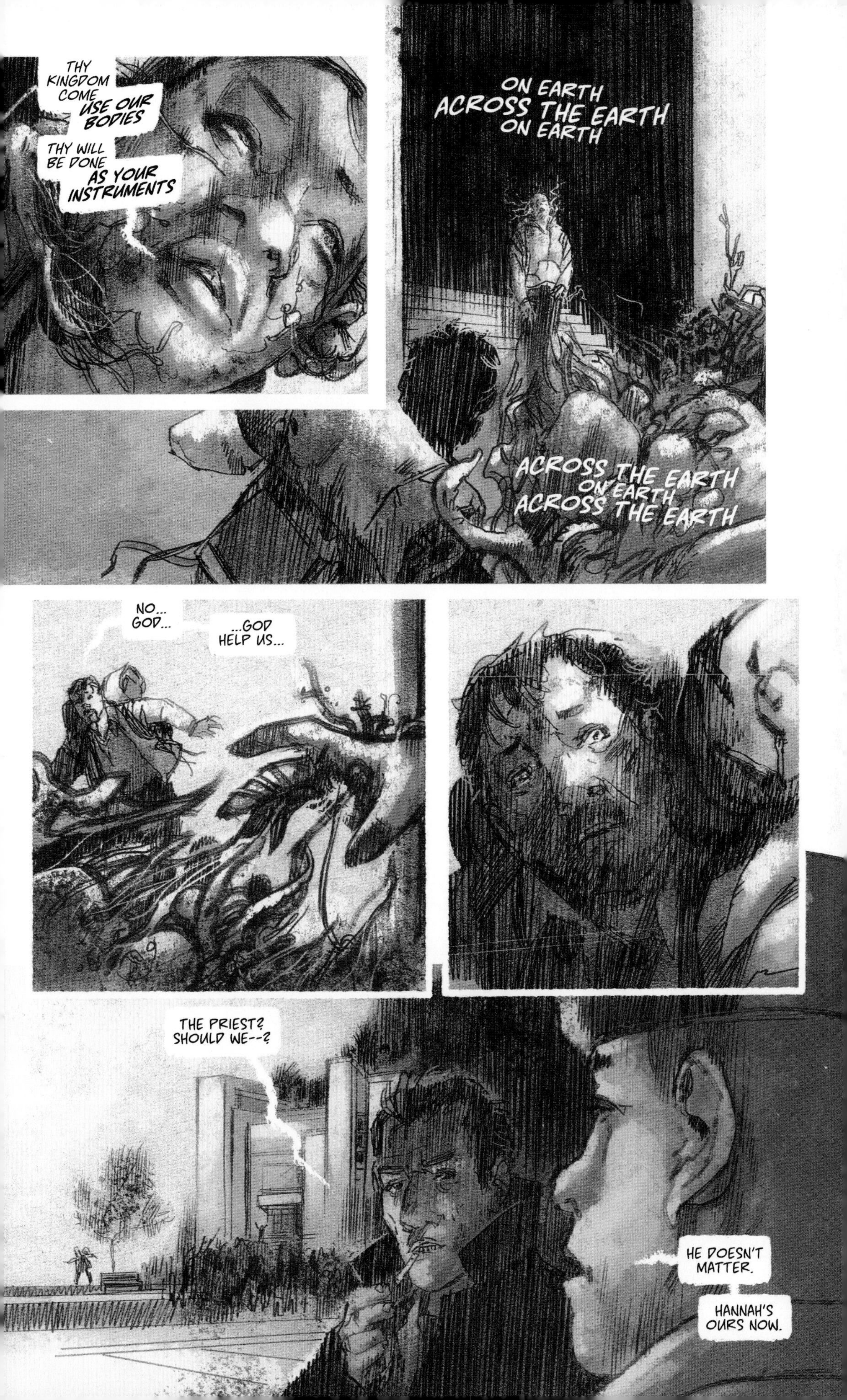
THY KINGDOM COME USE OUR BODIES
THY WILL BE DONE AS YOUR INSTRUMENTS
ON EARTH
ACROSS THE EARTH
ON EARTH
ACROSS THE EARTH
ON EARTH
ACROSS THE EARTH
NO... GOD...
...GOD HELP US...
THE PRIEST? SHOULD WE--?
HE DOESN'T MATTER.
HANNAH'S OURS NOW.

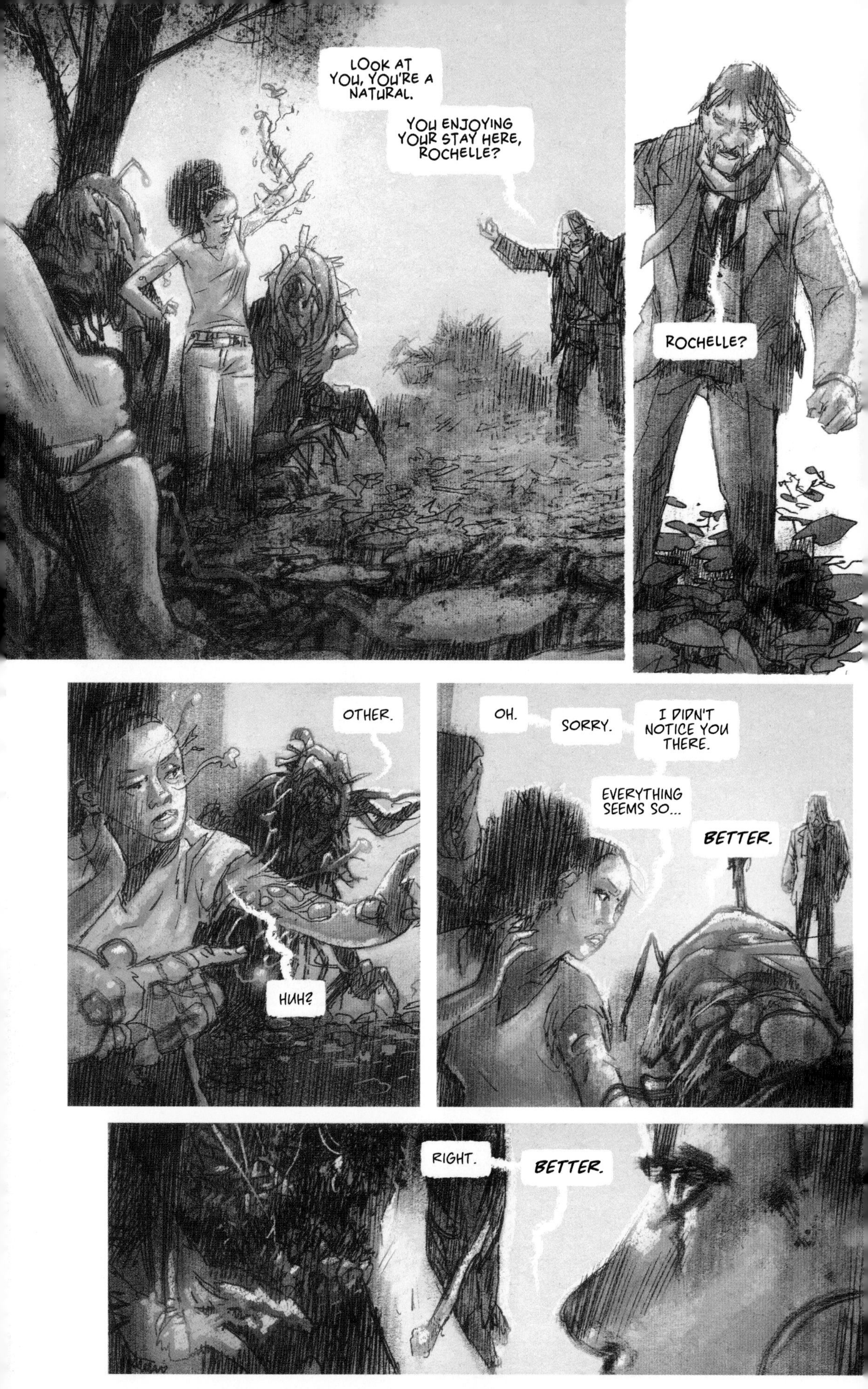
LOOK AT YOU, YOU'RE A NATURAL.
YOU ENJOYING YOUR STAY HERE, ROCHELLE?
ROCHELLE?
OTHER.
HUH?
OH.
SORRY.
I DIDN'T NOTICE YOU THERE.
EVERYTHING SEEMS SO...
BETTER.
RIGHT.
BETTER.

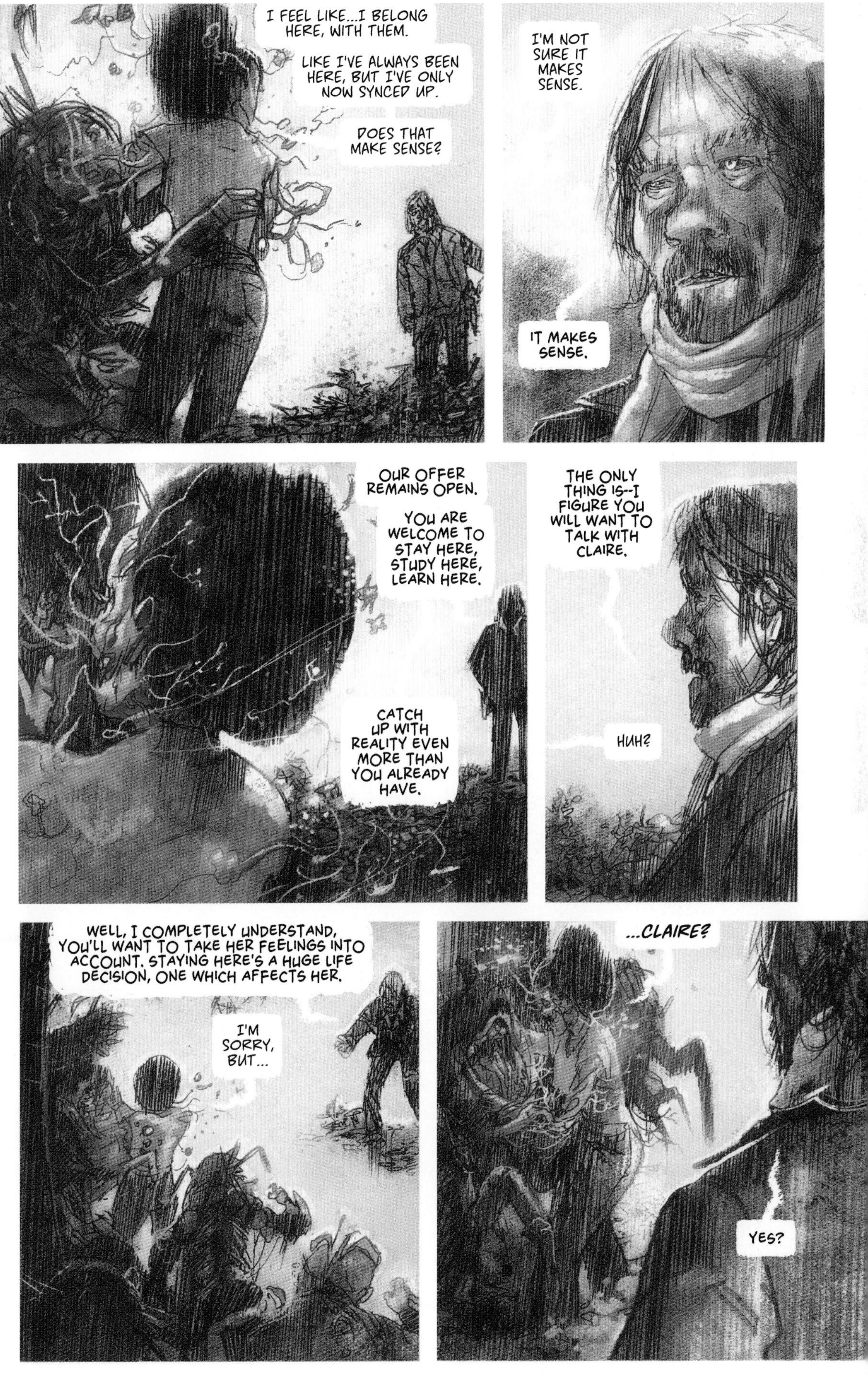
I FEEL LIKE...I BELONG HERE, WITH THEM.
LIKE I'VE ALWAYS BEEN HERE, BUT I'VE ONLY NOW SYNCED UP.
DOES THAT MAKE SENSE?
I'M NOT SURE IT MAKES SENSE.
IT MAKES SENSE.
OUR OFFER REMAINS OPEN.
YOU ARE WELCOME TO STAY HERE, STUDY HERE, LEARN HERE.
CATCH UP WITH REALITY EVEN MORE THAN YOU ALREADY HAVE.
THE ONLY THING IS--I FIGURE YOU WILL WANT TO TALK WITH CLAIRE.
HUH?
WELL, I COMPLETELY UNDERSTAND, YOU'LL WANT TO TAKE HER FEELINGS INTO ACCOUNT. STAYING HERE'S A HUGE LIFE DECISION, ONE WHICH AFFECTS HER.
I'M SORRY, BUT...
...CLAIRE?
YES?

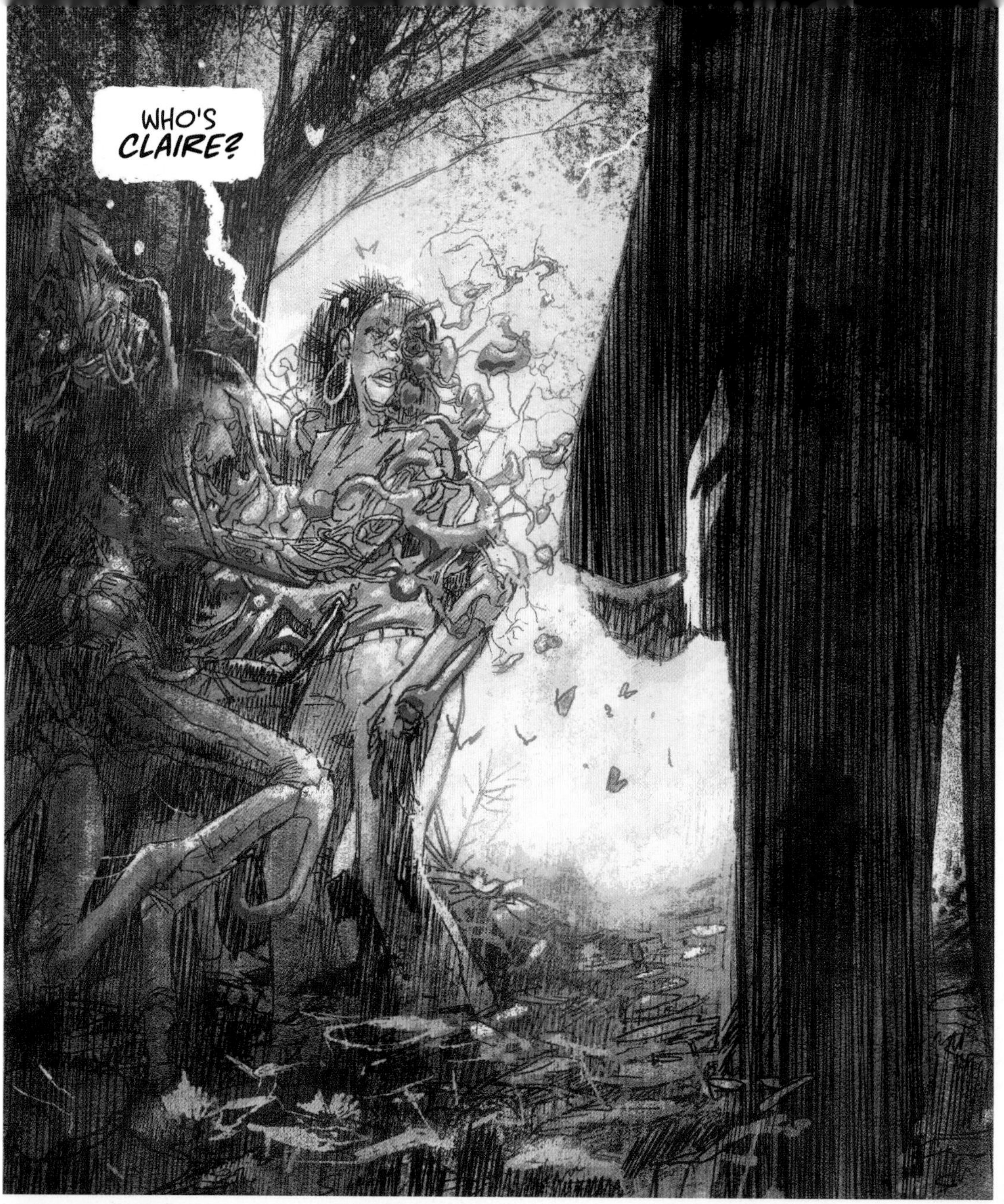
WHO'S CLAIRE?

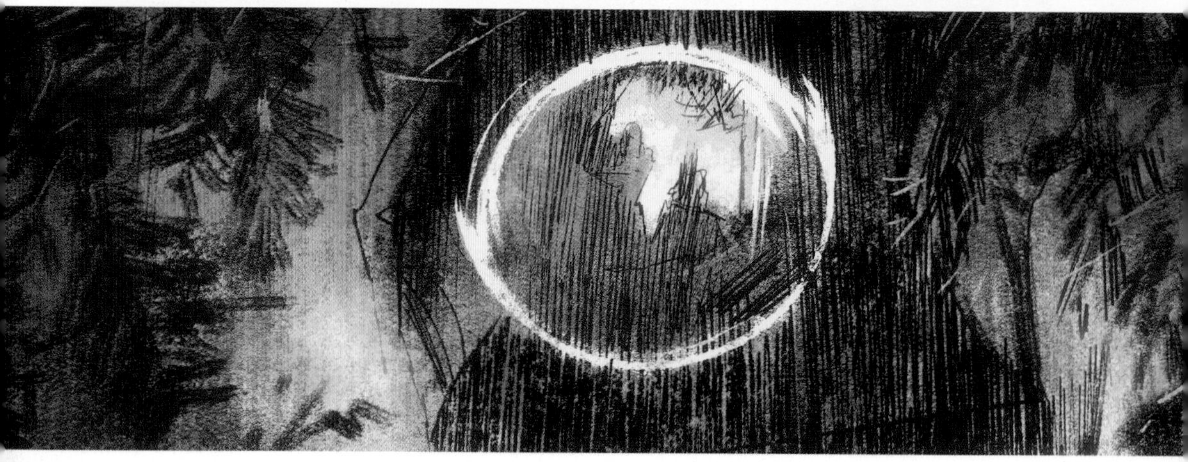

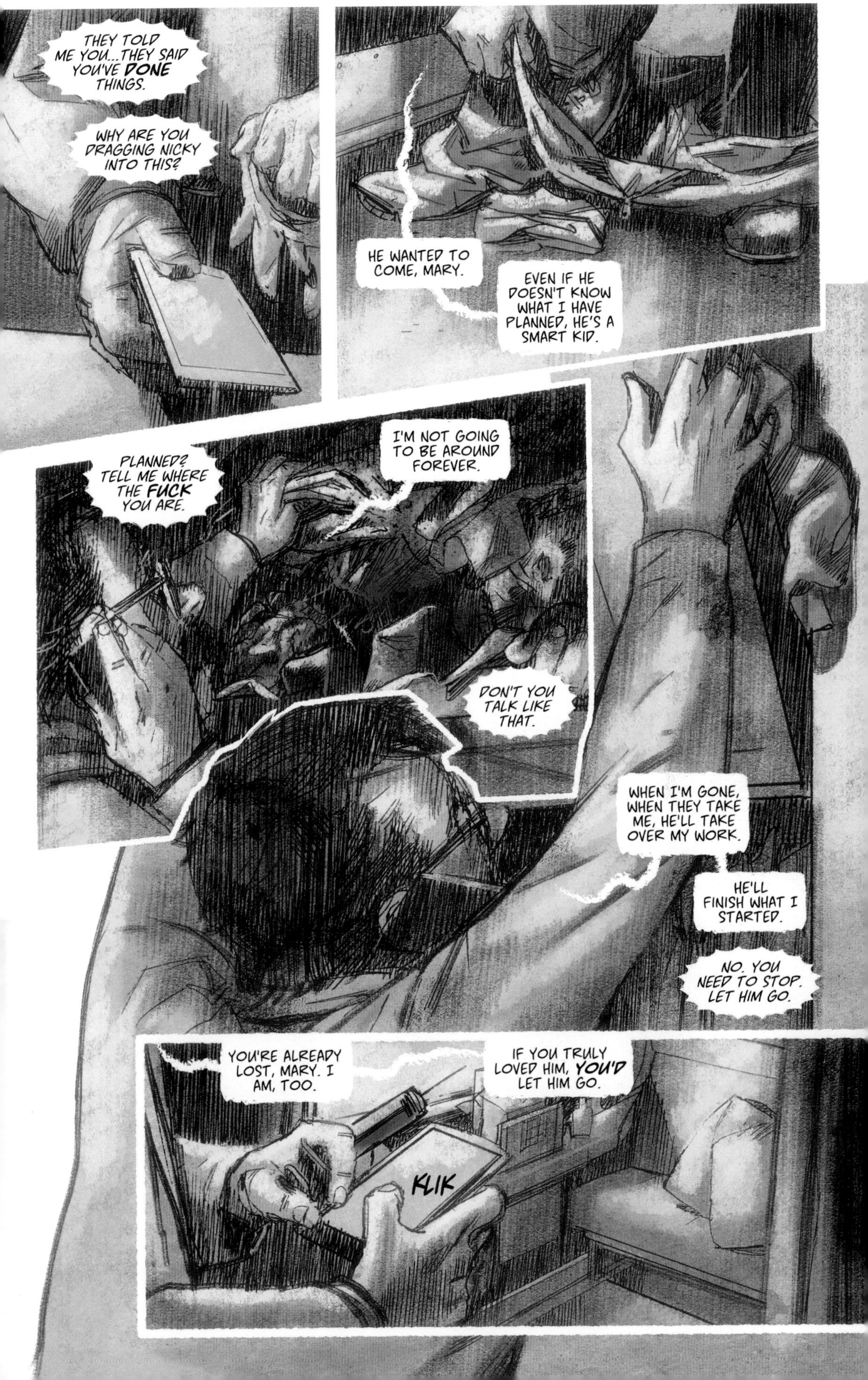
THEY TOLD ME YOU...THEY SAID YOU'VE DONE THINGS.
WHY ARE YOU DRAGGING NICKY INTO THIS?
HE WANTED TO COME, MARY.
EVEN IF HE DOESN'T KNOW WHAT I HAVE PLANNED, HE'S A SMART KID.
PLANNED? TELL ME WHERE THE FUCK YOU ARE.
I'M NOT GOING TO BE AROUND FOREVER.
DON'T YOU TALK LIKE THAT.
WHEN I'M GONE, WHEN THEY TAKE ME, HE'LL TAKE OVER MY WORK.
HE'LL FINISH WHAT I STARTED.
NO. YOU NEED TO STOP. LET HIM GO.
YOU'RE ALREADY LOST, MARY. I AM, TOO.
IF YOU TRULY LOVED HIM, YOU'D LET HIM GO.
KLIK

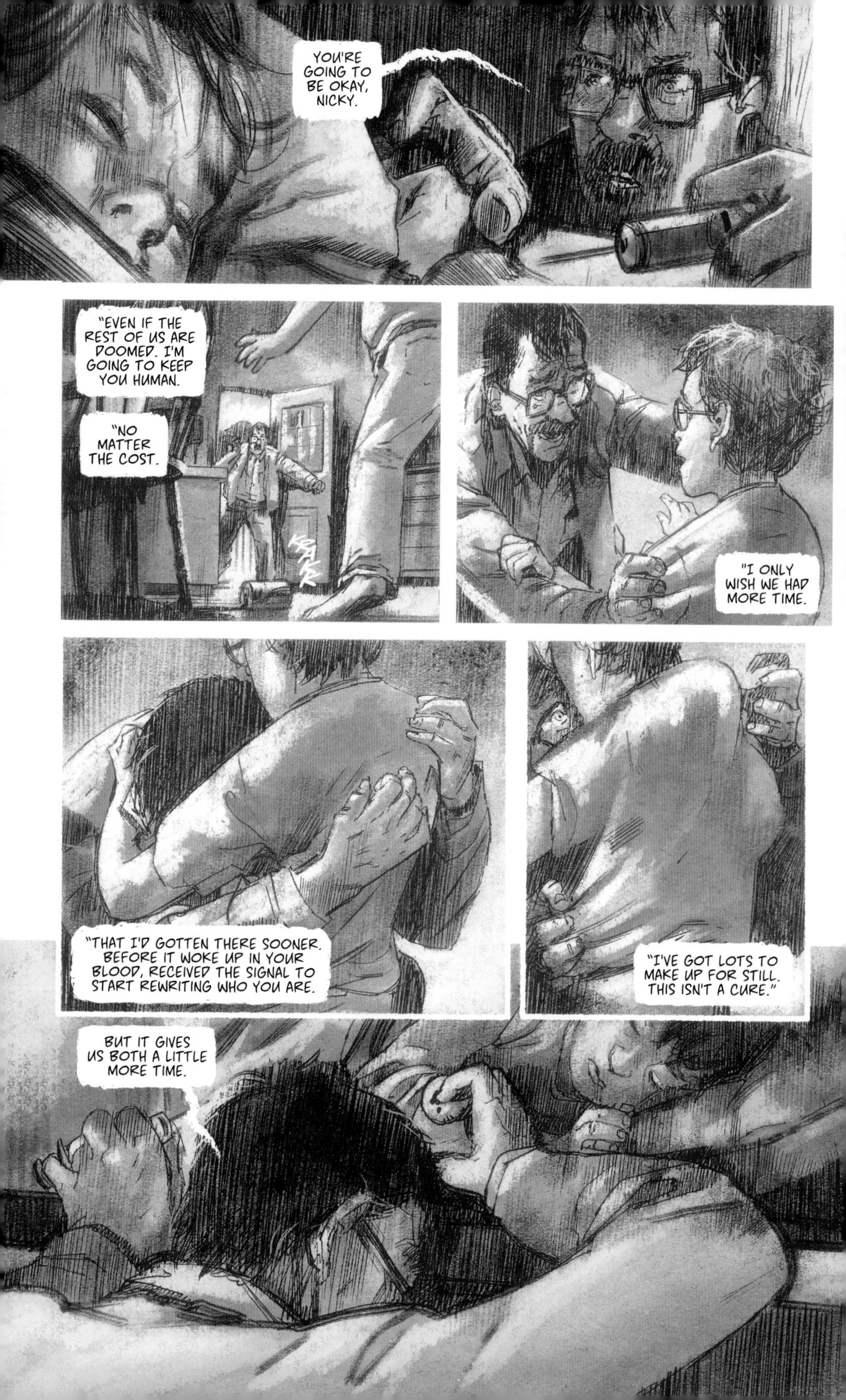
YOU'RE GOING TO BE OKAY, NICKY.
"EVEN IF THE REST OF US ARE DOOMED. I'M GOING TO KEEP YOU HUMAN.
"NO MATTER THE COST.
KRAKK
"I ONLY WISH WE HAD MORE TIME.
"THAT I'D GOTTEN THERE SOONER. BEFORE IT WOKE UP IN YOUR BLOOD, RECEIVED THE SIGNAL TO START REWRITING WHO YOU ARE.
"I'VE GOT LOTS TO MAKE UP FOR STILL. THIS ISN'T A CURE."
BUT IT GIVES US BOTH A LITTLE MORE TIME.

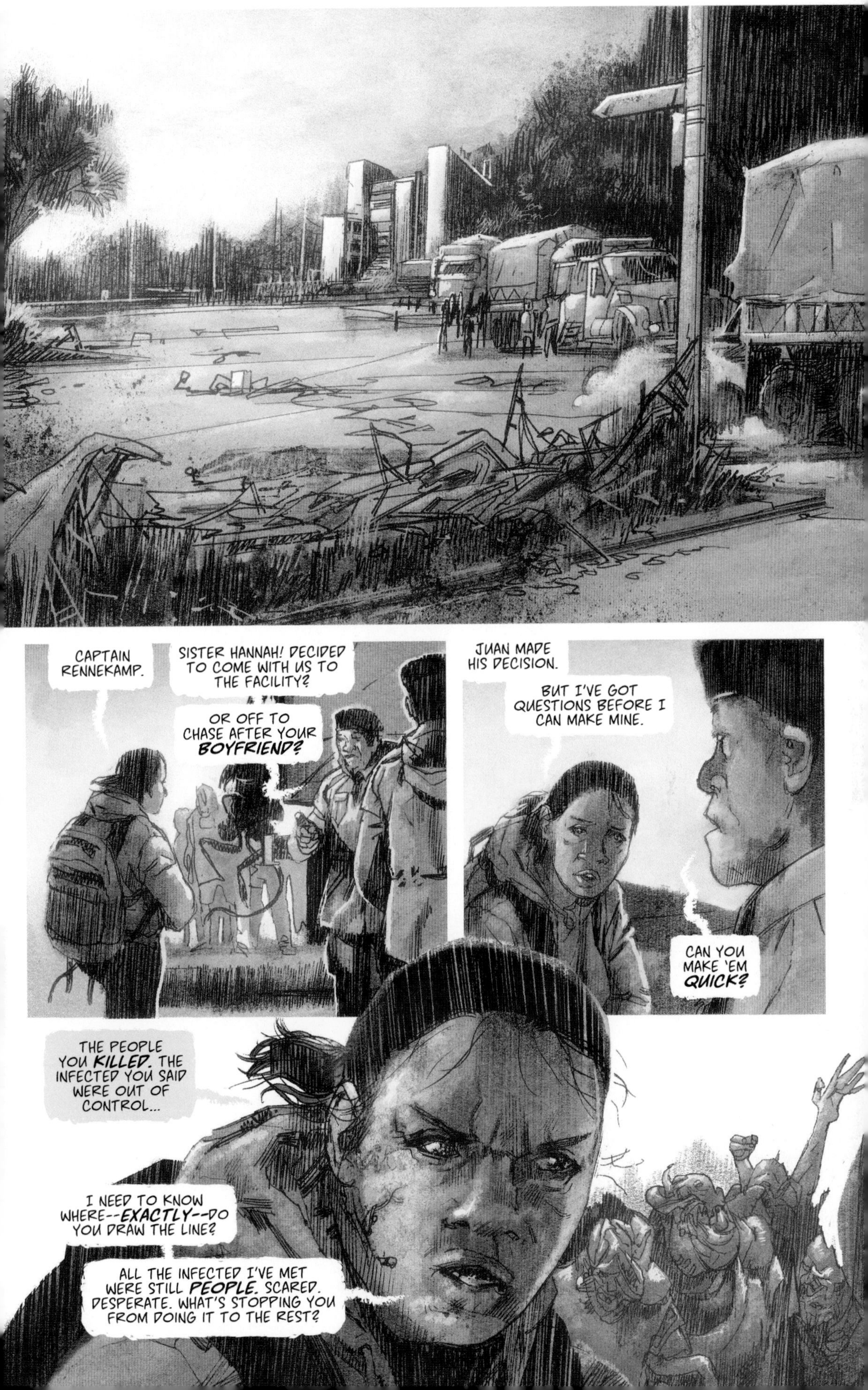
CAPTAIN RENNEKAMP.
SISTER HANNAH! DECIDED TO COME WITH US TO THE FACILITY?
OR OFF TO CHASE AFTER YOUR BOYFRIEND?
JUAN MADE HIS DECISION.
BUT I'VE GOT QUESTIONS BEFORE I CAN MAKE MINE.
CAN YOU MAKE 'EM QUICK?
THE PEOPLE YOU KILLED. THE INFECTED YOU SAID WERE OUT OF CONTROL...
I NEED TO KNOW WHERE--EXACTLY--DO YOU DRAW THE LINE?
ALL THE INFECTED I'VE MET WERE STILL PEOPLE. SCARED. DESPERATE. WHAT'S STOPPING YOU FROM DOING IT TO THE REST?

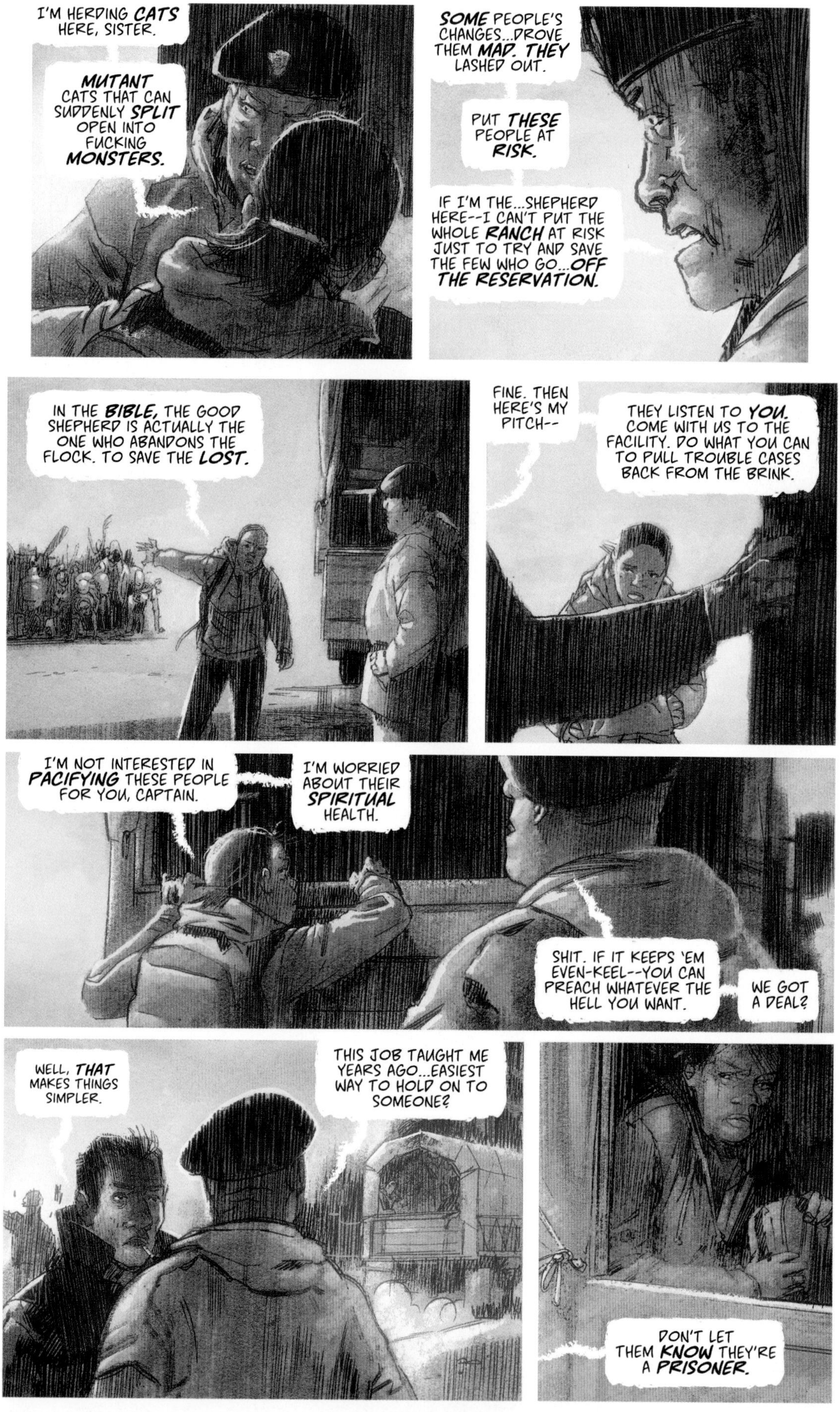
I'M HERDING CATS HERE, SISTER.
MUTANT CATS THAT CAN SUDDENLY SPLIT OPEN INTO FUCKING MONSTERS.
SOME PEOPLE'S CHANGES...DROVE THEM MAD. THEY LASHED OUT.
PUT THESE PEOPLE AT RISK.
IF I'M THE...SHEPHERD HERE--I CAN'T PUT THE WHOLE RANCH AT RISK JUST TO TRY AND SAVE THE FEW WHO GO...OFF THE RESERVATION.
IN THE BIBLE, THE GOOD SHEPHERD IS ACTUALLY THE ONE WHO ABANDONS THE FLOCK. TO SAVE THE LOST.
FINE. THEN HERE'S MY PITCH--
THEY LISTEN TO YOU. COME WITH US TO THE FACILITY. DO WHAT YOU CAN TO PULL TROUBLE CASES BACK FROM THE BRINK.
I'M NOT INTERESTED IN PACIFYING THESE PEOPLE FOR YOU, CAPTAIN.
I'M WORRIED ABOUT THEIR SPIRITUAL HEALTH.
SHIT. IF IT KEEPS 'EM EVEN-KEEL--YOU CAN PREACH WHATEVER THE HELL YOU WANT.
WE GOT A DEAL?
WELL, THAT MAKES THINGS SIMPLER.
THIS JOB TAUGHT ME YEARS AGO...EASIEST WAY TO HOLD ON TO SOMEONE?
DON'T LET THEM KNOW THEY'RE A PRISONER.

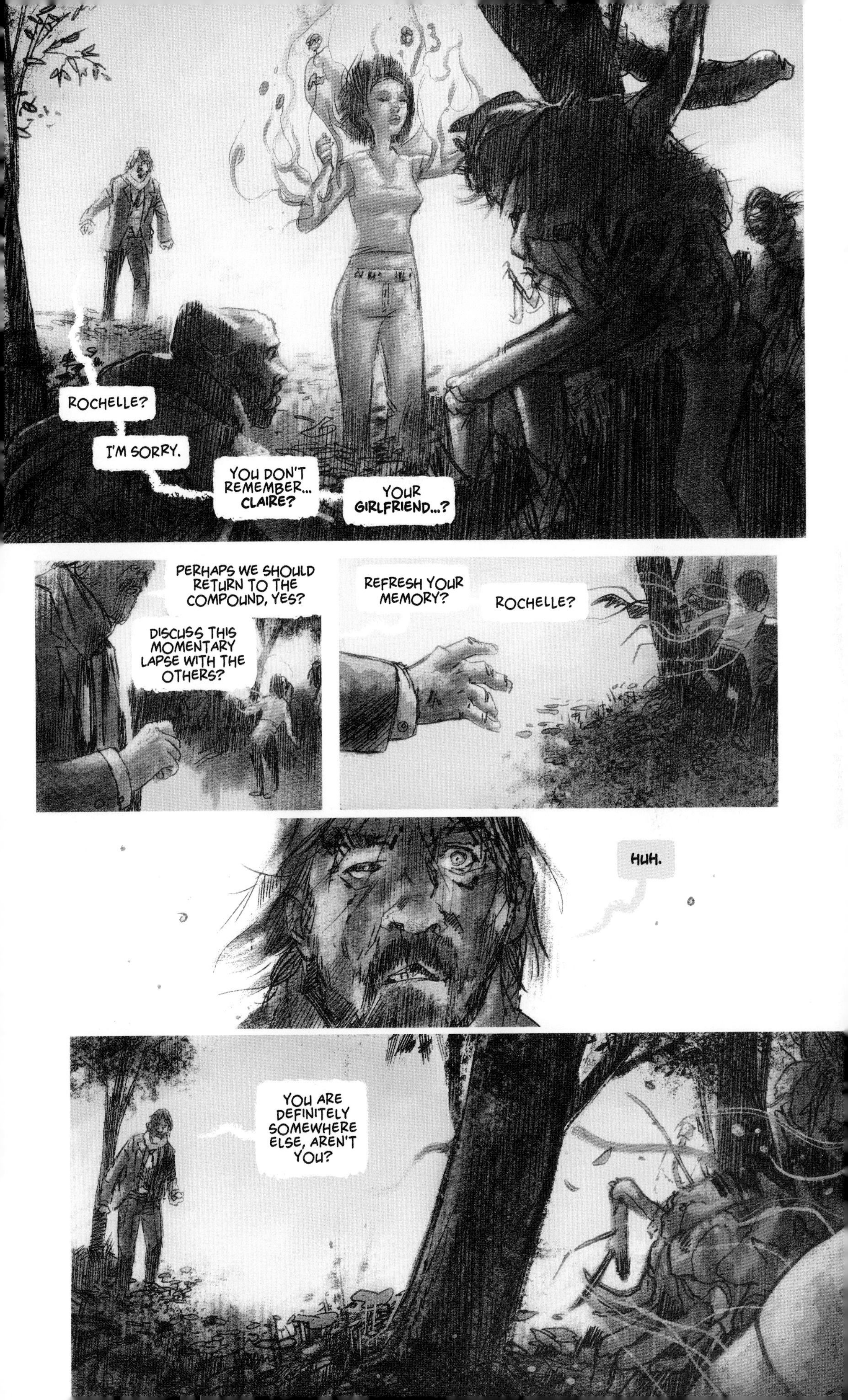
ROCHELLE?
I'M SORRY.
YOU DON'T REMEMBER... CLAIRE?
YOUR GIRLFRIEND...?
PERHAPS WE SHOULD RETURN TO THE COMPOUND, YES?
DISCUSS THIS MOMENTARY LAPSE WITH THE OTHERS?
REFRESH YOUR MEMORY?
ROCHELLE?
HUH.
YOU ARE DEFINITELY SOMEWHERE ELSE, AREN'T YOU?

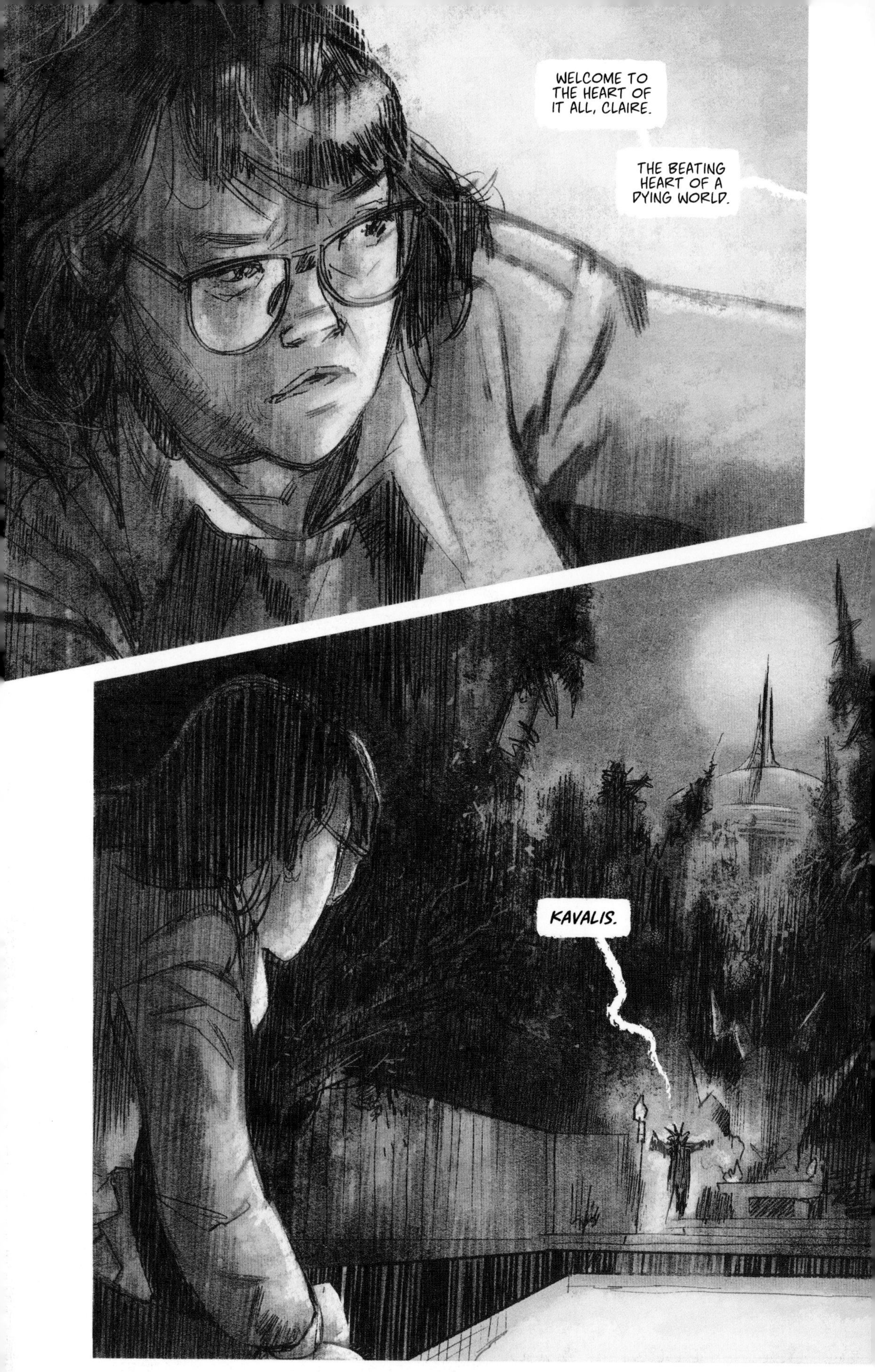
WELCOME TO THE HEART OF IT ALL, CLAIRE.
THE BEATING HEART OF A DYING WORLD.
KAVALIS.

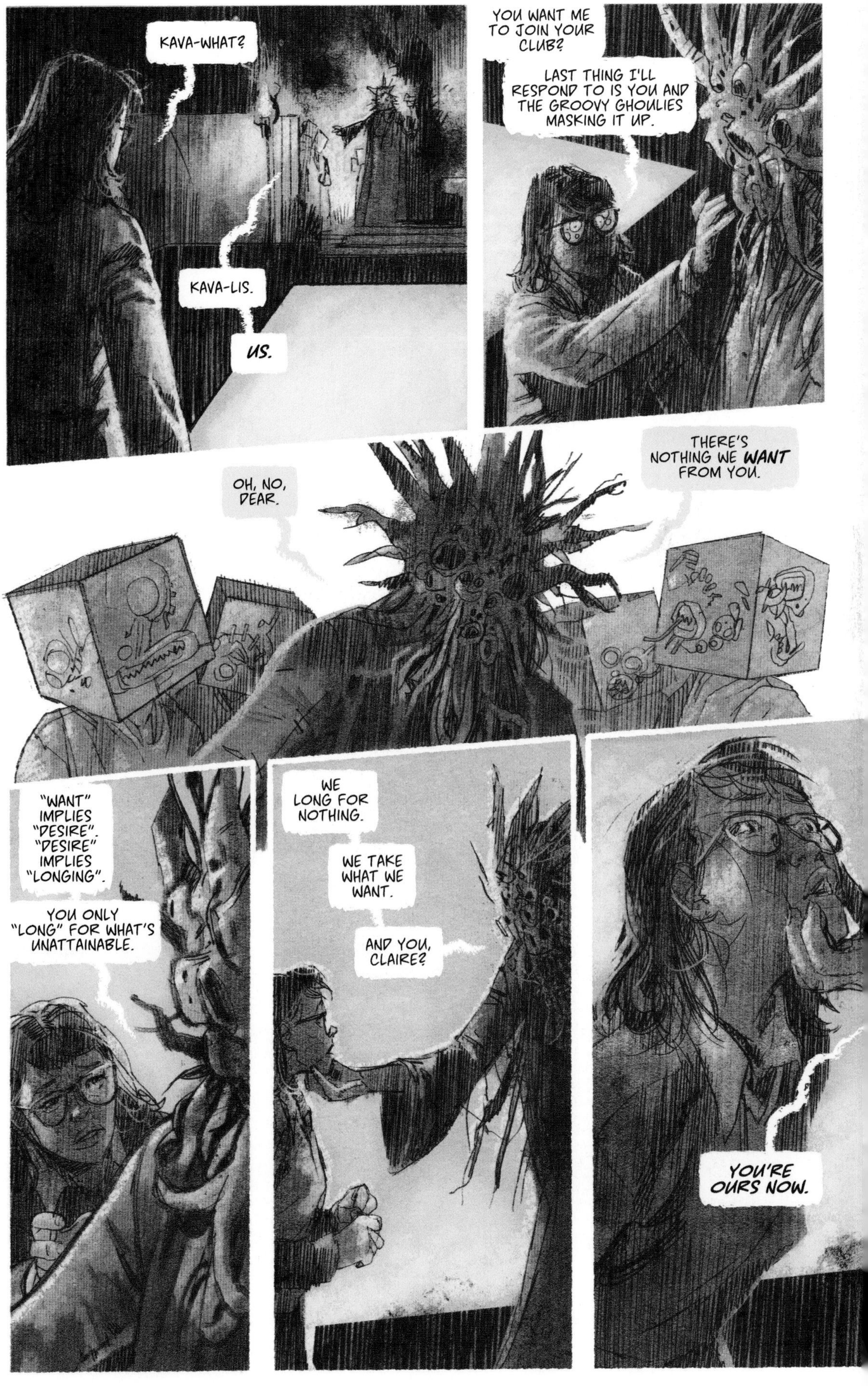
KAVA-WHAT?
KAVA-LIS.
US.
YOU WANT ME TO JOIN YOUR CLUB?
LAST THING I'LL RESPOND TO IS YOU AND THE GROOVY GHOULIES MASKING IT UP.
OH, NO, DEAR.
THERE'S NOTHING WE WANT FROM YOU.
"WANT" IMPLIES "DESIRE". "DESIRE" IMPLIES "LONGING".
YOU ONLY "LONG" FOR WHAT'S UNATTAINABLE.
WE LONG FOR NOTHING.
WE TAKE WHAT WE WANT.
AND YOU, CLAIRE?
YOU'RE OURS NOW.

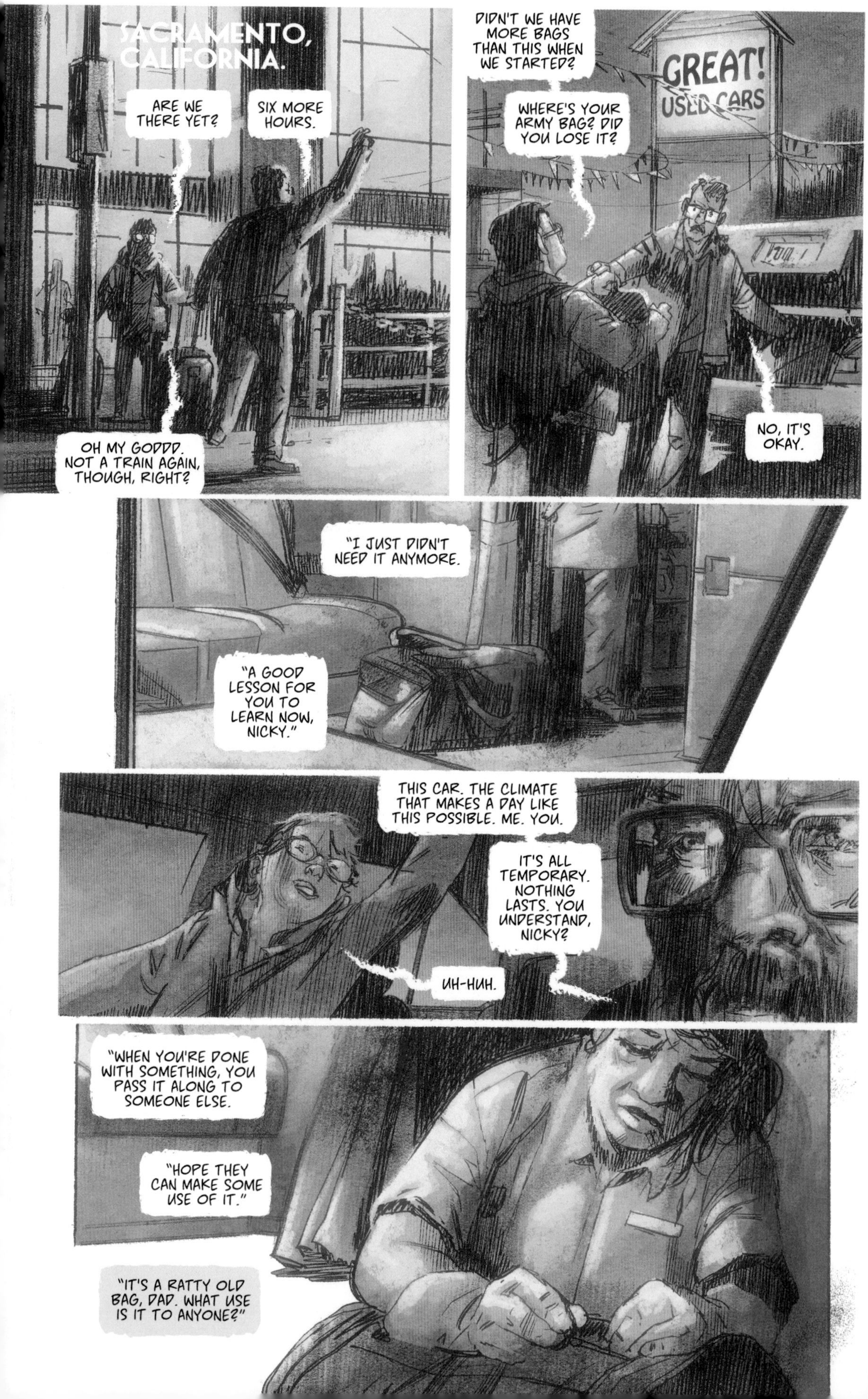
SACRAMENTO, CALIFORNIA.
ARE WE THERE YET?
SIX MORE HOURS.
OH MY GODDD. NOT A TRAIN AGAIN, THOUGH, RIGHT?
DIDN'T WE HAVE MORE BAGS THAN THIS WHEN WE STARTED?
GREAT! USED CARS
WHERE'S YOUR ARMY BAG? DID YOU LOSE IT?
NO, IT'S OKAY.
"I JUST DIDN'T NEED IT ANYMORE.
"A GOOD LESSON FOR YOU TO LEARN NOW, NICKY."
THIS CAR. THE CLIMATE THAT MAKES A DAY LIKE THIS POSSIBLE. ME. YOU.
IT'S ALL TEMPORARY. NOTHING LASTS. YOU UNDERSTAND, NICKY?
UH-HUH.
"WHEN YOU'RE DONE WITH SOMETHING, YOU PASS IT ALONG TO SOMEONE ELSE.
"HOPE THEY CAN MAKE SOME USE OF IT."
"IT'S A RATTY OLD BAG, DAD. WHAT USE IS IT TO ANYONE?"

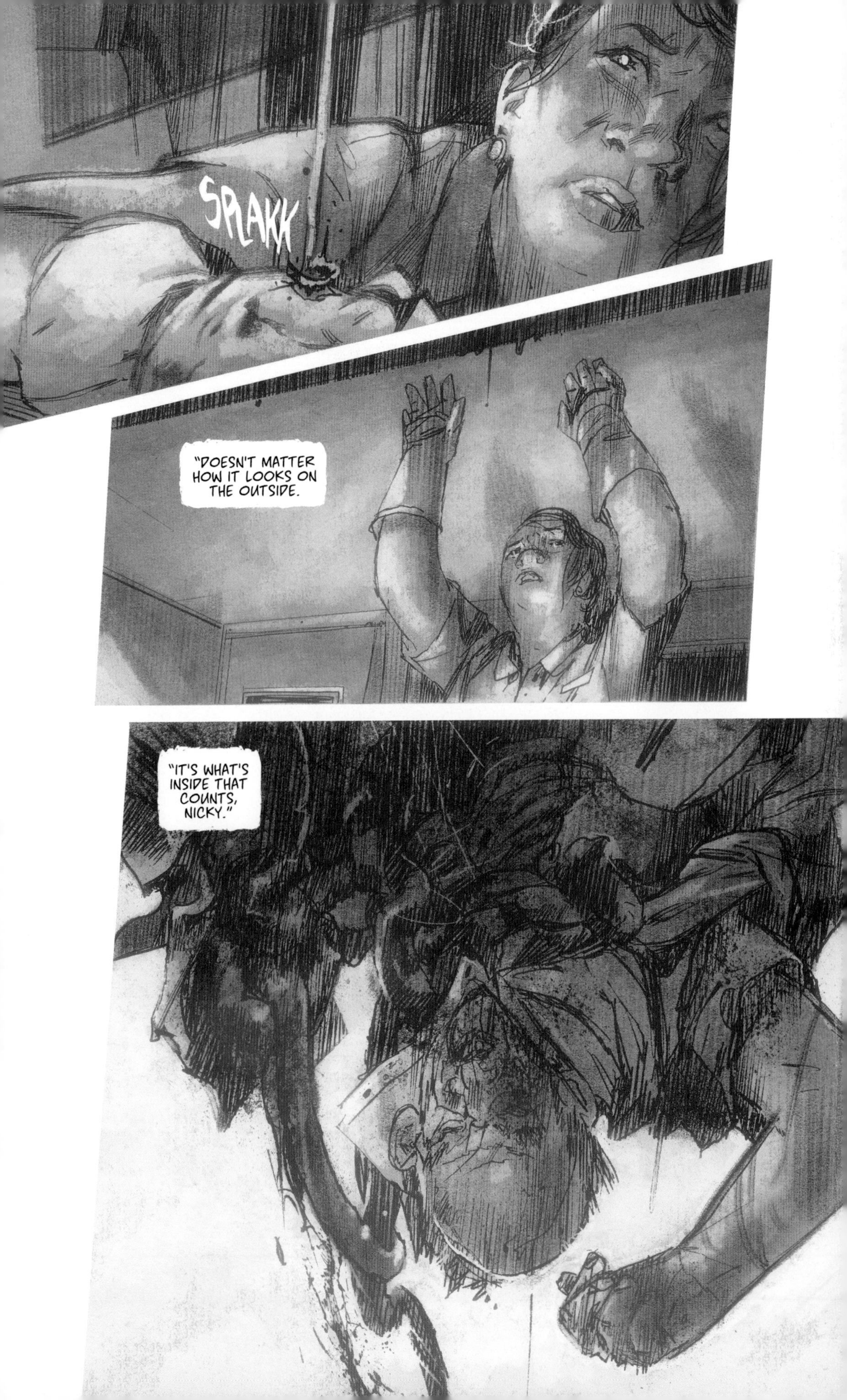
SPLAKK
"DOESN'T MATTER HOW IT LOOKS ON THE OUTSIDE.
"IT'S WHAT'S INSIDE THAT COUNTS, NICKY."

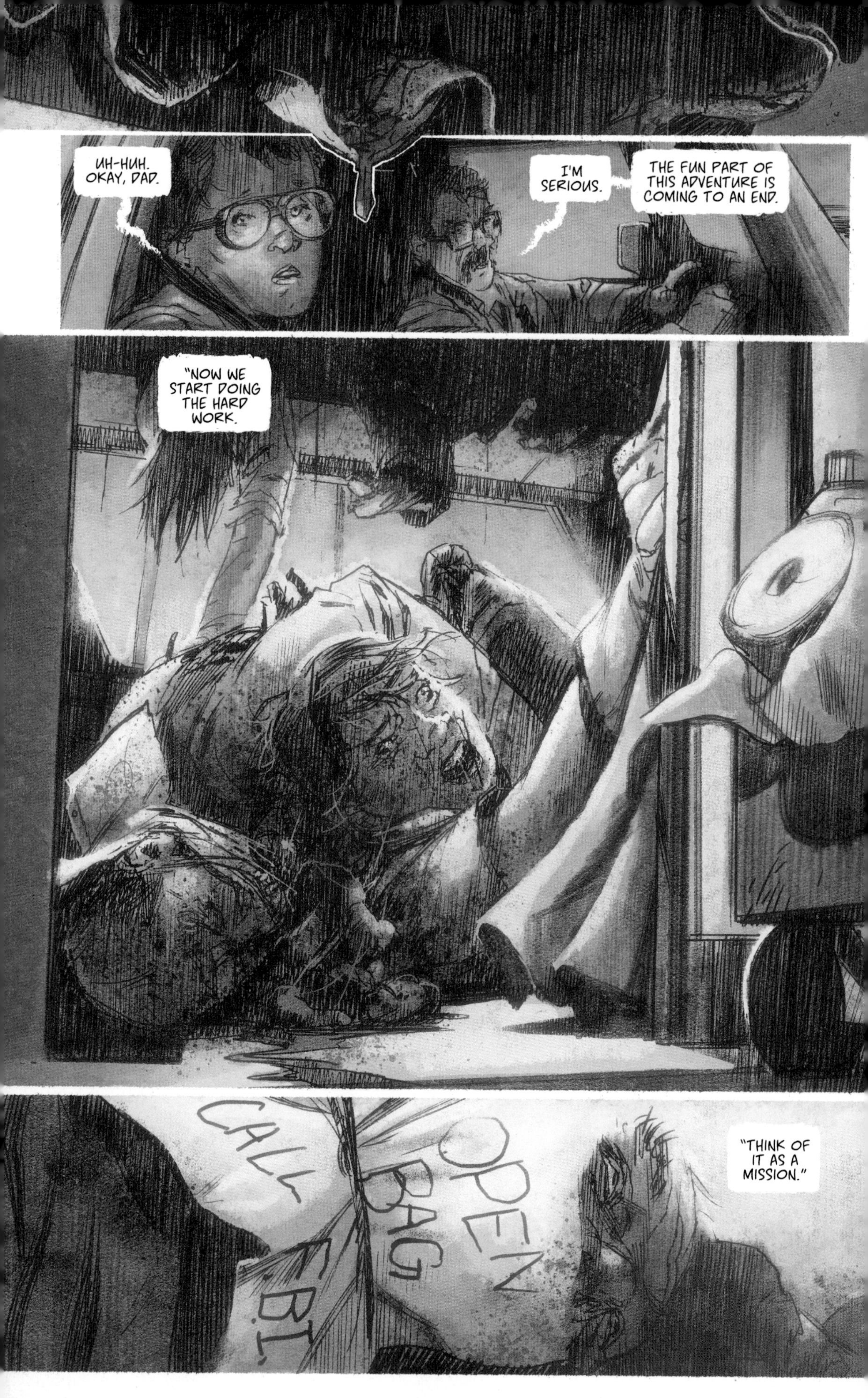
UH-HUH. OKAY, DAD.
I'M SERIOUS.
THE FUN PART OF THIS ADVENTURE IS COMING TO AN END.
"NOW WE START DOING THE HARD WORK.
CALL F.B.I.
OPEN BAG
"THINK OF IT AS A MISSION."

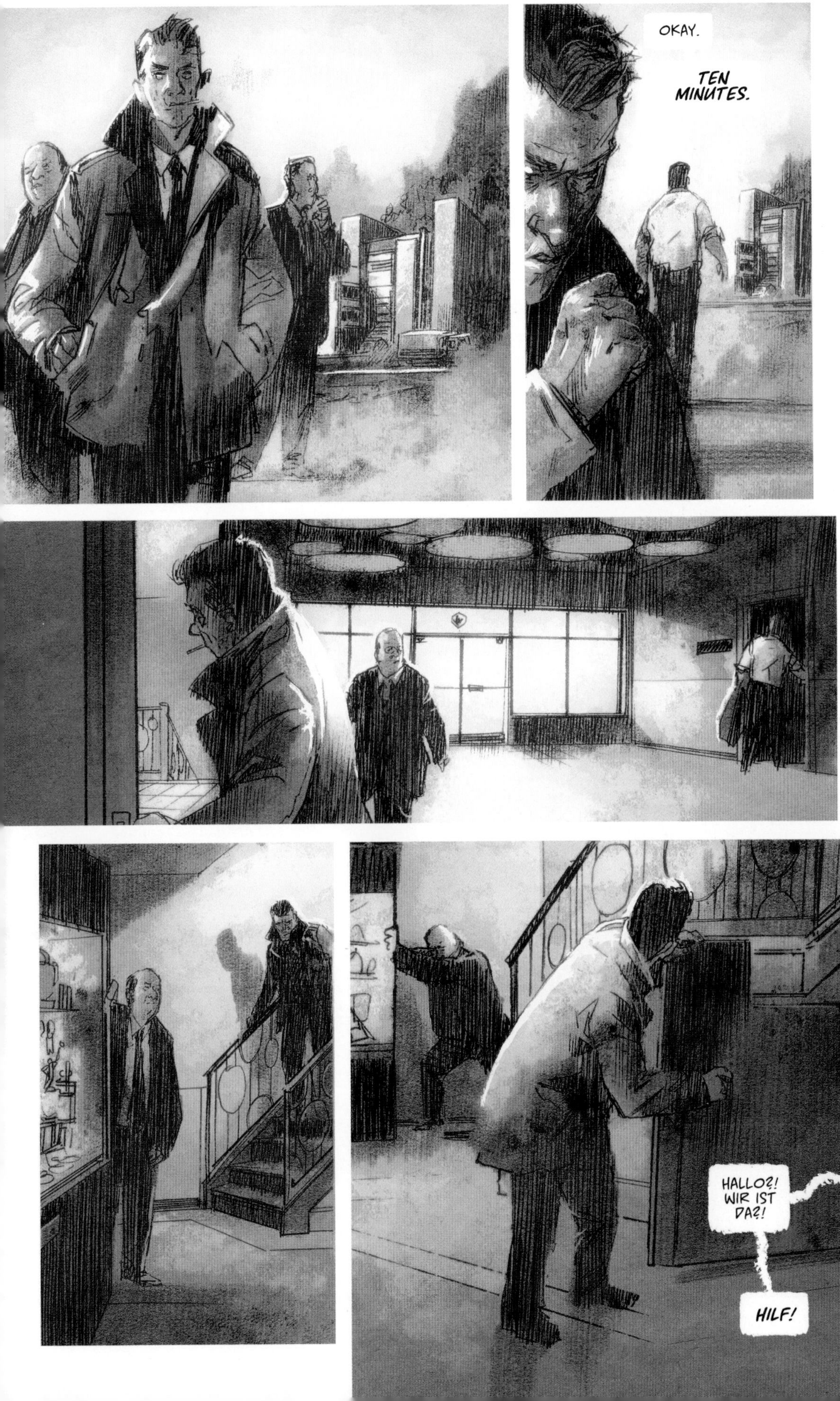
OKAY.
TEN MINUTES.
HALLO?! WIR IST DA?!
HILF!

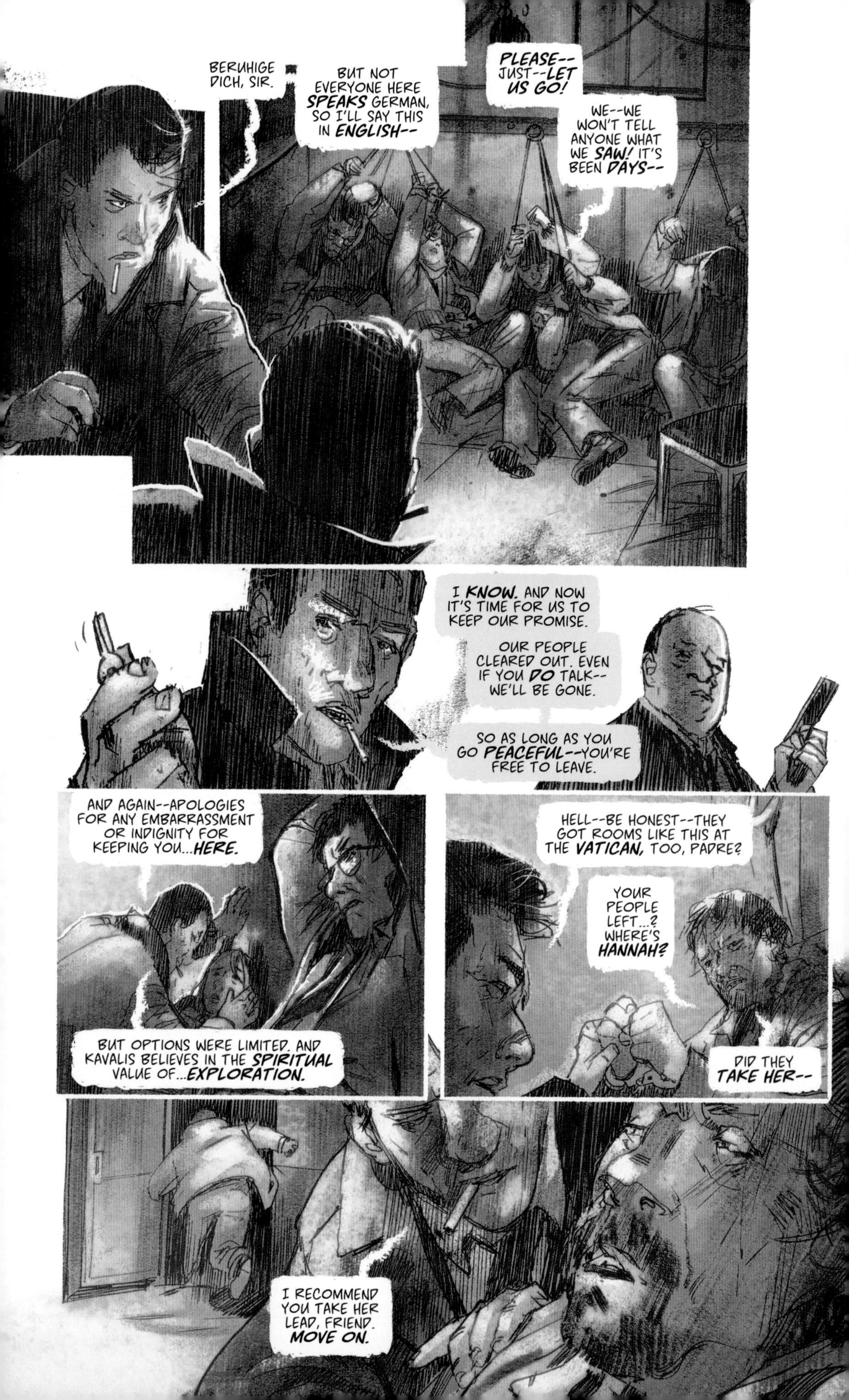
BERUHIGE DICH, SIR.
BUT NOT EVERYONE HERE SPEAKS GERMAN, SO I'LL SAY THIS IN ENGLISH--
PLEASE-- JUST--LET US GO!
WE--WE WON'T TELL ANYONE WHAT WE SAW! IT'S BEEN DAYS--
I KNOW. AND NOW IT'S TIME FOR US TO KEEP OUR PROMISE.
OUR PEOPLE CLEARED OUT. EVEN IF YOU DO TALK-- WE'LL BE GONE.
SO AS LONG AS YOU GO PEACEFUL--YOU'RE FREE TO LEAVE.
AND AGAIN--APOLOGIES FOR ANY EMBARRASSMENT OR INDIGNITY FOR KEEPING YOU...HERE.
BUT OPTIONS WERE LIMITED. AND KAVALIS BELIEVES IN THE SPIRITUAL VALUE OF...EXPLORATION.
HELL--BE HONEST--THEY GOT ROOMS LIKE THIS AT THE VATICAN, TOO, PADRE?
YOUR PEOPLE LEFT...? WHERE'S HANNAH?
DID THEY TAKE HER--
I RECOMMEND YOU TAKE HER LEAD, FRIEND. MOVE ON.

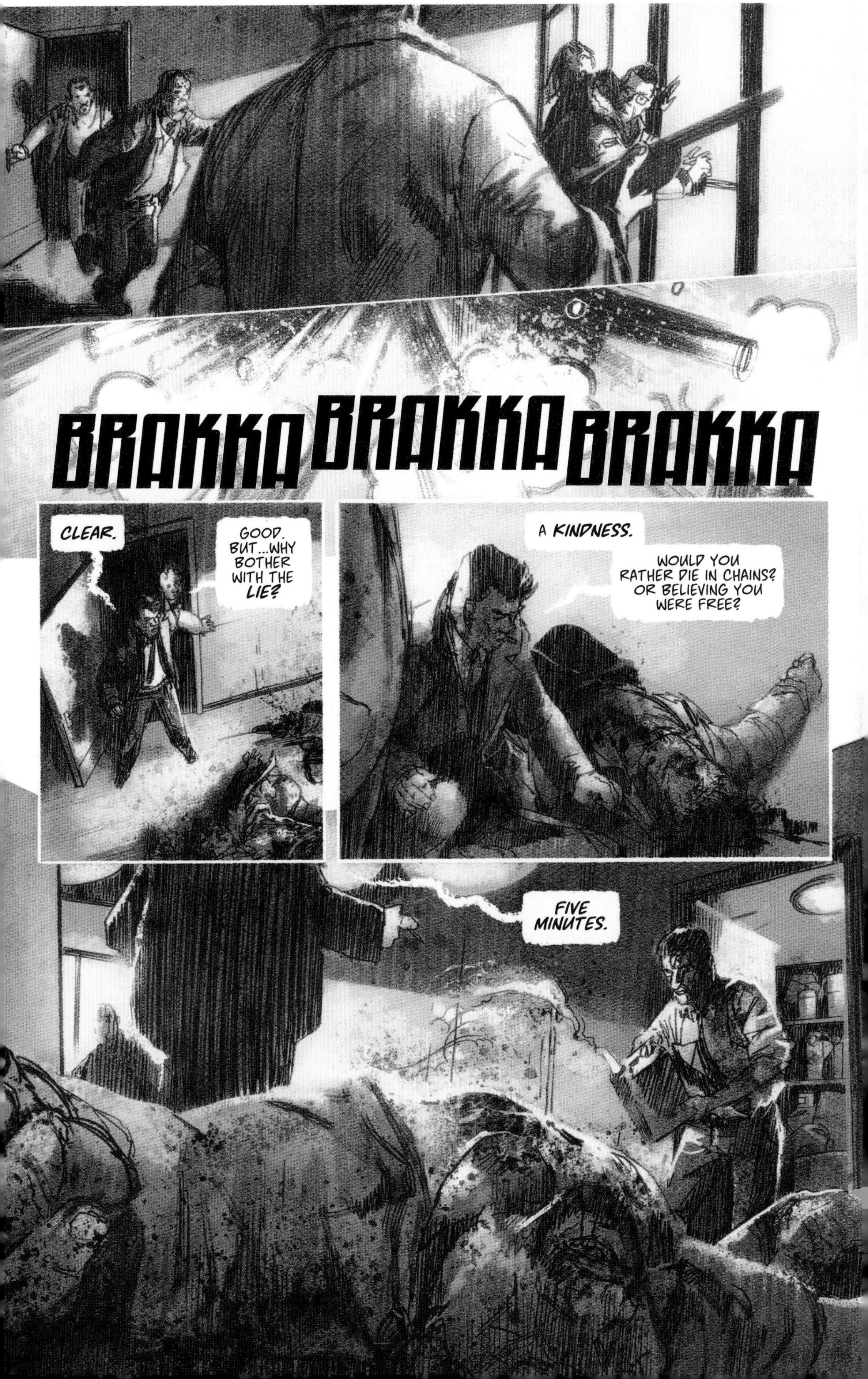
BRAKKA BRAKKA BRAKKA
CLEAR.
GOOD. BUT...WHY BOTHER WITH THE LIE?
A KINDNESS.
WOULD YOU RATHER DIE IN CHAINS? OR BELIEVING YOU WERE FREE?
FIVE MINUTES.

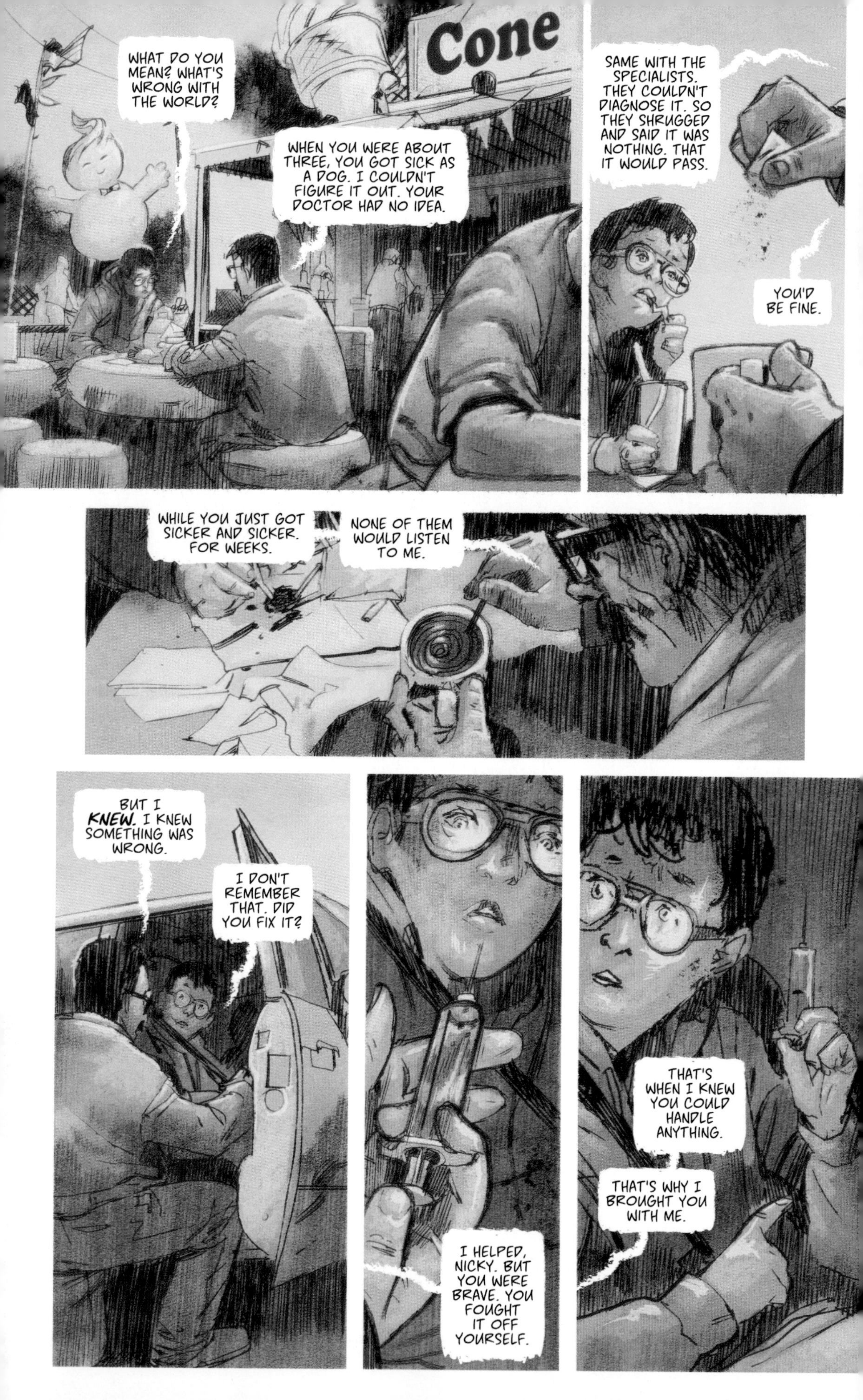
Cone
WHAT DO YOU MEAN? WHAT'S WRONG WITH THE WORLD?
WHEN YOU WERE ABOUT THREE, YOU GOT SICK AS A DOG. I COULDN'T FIGURE IT OUT. YOUR DOCTOR HAD NO IDEA.
SAME WITH THE SPECIALISTS. THEY COULDN'T DIAGNOSE IT. SO THEY SHRUGGED AND SAID IT WAS NOTHING. THAT IT WOULD PASS.
YOU'D BE FINE.
WHILE YOU JUST GOT SICKER AND SICKER. FOR WEEKS.
NONE OF THEM WOULD LISTEN TO ME.
BUT I KNEW. I KNEW SOMETHING WAS WRONG.
I DON'T REMEMBER THAT. DID YOU FIX IT?
I HELPED, NICKY. BUT YOU WERE BRAVE. YOU FOUGHT IT OFF YOURSELF.
THAT'S WHEN I KNEW YOU COULD HANDLE ANYTHING.
THAT'S WHY I BROUGHT YOU WITH ME.

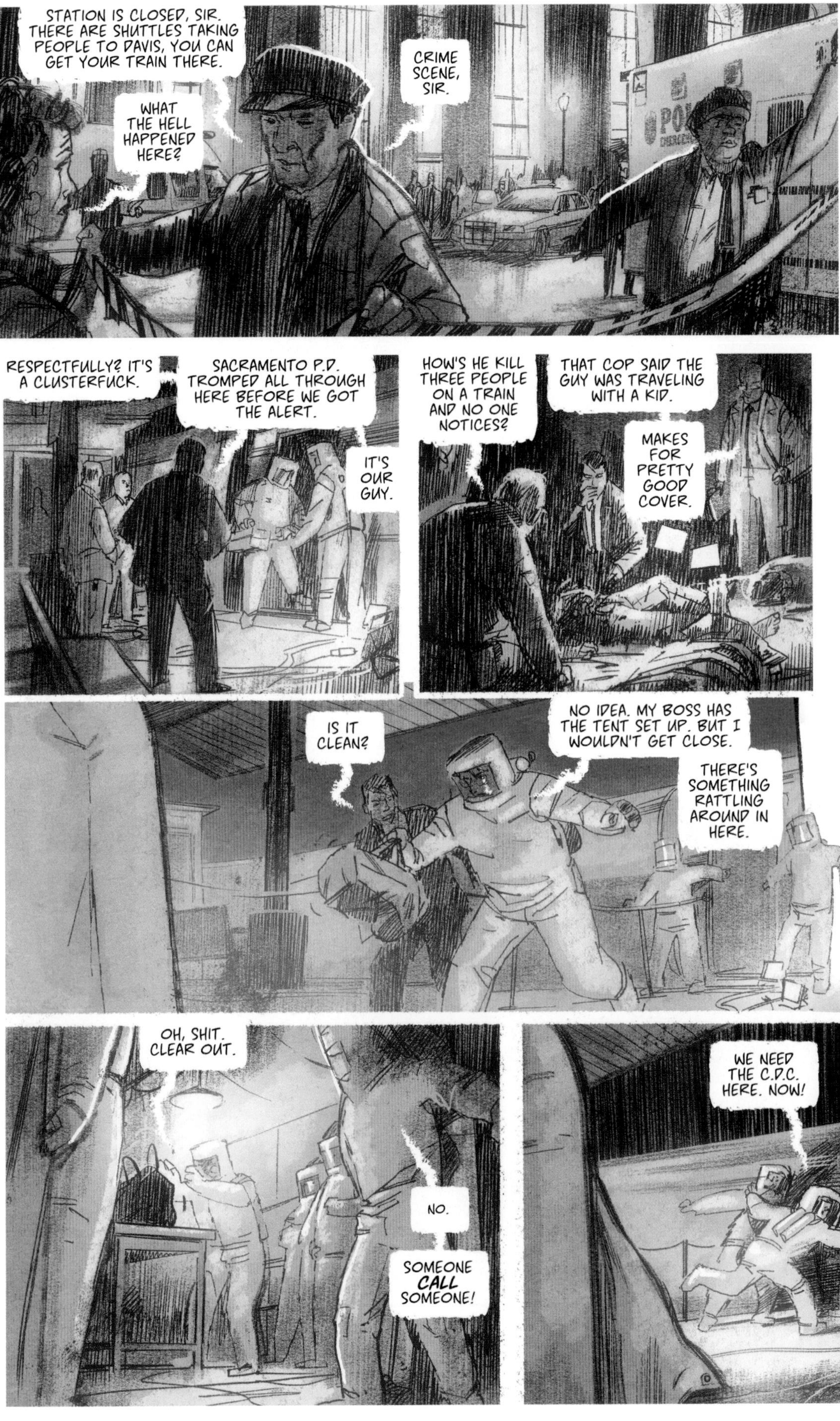
STATION IS CLOSED, SIR. THERE ARE SHUTTLES TAKING PEOPLE TO DAVIS, YOU CAN GET YOUR TRAIN THERE.
WHAT THE HELL HAPPENED HERE?
CRIME SCENE, SIR.
RESPECTFULLY? IT'S A CLUSTERFUCK.
SACRAMENTO P.D. TROMPED ALL THROUGH HERE BEFORE WE GOT THE ALERT.
IT'S OUR GUY.
HOW'S HE KILL THREE PEOPLE ON A TRAIN AND NO ONE NOTICES?
THAT COP SAID THE GUY WAS TRAVELING WITH A KID.
MAKES FOR PRETTY GOOD COVER.
IS IT CLEAN?
NO IDEA. MY BOSS HAS THE TENT SET UP. BUT I WOULDN'T GET CLOSE.
THERE'S SOMETHING RATTLING AROUND IN HERE.
OH, SHIT. CLEAR OUT.
NO.
SOMEONE **CALL** SOMEONE!
WE NEED THE C.D.C. HERE. NOW!

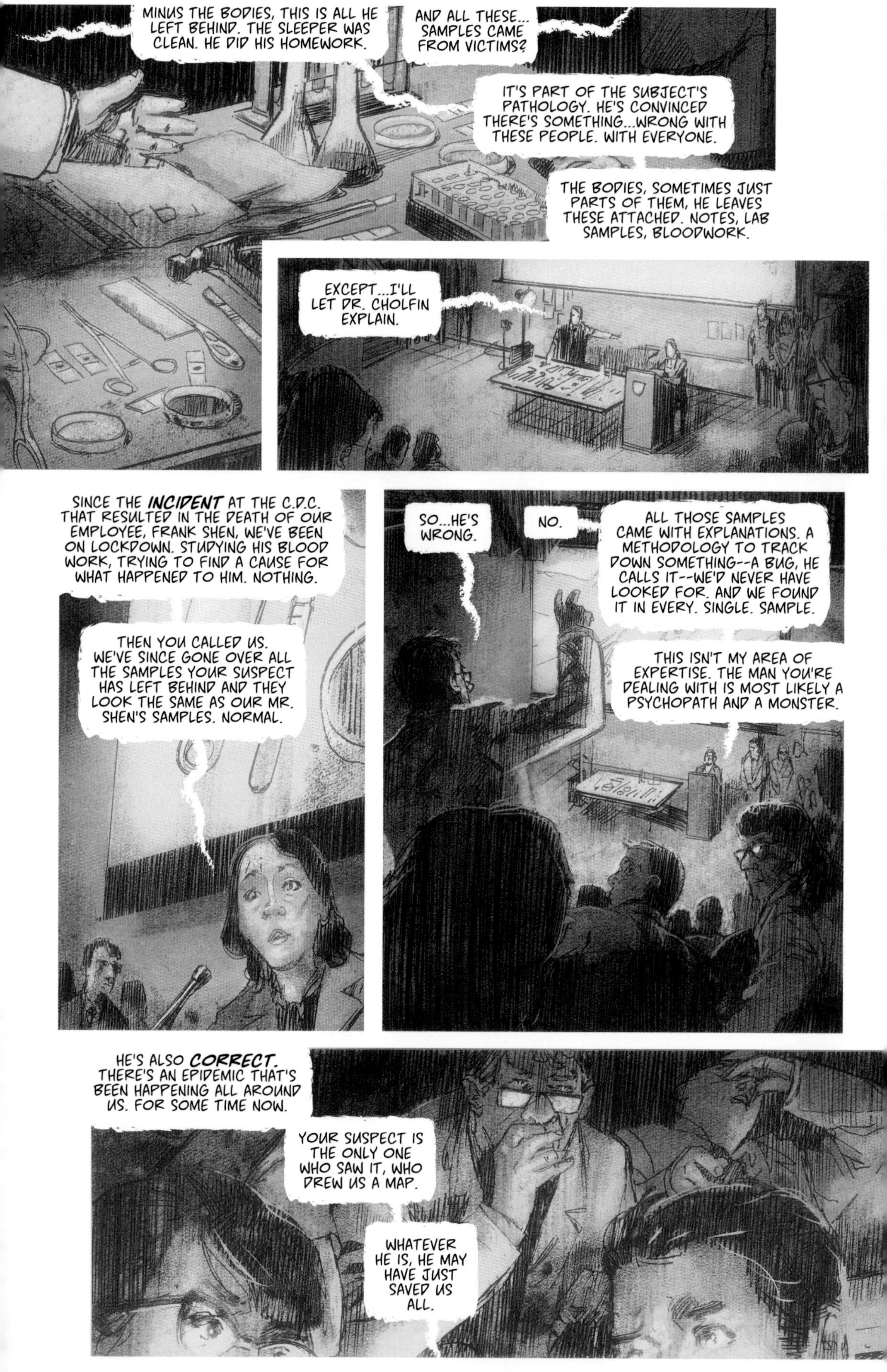
MINUS THE BODIES, THIS IS ALL HE LEFT BEHIND. THE SLEEPER WAS CLEAN. HE DID HIS HOMEWORK.
AND ALL THESE... SAMPLES CAME FROM VICTIMS?
IT'S PART OF THE SUBJECT'S PATHOLOGY. HE'S CONVINCED THERE'S SOMETHING...WRONG WITH THESE PEOPLE. WITH EVERYONE.
THE BODIES, SOMETIMES JUST PARTS OF THEM, HE LEAVES THESE ATTACHED. NOTES, LAB SAMPLES, BLOODWORK.
EXCEPT...I'LL LET DR. CHOLFIN EXPLAIN.
SINCE THE *INCIDENT* AT THE C.D.C. THAT RESULTED IN THE DEATH OF OUR EMPLOYEE, FRANK SHEN, WE'VE BEEN ON LOCKDOWN. STUDYING HIS BLOOD WORK, TRYING TO FIND A CAUSE FOR WHAT HAPPENED TO HIM. NOTHING.
THEN YOU CALLED US. WE'VE SINCE GONE OVER ALL THE SAMPLES YOUR SUSPECT HAS LEFT BEHIND AND THEY LOOK THE SAME AS OUR MR. SHEN'S SAMPLES. NORMAL.
SO...HE'S WRONG.
NO.
ALL THOSE SAMPLES CAME WITH EXPLANATIONS. A METHODOLOGY TO TRACK DOWN SOMETHING--A BUG, HE CALLS IT--WE'D NEVER HAVE LOOKED FOR. AND WE FOUND IT IN EVERY. SINGLE. SAMPLE.
THIS ISN'T MY AREA OF EXPERTISE. THE MAN YOU'RE DEALING WITH IS MOST LIKELY A PSYCHOPATH AND A MONSTER.
HE'S ALSO *CORRECT.* THERE'S AN EPIDEMIC THAT'S BEEN HAPPENING ALL AROUND US. FOR SOME TIME NOW.
YOUR SUSPECT IS THE ONLY ONE WHO SAW IT, WHO DREW US A MAP.
WHATEVER HE IS, HE MAY HAVE JUST SAVED US ALL.

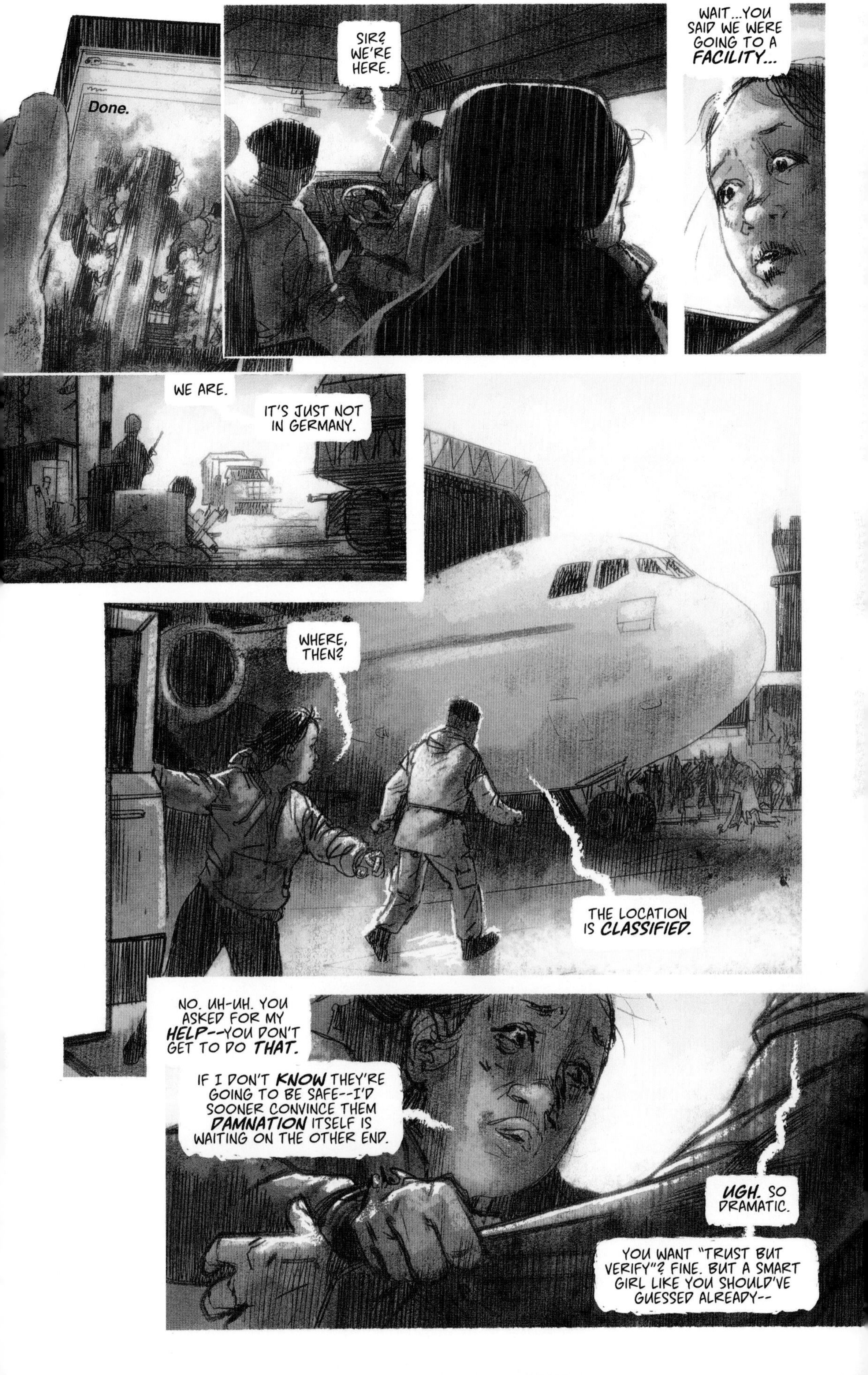
Done.
SIR? WE'RE HERE.
WAIT...YOU SAID WE WERE GOING TO A FACILITY...
WE ARE.
IT'S JUST NOT IN GERMANY.
WHERE, THEN?
THE LOCATION IS CLASSIFIED.
NO. UH-UH. YOU ASKED FOR MY HELP--YOU DON'T GET TO DO THAT.
IF I DON'T KNOW THEY'RE GOING TO BE SAFE--I'D SOONER CONVINCE THEM DAMNATION ITSELF IS WAITING ON THE OTHER END.
UGH. SO DRAMATIC.
YOU WANT "TRUST BUT VERIFY"? FINE. BUT A SMART GIRL LIKE YOU SHOULD'VE GUESSED ALREADY--

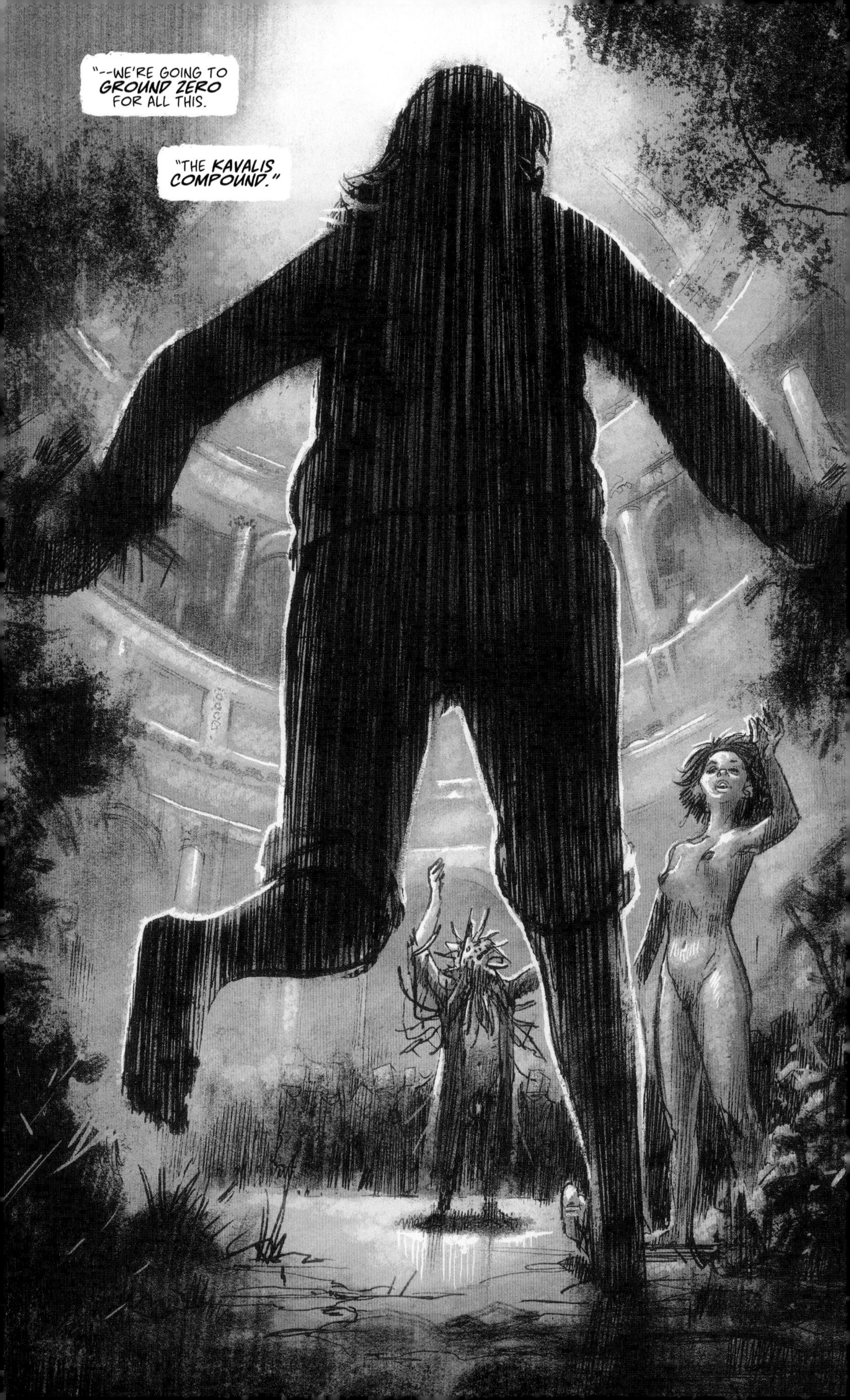
"--WE'RE GOING TO GROUND ZERO FOR ALL THIS.
"THE KAVALIS COMPOUND."

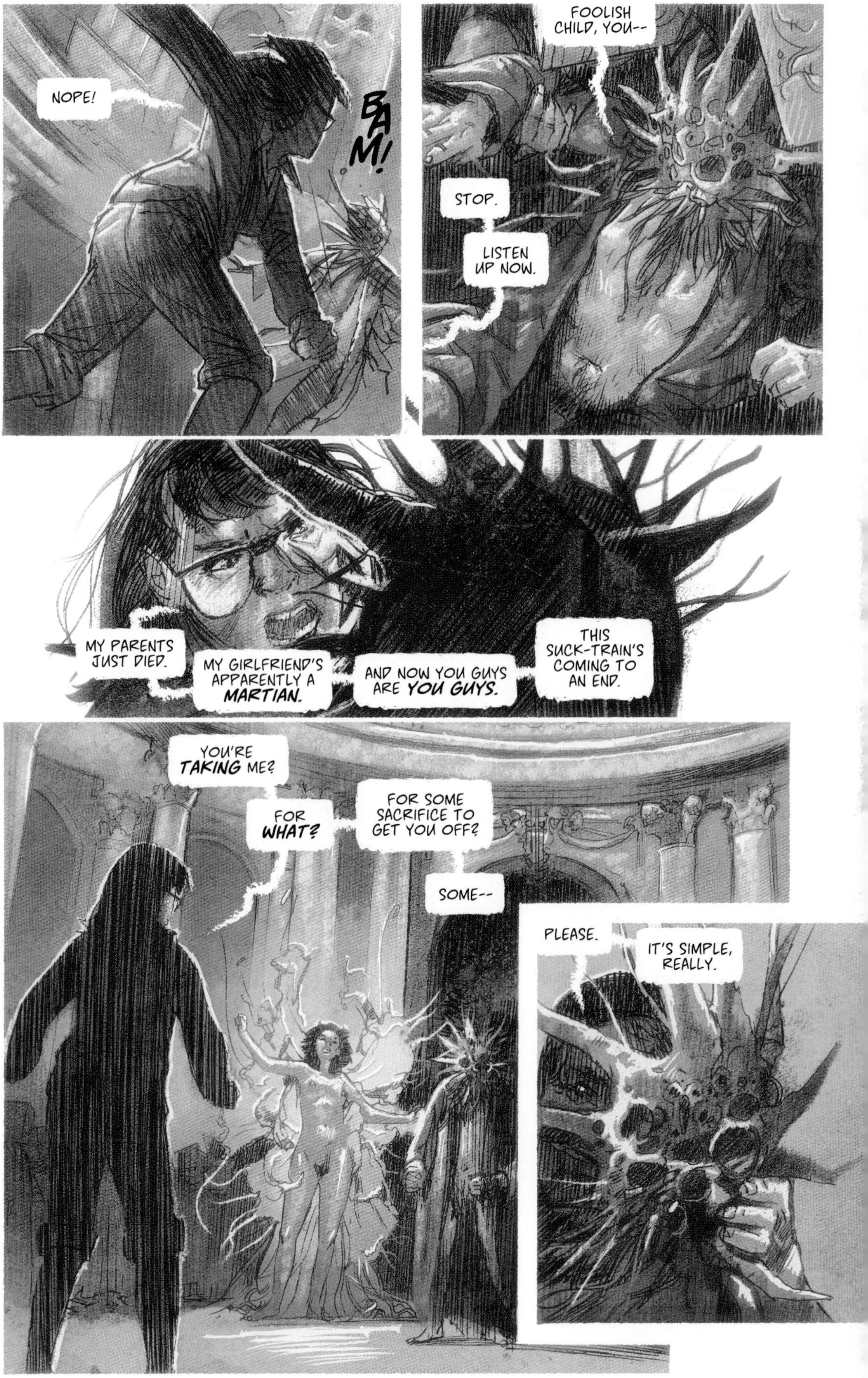
NOPE!
BAM!
FOOLISH CHILD, YOU--
STOP.
LISTEN UP NOW.
MY PARENTS JUST DIED.
MY GIRLFRIEND'S APPARENTLY A MARTIAN.
AND NOW YOU GUYS ARE YOU GUYS.
THIS SUCK-TRAIN'S COMING TO AN END.
YOU'RE TAKING ME?
FOR WHAT?
FOR SOME SACRIFICE TO GET YOU OFF?
SOME--
PLEASE.
IT'S SIMPLE, REALLY.

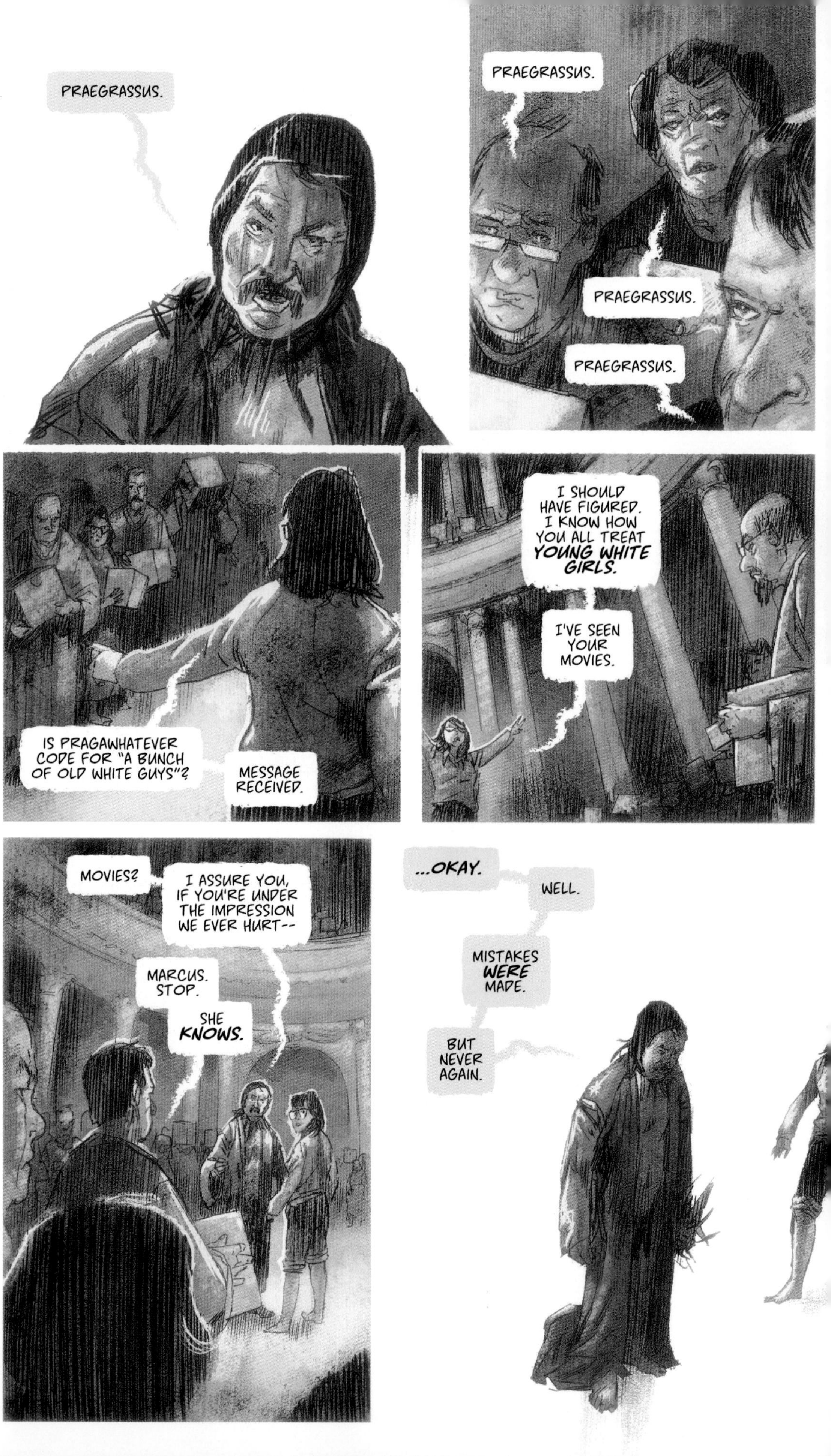
PRAEGRASSUS.
PRAEGRASSUS.
PRAEGRASSUS.
PRAEGRASSUS.
IS PRAGAWHATEVER CODE FOR "A BUNCH OF OLD WHITE GUYS"?
MESSAGE RECEIVED.
I SHOULD HAVE FIGURED. I KNOW HOW YOU ALL TREAT YOUNG WHITE GIRLS.
I'VE SEEN YOUR MOVIES.
MOVIES?
I ASSURE YOU, IF YOU'RE UNDER THE IMPRESSION WE EVER HURT--
MARCUS. STOP.
SHE KNOWS.
...OKAY.
WELL.
MISTAKES WERE MADE.
BUT NEVER AGAIN.

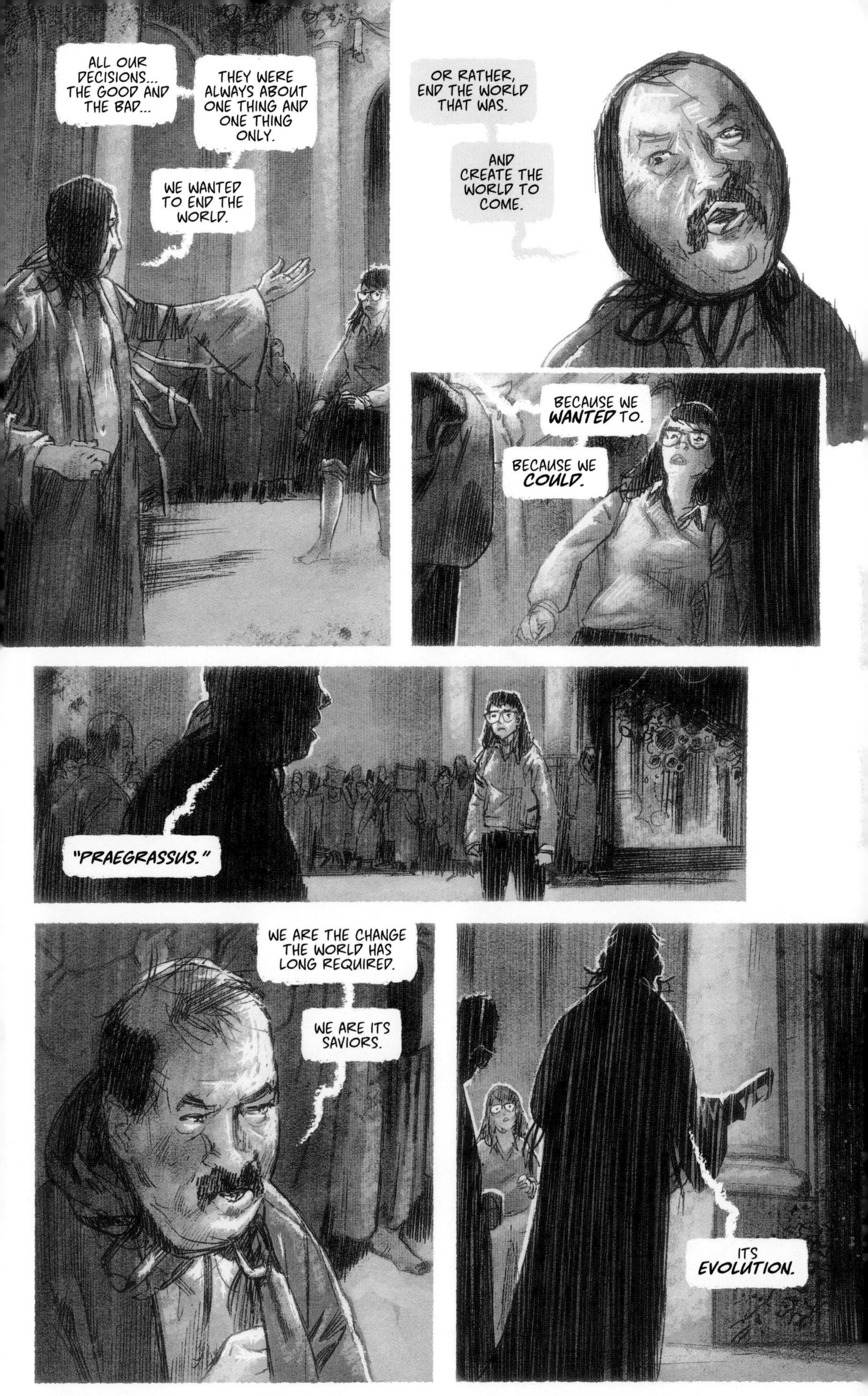
ALL OUR DECISIONS... THE GOOD AND THE BAD...
THEY WERE ALWAYS ABOUT ONE THING AND ONE THING ONLY.
WE WANTED TO END THE WORLD.
OR RATHER, END THE WORLD THAT WAS.
AND CREATE THE WORLD TO COME.
BECAUSE WE **WANTED** TO.
BECAUSE WE **COULD.**
**"PRAEGRASSUS."**
WE ARE THE CHANGE THE WORLD HAS LONG REQUIRED.
WE ARE ITS SAVIORS.
ITS **EVOLUTION.**

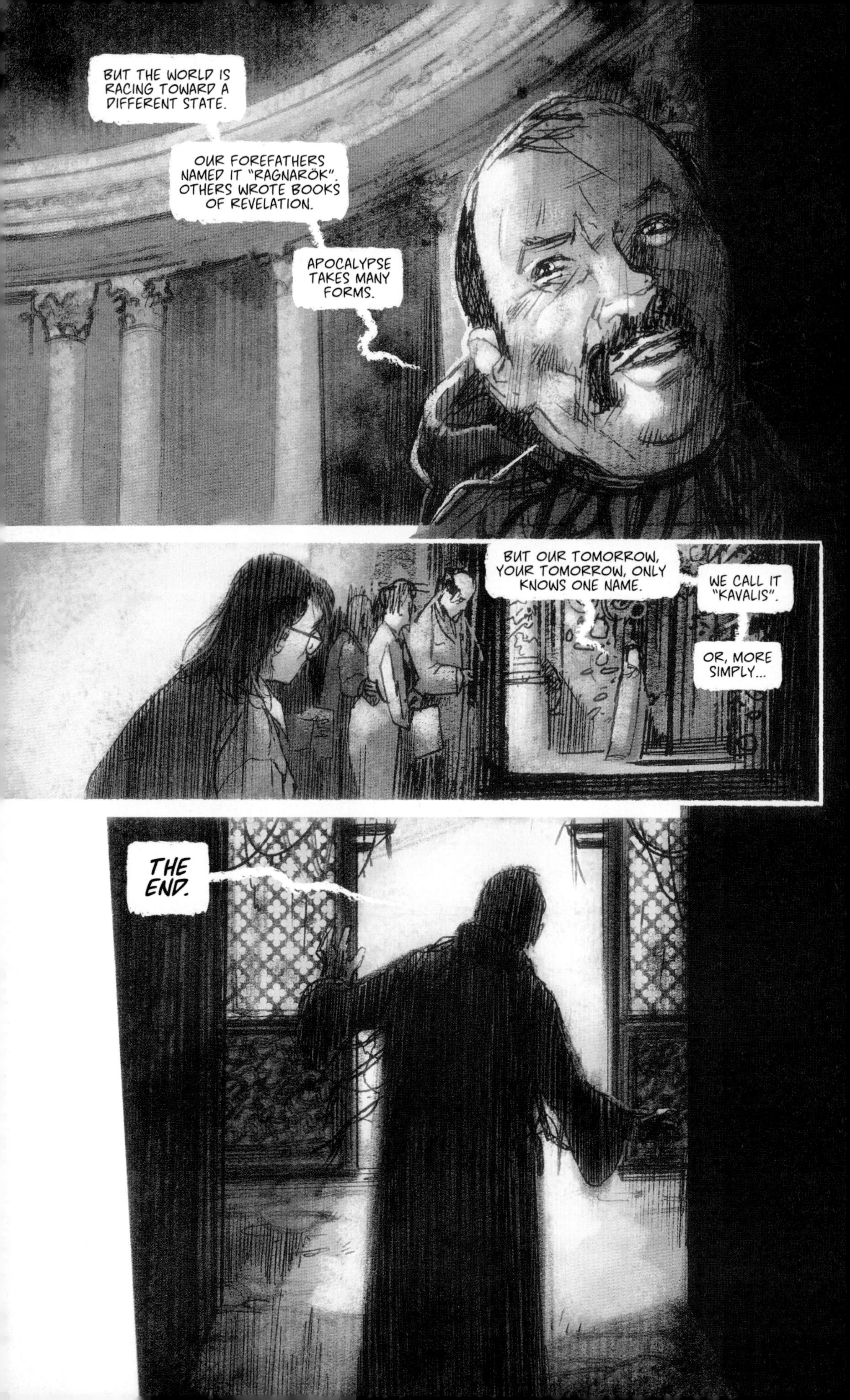
BUT THE WORLD IS RACING TOWARD A DIFFERENT STATE.
OUR FOREFATHERS NAMED IT "RAGNARÖK". OTHERS WROTE BOOKS OF REVELATION.
APOCALYPSE TAKES MANY FORMS.
BUT OUR TOMORROW, YOUR TOMORROW, ONLY KNOWS ONE NAME.
WE CALL IT "KAVALIS".
OR, MORE SIMPLY...
THE END.

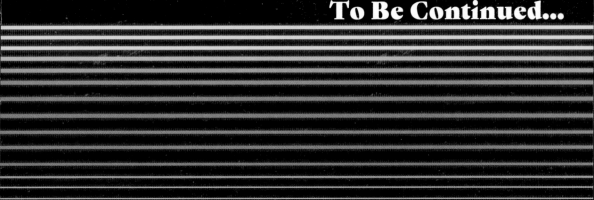

To Be Continued...

# "As bad as things are right now?

# They're about to get a whole lot worse."

# For more tales from ROBERT KIRKMAN and SKYBOUND

Daniel Warren Johnson Mike Spicer
EXTREMITY
VOLUME TWO WARRIOR

REDNECK
Donny CATES Lisandro ESTHERREN Dee CUNNIFFE
VOLUME TWO
The Eyes Upon You

**VOL. 1: ARTIST TP**
ISBN: 978-1-5343-0242-6
$16.99

**VOL. 2: WARRIOR TP**
ISBN: 978-1-5343-0506-9
$16.99

**VOL. 1: DEEP IN THE HEART TP**
ISBN: 978-1-5343-0331-7
$16.99

**VOL. 2: THE EYES UPON YOU**
ISBN: 978-1-5343-0665-3
$16.99

BIRTHRIGHT

**VOL. 1: HOMECOMING TP**
ISBN: 978-1-63215-231-2
$9.99

**VOL. 2: CALL TO ADVENTURE TP**
ISBN: 978-1-63215-446-0
$12.99

**VOL. 3: ALLIES AND ENEMIES TP**
ISBN: 978-1-63215-683-9
$12.99

**VOL. 4: FAMILY HISTORY TP**
ISBN: 978-1-63215-871-0
$12.99

**VOL. 5: BELLY OF THE BEAST TP**
ISBN: 978-1-53430-218-1
$12.99

**VOL. 6: FATHERHOOD TP**
ISBN: 978-1-53430-498-7
$14.99

Gasolina

**VOL. 1: BIENVENIDOS TP**
ISBN: 978-1-5343-0506-9
$16.99

**VOL. 2: FIESTA TP**
ISBN: 978-1-5343-0864-0
$16.99

MANIFEST DESTINY

**VOL. 1: FLORA & FAUNA TP**
ISBN: 978-1-60706-982-9
$9.99

**VOL. 2: AMPHIBIA & INSECTA TP**
ISBN: 978-1-63215-052-3
$14.99

**VOL. 3: CHIROPTERA & CARNIFORMAVES TP**
ISBN: 978-1-63215-397-5
$14.99

**VOL. 4: SASQUATCH TP**
ISBN: 978-1-63215-890-1
$14.99

**VOL. 5: MNEMOPHOBIA & CHRONOPHOBIA TP**
ISBN: 978-1-5343-0230-3
$16.99

**VOL. 6: FORTIS & INVISIBILIA TP**
ISBN: 978-1-5343-0513-7
$16.99

VOLUME 6: INVASION
KIRKMAN
AZACETA

**VOL. 1: A DARKNESS SURROUNDS HIM TP**
ISBN: 978-1-63215-053-0
$9.99

**VOL. 2: A VAST AND UNENDING RUIN TP**
ISBN: 978-1-63215-448-4
$14.99

**VOL. 3: THIS LITTLE LIGHT TP**
ISBN: 978-1-63215-693-8
$14.99

**VOL. 4: UNDER DEVIL'S WING TP**
ISBN: 978-1-5343-0050-7
$14.99

**VOL. 5: THE NEW PATH TP**
ISBN: 978-1-5343-0249-5
$16.99

**VOL. 6: INVASION TP**
ISBN: 978-1-5343-0751-3
$16.99